The writing is swift and p  ices
on the edge of surreal ar   is

MW00626100

- B-Independent

The ending to **Rash** is completely shocking. After the first chapter, you think you have an idea of what was going to happen, but then at the end it takes a total turn, and you are left thinking, "How did all that happen?" This book has a great ending!
- ThroughTheseEyes.net

Rash is amazing, I was seriously blown away. This book is a masterpiece of underground culture.
- Flax Glor, producer of Radiation Nation Variety TV Show

Rash is a totally gripping, creepy, and (at times) downright sick little story. The character sketches are one of this author's strong points. Though spare, they hold exactly the right detail and information to create a vivid portrayal. The character descriptions alone were a treat to read. I intend to keep reading this author, I'm definitely hooked. I'm already itching for [**Talon**].
- Maximum RockNRoll

Rash progresses quickly and gains intensity at the turn of every page. The ending totally caught me by surprise, even though I had a taste of what was to come from the opening scene. The story unfolded and twisted back upon itself in preparation to strike, and strike it did!
- Jeff Leyda, Tess Records

For most of **Rash**, I felt I had a firm grasp on exactly what was coming. However when the expected scene arrives, the mechanics of the situation and the complex interplay of multiple plots absolutely blows you away. This struck me as a sign of true literary talent. Simply put, this book is awesome.
- Lethal Injection eZine

Rash, like its predecessor **Salad Days**, thoroughly engages the reader with its vibrant characters that seem to take life before one's eyes. There is a lasting snapshot in my mind of each of them that was introduced, however briefly. Even the darkest of them have their moments of humanity with which the reader can identify. Romalotti has a gift for storytelling.
- Dru, This Ascension

Talon has such well-written characters, you just gasp as you follow them through every suspenseful and sickening turn in the story. I loved it.
- Mistress McCutchan, Editor, Morbid Outlook Magazine

Rash is unnerving, twisted, and quite sick—lock this guy up!
- cevin Key, Skinny Puppy

Rash had an effect on me like some kind of hallucinogen. The descriptions are horrific...a very brutal portrayal of the lost and the sad and the damned. A twisted showdown like a bizarre disillusioned generation's idea of a Western shootout on Main Street.
- Jarboe, The Swans

Talon is a great follow-up to **Rash**. Romalotti does it again.
- Naika Malveaux, RealmGothica.com

Combining elements of thriller, suspense, and horror, Romalotti weaves a tale that reads like punk rock nightmares. The complex interplays will have you suspecting what may come next but never truly knowing. If you like SplatterPunk style writing, you'll enjoy this book!
- Wraith, The House of Pain

Talon is a realistic dark journey that is amusing and disturbing at the same time.
- Clint, Victory Records

The characterization within any Romalotti book is second to none, lending the individuals present within the book's pages a strong familiarity even before you get halfway through. You soon start to predict their thoughts, foresee their actions, and recognize speech patterns without being told who is speaking.
Talon is a compelling and tumultuous read, taking you on a ride to a world existing on the precipice of a hellish reality. Typically with Romalotti, things aren't quite as clear as they may initially appear. After a series of gripping incidents and interweaving plots (none of which follow the expected path), things are left perfectly balanced for an explosive climax in the last installment of the series, **The Stickler**.
- Scanner Magazine, UK

Romalotti has done it again. This third and final chapter in **Pariah [The Stickler]** brings back demons from **Rash** and **Talon**. As the lives of the characters unravel, the tale becomes darker and more complex. **The Stickler** answers a great deal of questions from **Rash** and **Talon** while providing readers with background information that explains the characters and what drives them. The way Romalotti writes is magical—the reader is under a trance which can only be broken by the last page.
- Dan Pugatch, UMass Torch/Manna 4 the Brain Zine

Romalotti definitely has a real talent for writing.
- Adam, H2O

PARIAH

CHARLES ROMALOTTI

Layman Books

Austin   San Francisco   Paris   Tel Aviv   Bombay

PARIAH – LAYMAN BOOKS
ISBN: 0-9679235-3-0

Edited by Daniel Smith
Cover art and layout design by Daniel Smith
Photo of Romalotti by Andrew Ellis

Available direct-mail from Layman Books for $8.

Layman Books
P. O. Box 4702
Austin, TX 78765-4702
www.laymanbooks.com

Romalotti can be contacted directly at layman@laymanbooks.com

Writing for *Rash* began January 1998, completed October 2000
Originally released June 1, 2001 (1,00 copies in print).

Writing for *Talon* began September 2001, completed March 2002
Originally released June 1, 2002 (1,00 copies in print).

Writing for *The Stickler* began September 2002, completed November 2002
Previously unpublished, first time in print.

Pariah release date: June 1, 2003

All testimonials on the back cover are for *Rash*.

Second Printing of Pariah

Printed in the United States by:
Morris Publishing
3212 East Highway 30
Kearney, NE 68847
1-800-650-7888

To my parents, Roberta and Clarence

Rash

Saturday, November 7, 1998
5:47pm

Austin, Texas

"Spare some change?" a young voice growled from the pavement.

Doctor Ronald W. Schtepp stared forward, intent on avoiding eye contact with the rugged youths sprawled along the sidewalk of the Drag. Their dirty bodies were intertwined in a mess of human limbs, enveloped in a deplorably wretched stench. He reached inside the pocket of his polyester pants and jiggled some change, advancing down the stained and broken sidewalk without forfeiting a penny. He enjoyed tormenting them—the ones known locally as the Dragworms. It sickened him how they preyed upon the compassion of liberals and naïve college students. He added it to his list of good fortunes that he was neither.

The cool wind whipped his thinning brown hair into a frazzled mess. His rotund fingers yanked it haggardly in place over his shiny bald crown as he rolled down the sidewalk. His brown vinyl jacket with the tanned elbow patches blended perfectly with the desolate street so aptly named. The cracked pavement was damp from an inconsistent drizzle that made the entire cityscape reek of decay and filth. The murky gray clouds seemed to threaten another chilling shower. He hoped to be inside his cozy Tarrytown home by then.

Strolling past the Church of Scientology, he entered the Bagel Shop on the corner of 22nd Street. Inside, it was warm and empty, as expected. He stepped to the steel counter, catching the eye of the tall man standing rigidly behind it. Their eyes met, and Ronald felt that strange feeling in his chest again. It made him smile, somewhat giddy like a giggly schoolgirl. He liked the feeling.

"Frank," he announced politely to the otherwise silent bakery. His strained voice was prominently male. "What's cookin'?"

Frank Smith raised his eyes and smiled, giving an ambiguous nod. "How are you, Ronald?"

"Not too bad," he decided quickly as he placed his hands passively on the counter's cold metal surface. He gave a proud smile that revealed a row of crooked, yellow teeth. "It's a fine day, though a busy one. Life is about to get much easier, I'm pleased to say. My work with the university is nearing completion, and everything is going extremely well."

"The skin stuff?"

Ronald smiled with a cocked brow that was as thick as steel wool. "My colleague and I are going to be rich, Frank. This is going to be big—you'll never have to scratch yourself ever again, Frank."

"I kind of enjoy scratching myself..." Frank dropped two pumpernickel bagels in a brown paper bag and lowered it into Ronald's limp, lazy hands. "I'm happy to hear things are moving along finally...I remember how frustrated you were recently. Where did you get the breakthrough, or are you not at liberty to say?"

"No details," Ronald insisted with strict confidence as he placed a dollar and some change on the hard metal counter. "I can tell you that the elusive chemical properties were extracted from known herbal cures." His smile intensified as he paused to reveal the clenching detail that apparently kept him up at night. "The product will be derived from a completely organic origin."

Frank smiled as if he found the subject very riveting. He didn't at all, though. He stood silently, waiting for Ronald to either continue or leave.

Instead, Ronald slouched at the counter obsequiously. "Now, weren't you away recently, Frank?" He stared into Frank's eyes, finding the intensity of his expression to be quite striking. He liked looking into his eyes. In fact, he liked it more than the bagels.

"Had to return to Kansas. Funeral last week."

"Oh...sorry to hear that." His facial expression fell sullen and ill, as if he felt great remorse. He didn't at all, though. "It does happen to the best of us, I'm afraid. Never know when our number is up."

Frank nodded slowly, deliberately withholding any sign of emotion. "Never know."

"Well," Ronald said as he tightly gripped the bag of bagels, "I suppose I should be on my way now. Maybe sometime we could make it out to one of those Ice Bats hockey games...it's a new season, you know."

Frank smiled politely.

"Well...we'll talk about it sometime," Ronald suggested as he removed his wiry glasses to wipe the surface clean. "I wouldn't be against paying."

"I'm kind of busy," Frank began, "with this place."

Ronald nodded, feeling a bit uncomfortable with his forwardness—then he looked into those eyes and knew exactly why he asked. In fact, he knew why he would someday ask again. "Have a good evening, Frank." He stumbled out the side door and down 22nd Street, feeling the cold breeze lapping against his pale, circular face as he staggered humbly to his car.

Pulling up to his quaint little home in Tarrytown, his attention was devoured by a black 1956 Plymouth Fury convertible sitting in front of the house. He paused momentarily, wondering whose it was and how long its presence would be allowed to desecrate his beautifully manicured lawn. He stepped down onto the wet street, locking the doors of his pearly white BMW before waddling proudly up the driveway. He immediately stopped when he discovered a blade of grass resting on the clean cement. He reached down and picked it up, placing it in his coat pocket until he could dispose of it properly.

As he fumbled for his keys, he rummaged through the day's mail. Several bills, and no new copy of *Sports Illustrated*. He loved that magazine, though he never read or understood a word of it. The pictures, he felt, were art. The sweat, the struggle, the passion, the muscles of men colliding... He suddenly felt something rubbing firmly and affectionately against his leg. When he looked down, his eyes met those of his housemate, Adonis. His cat.

"Adonis," he said as he reached down to caress his head. "How did you get out?"

No answer.

He slipped the key inside the lock, twisting it with a limp wrist and no resistance. To his dismay, it wasn't locked. As he pushed the door open, he stood cautiously immobile. No intruders to be seen, only the cold emptiness. The place was just as he left it, spotless and clean. Authentic posters of Broadway musicals were housed in steel frames, secured to the chalky white walls. The thick brown carpet still bore the tracks of the sweeper from earlier in the morning. The artificial scent of lemon was strong, and the atmosphere was painfully cold.

"Silly me," he said to Adonis as he stumbled inside. "Seems I failed to lock the door. I would've forgotten my head if it wasn't attached...are you a hungry kitty?" He pushed through the swivel doors of his bedroom where the walls were painted icy blue and the bedspread was an appropriate match with patterns of icebergs and penguins. The swivel doors squeaked annoyingly behind him as they closed once again. He removed his coat and placed it amongst his small collection of drab business attire and pastel lingerie. He could smell the fragrance of Shalimar in the frigid air. The scent of Lucinda. The thought of her brought a warm smile.

Adonis meandered between his feet, rubbing passionately, begging for attention.

As he stepped away from the closet, he noticed that a message was flashing on his answering machine, opposite his Queen-sized bed. A picture of his ex-wife towered over the machine. He refused to remove the photograph, if for any other reason than her dress in the picture matched perfectly the pattern on the quilted nightstand.

He pushed through the squeaky swivel doors and lumbered to the kitchen. A strange feeling of discomfort infected his environment, though he spoke what came to mind: "Hungry kitty." As Adonis fed from the tin can that rested in the palm of his hand, he felt a crisply cold draft creep up his spine. He turned quickly, to nothing. Yet, a draft had penetrated somehow, as if a window were open, and that uneasy feeling of being watched... "ESPN tonight, Adonis. Boxing..."

4

He lowered the tin can to the icy cold counter and crept back to the bedroom. The doors squeaked mercilessly as he passed through them. Someday, he resolved, he would hire some young man with impressive tools to fix that obnoxious squeak. The thought of it brought a mischievous smile. He lowered himself to the bed, avoiding looking at the picture of his ex-wife as he pressed the play button on his answering machine. The caller ID showed it to be his business colleague, Vaughn Richter. He figured as much. No one else calls him.

"Ronald, I need you!" Richter's voice exclaimed desperately, breaking the silence of the cold room. "I need to speak with you—now. Please call me immediately. She's dead. Purty's dead. I've killed her... I don't know what to do..."

His voice faded quickly to silence, leaving a stale chill in the air. Suddenly, like nails on a chalkboard, the sound of the squeaky door sent a tremor of fear through his hefty frame. As he turned, his eyes widened with horror.

"Purty?" he gasped. "Is that...you?" He could barely recognize her to be human. Her rotting skin seemed to drip from her emaciated body. It appeared that she had been skinned, nothing more than a bloodied carcass with the flesh still dangling from slick muscle.

"I want the antidote," she growled. Her bottom lip hung freely as though it was partially severed, making her speech relatively indistinguishable. "Cure me."

"I don't know what you're talking about."

"You don't know?" she hissed.

"No," he replied with a trembling, terrified quaver. "I don't know."

The crackling thunder of gunfire ripped through the room as the bullet penetrated his head, splattering his brains against the wall behind him, splitting his head like cracked watermelon.

This was how Ronald W. Schtepp died.

Sunday, August 16, 1998
4:03pm

Tucson, Arizona

Dirty fingers quickly sifted through the stacks of vinyl records, ignoring any release not of an independent origin. The electronic rhythms of early Industrial music pulsated throughout the Toxic Ranch record store as Jobie Wallace stood alone, immersing himself in a subterranean world of seven-inch singles. His poorly managed long fingernails retained a layer of grime over chipped black nail polish.

He inhaled deeply, absorbing the musty scents of his surroundings. This store was as much his home as anywhere else, though he had never set foot in Tucson until earlier that day. It was the contents of the store rather than its locale, containing the music and literature of the anarchist philosophy that pushed the blood through his young, thin body. He held firm the staunchly liberal beliefs of bands like Naked Aggression and Capitalist Casualties. He considered himself a political advocate, an anarchist with a mission. The only shirt he owned, the one on his back—a sleeveless Crass T-shirt, once black, though now it had a brownish tint from months of filth, displayed proudly his political colors. A large tear zigzagged across his back, sewn haphazardly together with dental floss. The slogan *Fight War, Not Wars* stretched across the back of his shirt, a sort of rally cry to all those who stood behind him. The rest of his outfit was the last of his clothing as well. A plaid flannel kilt draped over his bony legs. It was an image inspired partly by heritage and partly by influence of a punk rock band known as the Real McKenzies. His toes peeked through an ancient pair of combat boots that were wrapped with duct tape to keep his soles intact. He showered infrequently, if ever. He felt people kept their distance based on his ragged appearance. He was mistaken.

The expression on his face was rigid and speculative, by choice. It was part of the uncivil, streetwise image he wished to portray for himself. His bony face was splotchy with acne and razor stubble. Jailhouse-style tattoos of cobwebs spanned from the peak of his nose down across his narrow, pasty cheeks. His hair was short and disorderly, with the left portion dyed black while the right was bleached a stunning white. Despite his adverse sense of style, and to his dismay, his most striking features were those given at birth—piercing icy-blue eyes that could penetrate the coldest of hearts. His smile was very enticing as well, though he chose to restrict such expressions as often as possible. As he saw it, there was no place for smiles in a world so malicious and destructive. Such an expression would be turning a blind eye on the hard truth. Jobie considered smiles the badges of weak and trusting servants of a corrupt and barbaric fascist order. He was proud of the fact that he lived outside the system. He held no job and paid no taxes. He depended on nothing and no one—except those who mercifully supplied their pocket change daily for much needed meals.

The nation's highways were his home, resting nightly on the soil he spurned so adamantly. On his eighteenth birthday, just four months earlier, he and his younger brother Rik left their abusive home life in Tacoma, Washington in favor of freedom and adventure. Jobie's pockets contained a collection of four rocks—one from each state they had traveled to the present. Forty-six remained uncollected.

His other two possessions remained closely at his side—a collection of Noam Chomsky's writings and his own work in progress, *The Apolitical Manifesto*, which was more or less a glorified journal of rhetorical ranting. It was filled with second-hand perspectives on blind consumerism and the corporate censorship of mass media.

His eyes widened and his fingers ceased as he gazed happily at an orange and yellow record. It was a curious sight, the type for which he lived. It was an unknown record from an obscure punk band featured recently in the *Lost Legends* section of *Maximum RockNRoll*. They were called the Jerk Offs—a band that had stumbled briefly onto fleeting notoriety after their vocalist, Norman Malley died tragically over ten years ago. Strangely, this particular seven-inch had a different singer, which wasn't mentioned in the article. He wondered what circumstances buried this portion of the band's history. He often contemplated the fates of these people, the ones who pioneered the vision to which he so passionately subscribed. How did they learn to survive in a world that so radically contradicted the movement's philosophies?

He walked the record to the counter, examining its simple cover art. "I want to listen to this record."

The clerk grudgingly gestured to a stereo with a set of headphones.

"Why does this store carry corporate merchandise?" Jobie asked. "I mean, you have a section for the Media Whores—total sell-outs. Isn't this an independent record store?"

The clerk stared without reply. He had grown tired of responding to Jobie's menial questions and accusations. It was almost as if Jobie sensed a conspiracy, as if there were any other reason to stock a product beyond the general principle of supply and demand. After hours of interrogation, the silent approach seemed to be the best response.

Jobie sneered at him with slit eyes, clearly marking his disapproval. He'd break something before he left.

He carefully placed the record on the player and fastened the headphones over his large ears. The gnawing background noise dissipated behind the crackling pops of the record. He watched the clerk staring at him with contemptuous eyes. Without warning, all his thoughts were devoured by a thick wall of passionate anxiety surging through the headphones. Goosebumps covered his arms as a smile formed across his face, though it was quickly extinguished by his own sense of reason. This was it. That new high, delivered by a recording over a decade old. He lived for such a rush, and hardcore was his drug of choice. Such a pure high, yet only as good as the unfamiliarity of the music. Comprehension brings immunity, carrying with it the craving of a newer, faster, stronger, and harder high. If he could only find a way to steal this record...

A stiff finger tapped him aggressively on the back. He didn't even flinch—he knew it was his brother.

"What?" he asked.

A more aggressive tapping came as a response.

"What?!" He removed the headphones, glancing over his shoulder at a pair of fiery red eyes. Not bloodshot, but candy-apple red—from a pair of artificially colored contact lenses. Red and green eye make-up seemed to explode across his face in a nuclear sunburst. The result was something close to a demon from a B-movie sci-fi flick. His hair was shaved over his ears with the rest extending toward the lighting fixtures in a ratted mess of burnt orange and black. From the neck up, he looked completely and convincingly alien. A skin-tight black mesh shirt hugged his pale and thin body. A black cheerleader skirt fanned out at his hips. Blood red cotton leggings seemed to drip inside patent leather neon-green boots with three-inch heels and enormous silver buckles.

"She's here," he spoke strongly through a pair of thick blackish-purple lips. "Outside."

"Have her come inside."

"She hates music. She won't come inside."

Jobie grumbled as his face scrunched with irritation. The web tattoo condensed with his tightened skin. "No one hates music."

"Apparently she does."

"Is she a Betty?" Jobie pried. "Is she hot?"

Opaque shook his head as he turned to walk away. "Chasing Betties, always chasing the skirts," Opaque caustically mumbled to himself, "Nothing better to do...chasing Betties...writing terrorist manuals..." He casually returned to the blazing heat of the desert.

"Hold this record for me," Jobie demanded the clerk as he removed the headphones. "I'll be back to get it." He continued out the door, following the lead of his younger brother into the dry heat of Arizona.

There, standing next to the curb was the most attractive misfit youth he had ever seen, and it certainly wasn't his brother. His eyes widened and the pace of his heart intensified as he stepped forward to join them. He clutched *The Apolitical Manifesto* with tense fingers as he swaggered up to them in steady cool reserve. He could feel his brother watching him, studying him. He knew that his brother was keen to every thought, every feeling. He always was.

The young girl stood smiling with a postcard perfect expression of bliss and ease. She couldn't have been more than seventeen years of age, though her youth seemed timeless. Jobie felt an immediate and desperate yearning to be a part of her world, her happiness. He had seen so little of it in his life.

"Hello," she greeted him clumsily with a high-pitched voice that mirrored a child's. The sharp angles of her cheekbones seemed to almost protrude uncomfortably under her fair skin. Her smile was intoxicating and graciously innocent, like a Catholic schoolgirl. A long and slender nose seemed to offset the proportions of her tiny chin. At an angle, her nostrils seemed enormous. Her over-sized brown corduroy pants concealed any suggestion of legs, though he assumed they were as thin as her gaunt, though pretty horse-like face. A shiny, tight lime-green Adidas T-shirt did show that she needn't wear a bra, and it was clear that she didn't by the way her firm nipples poked under the thin fabric. Her posture was awkward, pigeon-toed with slumped shoulders. The bones of her shoulders and elbows were as sharp as pencils. "Are you Jobie?"

He nodded affirmatively while squinting in the harsh sunlight.

"I'm Treva Rifkin," she announced timidly as she ran her bony fingers through her messy burgundy-colored, shoulder-length hair. She teased her bangs nervously as she giggled. And giggled. She tapped her chest with a stiff finger, giving a visual aid to her introduction. She seemed perfectly incapable of speaking without her hands. Every word was aided and accentuated by elated gestures. "I met Opaque this morning out front of the Bison Witch." She aimed her slender finger down the street, jabbing at the dry air as she closed an eye to focus on the nearby intersection of 4th Avenue.

Jobie shifted his attention briefly to his brother, Rik, or as he obviously preferred, Opaque. Jobie laughed aloud, bringing their conversation to a sudden halt as he humored himself at his brother's expense.

Treva stared at him, calculating his mocking laughter. She didn't like it. There was something vindictive and judgmental about it. She felt it was aimed at her. Anger spontaneously burst inside her skinny body, ignited by his apparent scrutiny. She hated to be laughed at, and she felt hatred toward him for laughing at her. Her large green eyes flared with a neurotic ferocity. Her face suddenly flushed red, speckling her fair skin with an uneven splotchiness. "What are you laughing at?!"

"Nothing," Jobie shrugged with a belligerent and self-gratifying grin, devoid of the knowledge that her mood had completely shifted. "Just…my asshole brother."

She turned to Opaque who nodded politely at her in compliance. She could sense in his compassionate, yet burning red eyes that she had misread the situation. His sensible awareness put her immediately at ease again as if nothing had stirred her. His perceptiveness was clearly a quality lacking in Jobie. "Oh," she mumbled with a belated sigh. Her shoulders slumped forward as her massive eyes twinkled once again. No sooner had her skin discolored, it completely faded back to its smooth delicacy. Her smile followed, revealing a set of awkwardly large teeth. "Your brother tells me you've got something I've been trying to find."

Jobie raised an eye and pursed his lips as he gave a short nod. "Oh really?"

"So I've heard," she told him. "That's what a little birdy told me anyway." Her finger quickly shot toward the tops of the buildings, as if tipping them off to the whereabouts of birds. She raised her bushy brow and batted her long lashes. "Haven't smoked in days."

Jobie glanced down the street, checking for any wandering eyes that may be upon them. He pulled a plastic bag out from his pocket and laid it in her bony hand. "Good stuff," he promised.

She took a quick look at the bag's contents before handing it back to him. "No seeds, no stems..." she mumbled with her sweetly innocent voice that flowered the air around them. She was quite aware of how smitten Jobie was with her. She would play it for all its worth, for all her ego's worth. "Are you a cop?"

His chilling laughter rang loudly through the desert's heat. "A cop? How dare you insult me...if I was a cop I'd have to kill myself."

She let out an awkward and submissive giggle that she quickly stifled by covering her thick lips with a bony hand. There was genuine warmth in her laughter that infected both of them. A silent exchange of smiles followed. "Had to ask. So how much?"

"Forty bucks a quarter."

She looked to the ground, as if seeking the words that rested so comfortably on the end of her tongue. "That's more than I have."

Jobie felt discouraged, even insulted. Had he not found her so attractive, he'd have simply walked away at that moment. "How about thirty-five? Come on, that's a steal. It's worth more."

She gave a relaxed and girlish giggle that again deceived her age. It was one that belonged on a playground. Yet it was her childish demeanor and cutesy little-girl voice that drove Jobie's hormones to the brink of a meltdown. It made him want to conquer her, to chastise her purity with a violent and passionate struggle that she would not win. He wanted that power over her, to destroy the very thing he found so enticing. He felt morbid and twisted for such thoughts. He liked the feeling.

"I'm kind of broke—I only have twenty-five dollars," she confessed. "See, I'm passing through from Colorado—"

"Where you heading?" Jobie interjected.

She shrugged her shoulders. "Beats me."

10

"We're traveling also," Jobie told her. "We're going to visit every state of the union, before hitting Europe, eventually. We've seen a lot already. In fact, we were in San Diego just yesterday morning. I believe we're going…" He looked to Opaque, who returned the gaze with casual indifference. "We're going to New Orleans. For Mardi Gras."

"Wow! Cool!" she exclaimed excitedly. "Can I go too?"

Jobie's eyes lit up, as she expected.

"February," Opaque muttered with a firm and commanding voice. "Mardi Gras isn't until February."

"Oh," Treva sighed. "That's too bad…"

"Well, let's just take the scenic route," Jobie suggested.

Treva looked at him, at the spider's web tattoo spanning his hollow cheeks, at his messy hair with the cheap dye job. She studied his powerfully hypnotic eyes that squinted in the heat of the desert. They seemed to be undressing her, violating her. The thought made her smile. He was exactly the kind of guy that her father would despise. "All right," she declared with excitement. "Let's find a ride."

Monday, September 7, 1998
10:47pm

Outskirts of Kyle, Texas

"This is it," Cindy Dunne resolved. "This conversation will be our last."

Tamika Tovar fell silent, writhing in discomfort as she clutched the phone against her ear. She didn't want this, but she seemed to never get what she wanted from life. Misery seemed part of its endurance, with death the only release. These thoughts had been the source of many intimate conversations she had shared with Cindy, but as the final hour approached, it all seemed very irrational. She didn't want this, she never did.

"Tamika, you're not talking to me," Cindy complained. "Are you still there?"

"I'm here." Tamika pulled the black sheets up to her thick neck. She felt somewhat more at ease, simply knowing that her obese body was covered from view, despite her solitude.

The heat of the night penetrated the boxy trailer. Black tapestries hung from the walls of her room. White and red candles dripped over ornate iron fixtures secured to the thin wall. The room was otherwise dark. *The Taste of Cindy* by The Jesus And Mary Chain played softly from a nearby cassette player. It was a significant song—it was their song. The seventh on the *Psychocandy* album, it took nearly half the tape to find the courage to give that first kiss. But that was years ago, long before the tumultuous ride that their relationship had become. Cindy's violent mood swings and erratic panic attacks seemed to always keep happiness beyond their reach. At seventeen years of age, Cindy decided she had had enough of life. As the only love of her life, Tamika agreed on a similar fate. She always told her that she would give her life for the love she felt. Now the clock ticked…

"Soon I'll know the answer to the big question," Cindy marveled optimistically. "Where we go from here. Do you think we'll meet, or do you think the lights will just go out?"

"I don't feel well," Tamika said solemnly.

Cindy laughed. "Oh, listen to you! Like it's going to matter. We'll both be dead soon. What difference does it make?"

"None?"

12

"Right, none," Cindy insisted. She had expected Tamika's hesitation. She knew that Tamika never followed through with anything she ever promised. Her poor self-esteem was always the overbearing deterrent to all her endeavors. No, Tamika wouldn't do it, and they both knew this. Likewise, both were aware that this was their final conversation. Cindy didn't share Tamika's passive nature. Cindy's word was her honor, despite how infrequently she gave it. "Tamika...thank you for being my friend."

Tamika sat perfectly still, numbed by the words. It was the closest Cindy had ever come to telling her that she loved her.

"I've got to go," Cindy's voice trembled awkwardly. Her anger quickly surfaced, ignited by her inability to control her emotions. "Fuck it..." She slammed the phone down violently. These were the last words ever spoken between them.

In the morning, before the sun surfaced, Tamika crawled out of bed. She hadn't slept. Her round face was puffy from all the tears she'd shed the night before. Her kinky curly black hair was a frightful mess, as always. She grabbed the length of it with both hands, twisting two pigtails together behind each ear, tying her hair with thin red satin ribbons. She slipped a long flowing black velvet gown over her shoulders as she gazed dully out the window. The sirens hadn't come yet, but it didn't surprise her. Knowing Cindy's parents, it would take them days to find her body in the camper on the front lawn—her bedroom. And knowing them, there'd be a party later that night.

She stumbled over to her dresser, removing all her favorite outfits, which didn't amount to much. She crammed them inside an empty pillowcase, stuffing her small collection of cassette tapes with it. She diverted her attention in the dim light to the plastic baby doll on the nightstand. It was the only thing Cindy ever gave to her, something she found alongside the road one drunken night. She tucked the doll inside the pillowcase and left the room.

Darkness filled the confines of the tiny run-down trailer, but she knew her way quite well. This had been home her entire life. As she passed through the living room, her large brown eyes squinted at the sight of the snowy static on the television set. Her mother was passed out on the couch, still clutching a glass of tequila that she had partially spilt on herself. The ashtray was full of butts from the night before. She had a visitor, it was clear, but there was nothing new with that. Her mother based her identity on the men she acquired. Tamika was quite aware of her reputation throughout the trailer park. Anyone needing a good time knew where to go. Her mother claimed that it was in her Hispanic blood to be so sexually active. Tamika never understood why she didn't share the same affliction, unless the African-American blood of her father's stifled her *Hispanic fire*.

She crept through the living room to the front door. On the plywood display next to the door was a photograph of herself, taken at Christmas many years earlier. The child in the picture was coming out of her skin with

13

excitement, clutching a wrapped package with tiny fingers. Her expression was almost constipated with excitement—her lips were stretched into a long, thin horizontal line. The process of taking the picture had clearly delayed the opening of the gift, therefore perfectly capturing her impatient enthusiasm. The photograph had always haunted her—that child had died long ago. She removed the photograph from the shelf and stuffed it into her pillowcase. She took one last look at her mother before leaving.

"Thanks for nothing, bitch," she mumbled as she left, never to return again.

The air was already warm and the sky was beginning to glow a pale blue. The sun would be up soon.

As she stumbled up the gravel road in the quiet darkness, she thought it interesting how strangely inhibited she felt. There were no eyes watching her, yet she felt grossly analyzed. She felt repulsive and disgusting, fat and ugly. She figured her poor appearance was based on the amount of food she ate. Well, she wouldn't have to worry about that. She wasn't sure exactly where she was going, but she knew wherever it was, food would be scarce. She liked the idea. She finally smiled, stumbling to the top of the hill where the lights of all the trailers scattered the horizon, as far as she could see. This was hell, she estimated as she continued to the main light source, the nearby Diamond Shamrock gas station. The sky was coming alive, transforming from blue to deep purple and orange.

She wondered if Cindy's spirit was following her. She hoped as much. She knew that Cindy would take care of her. Cindy was the only person who ever did.

By the time she had arrived at the gas station, the sun was already peaking on the horizon. Old pick-up trucks with full loads idled before every pump, readying for a day of hard labor. She stumbled into the harsh fluorescent lights, feeling absolute discomfort in her obese body. She spotted a familiar man pumping gas, a man she found passed out on her mother from time to time. She was amazed that she could even remember all those men, all those faces. He looked at her as she approached, squinting while rearranging his chew with his tongue.

"Shouldn't you be on your way to school, young lady?" he asked her with a distinct Texas twang.

"I need a ride," she told him.

"I didn't figure you were going to school, not with that bag over your shoulder. Where you heading?"

"Where you heading?"

"San Antonio."

"Sounds good to me," she said. "Can I get a lift?"

"What you got to offer me?" he asked.

She looked to the ground nervously, and then raised her head sheepishly. "Nothing."

14

"Gas, grass, or ass, sweetheart," he recited from memory, impressed by his own cleverness. "No free rides in this world."

"No thanks, then," she told him as she continued to the station, toward the blinding white lights. She eyed all the backward country folk walking in and out of the small store. It was a pleasant reminder of why she felt such a need to leave. She didn't belong. She didn't really belong anywhere, but she knew that this was definitely not the place for her.

"Darlin'," a woman's voice shot from a nearby pump. "If you're needing a ride somewhere, I could take you to Austin. I work downtown. State Capitol building."

Tamika smiled, overwhelmed with relief. "Thank you."

The woman lit another cigarette while fluffing her enormous bangs into place. The signs were clearly marked *No Smoking*. "Why you leaving?" she asked Tamika as they stood outside her primer-colored Ford Escort.

"Look around you," Tamika said.

The woman laughed. "Climb inside, it's unlocked."

The journey to Austin was rather quick, aided by the comfort of silence. The construction along Interstate 35 was a good distraction, though it slowed traffic to a near halt. They listened quietly to the morning program on KVET.

"This city is growing too fast," the woman said as she lit up another cigarette. "No place I'd want to live. In ten years this city will be enormous, like Houston."

Tamika smiled briefly as though she had any interest at all.

"It's a hard world, darlin'," the woman told her between drags as they slowly progressed through the morning's traffic. "Ain't nothing comes easy."

Tamika nodded timidly.

"There's a place in town you may want to check out," the woman continued. "Find a lot of kids that wear the same kind of dark clothes you do. There on the Drag. Ever been on the Drag?"

Tamika gave another passive nod.

"I think you should spend some time down there, get a feel for the world before you take off too far. You may find that you'd be better off where you were. Anyway, I can take you down there, but you're on your own, then. I'm sorry. I wish I could help more."

"Thank you," Tamika told her kindly before they fell into silence again. She didn't speak another word until she was dropped off in front of the Church of Scientology on Guadalupe. "Please don't mention this to anyone."

The woman smiled. "You're safe with me. Now take good care of yourself."

Tamika thanked her once again before slamming the door.

Guadalupe Street was vibrantly alive with young students rushing to their morning classes. The businesses already open for business, serving breakfast and coffee to the tired faces of the real world. The street smelled of grime, much like a real city. She liked the smell. A group of young disheveled kids were splayed on the corner in front of the Bagel Shop. They were sound asleep like a pile of dirty dogs—all but one that stared at her with fiery red eyes. The stranger's eyes locked onto her—eyes that were surrounded by a vicious war-paint of cheap cosmetics. A burnt orange and black frightwig rose above the person's head like the feathers of an Indian's headdress. Then he smiled at her, his black lips curving into the most natural expression she had ever seen. She returned the gesture comfortably as she wandered closer. He sat up and studied her as she stood over the sleeping mound of dirty youths.

"Hello," she whispered to him. She realized he was quite young, yet strangely intuitive in his observations. "I'm Tamika Tovar."

He bowed his head gracefully. "Opaque," he introduced himself with an unexpectedly strong voice. "Have a seat. Join us."

Friday, September 11, 1998
10:33pm

Austin, Texas

The rain dripped down the tall pane windows of the Palmer Auditorium, smearing the lights of the city to the rhythms of the Austin Symphony. Soft lights caressed the stage with delicate layers of pastels. Behind the musicians was a banner listing all the corporate sponsors of the event, *The Third Annual Swing Symphony*. Judging by the immensity of the audience, the symphony fund-raiser was a success.

Professor Vaughn Richter leaned back in his chair as he studied every movement of the conductor's baton, yet he witnessed nothing. It was all felt deep within where dreams and passions materialize. He thought back to a time early in his life when the seeds of his inspiration were sown. His recollections were vivid. He could almost feel the breeze blowing through the rusty screen, whipping the caramel colored curtain in slow swirls. His father sat at his desk, reading one book while holding his place in another. His back was turned to him, much as it always was. He knew this part of his father quite well, but his eyes were shrouded in mystery. In fact, he had no recollection of what color they even were. From a nearby radio, the music of Hoagy Carmichael filled the air with tones as rich as the fragrance of wildflowers. It was the first time he really remembered the impact of music, how it controlled his heart and steered his emotions. That very moment seemed somehow orchestrated by the music that solidified his past, secured in memory like a velvet bookmark. His love began from that moment on, both in music and in his determination to be the great man he considered his father to be.

Generous applause showered the conductor as Gershwin's *Nice Work If You Can Get It* came to a close. The rain slammed mercilessly against the massive green domed roof. The conductor took an appreciative bow before turning his baton to the orchestra.

As a devout enthusiast of the genre, Vaughn could attend a performance like this every night of his life. In an age so far removed from class and elegance, an event such as this sadly came but once a year.

He was rather disappointed that the program contained not a single work from his favorite composition team, Rodgers and Hart. Their unlikely union defined the humble lives of a lost era's working class. They were the perfect combination, with Richard Rodgers' flawlessly crafted music supplying the foundation for the most sincere and thoughtful lyrics ever penned to song. Lorenz Hart was a poetic genius, a man whose words melded to the core of the human soul.

Across the circular table, he could feel the eyes of Doctor Schtepp. He needn't look to know they were upon him. He could feel their presence, trying desperately to penetrate his psyche, to force an insight into his sacred identity. Schtepp was the perfect colleague—determined, intelligent, comprehensively researched, and highly educated. He had a strong work ethic that perfectly matched his own. Otherwise, there was little more to be said. He believed that if you hadn't a good thing to say, there was no use for words. On a non-professional level, he kept his silence in regard to Doctor Schtepp.

Sitting next to his colleague was Virginia Jahnke, the development director of the Austin Civic Opera. She was an attractive woman, despite her slight obesity. The beauty of her face was somehow reliant upon its fullness. He couldn't imagine her appearance any other way. She was sophisticated and savvy, with a flair for style and a genuine artistry with cosmetics. She seemingly had a weakness for Schtepp, which Vaughn assumed was based on his pathetic nature. He was a man with money and little more. Her kindness to him, he believed went no further than the hopes of his generosity toward the Opera. She seldom spoke with Vaughn, considering him either too modest or too frugal to become a notable donor to the arts.

As the conductor delivered his stale and over-rehearsed humor to the warmly receptive crowd, Vaughn was reminded of the ceremony for his undergraduate degree many decades ago. The same tacked-on charm. Same rhetoric. He clearly recalled the feeling of that stuffy auditorium, enduring the words that parted him from the reason for his attendance. Unlike those times, his personal research projects had intensified in public value beyond the chemical formula for lysergic acid diethylamide. His life, as he had always dreamed, finally would make a difference on mankind. His father would have been proud.

He glanced at the program once again to see that it was the last song of the night, Cole Porter's *Begin the Beguine*. It was one of his all-time favorites. He pondered the cumulative worth of the memories that defined his life, and how this song seemed to somehow thread itself throughout. As the music stirred life into the still atmosphere, Vaughn leaned forward and smiled. It was almost as if he could reach out and touch the fogged windows of his father's Chrysler Imperial. That is where the song took him. The summer of 1966, a night he would not forget. It was that very night that he resolved this song to be his favorite, as it played softly over the radio—his only contact with the outside world. The image of the twisted oak trees swaying in the cool breeze stood erect in memory like a statue of honor bearing his name. Outside the car, the crescent moon shined on a vast and empty countryside road, with every shimmering star visible in the blackened sky. In the expansive backseat of the car, alone and far from civilization, Lenora Craig was losing her virginity. And so was he.

He raised the wineglass to his lips, sipping the smooth pinot noir as he watched the bows of the violins move in one great, synchronized motion. The moment he received his Masters degree, the moment he accepted his life's career as a chemistry professor at the University of Texas—all chained together by the memory of this one song.

He glanced across the table at the other faces that shared his space. He could see in their eyes that his exuberance was not shared. Doctor Schtepp was far away in thought, as usual—probably scheming ways of spending more time with him. Virginia Jahnke smiled, as she always did. Her eyes studied the occupants of a nearby table—the board of directors for the Vi-Tel software corporation. Otherwise, she was completely oblivious to the fact that timeless romantic music played, calling upon her own spent youth. So far was it lost from her that she failed to even recognize its voice harkening through the rhythms like the ghost of a childhood friend. It was a game to them all. A fashion show, of sorts. The music was there only for ambiance, for its role in the prestige they sought to obtain. Few noticed, and even fewer cared. Vaughn cared, he cared a great deal in both regards—not just for the wonderful music, but also for the prominence that he would soon acquire. In just one year, everything in his life would be quite different.

When the music left the auditorium, the people followed, shuffling themselves slowly into the lobby with impersonal smiles.

"Would you care to join me for a drink?" Schtepp asked Vaughn as they stood by the doors in the lobby. The rain trickled down the glass, bleeding the outside world of all its color. "Maybe at the Elephant Room?"

"Oh...not tonight, I'm afraid," Richter responded politely with a firm and deeply rich voice. His vocal cords would've suited an opera singer. The strength of his voice was amplified by the determination that illuminated from his deep-set eyes. "It's been a long day."

Schtepp nodded dejectedly as he adjusted the hair that rested over his bald crown. He looked up at Vaughn's face, atop his tall muscular frame. He found himself drowning in his eyes. He felt himself lose his own identity briefly as he floundered to escape the comfort of his comrade's towering confidence. Yet, there was nothing he wanted more than that loss.

"Did you enjoy the show?" Vaughn asked calmly.

"Yes, yes I did," he replied as he scooted closer to the front door. He held it open for Vaughn, watching as he glided through it with the stature of royalty. Once outside, Schtepp opened his black umbrella and turned to Vaughn, staring at his perfectly sculpted face, his handsomely male features, and the gray beard that gave his pronounced jaw a sublime dignity. He could tell by his thick and dark eyebrows that his short gray hair had once been the same dark shade.

Together they stood under the umbrella as the rain formed an arc around them. It covered them like a webbed claw. Schtepp looked up at him and nodded. "Well, have a good night."

Vaughn smiled politely as he pulled his emerald-colored jacket closed. He looked at his watch, realizing that it was already eleven-fifteen, much later than he had anticipated. When he glanced back up, lightning ripped across the sky, followed immediately by a deafening thunder. "We'll talk again on Monday." He turned away and walked briskly through the parking lot as the cold rain streamed down upon him like confetti.

11:01pm

"Thunder freaks me out," Tamika confessed as the rain streamed over the Bagel Shop's green awning. She was crouched in the corner of the deck, safely tucked away in the shadows. She cradled her legs in her arms to conceal her weight. Her pillowcase sat nearby, safely dry under a wooden table. The plastic head of the doll peeped from within, floating in a pool of dark clothing. "I hope it stops soon."

Jobie stretched his dirty hand outside of the deck, reaching into the cold water that descended from the colorless sky. He inhaled deeply, breathing in the grimy stench of the city that intensified with the rain. It smelled of an aged society, used like a whore. "I can't see this rain lasting long. I don't think it ever rains this much here in Texas." It didn't even occur to him that Tamika would know. In fact, he was hardly aware of her presence. To him, it was just Treva along with two other spectators. He leaned back against the wall and propped his bare feet up on one of the wooden tables. "We're not staying in this town very long."

Inside the bakery, it was completely dark, closed for the night. Quiet, as was the rest of the Drag.

"How did you guys get all the way to Texas?" Tamika asked. She hoped her questions would bring her closer to their tight circle. She felt like an outsider, unsure of the club's secret handshake. She looked over to Treva and smiled. In her she saw a potential companion, if for no other reason than the fact that she found her to be prettier than herself.

Treva sat on the floor in demure posture, rolling a fat joint as she sipped from a Diet Coke. A cigarette burned slowly, hanging from her mouth, quenching her appetite. "We couldn't find a ride." Her cheerful voice trembled like a feeble child. She licked the edge of the fine paper, finishing the joint that would relinquish Jobie's once impressive supply. She glanced at Tamika, thinking that she could see the two of them becoming closer. If for no other reason than the fact that she knew she was prettier than Tamika. "We found a freight train eventually." She reverted her attention back to matters at hand, the lighting of her joint. A dead silence followed.

"How about a game of truth or dare?" Jobie suggested, bored with their trite discussion. His question was clearly aimed at Treva, hoping to pry vital information pertaining to her morals.

She hadn't even noticed him speaking. She was too preoccupied trying to light the joint with her cigarette. Her face was scrunchy and focused with one eye closed and a cocked brow. He waited until she had it lit before rephrasing the question to be more direct. "How old were you when you first had sex, Treva?"

She took a hit off the joint before passing it over to him. She let out a deep cough before taking a drag off her cigarette. As she released the smoke into the sticky air, she smiled diffidently. "I was pretty young, and to be honest, I'd really rather not say." She turned to Opaque, raising her brow to pose the same question.

Opaque was centered on top of the middle table with a black comforter shrouding his thin body. He towered over them like an effigy. He shifted his silent attention to her, feeling her thoughts, studying her feelings. His enormous military bag sat at his side, overflowing with all of his expensive and eccentric clothing. He returned her gaze with confidence, masking his thoughts behind ghoulish make-up and a hollow expression. He kept his emotions well tempered, though his opinion of her was souring by the day. He honestly wished he had never introduced her to Jobie. He had been the third wheel ever since. "I'm not into sex, and I'm not one to tell. Tamika?"

Tamika's eyes widened as the question came to her. The honest answer wasn't an easy one. Not for her ego. She'd have happily given away her virginity years ago, had someone wished to take it. There were many boys with whom she would've shared the experience, but the feeling was never reciprocated. She still harbored bitterness about it, and now that the years had passed, she felt she had somehow missed the boat. She couldn't turn back time, and there wasn't any girl her age that she knew who hadn't already lost her virginity to a man. Even her friend Cindy would occasionally have sex with a much older man, a fact that caused an unbearable rift in their trust. It not only derailed Tamika's confidence, but also made her green with envy. Her chastity invariably became a conviction, a cover from the difficult truth she kept close to herself. "I'm a lesbian," she told them proudly. "I have no interest in men. My first experience was with my friend Cindy *years* ago, like maybe when I was fourteen."

Jobie nodded his head casually as though he cared. His lungs were still filled with smoke as he passed the joint back to Treva. "Don't bogart the fucker, Treva," he requested, knowing that she had practically consumed his entire bag on her own. He turned to Tamika, who stared with those frail, puppy dog eyes. Her low self-esteem annoyed the hell out of him. "I was fourteen also."

"How did you get your nickname, Opaque?" Tamika asked timidly.

"I made it up."

"I used to have a nickname," Treva exclaimed between hits as her arms suddenly exploded into the misty wet air. Her fingers wiggled with excitement. "My mother always called me Purty. Isn't that ridiculous?"

Everyone laughed, mostly at her ostentatious behavior. Jobie's quiet comment went undetected under the cackling laughter. "Fitting."

"I always liked my mother," Treva said as she passed the joint over to Jobie before taking a quick gulp from the Diet Coke. Her high-pitched, childish voice absorbed the entire focus of their attention. "My father..." She shook her head slowly before she continued, "what a dick."

"Why don't you like music?" Jobie asked her out of nowhere. "How can anyone not like music?"

"My family *loves* music. In fact, believe it or not, my grandmother was once in a band! Way back in the fifties, they were called Strawberry and the Milkshakes. She was Strawberry, because of her hair. Just like mine. My grandmother was a wacko. A different kind of crazy than my dad...I fucking *hate* that asshole. *Hate him.*"

Opaque watched intently as the anger burst inside her. He had seen it several times before. Her brow furrowed and her teeth grated while she studied the ground, locked into a memory. He imagined the scenes that played out in her mind, the horrors of her past that she struggled to contain in a locked box. The anger took ownership of her, enflaming her body with a coarse ruddiness of dappling hives. Her skin discolored slightly as if lava from an internal volcano seeped from her pores. It spread quickly, flowing down her arms to her bony fingers. Her expression was lethal and venomous. For a fleeting second, she almost appeared monstrous—then suddenly her innocent smile reappeared, extinguishing the negativity altogether with one quick breath. Her tense, splotchy complexion dispersed as well, residing below the surface of her skin, waiting for the next manic tremor.

"Yeah...my father," Treva said as she examined her arm, scratching it nervously to quench the hives spawned by her own neurosis, "he *loved* music."

Jobie passed the joint back to her. He hadn't noticed a thing. "What's the wildest thing you've ever done sexually?"

She smiled innocuously as she took a quick hit from the small roach poised between her thin fingers. Jobie smiled briefly as well, waiting to reveal his amazing exploits, like the time he made out with two drunk girls after a punk show.

"I swear," Treva began, "I was always interested in sex, even at a young age. I knew men wanted it, and I knew they wanted me. I remember when I was in fifth grade I used to meet with a group of boys in the alley after school. They'd skip lunch so that they could give me their lunch money to see me naked." She took the last hit off the roach before flicking it into the rain. "Soon the small group became half my class! I was a celebrity!"

Jobie glanced down at his kilt, checking to see if his erection was obvious. It wasn't. If he had a dime to his name, he'd have offered a trip to the back alley, just like the old days for her...

"I got really good at reading men," Treva admitted. "I remember being in a mall once at about the same age, and I could tell which ones would, and which ones wouldn't—all from a look in their eyes."

"How do you know you were right?" Tamika asked.

"Experience. Besides, I've seen that look my whole life. I know it when I see it." She peered into Jobie's striking eyes, reaffirming her statement. She smiled for a brief moment before she continued. "I didn't even need birth control back then—I had never even had a period! I remember fantasizing about telling my dad that I was pregnant at that age. I really wish I would've been. His response would've made it all worth it. Sex is such a powerful thing."

"Who showed you that power?" Opaque asked, following the lead of suspicion.

She avoided the question, hiding behind a phony facsimile of a grin.

Jobie raised his eyebrows as his heart rate quickly increased. Treva could sense this—she didn't even need to look at him to know. His interest in her seemed to seep from his pores.

"I wanted to be good at sex. I was determined to be the perfect lay." She paused to sip from her soda as her small audience waited in uncomfortable silence. "Once...I believe I was in seventh grade at the time, I was having sex with my father's friend. He wanted to keep it a secret, but all I wanted was to have his child so my father could never forget. Didn't happen, and I agreed to be quiet about the whole thing. The following year at a camping trip, my father packed the camcorder for whatever reason...I hid it in my tent under some clothes and left it running. It was at the perfect angle, though the lighting wasn't very great. As I expected, my father's friend came to my tent for a visit in the middle of the night. Caught the whole act on film! I wish I still had it. Unfortunately, I left it for my father to find after I ran away."

Everyone rearranged themselves from awkward discomfort as the rain trickled from the awning, splattering against the filthy sidewalk.

"This may sound like an odd question," Tamika offered obliquely, "but have you ever had an orgasm?"

"Hmm..." Treva contemplated as she took a quick sip from her Diet Coke. "I'm not sure. I suppose not." She shrugged her shoulders as she lit another cigarette. The question seemed irrelevant to her train of thought. "You know," she continued, "whenever someone pissed me off, I always found a way through sex to get even, usually ten-fold. For instance, I had a classmate whom I hated. She was one of those annoying popular bitches everyone wanted to fuck. I hate girls like that. She had heard from a friend that the football team had pulled a train on me—which was only partially true. Two players, and I only did it to keep up my reputation at the time. Anyway, she insulted me in front of some of my friends. She called me a whore to my face, the stupid bitch. I wanted to kill her. That weekend, I went out of my way to score one of the players that I hadn't yet—her boyfriend. I found out afterward that I had actually taken his virginity. Word about it got out, thanks to my big mouth, and they broke up."

Tamika leaned forward uncomfortably to check the clock inside the bakery just as lightning ripped across the sky, trailed by bellowing thunder. "It's eleven-fifteen."

"So what about you, Jobie?" Treva asked with her sweetly juvenile voice. "What's the wildest thing you've done sexually?"

Jobie leaned back, placing his hands behind his head. "I'm not the type to kiss and tell."

Saturday, September 12, 1998
1:16pm

Treva strolled carelessly down the Drag as a sparse rain trickled from the misty gray sky. She swung a can of Diet Coke in her claw-like hand as a cigarette dangled from her smiling lips. The rain dampened her dirty scalp, pasting her raspberry-colored hair to her prominent cheekbones and fair skin. Her wet shirt clung to her bony ribcage, accenting the perkiness of her hard nipples under the thin lime-green fabric.

Her cheery disposition shined amongst the dour faces shielded beneath colorful umbrellas. Women gave passing glances of discontent like drenched kittens, mortified that their cosmetic allure had washed away with the rain. The men, on the other hand, secretly ravaged her body with their sordid imaginations. Their lascivious attention fertilized her ego, building upon her personal identity of objectified beauty. She held their gaze, flirting shamelessly with bedtime eyes that beckoned decadently sinful pleasures. It had been months since she had allowed a man to have custody of her body. She humored the idea of luring one or two young students to the alley where they could have their way before leaving her naked and neglected, discarded like trash. The thought brought a smile to her meager face.

"Spare some change?" a young girl asked from underneath the Eckerd awning.

Treva stopped in mid-stride as she placed her wrists to her scrawny hips. Her posture spoke sassiness. "You're asking *me* for money?" She pointed to the pavement with a stiff finger before dramatically poking at her own flat chest. "You're loungin' in *my* bedroom!" Her tiny giggle reduced her confrontational manner. It screamed of innocence. She raised her shoulders with heavy exasperation as she rolled her eyes dramatically. "Whatever..." She strutted back down the sidewalk with a meandering liquid-like motion, haphazard and carefree.

Her gaze fell to the concrete that collected pools of water in its broken surface. Several layers of cement comprised the sidewalk in its entirety, each from a variance of construction throughout past decades. The result was a patchwork of dissimilar grays that unified into a solid singular surface, an olla-podrida of design.

There came a rift in the flow of pedestrian traffic as she approached 22nd. A dark male presence stood in her path with crossed arms and a daunting scowl.

25

He raised his eyebrows salaciously at the sight of her, allowing his forehead to crinkle unnaturally over acne scars. He was tall and muscular with menacing, angry eyes. His attire was black, including his back-turned baseball cap that concealed his greasy orange hair.

"Who are you?" he hissed at her. His voice was shrill, a near caterwaul.

Treva smiled comfortably as she sucked the final drag from her cigarette, flicking the butt of it into a stream of water that raced toward a nearby gutter. "Why?"

His expression hardened like block ice. "Because I asked."

"My name is Treva," she resigned with her silly sweet voice. "I just came to town. And your name?"

His eyes rolled with sheer disappointment. His lips pursed like a sphincter. "You don't know?"

She raised her hands into the moist air while shaking her head emphatically. "I don't know...sorry."

"You need to know who I am," he told her flatly. "I'm Dickhead." He looked to gauge her response. "Got it?"

She nodded, though she didn't get it at all.

"See all these people around here on the corner?" he asked her, gesturing to a gregarious bunch of filthy kids loitering in front of the Bagel Shop. "Ask them about me, they'll tell you."

"Hmm...I'd rather you tell me. What is there to know?"

He smiled proudly, revealing his chipped and stained teeth. "Let's go have a seat." His voice was as enticing as grating metal.

She followed him to the arcade where they sat on the dry walkway alongside the inner wall of the Scientology building. She took a quick sip of her Diet Coke and faced him directly.

He raised his voice to a steady monotone. "What do you want to know?"

"Obviously what you want me to know," she replied with contrasting vivaciousness. She could see in his indignant eyes that he'd rather she hear from someone else, just to add to his mystique and validity. She could tell that she wasn't playing along very well. "Come on, tell me about it."

"Well..." he began slowly as he forced himself into a relaxed pose against the crumbling white wall, "I came from Atlanta, I've been here around a year, maybe longer."

She nodded supportively.

"When I got here, a lot of the businesses were coming down on us because of the Oogles, and there was a lot of tension out here. Shops would give us shit, the cops were starting to enforce the *no-camping* laws to keep us off the streets. I don't know how it all came down, but it's kind of history down here anymore...one night a group of about half a dozen Straight Edgers came to the Drag and started bustin' people up. They don't like us."

26

"What is that?" Treva asked anxiously, pleasantly enthralled in the direction of his story. "Is that a gang?"

"Kind of," he told her. "Straight Edge, the vegetarian assholes who live some puritan lifestyle…they're as much a gang as skinheads are, but they just don't drink like the skinheads."

She nodded as if she knew anything about what he was telling her. All that mattered to her was the word *gang*. She always fancied the thug lifestyle.

"Some of my friends ended up in the hospital, it was bad. Really bad. As the legend goes, I organized a couple of the tougher Crusties, we had about four of us, and we stayed on guard each night until they returned. They never did, but from that moment on, anytime we ever got shit from anyone, my boys would keep the peace for us out here. When the stores would give us trouble, I'd bust out their windows after hours. The cops would talk to us, but no one knew any different, they had no proof…so we started getting more respect. Do you get what I'm saying?"

Treva nodded. "Have you seen the other gang since then?"

"Nah," he shrugged half-heartedly.

"So who all is part of your gang?" she asked.

"We're not a gang," he decided. "We're generally pacifists. Just don't mess with us."

"What is a Crusty? And what is an Oogle?"

"Crusties are the real thing. We live on the streets, we move from city to city—it's a lifestyle. Oogles are posers. They're kids from the suburbs pretending to be street. Mommy brings them money and picks them up when it rains. Like I said, posers."

"Have you been a Crusty very long?"

"Long enough," he replied defensively. "I was part of the Five Points crew in Atlanta. I was in Athens, Asheville, Philly…I spent some time with the spider punks in New York."

She almost didn't want to ask, fearing that her redundant inquiries would diminish her own street credibility. It was clear that the word punk seemed synonymous with renegade. "What's a spider punk?"

"They live in the trees, they sleep in hammocks way in the tops, no one knows they're there. They live in Central Park."

"I think Jobie is a Crusty punk, then," Treva mumbled aloud, speaking her random thoughts for no apparent reason. "But he doesn't sleep in trees."

"Boyfriend?" His fists clenched briefly.

"Not really." Her mind quickly went from Jobie to his empty bag of pot. She could use a new hook-up. "Do you smoke?" she asked under her breath with a coy and playful smile.

He grinned pompously. It almost seemed like a taxing effort for him. "Looking to get high?"

She nodded her head quickly, excitedly. "Do you know anybody?"

"I know a lot of people," he boasted.

"Can you get acid?" she whispered with bright enthusiasm.

He smiled confidently, though his eyes were still tense and bitter. He casually reached inside the pockets of his black jeans and unfolded a flier. "Skin Ensemble show tonight...remember this name, and you can tell Talon that Dickhead sent you, he owes me a big favor..."

1:17pm

Tamika glanced over her shoulder, out the Metro coffee shop's second-story window overlooking the Drag. The window's glass was streaked from the rain that was in a current state of submission. On the street below, the traffic scooted slowly in opposing directions, clogged and congested. The windshield wipers of each car alternated to a different rhythm, scraping across dry glass as if anticipating another shower at any second.

She rearranged herself in the hard metal chair that was shaped like a box with harsh right angles. The backrest was made of separated metal, making tiny waffle patterns on her elbows and arms. She leaned forward on the glass tabletop, admiring the blue shadowing of Opaque's cheeks. His face was flushed white, his lips a blackish-purple, his cheeks shadowed with a misty dark midnight blue that somehow blended up to the circumference of his smoldering red eyes. His color scheme was almost patriotic.

Over the metal guardrail, she could hear the occupants of the coffee shop laughing happily as the music of Clan of Xymox's album *Medusa* played over the speakers. She wished they would go away.

In the distance she could see the black metal tread-plate stairs that separated the two floors. The bottom floor was softly lit by rows of track lighting that reflected dully off the polished cement. Upstairs felt like an attic, with the entire shop being nothing more than a modified warehouse. The brick walls were the color of ash.

"We're not staying in Austin long," Opaque told her flatly as he slowly stirred his café mocha. His arms were completely lost inside elbow-length, black satin opera gloves. They hugged his pale skin tightly. Silver claws like those of a buzzard extended from his fingers, clicking against the ceramic mug to the lethargic rhythm of the music. "We'll be leaving here soon."

"Where are you going?" she asked.

"Everywhere." He took a dainty sip of his simmering drink as his eyes followed the perimeter of the glass tabletop. Its shape reminded him of an amoeba. "Heading east to New Orleans."

"Sounds exciting."

"I'm excited to go," he told her. "Hopefully our luck won't change for the worse."

She glanced up at a young couple, both doused in heavy black garb. She glared with envy at the young girl's thin shapely body before returning her attention to Opaque. He was watching her. In his eyes it was clear that he had seen right through her thoughts. She could see the judgment in his eyes, though she didn't fear the verdict. He was merely observing and understanding who she was. Apparently understanding too well. "What made you want to leave home?" she asked him.

His eyes squinted and his mouth tensed as though he had swallowed his tongue. "Had to."

"Why?"

"Our family had trouble," he admitted. "It was always Jobie. He and my dad had some problems. I never understood why, and if there was a reason, I never knew. My dad drank too much, and then there'd be some problems...it was sometime in the spring, possibly April...I remember that the night was chilly and there was a terrible wind. It really seemed like it was going to rain. I remember it well. It never did, though." He sat quietly a moment. "Such a strange memory, but it's the tree that I remember the most. Funny...the tree was being blown really hard, the branches were banging against the house...the sound of the wind drowned out the screams coming from the other room. I opened the window. I was scared. I was always scared. Scared that dad would come after me next. I climbed out onto the roof and to the largest branch, hiding in the tree as I had since I was a little kid."

Tamika watched him, seizing the discomfort that he felt by reaching out and grabbing his hand. It was tight and rigid.

"I clung to the branch, and the wind was whipping the whole tree, I felt as if the entire world shook with instability. I could see inside Jobie's room, I watched dad beat him. I had never seen it before, and I will never forget it. When dad left to go downstairs, I climbed onto the roof and knocked on Jobie's window. I watched him cry...I had never seen that before. My image of him shattered, and I liked what stood in place—he was scared, just like me. I climbed inside the window and he told me dad was coming back, that I had to leave. I asked what happened. He wouldn't say. I could feel the wind pushing me around as I watched him lay in a curled ball on the floor. His lips were bloody. I asked him to get up, to go. I didn't have any idea what I was saying." He took a sip of his smoldering drink and stared into the dark liquid.

"Did he get up?" Tamika asked.

"He asked where we'd go, and it was clear he wasn't sold on my idea. Honestly, I wasn't either. I suggested Portland since he had a friend there. He visited regularly, doing research for his book at the Liberation Collective on weekends...he got up, and he was obviously in pain, holding his gut, limping to the window. My heart was racing, I was so scared. Everything was chaos. Dad would come up soon. We had to leave. We had only a few minutes. I stumbled across the roof and back into my room, filling a military bag with all my clothes and keepsakes. Then came the sound of dad's footsteps, slowly, drunken…up the stairs again. They were angry belligerent steps."

Tamika stared with wide eyes that begged him to continue.

"I tossed the bag out the window so that it rolled onto the lawn below. I helped Jobie climb out his window. He was in a lot of pain. Dad could've killed him, and maybe he would've. I put my arm around him and helped him to the tree, pushing him up into it as dad opened the window and screamed at us. He was violently angry, but too drunk to follow us. I stood there staring at him, consumed with fear and humility and an enormous feeling of failure to him as Jobie climbed down the tree. Dad was disappointed with me—I could see it in his eyes. I began to second-guess my motivations, and then I thought of Jobie. I had to leave, I had to get him out of there. I knew dad would follow, he'd go downstairs and out the front door just in time to catch Jobie and beat his ass. But he didn't. He just stared at me, hurt. His eyes said everything. He needn't speak. We looked at each other for what seemed like hours, and I will never forget. I climbed down the tree to the front yard, grabbed my bag, and together we raced down the street, running through fields and searching for darkness. We clung to the darkness for days, living in the shadows, traveling at night. A few days later, we were in Portland."

"Did your dad ever try to find you?" Tamika asked.

"If he did try he failed, so I'm not sure. We stayed in Portland for a few weeks, bumming money on Burnside, thinking we would find a place to live there. We had no plans to go anywhere else…then Jobie spent a weekend in Eugene. Before we knew it, we were staying in Eugene. Jobie really liked it there, I didn't. Too many hippies. Too small. I like living in the city. After about a month, we found a ride down to Berkeley. At that point, we decided that we would simply travel from city to city, state to state. Leaving was the hardest. The rest has been easy."

"Do you always agree on your destination? Do you ever argue?"

"We try to give each other plenty of space," he told her. "I tend to be a loner, I like my personal space. I need privacy. I tend to not mix well with others. I obviously don't fit in on the Drag."

"Do I bother you?" she asked.

"Actually, not at all. Now, Treva bothers me."

"How can you not like Treva?" she asked. "She is always so happy, always laughing."

"But she never laughs at anything funny!" he pointed out. "She just laughs. I mean, how weird is that?"

"What do you think of Austin?" she asked him.

"I like it." He looked down the length of the coffee shop, at the dark and empty stage at the far end of the balcony. The ceiling was naked with crisscrossing patters of wooden planks like the ribcage of a gutted carcass. The blocky metal tubes of the ventilation system clung to the bottom of the wood blowing cold air upon them. "The Drag isn't my scene, but Jobie seems to like it. It works for now."

"I don't think I fit in well here, either." She glanced out the window once again, seeing the same cars still lined up in traffic. The Eckerd sign suddenly lit with an electrical glow. Its light reflected in the water droplets on the windowpane, sparkling like glitter. "Where are you going after New Orleans?"

He smiled. "Who knows? We'll decide that at the time."

"Sounds like a blast. I should do something like that someday. I could just leave here, and why not?" She let out a deep exhalation that determined defeat. Her enthusiasm had completely derailed, her slumped shoulders and poor posture revealed this. "I'm not sure I could do it on my own."

"Why don't you join us, then," he offered loosely as he tapped the metal tabletop with his silver claws.

Her eyes widened with excitement. She could hardly believe it. "Really?"

He nodded casually.

She stared down at the old wooden floor, deep in contemplation, high on flattery. She was astounded, practically coming out of her dark skin. She looked up at him and smiled with all her straight teeth perfectly visible. "Yes, I'll go. But what will we do?"

"What are we doing now?"

"Wow...I've never been anywhere before...I've never even left Texas before!"

He smiled politely. "Here's your big chance. So what were your plans?"

"Right now or down the road?"

"You tell me," he told her.

"Someday I want my own home," she revealed with a pleasant smile. "A nice home. It wouldn't have to be big or fancy, just a nice house. A house, not a trailer."

He stirred his drink patiently as a smirk formed on his porcelain-white face. "Go on..."

"I want...maybe a dog, one that won't run away."

"What color is the house?"

She was quick to respond: "White."

"A fence?" he asked.

"Haven't really thought of that..."

"Well, think of it—a fence?"

"I guess not," she decided quickly. "Lots of trees, though."

"Would you want kids and a husband?"

"Oh yes," she replied. "Without any doubt I would."

He watched her as she fell into a deep state of introspection. She seemed at ease, it was the first time he had seen her this way. "Since when have lesbians sought husbands?" he asked.

She smiled.

"Busted!" he proclaimed proudly.

"Men don't like women like me," she explained disparagingly.

"What exactly is a woman like you?"

She shrugged her shoulders. "Men like waifs, they don't like fat girls like me."

"Actually, men don't like a shitty self-defeatist attitude like that."

"Well," she exclaimed, "it's the truth!"

"The truth is that you can be what you want to be. Look at me, every day I redefine who I am. I am the artist and I am the art. My expression, I'm like a statue. When I stand in front of a mirror, I can be the person I want to be. If you think you're overweight, then lose it. People do it all the time, why should you be an exception? You're as great as you want to be, and as worthless as you allow yourself to be."

"It's not that easy," she told him.

"Is it easier to just bitch about it? You're a beautiful person, Tamika. Share what you have with the world. It's such a colorless place anyway. Look around you, look at the sullen faces that fill the world. What better reason to have confidence than to simply accept that *no one* has it. That's the best reason I've found! How does that old song go...*wear your love like heaven.* You have so much to offer, there is so much color inside you just waiting to explode like an orgasm of rainbows. Let it out, liberate yourself."

She smiled at him, absorbing his kind words toward her. "I have a gift for you," she announced. "Do you want it?"

He nodded excitedly as his deep purple lips twisted into a very genuine smile.

"It's nothing fancy," she told him as she dug into her pillowcase of items. She pulled out her plastic baby doll with fair skin and no hair. "Here, it's yours...my best friend gave it to me, and I want you to have it now."

He slowly reached up and took hold of its waist, tenderly pulling it from her hands across the glass, cradling it in the clutches of his silver claws. "It's great."

She smiled happily.

"These clothes have got to go," he resolved with an impish sigh as the doll relaxed itself on the spread of his black gloves. "Can I dress it up?"

"It's yours," she said. "You can do whatever you want with it."

"I'll make it my own offspring, then," he said as he smiled from across the table. His warmth radiated through the layers of ivory make-up that covered his face. "Thank you."

Droplets of water covered the bumper's chrome like an assortment of lost contact lenses. Jobie ran his thin finger along the cold surface, peeling away the water like sweat. It streamed down his arm, zigzagging like a snake before descending from his elbow to mud-soaked asphalt.

He slid forward from the curb, dropping himself on the edge of the street. The backside of his kilt absorbed the stagnant mixture of oil and rainwater from a small reservoir of stench trapped between the cracks of the dilapidated asphalt. A blue plastic bottle cap floated in the murky little pool, seemingly drawn to him like a life-raft seeking refuge from the filth and decay. He picked it up and examined it, noticing an inscription on the hidden underside. It read *You Are Not A Winner.*

Across the street, small children ran wildly in circles on the small lawn of the University Baptist church daycare. Black metal bars restrained the children from the world, or was it that the bars restrained the world from the children? Jobie assumed the latter by how the elders nervously watched him. He imagined what they saw in him. He liked what he assumed they feared, finding comfort in the murkiness of their prejudice. There was safety there, a guaranteed distance from vulnerability. The irony was that he would give anything to be behind those bars. He had been taken away from such comfort at too young an age. As he watched them frolic with bliss and disregard, a wave of remorse swept over him. The safety of those confines, he could scarcely remember his own comfortable structure. The cage through which he now peered, it wasn't constructed from love, but rather fear and hate. Those children, he thought, they would spend their entire lives trying to return to this. Now, for him, it was too late. He was a monster, what the parents feared most, yet the reality was he had never changed. Only they had.

"What are you doing?" an innocently sweet voice asked over his shoulder. Before he could turn, Treva plopped herself gleefully on the curb.

"Why are you sitting in a puddle in the street?" she asked.

"Why not?"

"What are you doing?" Her soft, feminine voice blended with the children's innocent chatter.

He shook his head loosely. It was a stern, confident gesture. "Nothing."

"I've met some people," she announced quickly. "I like it here."

"Don't get attached, we're not staying." He turned to face her, peering into her eyes. She smiled at him. His tattooed face was straight and narrow.

"You never smile," she pouted. "Why do you never smile at me?"

He looked quickly over her shoulder to nothing, anything to lose eye contact. "Why do you ask questions like that?"

33

She shrugged her shoulders. "You never smile…"

He turned to face the children once again. Knowing she wasn't watching, he smiled, but only to himself.

"We're going out tonight!" she exclaimed loudly with a deafeningly sappy voice. Sweetness seemed to pour from her mouth like sugar.

"Where?"

"Um…I forgot, but I have a flier right here," she told him as she searched each pocket. "Right here…Ohms…they're actors or something…they're called Skin Ensemble. Not that I care about that, but we're scoring some acid. We're supposed to meet someone named Talon, we'll need to tell him that Dickhead sent us."

"Who is Dickhead?"

"That's who I met…that's what I'm trying to tell you," she said irritably as she extended her arms in the air. "See, you never listen to me…"

He shook his head as he sighed loudly. "Who is Dickhead?"

"Some guy."

"Some guy?" he asked as he turned to her quickly with a sharp eye.

"Yeah…just some guy. Why?"

"Why are you trying to meet other guys?"

"Why not?" she asked.

"What am I here for?" he demanded. "Why are you even hanging out with me, then?"

She sat quietly.

"Why?" he repeated.

"Don't talk to me that way, Jobie," she mumbled uneasily. "I don't know…everyone knows him down here. On this corner, he seems to be the one who watches after things."

Jobie laughed coldly. "Watches after things?"

"Seems that way. He kind of has a gang, they fight another gang called the Straight Edges."

Jobie laughed. "Straight Edge is not a gang…this guy isn't in any gang…he's just trying to get into your pants."

"I don't know," she returned quickly as she raised both hands out to the humid air once again.

"Sounds like he earns his name, if you ask me," Jobie decided.

She shrugged her bony shoulders as her thoughts wandered a different path. "What was the name of your hometown again? I forgot."

"I've told you."

"I have a lot on my mind…I'll remember this time."

"Tacoma," he said quickly as he stood, disappointed. "Puyallup, Washington." He reached in his sporran and pulled out six rocks. "One from each state I've been through."

She reached out her bony hand. "Let me see them."

He grabbed her hand with his other, holding it for a second to see her reaction. She clamped hers around his and smiled at him.

"Can I see them now?" she asked politely, patiently.

He nodded as he placed them in her hand. He watched as she studied each one, drinking his past, wishing she had been part of it then. He loved watching her, memorizing her warm smile, consuming her cheerful disposition.

"Can you tell where each is from?" she asked as she raised one to him. "This one?"

"Arizona..." he said quickly. "I got it about three minutes after I met you. It was right out front of the record store. It's my favorite one, it reminds me of you."

She smiled. "And this one?"

"Oregon. Before I met you."

She laughed. "So are these marked by whether or not you knew me yet?"

"Basically," he admitted.

"Is this everything you own?"

"No," he told her swiftly. "I have my writing and a book I stole in Tucson by Howard Zinn."

"Really? You stole it?"

He nodded proudly. "All property is theft anyway." He watched her as she contemplated his words. It made him feel proud, as if she were acknowledging something about him, maybe his intelligence, but he wasn't really sure. He just knew he liked it—her thoughts, his words. "I keep it hidden along with my writing, I don't want anything to happen to them, they're all I have."

"I see," she said. "Man, I could sure use a cigarette. Those kids are loud...they annoy me."

"Then I must annoy you," he told her. "Who is Dickhead, point him out to me."

She rolled her large eyes. "Why do you keep asking that?" She looked over her shoulder, down 22nd Street. "He's not here. If you want to meet him— "

"I don't," he said as he swiped the rocks out of her hand. He turned and walked away, leaving her alone on the curb. He glanced briefly at the children behind the bars and thought of what he'd give to go back, anything to go back.

11:57pm

Jobie slovenly leaned against the bar, cleaning the dirt from underneath his chipped black fingernails. Tiny red and blue Christmas lights were strung over the bar, painting the air a mixed violet. Black neon lights bathed the sparse white clothing of the other patrons in a purple glow. The venue was dark with misty smoke clinging to the stale air. Silhouettes danced somberly like ghostly apparitions on the nearby dance floor. Opaque was among them.

"Should I get my fortune told?" Treva playfully asked Jobie. She was perched on a barstool, pointing to a nearby table covered with stones. She read aloud the sign over the table: "Rune...Stone...Fortune...Teller." She repeated it twice to herself. She kept her wandering eye on the long line of people waiting to pay five dollars to receive a flogging from Mistress Lakasha. A shirtless man stood before her with his extended hands cuffed to the wall by chains. His head was bowed and his muscular back streaked with red welts from the tresses of the cat-style whip.

"They'll tell you that you'll be going to New Orleans soon," he told her over the gritty pulse of Industrial dance music. He glanced over at the fortune-teller. A wineglass sat at the center of the table. In it was a candle with most of its red wax melted into liquid like red wine. Red wine, with a flame dancing on the surface.

"Just you and me going to New Orleans?" she asked. "That's what I see. I feel like we'll be leaving Austin alone."

"You'd have to ask the bitch with the stupid-ass rocks." He looked out at the dance floor to find his brother. He could sense the attention that Opaque seemed to absorb from those who surrounded him. He was sporting a skin-tight leather outfit that accentuated his body's frail form with satisfying results. His arms were wrapped with tight fishnet that extended from his shoulders to his fingers. His face was flushed white with base and his red eyes seemed to be floating in a cesspool of black eyeliner. It was an unspoken rule of his to avoid color while out clubbing. Only black and white—latex or leather.

Dancing close to Opaque was Tamika, hovering over his every move. The DeeJay booth towered over the dance floor with an open wire mesh screen surrounding it like military netting. Two iron cages stood before the DeeJay booth. Pale young girls with bobbed raven hair danced inside them, wearing only black leather bikini bottoms and a single strip of electric tape across their nipples. Large speakers hung from links of chain with radioactive symbols painted on each. There was a girl with long, pink dreadlocks controlling the center of the dance floor. In each hand she gripped a length of chain, the ends of which burned in bright flames. She twirled them around her body and over

36

her head in unison like bayonets. The orange glowing orbs of fire circled around her rhythmically like fireflies.

On the back wall of the stage was a large screen displaying a grainy black and white film's negative of a vivisection interspersed with transsexual pornography. It was difficult to distinguish the images from another based on the low quality of the footage. Blue orchids lined the front of the stage that contained only a single metal chair.

The music throbbed with an irritating screech, mechanical in origin with the accuracy of a computer. It was a systematic pulse, clamoring like machinery, droning. Heads bobbed and bodies slithered, grinding to the methodical rhythm as white stage-lights exploded with blinding intensity. Then suddenly darkness. The room was invisible, lit only by random candles as the rhythm of the machines grated into a convulsing surge of power like the passions of an android orgy.

On the screen behind the stage were the words *The Skin Ensemble* glowing a faint gray, barely visible. A sullen silhouette of a man stepped onto the empty stage, followed by a woman. The crowd edged close to the stage, standing before the blue orchids. Smoke rolled onto the floor, rising in a swirling haze.

A flash of light ignited from the stage floor like a fiery fountain. In its glow was a tall and lean man wearing only a pair of leather jockey shorts and crisscrossing leather straps that were joined with silver hoops from his navel to his chest. His face was ghastly, near death and painfully thin. His eyes were closed with only the concave of his sockets painted with black eyeliner. There was no trace of hair on his head, including his eyebrows—completely waxed. A tattoo of a snake seemed to slither down the middle of his head like a mohawk. The tongue of the snake split in place of his widow's peak, lapping at his narrow forehead. Its green rapturous eyes were clearly present, even in the stark lighting. He slowly raised his hands outward from his body as the music grated around him. He appeared ominous and evil, like a servant of the underworld, fresh from death. In his hands were two leather floggers, and as he slowly raised them over his head, the tresses covered his face like a leather veil. The music stopped and the lights went out again. The crowd cheered with lewd anticipation.

Treva assumed this mysterious person was whom she had come to meet, Talon. Treva stared with unbridled enthusiasm, eagerly awaiting the return of light to her world. She wanted him to use those whips on someone—she wanted to see their pain. Her breathing became irregular. She squeezed her legs tightly together as she imagined being on all fours in front of him with an arched back, submitting to the leather. She yearned for the structure of the lash.

The music returned, grinding, throbbing…lapping at the audience with swift strokes of brutal punishment like cold metal on hot, sticky skin. The lights exploded once again, revealing two topless young girls bowing at Talon's side. With an unyielding expression and a calculated sense of motion, he advanced toward them.

He grabbed the bleached hair of the first one, coiling a hard fist in her clean hair. He yanked her head back forcefully, albeit gently. She looked at him uneasily, though perfectly relaxed. He moved his lips close to hers, slowly, passionately. He stopped within an inch, keeping her edged with desire as she stared at his mouth. He gave no expression, and no indication of a single thought. He then spit on her face and yanked her head so that she stared helplessly at the ceiling. His saliva dripped from her chin as he pulled his other hand back over his shoulder, lashing her back with his leather flogger. It cracked against her frail skin, ringing clearly over the music that scratched its way through the club's stone walls. She arched her back with desire as he pulled her head close to him once again. He leaned over her and stuck out his tongue, allowing his saliva to drip down into her open mouth. He relentlessly whipped her across the back several times, forcing her to grimace in painful desire. He let loose of her hair and stepped forward to the other young girl.

She stared at him uneasily, though she seemed strangely anxious and excited. A smile worked its way into her expression until he slapped her gingerly across the face. Her expression changed briefly, then the smile returned. She beckoned the scourge to be repeated. He gave it to her, leaving her cheek rosy red. She craved more. He could sense this, and therefore he returned to the other girl, leaving her wanting, frustrated with desire.

He swiftly grabbed the blond by her shoulders and raised her to the metal chair. Twirling his flogger in his hand, flexing his pale muscular body, he looked up at the audience that gave their undivided attention. With tremendous force, he slashed the tresses across her body, leaving a red streak across her flat chest. A second blow wrapped around her ribcage, staining her side with a throbbing bruise. His strike was otherwise precise. As the music lost its momentum, so did he. He left her propped against the chair with her petite hand dangling passively to the floor. Her chest was lined with red streaks like a grid.

The lights faded quickly as coldwave music swiftly changed the mood. Tension filled the air with awkward enthusiasm. Slowly, red lights flooded the small stage. Talon was on his knees with his hands behind his back. His body was speckled with sweat. It dripped from his brow onto the stage. The young girls were gone. He was alone, kneeling in a pool of red light with his head bowed to the ground.

An Asian woman glided onto the stage, shifting her hips from side to side with a saucy sway. Her black hair was straight and long. A tight black latex dress was all she wore, though generously revealing it was. Over her small chest was a pattern of tattoos of leopard spots that crawled up around her neck and down the spine of her back. Just how far they went was only decided with a strong imagination.

She leaned down to his bald head and licked the sweat from his hot, clammy skin.

As the aggressive Industrial beats ignited once again, she raised her hand, holding up a silver hook to the crowd's delight. A white string dangled from the end of it. She brought the hook to her partner's skin, caressing his muscular back with its cold metal surface. Her black hair fell over her pale shoulders, arriving on Talon's hairless head. She suddenly sunk the hook into the pale skin of his back, releasing a small stream of blood as she shoved it through and back out his skin. His expression maintained like a statue as she yanked on the string, pulling his skin firmly. She raised another hook to the riveted crowd. Without hesitation, she plunged the hook into his skin on the opposite side of his back, allowing the blood to drip down his spine. She bowed to her knees, licking the blood from his body, cleaning the wounds with her tongue. She glanced up at the crowd with red lips that seemed to drip from her mouth, down her chin. Her face was free of feeling, free of emotion. It aroused the crowd. It aroused Treva. Her hands became coiled fists as she squeezed her legs tightly together, grinding them against each other under the bar.

"This is some fucked up shit," Jobie mumbled to her.

Treva nodded slowly as she moistened her lips with her firm tongue.

The Asian woman yanked upward on the hooks, forcing the man to his feet. She pulled his face to hers. They stared into each other's eyes longingly before she revealed to him a long silver needle. She placed it in his hands before kissing him. With their lips locked, she lowered the needle between their noses, firmly through their overlapped lips. The crowd cheered as they remained pierced together, connected by the needle. The music grated and the lights diminished around them.

The Skin Ensemble show was over.

The music continued with its blistering madness of modern mechanized grit. The dance floor filled once again.

Treva grabbed Jobie's hand, pulling him to the stage. She led him through the darkness with her hormones piqued by desire, finding the foot of the stage amongst the blue orchids.

Green lights suddenly lit the stage, sending a glowing hue through the club's artificial fog. Treva looked up only to find Talon towering over her, looking down upon her with hollow eyes. Two holes dripped fresh blood from his lips onto the blue orchids.

"You have something we want," Treva screamed in vain over the music. "Dickhead sent us."

He crouched to the edge of the stage, showing recognition of her statement. He grabbed her hand and pulled her up to the stage, leaving Jobie alone with his Asian partner. Jobie climbed the stage as Treva was cavorted off to the rear by Talon. Jobie stood next to the Asian woman, staring at her. She could sense his confusion, though not a word came from her bloodied lips.

"I liked the show," he finally told her.

She stared at him evenly, not even blinking.

He looked to the ground, waiting uncomfortably for Treva to return. "My name is Jobie."

She simply stared at him, allowing the blood to drip from her chin onto her latex outfit. He followed its course, watching the blood trickle down her sweaty chest.

"Nice tattoos." He wasn't sure if he was speaking to a human or a machine. He decided on a different approach to instigate a reaction from her otherwise tacit front. "I like your tits, can I see them?"

She shook her head evenly.

"Do you have a name?" he asked.

She stared silently, unmoved.

"I said I like your tits, can I see them?"

She shook her head again.

Treva emerged through the darkness with a silly-girl grin. She wandered across the stage, smiling shamelessly into the crowd. She shot a fist into the air as she stepped up to Jobie. "Score!" She held out four hits of acid. "Where is Opaque and Tamika?"

"I don't know," Jobie said. "Give them to me, I'll find them. These people are weird."

Treva placed the small cutout papers in his hand, taking one for herself and placing it on her tongue. Jobie wandered through the crowd, seeking out his brother and Tamika.

Talon grabbed Treva's bony fingers with a tender grip. She looked into his eyes, wading through the darkness of his soul.

"I liked your show," she giggled innocently to him.

His face was coarse and hard, frozen. The blood colored his lips like cherries. He softly gripped her fingers. His Asian counterpart stood at his side somberly.

"I understand it," Treva said, not fully knowing what her words meant herself. "The discipline over pain, it's spiritual, isn't it?" The cold hardness of his eyes answered her question without words. "I'm Treva," she sang happily, introducing herself to both of them.

Talon pulled her hand, bringing her off the stage to a back room—a green room painted black. The Asian woman closed the door behind them, locking them inside. One light bulb dangled from the ceiling, sending hard shadows over their faces. There was a pungent odor to the room. The stench of it was sickening.

"Spiritual..." the Asian woman said aloud as he glared at Treva's bright eyes. "How far would you look to find God?"

"I don't believe in God," she admitted. "God wouldn't have allowed certain things to happen to me. Even if he existed, I couldn't believe in him."

"You don't need to look any further than this room to find God," Treva was told.

Treva raised a brow of disbelief. There was a silence that surrounded them, though the music vibrated through the walls. The stench of the room was revolting. And the bright light blazed over a scratched mirror, burning their tender eyes into tight slits. Treva felt like a tourist in their presence, though she wasn't sure where the trip would be taking her. The atmosphere felt synthetic, a byproduct of their ritualistic behavior.

"I don't even know both your names," Treva said with a throaty laugh. Her voice was trill.

"I'm Talon. This is Phaedra Lin." The timbre of his voice was like a raspy whisper. Barely audible, even in the awkward silence.

Treva bowed her head politely to Phaedra. The gesture was not returned.

Talon wandered over to a wooden desk. He opened a drawer and removed a small leather pouch. He returned to the two of them, standing uncomfortably close to Treva.

"You're right," he breathed softly to Treva. His soothing voice was hollow with what seemed to be indifference. "Spiritualism."

Treva smiled. "I suppose so. You're never really doing something bad until someone tells you that you are…right?"

There was no reply.

"I mean, that's why you do it," she decided. Her discomfort was numbing, she wanted nothing more than to leave, but something kept her. "Where is this…this thing that you talked about?"

"Thing?" Phaedra asked with a pointed glare.

Treva grimaced at her expression. She found her to be stunningly beautiful, and it made her sick with jealousy.

Phaedra looked to Talon and nodded. He received her wordless thoughts clearly, and his own silent expression displayed his approval. He grabbed Phaedra's hand and pulled a hypodermic needle from the black pouch. He pricked her finger with it, digging deep into her skin until the blood flowed readily. Taking hold of Phaedra's wrist, he moved it to Treva's mouth, placing her bloody finger on Treva's limp lips. Treva stuck out her tongue, licking the fluid that soured her lips like salt. She sucked Phaedra's finger deeper into her mouth, drinking the blood, devouring it with a thirst she had never known. Talon lifted Treva's hand and pierced her finger with the needle. He plunged it into his mouth, sucking the blood from the small wound. He punctured his own hand before placing it in Phaedra's receptive lips. Together they stood in silence, drinking each other's blood, feeling the life pour down their throats.

Treva's heart intensified its pulse as she licked and sucked on Phaedra's bony finger. The blood pooled at the base of her tongue, igniting her senses with sapphic prurience.

Phaedra reached up and grabbed Treva's upper arm, squeezing it tightly. She could feel the pressure of blood swelling in her arm. She closed her eyes and concentrated on Phaedra's digits that bled inside her lips. She felt a prick in her upper arm, shocking her. She opened her eyes to see that Talon had plunged the hypodermic needle deep into one of her throbbing veins. She gasped uneasily until the fluid entered her body. She could feel it moving up her arm, changing her entire chemistry into grand divinity. The gritty atmosphere of the poorly lit room suddenly transformed into the most beautiful place she could ever possibly imagine. She was surrounded by love—a hyper-orgasmic sense of love and being that was perfectly alien, perfectly perfect. Truly blissful, euphoric. The release of death couldn't be any better, heaven couldn't even be close…the vomit itself, warm and filled with blood, it was absolutely breathtaking…a trip to Eden, a dance with angels.

They were absolutely right—she had embraced divinity.

The following morning, she awoke on the Drag against a beer-stained wall that was tagged with graffiti. Her stomach ached and she felt she was truly in hell. Her comrades were at her side, fast asleep. Her body was quaking, and hives covered her body like acidic burns. She examined her arm briefly, realizing that Talon's pager number had been carved into her arm with a razor blade the night before.

She pulled herself to her feet uneasily. She was in hell, no doubt about it. She lunged herself forward at a pedestrian, grabbing an unsuspecting girl's coat and clinging.

"Please help me," Treva begged the horrified student. "I need to call someone, please…give me some change."

The girl reached nervously into her pocket and pulled out a modest handful of silver coins. Treva reached anxiously for it, knocking it all to the broken sidewalk. As the girl quickly rushed away, Treva fell to her knees and collected the change as her body ached and her mind struggled to control itself. She didn't want the control—she needed the *loss* of control. She owned heaven the night before…now this hell.

The anxiety of the craving caused her skin to splotch and discolor. Hives spread across her body like flames.

She desperately stumbled down the Drag to a pay phone where she dialed the pager number with maddening impatience. A lifetime passed before the call was returned. She picked it up on the first ring.

"Talon!" she screamed into it.

"Yes?" he breathed softly. His voice was icy and calm.

"Help me, I need help."

There was a brief silence followed with the sigh of words: "Where are you?"

"On the Drag, by Tower records."

"Do you have any money?"

"No," she replied dejectedly.

He paused momentarily. "Get money—you'll need it. I'll be down there in thirty minutes," he told her before he hung up.

"No, I need it now, I *can't* wait," she cried as she slid down the hard stone wall. "I need it now... *now*..."

Wednesday, September 16, 1998
4:47pm

The University of Texas at Austin

"I believe I'm done for the day," Chasey Novak told Vaughn.

He raised a stiff finger to request her patience as he finished the last paragraph of the article on the chemical components of Tea Tree Oil. He looked up at her and smiled while rubbing his bloodshot eyes. "It's been a long day."

"The day is not nearly long enough," she replied as she placed her clipboard on his desk amongst the copies of scientific journals. Her face was perfectly composed and relaxed, brimming with complete self-control. She was in her environment, amidst the chemicals, formulas, and grand visions of biological manipulations for the advancement of mankind. Her long straight blond hair was pulled back into a ponytail, wrapped with a baby blue scrunchy. A few strands had escaped and were dangling over her beautifully fair skin, clinging to her naturally full red lips. The color of her blond eyebrows almost blended with her skin tone, and her pale blue eyes seemed to be the entrance to a vast and impressive wealth of scholastic knowledge. Her white lab coat was immaculate, as were her khaki Docker's pants and Adidas jogging shoes. A gold crucifix hung around her neck, resting above her modest cleavage. "Do you have any idea when the samples from the Burdock root are going to arrive?"

"I'll need to contact Schtepp," he told her, a bit discouraged. "I was promised they'd arrive today."

"I can't finish my report until that package arrives."

He leaned back comfortably in his old wooden chair, feeling a sudden relief in his intern's irritation. He liked her diligence. It put him at ease knowing he could depend on her. She would make a fine biological researcher some day. "We're very close. The new serum with extractions from the Evening Primrose Oil and Capsaicin is, in my opinion, ready to be tested on human subjects. What we have at this point is practically marketable, regardless of the improvements we have yet to make."

"I don't believe it's ready, but that's just my humble opinion, and maybe I'm too cautious. The Burdock root," she interjected assuredly. "That will finish it. I just wish those samples…"

44

"I'll get on them. By tomorrow morning, no later."

"I'm sure you can't wait for this to be completed," she said to him with whimsical optimism. "This is your dream, after all."

He nodded proudly. "Indeed so. And no, I can't wait."

She laughed aloud suddenly, chasing her train of thought. "Your ties with Doctor Schtepp will be severed."

He smiled, sharing with her the thoughts they both agreed upon. "Poor old fool. What will he do without me?"

"Well, he does have that woman he speaks so highly—what's her name? Lucinda?"

"Ah, yes...Lucinda. I bet she's a looker," he joked.

"Ah, what's in a look? Beauty is fleeting. She's probably a very nice person."

"Probably so," he responded callously. "Well, have a good night. Any plans?"

"Church choir practice. In fact, I'm almost late."

"I just need to finish up here, I'll be another half hour at least. I need not keep you, you're free to leave."

"Okay, thank you," she offered politely before grinning sheepishly. Her coy expression was indicative of a rare comical thought, or as close as she came to it. "Will I see you at church?"

"Hmm...probably not."

She nodded her head, happy with her casually dull wit. "Well, I'll have you in my thoughts and prayers."

He didn't want to admit how often and under what circumstances he'd be thinking about her. "Take care."

The phone rang as she walked swiftly out the door.

"Hello?"

"Ah, you're still there," Schtepp breathed heavily through the phone. "I thought I'd catch you."

"Have you heard anything about the samples?" Vaughn snapped. "They promised me they went out overnight."

"Hmm..." Schtepp took a moment before replying as he savored the forceful determination of Vaughn's large voice. Every word spoken left him enamored by the simple eloquence and overall sophistication of his entire being. "I'll give them a call. Don't worry about it, I'll handle it."

"I would appreciate that," Vaughn told him flatly.

"Would you care to have dinner tonight?"

Vaughn sighed with irritation, though his words gave no indication of it. "Oh, not tonight, I'm afraid. Long day, I'd just like to watch a movie and call it a day rather early."

"I understand," Schtepp shrugged uncomfortably.

"How about your friend Lucinda? You could ask her."

"She's here right now, as a matter of fact."

"Well, then, I shouldn't keep you," Vaughn said. He thought a moment, wondering who she was, what she looked like, and why he had never met her before. He knew that there was some type of close intimacy involved because he could sometimes smell her perfume on him. Little did he realize that his visualization of the scene on the other end of the phone was far more intriguing than he could scarcely imagine.

"You're not keeping me at all," Schtepp replied softly with a pair of red painted lips. His skin was powdered and pretty, covered with a fair amount of blush and gaudy green eye shadow. A flowery blouse covered his large torso, highlighted with a pair of spongy foam breasts that were shaped like torpedoes. An orange skirt, starched and ironed, covered his stumpy legs that were fitted within a large pair of dark nylons. His free hand caressed the high-heels on his large feet—Lucinda's large feet. "Maybe sometime this weekend, then, possibly dinner at my place?"

Vaughn opened his desk drawer and reached in the far back, under countless scientific publications. He pulled out a wrapped three-pack of bondage magazines. "I've got plans all weekend, actually," he told Schtepp as he considered the assortment of S&M video rentals that awaited him at home. "Thanks for the offer, though."

"Well," Schtepp whispered gracefully into the phone as he reached down and picked up a package from Federal Express, "if the samples arrive after all, I'll let you know."

"Keep me informed," Vaughn said as he slowly, yet eagerly opened the plastic wrap of his sadistic magazines.

Schtepp smiled mischievously as he placed the package of Burdock root samples in his lap. Slowing the completion of the project only prolonged his time with Vaughn. He didn't need the money in the same way his colleague did, nor did he really desire the notoriety. The companionship was worth more to him than the professional foundation of their union and their supposed mutual goal. He knew it was his clout that Vaughn cherished—nothing more. He had his own ulterior motives. "I will deal with it, don't worry. You can trust me."

4:48pm

Wispy dark clouds rushed overhead, sliding under the belly of a gray evening sky. The clouds were too thin and sparse to hold rain, though they carried the scent of another miserably wet night on the streets.

Tamika sat quietly alone in the courtyard of the architecture building, sitting on the edge of a murky pool of filth that was once an impressive fountain. Pigeons fluttered in the palm trees around her, making horrendous noises as if warning of the impending storm that crept its way toward them. Gray feathers floated in the swarthy waters of the fountain, buoyant over the trash that lingered at the rust-tinged bottom.

The wind suddenly picked up, dropping the temperature several degrees. Tamika's velvet dress rippled in the wind, a wave of black flowing down her body. She watched the dress vibrate from the elements, feeling the cold wind raise the hairs on her neck. It felt like fingers running up her spine—thin, bony fingers that scratched for life, begging for recognition. Tamika whispered a soft *hello* to the open wind. Could it be Cindy's ghost, she wondered, still looking after her? Probably not.

The ripples glided across her dress like quivers from a post-mortem muscular reflex. The velvet was like a sea, and it surrounded her body until she became one with it. She was caught in its immobility, incapable of movement, unable to give the struggle for hope. There was nothing. Sadly, nothing had ever changed. This was her life, as it had always been.

She thought back to her lonesome childhood, of her negligent mother, and how often she was told that her life was an accident. Her existence was the worst thing that ever happened to her mother. She was glad to finally give the woman the peace she never deserved.

A long forgotten childhood memory resurfaced. It involved a bicycling accident one summer day. Though the injuries were minor—a scraped knee and wounded pride, the trauma of the experience held her in great captivity. She had been frantic, and she remembered well the feeling of fear as she limped home, crying uncontrollably. As she reached the lawn, she stopped. Her sobbing came to a quick halt as guilt consumed her—her mother wouldn't want to deal with this. She looked across the street where the neighbor's truck was parked in front of the doublewide trailer. How her mother despised the Griffin family, with their well-kept yard and lawn ornaments and Sunday barbecues…she slowly limped across the gravel road, looking over her shoulder every few steps to make sure her mother didn't see her stepping onto enemy land.

Tamika rang the doorbell, feeling like a complete traitor as she stood sobbing with blood running down her leg into her cheap shoes.

"Ma," the eldest son said loudly as he stood over Tamika in the front door watching her cry. "Something happened to the fat neighbor girl…"

Tears ran down Tamika's face, but not from the pain, rather from the humiliation of cowardly running to strangers for help. She was taken into the bathroom, a luxurious place so unlike that which Tamika had always known as a bathroom. It was spotlessly clean, just how she had always imagined hers would someday be. All of the lights in the fixtures worked, and the toilet paper was actually on the roll with the paper going over the top, just as she thought it should. The room even smelled clean, somewhat like bleach, and somewhat like citrus fruit.

"What's your name?" the woman asked as she cleaned the wound with a cotton ball and hydrogen peroxide.

"Tamika."

"Is your mother not home right now?"

Tamika sat silently a while, but before she could answer, the woman asked, "Would you like some cookies? I just made a batch yesterday. Do you like cookies?"

Tamika nodded passively with a sniffle.

"What's your favorite kind?"

"The ones in the brown box," Tamika replied with a beleaguered whimper.

The woman smiled. "The ones I made are peanut butter. Do you like those?"

Tamika nodded again.

"I think you're going to live," she told her. "This was a doozy crash, but I think we can salvage this leg." She put a bandage on it, one with Ninja Turtles. It made her smile. "Okay, that's the smile I was looking for...now how about some cookies?"

The rain began to fall, landing on her black velvet dress, the cesspool of sorrow in which she could find herself sinking deeper and deeper.

"Tamika," a feminine voice whispered with the wind.

She glanced over her shoulder, scanning the dark. Treva's gaunt and pasty face smiled from the courtyard entrance, shining in the cold drizzle. She sauntered up to Tamika, standing over her, momentarily shielding her from the rain. "I need to borrow money."

Tamika immediately handed over two dollars in pandered change without hesitation.

"Once when I was still living in Colorado, I was at this pond," Treva told her as she stared down into the murky fountain. The rain sizzled upon its water, pocking its surface. "There were some ducks down in the pond, and I was fairly young, I liked ducks, you know."

Tamika glanced up at her politely, attentively. She couldn't help but notice her dry and irritated skin. She seemed to be covered with tiny flaking scales. The rain, she hoped, would do her souring complexion some good.

"Suddenly the male ducks overpowered this female duck," Treva told her. "And they all took turns savagely raping this bird. But when the bird had the opportunity to escape, it just laid still, it didn't have any interest in getting away." Treva turned to Tamika and raised an eyebrow that revealed her tired, bloodshot eyes. "Have you ever craved pain?"

Tamika shrugged. "Not really."

"I believe humans instinctually crave pain. Consider the fact that in the course of human history, we've only been out of the caves for a fraction of that time. Of course, cavemen weren't able to buy a woman a drink at the local bar, so they had more direct ways of getting action. For our species to exist, don't you think that there is something built into the design of women to crave this aggressive approach? If not, wouldn't all the women have congregated to the hills, hiding from men? I have this theory about women," Treva resolved. "Show me a woman who claims she isn't drawn to the idea of violently degrading sex, and I'll show you a liar."

Tamika sat quietly as the rain cleansed her body. She didn't want to lie.

"Thanks for the money," Treva said innocently before leaving.

9:10pm

Jobie stood in the shadows, drinking Lone Star beer from a bottle, watching Treva as she waited on the street corner. Every second that passed filled him with pain. He knew she was waiting to meet someone, and it wasn't him. He looked to the ground and kicked some rocks against the stone wall of the alley. In black letters spray-painted across the wall were the words *Chumps Rule*. The rocks ricocheted off the wall, falling to his duct-taped shoes.

A black convertible Plymouth Fury pulled up to the curb. Treva stepped forward and climbed inside. It was Talon and Phaedra. He poured the beer down his burning throat as the car slowly crept down the street with its red taillights aflame.

Propped against the far wall in the darkness was his small fortress, a stack of wooden pylons that held the shrine of *The Apolitical Manifesto*. He stumbled over to it, drawn as if it was the luring finger of his lover. His writing was the only thing in his life that had ever been true, that had never let him down. He leaned his weight against the pylons in silence as he clutched the bottle of beer. He also loved beer. Beer and writing.

Memories fixed themselves upon him. Not the typical ones of locker room torment and brash insults from the class elite, but the more recent memories of his journey to freedom. Treva's effortless smile as the desert wind whipped her raspberry hair in a furious mess. The way the freight train rumbled beneath them as they ventured eastward into the darkness. Jobie faced the rear, watching where they had recently been, uninterested in their direction. Behind Treva, a storm brewed on the western horizon, and the rain could be seen falling from the dark clouds onto barren mountains. The sun was setting behind it, visible only as a fractured blur of hot pink through the distant storm. Its color was a perfect match for Treva's hair. Its natural beauty was also on par. The moment was a perfect start to a perfect end.

He remembered at the time feeling hopeful and optimistic, free from the past.

"Hey!" a raspy voice came from behind him. "Who's there?"

Jobie looked over his shoulder—he was startled—it sounded like his father's voice. Two young men, roughly his own age, stood side by side with crossed arms, blocking the entrance to the alley. One stepped forward, clearly marking himself the owner of the voice. His black shirt was tight and old, torn strategically, revealing firm muscle. His black jeans were of the same quality, and his cheap sneakers, equally so. His orange hair was messy and his face filled with anger. Acne scars covered his jaw like a beard. His friend, an obese mama's boy with thick glasses, long clean hair, and an *Evil Dead* T-shirt, stood with his hands tucked loosely in the pockets of his blue jeans.

Jobie dropped *The Apolitical Manifesto* down on the pylons as he stood to greet his visitors.

"Who are you?" the smaller, more rugged guy asked aggressively. His voice was gritty.

Jobie scoffed with a condescending glower. He crossed his arms to show his casual indifference.

"I asked you a fucking question," the guy said as he stepped closer, edged with explosive anger. "When I ask you a question, you answer. Got me?"

Jobie laughed.

"Do you know who I am?" he asked Jobie.

"Nah...you got it wrong," Jobie responded with a drunken slur. "The question is, do *you* know *me*? Obviously...you do not..."

His face ruptured with heated angst. He reached inside his pocket to retrieve a shiny steel butterfly knife. "My name is Dickhead. I'll tell you the deal...you will show respect." He closed the distance to where they could see each other's bloodshot and mutually hostile eyes.

Dickhead's partner stepped up beside him, besetting Jobie in the corner against the wooden pylons. Instinctively, Jobie smashed his beer bottle downward against the stone wall—a trick he learned years ago. It was the best way to get a jagged edge on a broken bottle. Its loud crash echoed through the alley.

"Come on," Jobie threatened as he raised the bottle to Dickhead. "Let's go, mutha-fucka!"

Dickhead shook his head, unamused by Jobie's drunken swagger. "Drop the bottle, I'll drop the knife. We'll fight like men."

Jobie shook his head. "Negatory, pal. Come on, let's go."

"There's two of us."

"And there's only one of me," Jobie reminded him boldly.

Jobie scooted forward, slashing the air with his broken bottle, swiping it within an inch of Dickhead's face. He saw no counter-attack, but felt the knife barely graze his arm as the blood quickly slipped off his elbow. He looked down at the wound just as a swift kick from Dickhead's friend sent him against the wall. He felt his face mash into the brick as fists rained upon him with violent force. With each impact, he could feel the numbing pain of blood and bruises coloring his pasty body. He covered his head as he slid to the pavement, cradling his body like a baby as they stood over him, kicking and beating. As he lay in a huddled mass, all he could see was Treva holding him tenderly, pampering him, loving him. She was nowhere around. He gasped for air as silence fell upon him. He felt alone, he had no idea where they were, he couldn't see anymore. His eyes were swelling.

The blows had ceased.

He felt warmth trickle down his face, over his neck. Urine. It burned his bloodied cheek like saltwater. It bathed him, penetrating his open wounds—he flinched and floundered against the wall of the alley, but he couldn't muster the strength to crawl away. He stopped resisting as he struggled to breathe, all the while feeling the piss stream down onto his face. Cold laughter filled the air, and he listened to them, laughing so proudly at his pain. His eyes were swollen shut. He envisioned Treva's uncalloused smile radiating through him, but she was nowhere near.

Through the ringing in his ears, he could hear footsteps. He cracked open a swollen eye and saw them strutting away. He placed his hands on the ground that was now saturated with their urine. He tried desperately to raise himself.

"Come here!" he screamed desperately. He didn't look up, but he could hear that they had stopped walking. "*Motherfuckers...*"

"Are you talking to me?" Dickhead squealed.

Jobie pushed against the cold cement, hoisting himself inches away from the ground. "Get back here, you...fuckers...I'm not through..."

Dickhead looked to his friend, then back to Jobie's beaten body. He shrugged his shoulders. "You want more?"

Jobie lifted himself to his knees. From there he leaned back against the wall, facing them with one eye slightly cracked open as he gasped for air. He could see in their expression that they had worked him over pretty well. They seemed to have lost their anger. Jobie hadn't, though. "Next time...you won't know...what hit you...motherfuckers..."

Dickhead grabbed Jobie's head and pushed him back against the wall. The impact ignited the pain of every injury. One last kick to the chest put him back to the ground. He could smell the blood in his throat, he could taste the urine, and he could see Treva's lovely face, smiling, full of love...her eyes cloudy with simplistic beauty and absolute joy for him. He raised himself again. He wouldn't fall, not for these guys.

"Ah, what's this?" Dickhead said in Jobie's blindness. "Must be yours."

Jobie could hear the tearing of paper as pieces of *The Apolitical Manifesto* showered upon him. He reached into his sporran as he looked down at the shoes that encircled him. He cupped the largest rock, the jagged California rock. It was long and slender with sharpened edges. He tucked it under his kilt away from sight. He crawled to the pylons that were now surrounded with ripped paper.

Jobie jabbed the jagged edge of the rock deep into Dickhead's calf. Caught perfectly off guard, he twisted sideways off balance from the explosion of pain. He teetered to the wall, holding his leg.

Jobie found the strength from adrenaline to lift himself to his knees, just in time to shove the rock straight into the other's crotch. The impact sent him back a few steps, crashing into the pylons, doubled over and near useless.

Jobie stared in amazement through his one good eye. He could almost feel the pain flee from his body. He struggled to climb to his feet to defend his honor. Then came the slashing of the knife, missing his face by only so many inches. As the knife cut at the air, he realized that he had only served to anger them.

Dickhead connected his left fist with Jobie's jaw, sending a fountain of blood from Jobie's bitten lip. He fell to the ground, held down by all the pain that returned with a vengeance. He was motionless in defeat, beaten and humiliated. Dickhead tucked the knife back inside his pocket and spit upon Jobie's bloodied face.

"Come on," Dickhead gestured to his sidekick. "Let's leave."

Thursday, September 17, 1998
9:47pm

Hyde Park in Austin, Texas

Dark shadows slithered along the cedar walls of the cramped study, born from the light of a gallery of lilac candles. An impressive array of collegiate books with bent spines filled the limited space of the boxy room. The books seemed to flow from the shelves, dripping into towering stacks of concrete knowledge onto a nearby wooden table. A small forty-watt bulb hung from a fixture that dangled over Vaughn's head.

Blossom Dearie's juvenile sweet voice crooned through a haunting rendition of Rodgers & Hart's *To Keep My Love Alive* from a small stereo in the other room. The song, about a woman who routinely murdered her lovers before the passion faded, was one of Vaughn's favorites, though the sentiment had temporarily lost its luster to an unfavorable mood.

His eyes squinted irritably as he reread the report. He paused briefly to take a sip of chamomile tea as he contemplated its supposed urgency. *Risks of Compositional Contamination* by Chasey Novak. Her caution insulted him. Such nerve for a mere understudy to challenge his experience... He wasn't about to postpone the tests—they had come too far, spent too much money already. Time was not on their side—not with the increased popularity of herbal cures and antidotes. Experiments such as these were being conducted all over the world—the slightest delay could set them at a permanent disadvantage. The additional month requested by Chasey was out of the question. They were ready for the testing now. Any alterations in the serum's formula could be made along the way.

He placed the report on the armrest of his recliner while he took a moment to finish the cup of tea. He dangled the empty ceramic mug in his relaxed fingers as he glanced about the room for his own research notes. They were nowhere to be seen.

He closed his eyes, tense with frustration. The notes were still at the university, and with the hour approaching ten...it could wait until morning.

His deceased father's face flashed through his mind—not the face he had remembered as a child, rather the decrepit ruin of a man whose life was slipping away. It was a ghastly shell of a memory, a sick conclusion to an otherwise enviable existence.

"Son," his father said gravely, "I spent years in the field, I gave my life to my work." He paused a moment as he breathed slowly, summoning the air to finish his thought. "My name will soon be forgotten. I leave the world nothing...I leave only you." He pulled Vaughn closer. "You will be successful...my name will be remembered...through you."

"I won't let you down," Vaughn promised. "I give you my word."

Vaughn sprang from his chair with a rediscovered vitality. He checked his pockets for his car keys and quickly made his way to the door.

9:48pm

"Money first," Treva insisted.

The young student eagerly extended a dollar bill. She swiped it away quickly, tucking it inside her deep pants pocket.

"It's dark in here," the other, more cautious student complained as he gazed uneasily down the alley. "Step into the light."

She stared at him, hating the thought of succumbing to this or any other request. But she needed the money—her pride would have to subside. She took one firm step forward as she glanced down at her shirt, making sure that the light would in fact be on her body. "Ready?" Without waiting for a reply, she raised her shirt to her shoulders, watching their eyes widen at the sight of real bare breasts. "Do you want to see more?"

They nodded.

She put her left hand down over the crotch of her pants. "Want to see what I have in here?" She revealed the metal teeth of her zipper. "Ten dollars."

"Five," the less cautious one told her confidently, asserting his presence in a vain effort to control the situation. "You give me head, I'll give you twenty."

"You don't want her to suck your dick, man," his friend said aloud with perfect disregard. "She's probably diseased. Look at her, look how fucked-up she is. Look at her skin, something is wrong with her. You don't want her to touch you."

Treva looked down at her arm, at the rash that covered her body like rust. "I'll show you my pussy for five."

The two exchanged a glance before shaking their heads. "No, thanks."

Treva stared in disbelief as they turned to walk away. She couldn't fathom their lack of interest. It was a foreign tongue—venomous and scathing, poisoned with disinterest. She felt her skin crawl as though parasites were feasting on her flesh. She ran her fingers down her arm, scratching her skin until it pulled up under her nails in bloody streaks. The texture was coarse and dry, like that of a serpent. She impulsively scraped at her skin, shoveling it from her arm with brittle claws. She couldn't stop herself. Her skin blazed like fire, she wanted it off her body.

She slid to the blacktop, shrouded in darkness, thirsting for the impurities that deliver divinity in a charred spoon. She desperately needed money. She would do whatever was required to embrace the angels once again.

10:21pm

"Spare some change?" the grubby street kids recited glibly.

Vaughn turned reticent to avoid a confrontation. It angered him to see the depths to which the country had fallen since his youth. It was those damned liberal politicians that set the machine into self-destruct mode, he surmised, starting with socialized medicine, back with the New Deal.

As he lumbered down the back streets toward the university, he humored the idea of a vigilante ridding the streets of these vile iconoclasts. There is no life without purpose, he figured, yet there is clearly no purpose in their eyes. Useless and lost, a debit to a once great nation.

His gait was quick and firm. Each step seemed absolutely deliberate with focus and meaning. He stared forward into the night, beyond the commonplace truancy of the Drag to his destination at the university.

He abided by a personal philosophy he termed *fundamental naturalism*, or the virtues of barbarism. He considered capitalism an extension of this, and thus the reason for its effectiveness. He scoffed at the notion that humans are inherently peaceful creatures. No other species on the planet kills for sport. Humans kill without purpose. Humans kill for reasons outside of necessity. We do it because it's fun.

As he stepped foot onto the Drag, he pondered how easy it would be for someone to kill one of these malodorous runaways. He was surprised that it didn't happen more often. If he was in a particularly foul mood, he sometimes found himself sketching out the process of it in his mind—how he'd do it, and how he could get away with it. These kids had chosen this lifestyle. They had severed ties with their families to live out here. Their families probably didn't even know how to find them. Yes, it would be easy—and thrilling. Although with the distance he kept himself, there was no danger of temptation.

"I'll show you my tits for five dollars," a warm, friendly voice offered.

He stopped a moment, shocked by the flagrant words and youthful voice from which they came. He looked down to see a pasty young girl leaning passively against the wall. Her left arm was striped with the trails of bloody scratch marks. An under-aged tramp. "No thanks."

"Then I'll give you head for twenty," she offered with her juvenile voice, sweet as candy.

His lips scrunched unevenly as if he had bitten a lemon. "Your frankness appalls me. Again, no."

She giggled. She liked the silver tint to his hair. Even in the dark, it was quite striking. His eyes had a subtle ferocity, and he had that look. That look that said *yes*, despite the firm resonance that gave weight to his words. "I'll do it for ten," she offered. "Just for you."

He glanced at her arm, at the red streaks that appeared as welts. Her skin looked like chipped red clay. Tiny specks of dried blood from recent needle injections dotted the bend of her arm. "Poison ivy?"

"Ten bucks," she repeated like a used car salesman. "Just for you."

He reached inside his pocket and pulled out his leather billfold. He thumbed through the bills, pulling out a crisp new ten-dollar bill. "I'll give you this money if you answer three questions honestly."

She nodded her head excitedly.

"You have to be honest," he demanded.

"Promise."

"Poison ivy?"

She shook her head. "Comes and goes with stress."

"It's psychosomatic?"

"It's nerves," she corrected him.

He smiled at her ignorance, though he didn't find it cute in the least. It simply gave credence to his presumptions of a deteriorating America. "Looks pretty bad this time."

She examined her own arm. She didn't like his questions or his condescending tone, but the bill that awaited her tenuous claws reinforced a more cooperative attitude. "It is pretty bad this time, but in one hour I will have the skin of a baby."

"Why?"

Her bright smile stretched across her dry face. "I'll be high again."

"Question number two," he said brusquely as he looked over his shoulder to make sure they were alone. He knew he'd need a greater lure than money. "Have you ever tried a pharmaceutical drug called dilaudid?"

"No. Chiva, nothing else."

"It's the cleanest high you'll ever have," he informed her.

She smiled, unsure of where he was going with all this. "Do you want to fuck me or what?"

"That's where the third question comes into play...are you busy this weekend? And no, I don't want to copulate with you...I value my own health." He pulled all the money from his billfold and flipped through the small stack of twenties. "I will give you thirty dollars to meet me tomorrow night, at which time I will promptly give you an additional fifty dollars. That's a total of eighty dollars. All you have to do is sit and watch the television while I take your blood and give you vaccines that will help cure your skin problem—cure it forever."

"What about the dilaudid?" she asked.

"We'll negotiate that later. I'll require your assistance often, if you're willing to give it. Maybe we can strike a better deal for future meetings."

"You're going to want to fuck me, aren't you? I mean…you want to give me a vaccine? That's it? I find that hard to believe."

"Why is that hard to believe?"

"That sounds like work. You'd rather work than fuck?"

He nodded with a straight face. "Different priorities. I live for more than a cheap thrill."

"Thrills aren't cheap. How can I be sure I can trust you?" she asked. "How do I know you aren't a serial killer?"

He shot her a devious grin. "I'll require a lot of blood work from you, but I sense you don't have problems with needles. You'll be dizzy and light-headed—that's the worst of it. Trust me."

She looked at his firm jaw and the gray beard that covered his sculpted face. His hands were powerful and strong. And the look in his eyes…he had that look. She had seen it before, and she knew it well. It wasn't pure or pious—there was a dark intent stirring in the shadows of his mind. It beckoned her with a raspy, wretched whisper of foreboding danger.

"There's a food stand on the corner of 24th and Speedway, right on campus," he told her. "Just a few blocks away from here. Do you know how to get there?"

She nodded affirmatively.

"Meet me tomorrow at six o'clock in the evening. I will return you to the same location at the same time on Sunday. Can you do this?" He held out thirty dollars. "Fifty more tomorrow night. Don't be late."

She snatched the money from his hands. "No more questions, mister."

"Nice doing business with you…"

She thought a moment, trying to come up with the appropriate nickname for which she would like to be identified. "Purty."

"Purty, eh?" he said with an involuntary laugh. "You can call me Professor Richter. This deal is exclusive to us, and only us—no one is to ever know. I'll see you tomorrow, Purty."

Friday, September 18, 1998
3:11pm

The Drag

The sensation of thorns scraping from underneath the skin teased and tricked Jobie's senses. It was a sensation he knew too well. He couldn't imagine another person more familiar with physical pain than himself.

He stirred his sludgy heap of navy bean soup—the bowl that Opaque was kind enough to have gotten for him from the Food Not Bombs van. Free food was always good food, he often said, but his boiling rage was struggling against his waning appetite. He felt he should be famished—he hadn't eaten since his confrontation with Dickhead. For that matter, he hadn't slept, either.

He set the bowl aside and looked up at the white painted brick wall over his head. A monster had been painted on it, a black rotund thing with a single eye splaying from a tendril that had over its comically beastly head the words: *Hi, How Are You?*

"Are you not going to eat?" Opaque asked without looking up at him. He was buried in a clean notebook, submerged in thought. Torn and maimed scraps of paper rested on his lap—the remnants of *The Apolitical Manifesto*. He had purchased a new notebook with panhandled money, an effort to bring life back to his brother's passion. "Eat the soup, asshole."

Jobie shut his eyes, concentrating on the needle pricks that caressed his feeble and beaten body. "I'm not hungry."

Opaque sat quietly a moment, trying to piece together the puzzle of mauled paper.

In his silence, Jobie suddenly fell onto the memory of a very fateful day from his past. He was in second grade, and comfortably part of a small circle of devoted friends. His parents were still together, although his father did drink quite a bit even back then, but it was a complete family that would pass any modern standards.

On this night that Jobie would never forget, his father didn't come home. There was a call late in the night, and his mother answered, but that's all he remembered. The next day in class, he learned that his father had been arrested. During a drunken conversation that turned sour at the favored watering hole, his father had come to blows with another regular patron. Jobie's father prevailed in the confrontation—the other man was hospitalized with a concussion and a couple of fractured bones. Everything changed for Jobie from then on. His father's opponent also had a child, Tina Murrow, the heartthrob of the second grade. She was devastated, and held Jobie accountable for her sorrows. Petty arguments flared over the jungle gym at recess with all the students taking sides on a conflict that was far beyond their understanding. Jobie stood against his class, his reputation tainted by what would become Tina's yearlong campaign to ruin his name. Her efforts were a success. He often wondered what his life would be like if his father's brawl had never happened.

Opaque looked across the street at the Dobie, a massive dormitory of aqua-blue glass with a mall and theater on the first two floors. A strange white mechanical contraption rested on top of the building like a dormant flying saucer. It seemed to tickle the underside of the ominous rain clouds. "Eat your food," Opaque mumbled again.

"I'm not hungry." He examined his arm where the blade of the knife had sliced him. A long, thin scab covered the wound with a dark purple crust. He was covered with the sort. He picked up the bowl again to show his appreciation. "Do you think that all the bruises and scars I've had in my life could cause permanent damage?"

"I doubt it," Opaque said as he tore his brother's thoughts from the crumpled paper that seemed to be covered with scribbles. He moved the pen across the new notebook with perfect legibility, transferring the words of the old rambling text with smooth precision. If anything, *The Apolitical Manifesto* would be a lot easier to read now. He glanced over at his brother, seeing the hateful scowl smoldering across his bruised face. "Tell me when you think this thing will happen," Opaque said, referring to the structural demise of the society caste system that his brother had written so much of in his journal.

"Within twenty years," Jobie said with a slight perkiness.

Opaque sighed with relief—he had taken the bait. He was so predictable, he thought, but he knew Jobie rarely had the chance to speak his ideas to someone who actually listened. "How will it happen?"

"Social revolt," Jobie said matter-of-factly. "The working class is slowly being edged out by computers. Within twenty years, computers will be the working-class. It will be like the Great Depression, millions out of work. There will be only an upper class and a lower class—things can't work that way."

Opaque turned to him, showing his interest.

"The only answer would be to dissolve the government that we now have and make a new one, a socialist government. At the age of eighteen, people who chose to continue their education would get a minimum allowance that would support their needs. As long as you educated yourself, you'd earn money, which is an incentive to better oneself. That money in turn would be put back into the system through their purchases, which would then be filtered back out as a percentage—rather than taxed, the business owners would pay a percentage that would be redistributed back to the people in the educational program. So the money would be in a constant flow." He paused to take a couple bites of the bean soup.

"Who would own the businesses?"

"Individuals, just the same as it is now. The only thing that would change is that you'd have something to fall back on rather than welfare. It'd promote positive values. If you wanted to invest in a business, you'd go the same route as you would now."

"And the government would be like what?"

"The government would be a group of randomly selected individuals that would oversee the polls."

"The polls?" Opaque asked.

He shoveled a couple of spoonfuls of the soup into his mouth before replying. "Every issue would be voted upon by the people through the Internet. Therefore the system would truly be by the people and for the people. We'd all have a voice. Take the Electoral College, for instance. Why on earth do we use such an archaic system in this age? We could vote on computers, then have the votes calibrated by one massive database for complete accuracy. It'd be easier for everyone, and way more effective and honest." He paused a while to finish the bowl of soup. "Besides, anyone who'd want the role of President is no one I'd trust."

"This is what I'm writing here, huh?" Opaque asked.

Jobie nodded with gleaming pride.

Opaque looked down at the empty soup bowl, then back at his brother. He watched as Jobie nodded his head in satisfaction, then the scowl returned forcefully.

"I'm going to find those guys," Jobie coughed spitefully. He eased himself back against the brick wall as his bruised and scabbed body screamed in vengeance. "They will pay."

3:12pm

Bleak deconstructivism. The interior designers of Urban Outfitters were obviously obsessed with the concept. The naked stone walls looked as though they had been swabbed with a mixture of turpentine and battery acid. Each corroded metal support beam was labeled with what appeared to be chalk, designating its function in some abstract numeric code. Japanese paper lanterns of varying pastels hung from the concrete ceiling. The pane glass front window was shattered evenly like a contorted web, intentionally broken for aesthetics.

"What do you think of this?" Treva chirped with a high and sweet voice as she held a pair of aqua-blue hip-huggers over her bony legs. Her plum hair was tied into two pigtails behind her petite ears. A thin black half-shirt clung to her body with a large silver star centered on her chest.

Tamika looked down at the tiny pants, making contemptuous gagging noises. "You'd look like a skeleton," she said with a subtle sarcastic bite.

"Since when have skeletons been blue?" She placed it back on the peg-board rack while her large eyes roamed the store. The metal steps leading to the second-floor caught her attention. The steps themselves seemed to have literally broken through the second floor, with the rusty wire frames fraying from the slabbed center of the concrete ceiling. Electrical wires and fixtures dangled from the depleted framework.

"How long did it take to make that?" she pondered aloud as she pointed to the ceiling emphatically.

Tamika started to follow the extension of Treva's finger, but was struck by the raw patches of skin that crawled up her friend's inner arm. "Do you have chigger bites?"

"Shhhh!" Treva said while ducking her head below the racks. "You can't say that in here."

"Say what?"

"You know…it's not right." She shook her head in disappointment. "You should say *chegros*. You of all people should know that."

Tamika's brow crinkled. "I don't think they're called *chegros*. I think chiggers is the proper word."

"Really?"

"Yeah."

"Hmm…" Treva focused on a display of zebra-striped handbags. "Are you sure?" She skipped forward three robust steps to a rack of half-shirts the color of ripe tangerines. "I could spend all day in here."

Tamika remained one step behind at all times, experiencing the thrill of shopping vicariously through Treva's immeasurable exuberance. She found it ironic that a store designed to cater to the counter-culture carried a product line almost exclusive to the waif look. Treva was right at home.

After rummaging through stacks of plaid skirts, Treva glanced upward into the glowing orb of the blue paper lantern dangling over her head. She found herself living in a fog between highs. She had lost her virginity to the needle, dined on the forbidden fruit, and sacrificed her soul for a brief glimpse into heaven. It was worth every second. If she could live the rest of her life high, she'd do it in a heartbeat.

"So how long have you been with Jobie?" Tamika asked her.

Treva shot her a bent face, not unlike one a child would make. "What?"

"Come on…it's obvious."

"What's obvious?" Treva asked. "Nothing is going on."

"I don't believe you."

"You don't have to," Treva resolved coldly. She picked up a black shirt with a pair of lusty red lips puckered on the front. "No, we've never even touched, and I've definitely never fucked him. Is that what you want to know, how he is in bed?"

Tamika cringed at the thought. "Not hardly."

Treva picked up another black shirt, this one with the number zero on it. "My lucky number."

"What's up for the weekend? Got any plans?"

Treva shook her head. The stubby pigtails flipped over her ears with each seismic head turn. "Not with Jobie!"

"With who?" Tamika pried. She scooted out of the way of other customers, bumping into a rack of dresses. She turned to the rack quickly, horrified at the thought of breaking something to bring all eyes upon her. It was there that she had finally found something in the store that caught her attention. A ruby red dress. It was made of thin cotton, knee-length, with a conservative cut that would cover the shoulders. It was both elegant and casual. "Wow, look at this."

Treva leaned over to look at it, reaching out with her scabbed hand to feel the soft texture of the material. "Yeah, nice. Better save those handouts. It'd take weeks of bumming change to pay for this."

That didn't seem unreasonable to Tamika. It'd be worth it. "I'm sorry, what did you say your plans were? I was listening, honest."

"I didn't say yet," Treva reminded her with her baby voice. Her eyes tensed for a moment as she raised her arms between them. Her skin looked as tarnished as the walls, boiling red. "Look at me," she whispered helplessly. Her face wrinkled with stress as tears formed in her eyes. "Something is wrong with me, Tamika."

"What?"

"I don't know."

Tamika couldn't disagree, she did look ill. Her face seemed tired, her eyes mere watery slits, and her whole demeanor was beaten and bedraggled. "What are you going to do?"

Treva sniffled as she shamefully tucked her arms under her skin-tight shirt. The black fabric stretched tight across her bony ribcage like a washboard. "I'm meeting a doctor this weekend," she noted optimistically. Her voice boomed with hope. "He's going to fix me."

"Really?"

She nodded brightly, slapping her pigtails against her perky shoulders. "I hope so." Her expression immediately fell desperate and sour as if the curtain had suddenly dropped. Her world had suddenly fallen into an eclipse. Her entire body responded with fatigued tension. She craved the needle, she had to find a phone—the doctor, she would be meeting him in a matter of hours, and he had promised this other new drug. Could she wait hours for another fix, though? "God, I hope he can fix me."

"You're meeting him tomorrow?"

"Tonight," Treva whimpered. "I stay all weekend. Don't tell anyone—don't tell the two brothers, especially Jobie." Tears rolled down her prominent cheekbones, dripping to the concrete floor. The redness of her skin was suddenly alive like fire, blazing across her body. She would match the ruby dress, she could become one with it.

"I won't tell them, I promise." She could see the pain and fear in Treva's bloodshot eyes. She placed her large hand on Treva's gaunt, bony shoulder. "It'll work. You'll be as good as new in no time."

"I hope so," she sobbed. "God, I hope so."

6:13pm

Chasey pushed through the front door of the Bagel Shop, ignoring the *Closed* sign hanging on the door. She stepped forward to a gentleman sweeping the floors. The eerie noise of indiscernible music was playing loudly from the tiny speakers perched high up the walls over enormous pane glass windows. Its gritty pulse tensed her body like steel.

"You've closed already?" she asked nervously over the racket.

Frank turned, somewhat alarmed to realize he was not alone. "Oh…well, we can extend the closing time by a couple minutes…I suppose." He stepped behind the counter and turned the stereo off, leaving a cold silence that brought the two intimately closer. "What can I get you—there isn't much left."

She looked down at the racks, bare and mostly empty. "I was told you have good pumpernickel."

"Bottom rack," he instructed. He waited for her to bend down to check out the remaining items. As she did, her loose shirt gave way to gravity, allowing a clear view down the neck of clothing to her silky white bra. It was a common recommendation from male bakers to beautiful female customers—bend over to look at the prized items on the bottom rack.

"I work for a doctor at the university…he swears by your bagels. He says he comes in every day, you may know him. His name is Ronald Schtepp."

"Oh, of course!" Frank said. "So you're doing the whole skin thing?"

She quickly looked up at him, almost alarmed. "You know?"

"Oh, not really. No details, but he keeps me informed of the progress."

"Hmm…interesting. I don't know about the pumpernickel. How about a garlic bagel, please?"

"Of course," he said.

She rummaged through her loose change, sliding forty cents across the cold metal counter.

He looked into her eyes—quite an attractive shade of blue—and nodded. "May I ask a question that's probably none of my business?"

"What's that?" she asked, anticipating the request for her phone number.

"What exactly are you working on over there?"

She smiled. "I can't just tell you."

"Of course you can! What, do you think I'll steal your ideas? I make bagels, give me a break! You can be as vague as you want."

She laughed. "Well, it depends on which of us you're talking about."

"How about you?" he asked. "What do you do?"

"I'm a glorified horticulturalist," she told him as she looked over his rugged face. She moistened her full lips and gave him a warm smile as she flipped her blond ponytail over her shoulder. "I grow plants."

He nodded slowly, confidently. His eyes stared deeply into hers, practically through her. He made her feel vulnerable, though completely at ease. Everything about his face was strong, and yet so reasonable and seemingly understanding. Very withdrawn, but she liked that in a man—it presented a challenge. He had the eyes of fire, she thought, but at the same time, she wasn't sure what that meant. Whatever it meant, he had them.

"I work with DNA." She chose to mask her interest with a steady forthright dissertation of fact. "We're taking known herbal cures for skin irritations and manipulating the DNA to bring out the components that relieve or cure the condition."

He lowered his brow in contemplation, perfectly unaware of the effect he had on her. "How do you know what is actually doing the work, chemically speaking?"

"That's the whole trick," she confessed with a smile she just couldn't contain, "we sometimes don't. So it's been hit and miss, mostly miss. Lots of guesswork. That's what my two colleagues do. They make the educated guess, I do what I can to bring results."

"So you're an intern?"

She nodded. "Until I can get a real job, yes."

"So if they make a lot of money by marketing this product?"

"Then I get credibility, nothing more."

"Really?" Frank asked, a little disappointed. "Doesn't seem fair."

"It's the way it works. Credibility in such a competitive field is nothing to frown upon, of course."

"So once you've messed with this DNA, you…"

"…I insert it into the gene and hope that the plant that is produced takes on the new characteristics."

Frank nodded hesitantly with a disapproving scowl.

"Yes, I'm not sure what I think of it, either…tampering with God's work."

"So how does it look?" he asked.

"How does what look?"

"God's work."

She smiled comfortably. "Magnificent. There is no question—this is all a very intricate design. There was a designer, I am certain of that."

"Did you ever question it?" he asked, looking at the silver crucifix hanging from a chain around her neck.

"No. Never."

"Are you getting close to what you're looking for?" he asked.

"Have I found God?"

He smiled. "No, have you found the right combination of chemicals?"

"Depends who you ask," she said, eyeing her watch.

"I'm asking you."

"Me? Then I would say no. Not yet. Close, but not yet. I'm more patient than my colleagues, but then again, I have nothing at stake here. Before this serum is used on a test subject, there are some things that need to be considered. How to combine the different compositions, at what levels—all of them artificially manufactured, none of them naturally occurring in nature...I just don't know if we're there yet. We're basically constructing a new form of life, and that's not to be taken lightly. Then we genetically combine this new organism with other strands of alterations...in the end, it will be a concoction of various genes spliced and manipulated—a completely new strand of life with characteristics that we know nothing about." She thought to herself a moment before getting slightly uncomfortable. "I'm saying too much, aren't I?"

"Not at all, but I get the picture if you'd like to quit while you're ahead," he said politely. "It's safe between us."

She nodded as she stared into his eyes, deep and understanding. She waited a second before saying another word, wondering if he had any more questions, such as her plans for the weekend. There was only silence. "Okay, well, it was nice meeting you, I'm sure I'll come in again."

"I will look forward to it," he told her. "Have a good night...and your name was?"

"Oh, I'm sorry!" she squeaked in tone that was much higher than her voice had been. She cleared her throat and replied with a lower, softer whisper. "Chasey Novak."

"Frank," he said as he reached out for her hand. "Frank Smith."

She lifted her hand gracefully, letting her fingers fall inside his firm grip. Making contact with his skin excited her with a cold and refreshing chill. His smile gave some indication that there was a mutual feeling involved. She let go reluctantly and mouthed the word *bye*.

As she walked away, he stared at the smooth skin of her legs, creamy and pale. She was not his type at all, far too pure, far too pale, and far too blond. Yet he couldn't take his eyes off her. She crept into his thoughts for the rest of the night.

6:14pm

Treva stared out the windows of Vaughn's car, watching the scenery of Hyde Park pass in a slow blur. The houses and neighborhoods north of campus were quite unlike those of west campus. These were much quieter, yet at the same time less somber. Each lawn seemed to boil over with a colorful array of flowers and vines. She considered how much she'd enjoy sitting on one of these old porches some hot summer evening with a glass of iced tea and a fat spliff burning in her hand.

She was disappointed to see that Vaughn's old house was one of the few without a porch. There was actually very little to it, just a small boxy thing with the overgrowth of ivy that scaled the white walls. The twisted and gnarled oak limbs spread like a canvas over the lawn, encompassing the green grass in shade. The grass thrived underneath, shielded from the blistering heat of the Texas sun.

She followed Vaughn to the front door with only the chirping of birds filling the air between them. No words were spoken until she entered.

"Take off your shoes," he insisted with a deep and firm voice.

She obliged without question. "Can I get a tour of the house?"

"No," he returned fervently. He led her to a back bedroom as he slowly removed his forest green necktie, allowing it to dangle around his thick neck.

She sat down at the foot of the King-sized bed, running her fingers across the smooth fabric of the beige comforter. She looked about the room, admiring its calm atmosphere. It had a rustic feeling to it, with its wood walls and floors and oil paintings of windmills. Aside from the pine dresser, a wooden chair, and an old footstool at the end of the bed, the room was comfortably vacant. It was as if she was inside a large wooden toy box, which seemed only fitting under the circumstances.

Vaughn stepped up to the foot of the bed, towering over her. She gazed into his hypnotic eyes as she stretched out across the bed and ran her eyes down the length of his body. His clothes were stylishly impeccable—pinstriped slacks and a pale green button-up shirt folded to the elbows. His leather shoes were polished to the extent that she could see the reflection of the wood floors.

"What are we doing first?" she asked him. "Are you going to take care of my skin, or are you going to fuck me?"

He laughed coldly as he looked down upon her. "I believe you have the wrong idea."

"Do I?" she asked, discouraged with his taut composure. "Are you not taking care of my skin after all?" She unfastened her street-sweeper corduroy pants, letting the fly spread to reveal her cotton white panties. She pulled her thin legs out of the pants, one by one. Her legs were splotchy red, like she had been splattered with tomato sauce that had dried on her otherwise fair skin. She tossed her pants aside to the floor. She looked him in the eye as she spread her legs far apart on the bed, showing him the crotch of her panties. "Fuck me."

His laughter reduced to a calm smile as he watched her without making any movement.

Her eyes tensed into hard slits. "I want you to fuck me. *Now.*"

"I don't have you here for that," he told her with thinning patience. His resistance to her lustful behavior failed to wane. "I'm old enough to be your father, young lady."

She reached down to her panties, pulling the fabric aside to reveal her moist vaginal lips. She spread her reddish-brown pubic hair apart to give him a better view. Her succulent lips parted somewhat, revealing the interior of her pink flesh. It glistened in the soft light. She slipped one of her long fingers inside her vagina, digging deep as she exhaled uneasily.

Vaughn's face restricted—the stench of her was enough to turn a virile man celibate. "I am not going to be having sex with you," he repeated calmly. "I can *promise* that much."

"Are you gay?" She looked to the crotch of his stylish pants. "You aren't even hard."

His condescending smile quickly washed away.

Suddenly it made perfect sense, the entire scenario. He was impotent. His promise was sincere—he couldn't have it any other way. She smiled at him, rubbing herself as she devised a new conquest. "Either you fuck me, or I'm leaving—which is it?"

"You need the money, you aren't going anywhere."

"You think so?" she asked as she prepared to stand up. "I'll leave right now."

"Sit down," he insisted with his commanding voice.

"Make me." She stood to retrieve her pants.

"You can leave if you wish. In fact, maybe you should."

"Coward…" She was ready to call his bluff. She held up her massive pants that appeared to be the size of a small tent. "Will you drive me to the Drag, I'll give back the money. I doubt this vaccine would've worked anyway. Nothing else has."

"Sit down." He grabbed her shoulders tightly, aggressively as a sense of wild exhilaration ignited within him. He stared at her blistered throat. He fought the temptation to wrap his hands around her veiny neck.

She looked up at him and smiled. She had successfully chiseled away a portion of his stoic exterior. "You like this, don't you?"

He let loose of her shoulders immediately.

"You want to throw me down on the bed, don't you?" she asked with a smile. "You want to cover my mouth while you pin me to the bed, fucking me like a dirty whore..."

This was already more than he had bargained. "Please keep your filthy body off the bed again until you have taken a shower. I can show you the bathroom..."

She tossed her pants aside again and jumped back on the bed. Her nipples were hard underneath her white tank-top, and her pubic hair jutted out from the edges of the cotton panties. She wanted to provoke him, to yank him from his throne of self-control. She crouched on his bed, pulled her panties aside, and smiled mischievously as a stream of urine splattered down her legs, onto his clean beige comforter.

Appalled and stunned, he lunged forward with anger, grabbing her bony shoulders once again. He yanked her violently to the wooden floor with a dull thud of young bones. "You disgusting bitch..." He grabbed her face, staring into her eyes with wild, roiling anger. The veins in his neck thickened. "What is wrong with you?"

She smiled as she lay on the wooden floor, helplessly in his clutches. She reached up and grabbed his crotch. He was excited by all this, just as she figured. She assumed he was desensitized by *normal* sex, probably a porn addict. "What's wrong with *me*? You're getting off to this."

He released his grip, allowing her to fall to the wood floor again. "You've ruined my bed."

She huddled herself on the hardwood, staring up at the maelstrom of havoc sweeping his body. She was pleased to see she had finally tipped his reserve. "You're going to have to contain me better. Maybe you should tie me up, restrict me. Maybe you should bind me, gag me, humiliate me...then fuck me. Tell me you want it, you want to fuck me, don't you?"

He shook his head with disgust. His ears were bright red. When he looked upon her, he saw vermin. "You have a serious problem."

She could see the conflict of violent interests eating away at him like cancer. She wondered how far she could push him—would he even strike her? She looked over to the wooden chair in the corner and pointed at it with her bony finger. "Tie me. You can stick me in the bathroom if you'd like," the tone of her voice suddenly shifted from seductress to helpless victim. "I'll cooperate, I promise. I'll take your medicine, I'll be good...I just want the dilaudid," she revealed with desperation. "Did you get it?"

He nodded. He was stunned by the sudden and extreme change in her demeanor. His own composure shifted with the confusion.

"I promise I'll cooperate." She stood submissively and wiggled helplessly over to the wooden chair. She dragged it and herself into the bathroom.

He followed her, watching her sit passively in it next to the sink.

"Tie my arms," she requested. "Keep me high and I'll do what you say, I promise."

He glared at her with utter contempt. Her mere existence revolted him. He had no qualms with what he intended to do to her.

"I'll do what you say," she repeated limply.

He quickly left the room, returning with several green handkerchiefs. He proceeded to chasten her as requested—something he now fully agreed was the best approach. He tied her hands together with one of the handkerchiefs, and then tied each hand to the back of the chair. He left the room for a moment, leaving her in silence fettered like an animal.

She could hear him shuffling things inside the refrigerator. He returned with a collection of vials in one hand, and a package of hypodermic needles in the other. Each vial contained a liquid of different color and consistency. Among those chemicals was the dilaudid, as he promised.

Her heart raced with excitement.

11:01pm

The black tires seemed to rip the water that glazed 4th Street. The white BMW crept forward, edging through the Warehouse District, the center of Austin's gay nightlife. Lucinda shot a quick glance into her reflection in the rearview mirror, smiling at the hot bitch behind the wheel of the sporty ride. Tawdry clip-on earrings hung from fat earlobes, sparkling in the dim light of the city. Her face was delicately painted to a fraudulent excess of formal frumpiness. She owned the look of high maintenance femininity—an image reserved almost exclusively for adolescent girls and Drag Queens seeking to embrace the pure essence of womanhood.

Highbrow intellectuals cluttered the walkway in front of Ruta Maya coffee shop as the smooth jazz poured from the deep chasm of a nightclub known as Cedar Street. Well dressed pedestrians—most of them in their late twenties, drifted back and forth across 4th Street, making an unruly mess of traffic.

Young gay men passed in front of the car, gazing inside, staring momentarily into Lucinda's lonely existence. Her eyes followed their paths across the street to a line that formed outside of Oilcan Harry's. Each of the men were doused in rich cologne, she could almost smell them from the street, all luscious and tasty and meaty. Their stiffly new clothing. Their hair firm and prickly with gel. Fine specimens, they were. As the old saying goes, the best looking men in the world are bound to the hearts of other men. Lucinda would have to agree.

As the white sporty beamer scooted across the intersection toward Congress, she smiled with excitement. She felt so alive, so young, so careless, and so perfectly free. Above all, she felt pretty. Her dress fit perfectly. Her feet were at ease in the platform heels. It was as though her costume for the week had been shed, tossed aside for her to flower over the weekend.

She gave another quick glance into her mirror as she winked at her reflection with a confident and robust smile. She glanced down at her passenger seat, at its emptiness. She would have to change that, she thought, as she turned north onto Congress.

11:17pm

Solid vines of steel ripped from the moist green earth in a single-file stretch like a row of crops. The peak of each black iron stem collapsed evenly upon each of the others in one unified link. They looked like lashes dripping with mascara. Yes, eyelashes—that's exactly what they were, Opaque decided. He logically knew it was merely the iron fence of the church, but on acid…they were eyelashes. And the street upon which he stood, the Drag, was the eyelid of the giant—the eye of the world. He was cautious to not make a single movement that might stir and awaken it. How enormous the eye must be, and penetrating—he feared what the eye would know. He glanced back up at the fence, watching the blurred tracers of dark nocturnal images blend in his shifting field of vision. The lashes, yes. Deep and black, but not the black of colorlessness, rather the blackened void of non-existence. To touch them would be to become a part of them, to become nothing. He had been nothing once. He had no memory of the world before his birth, and thus, he did not exist, not before the seventies—so why believe that he did now? How could he be certain that he was no more than a shadow, or a stain, or even a character in some book, brought to life only on a black and white page, existing only in the mind of the reader? He couldn't be certain…

A car passed down the street, consuming his attention with its blinding lights and roaring engine. It seemed so alive, so much more so than he was. After all, he was simply a machine, a product of the earth with the curse of self-awareness. Why had he never thought about the air that he breathed, exactly what he takes inside his lungs every second…and those sounds, they must always be there. Why does he never hear them? The buzz in his ear, the sound of leaves slapping one another with the wind, and those dogs barking. Everywhere, dogs barking. What were they saying to each other? Warnings of impending doom? Do dogs bark in the same language?

He stepped back onto the curb, onto the eyelid of the giant, onto its gray, solid skin. What a mess we've made of the earth...dogs barking everywhere. He looked upward, surprised to see a row of stars peeking through the gray clouds that seemed to spread like a tear in cloth, as if the whole sheet was tearing, and that buzz in his ear, it was from the stars. That's where it came from, he could hear them, the gaseous explosions of distant suns, carried with the solar winds...another car turned the corner, easing slowly through the darkness, its white surface shiny and covered with thousands of water droplets. It gave it a bumpy texture. He thought that the car had acne—yes, it was covered with zits. No, lesions. Cancerous lesions. Soon it would be dead.

The window rolled down, and an older woman stared at him with a smile. Her face was hard and haggard, rough and aged.

"Hello," came the somber voice with a deep and quavering fullness.

This was a man, Opaque realized suddenly. Typically, he'd have noticed immediately. He nodded his head slowly with wide eyes. It was an expression that was intended as a polite greeting.

"My name is Lucinda," she said. "Want to go for a ride?"

Opaque stared at her, watching her with his blazing red eyes. "Where?"

"You tell me," Lucinda offered boldly.

Opaque threw his hands in the air, uncertain about where he'd want to go—of all the places to go, where would he want to go? He thought a moment. Maybe he could go to the store to get Pixie Sticks, different flavors to bring color to the sidewalks—who was this person? Did he know this person? What was the question? Did he know this person? He looked down at the black tires, wondering what would happen if the eye of the giant—the car looked ill, it would not live long. "Can we go to the store?"

Lucinda smiled, wetting her thick lips. "Anywhere you want."

Yeah, the store, he needed a marker for the doll, it needed lipstick, the doll looked too—who was this person? "Do I know you?"

"Not yet."

Opaque stepped forward, looking inside the car. Its interior was black and dark, and the seats seemed so deep. Would he be able to feel the ground passing below him at such a depth? Of course he would. The black interior seemed thick and heavy—would he be able to move freely in it? Would his body become stuck inside it like wading through a vat of tar? How deep was it? Tamika, where was she again? She'd be back soon. Not too close to the lashes, a very dark pit of nothingness there, and the inside of this car—who was this person? "Do I know you?"

"Hop in," Lucinda beckoned.

Opaque stared at the lips, how they smiled, and how red they were. Blood? There was something not right—blood, or lipstick? No, he didn't know this person, he'd remember. "Waiting for a friend."

Lucinda shrugged her shoulders in a very male sort of way. Aside from the cosmetics and wardrobe, she wasn't much in the line of femininity. "You could make a new friend."

"No," Opaque said with a confident head shake, "I've got a friend, she's coming here, she's waiting for me...no, I've got a friend, I've got to stay right here. I can't move. Really."

Lucinda nodded. Discouraged, but not dejected. Lucinda was her own woman, flowing with confidence, passionate and alive. "Your loss, sweetie."

Opaque watched the car speed away, trailed by a blur of red lights that seemed to explode from the sickly machine. Red lights, red like her lips, red like blood. "Death rides in that car," Opaque whispered to himself. He was happy that he stood where he stood, firmly planted on the curb of the Drag, waiting for his friend to find him. If he moved, she may never find him...so he stood still, watching the black iron vines that seeped from the soil, twisting amongst one another in a great metal curtain. Yes, a metal curtain that refused to present itself to the hissing stars overhead. Why had he never noticed the stars before?

Saturday, September 19, 1998
11:17am

"Does there come a point when a statue becomes self-aware?" Opaque asked Tamika as they sat on the old concrete steps of the Tamale House #3. A layer of filth separated his legs from the asphalt, the residue from years of spilt salsa, soda, and melted cheese. Permanently stained. He looked to her, watching the last bite of migas slip inside her mouth. "After a piece of marble has been chiseled to represent the shape of a naked Greek man, and all the eyes that look upon it see not a rock but a naked Greek man...does the rock become something greater?"

"I suppose it's still just a rock."

"I think it becomes something more. The power of faith, mixed with our own perception of what we believe things to be...I think that a statue takes on a life of its own. Not that it can think or breathe or move, but it will acquire an aura."

"Maybe." She sat the empty plastic tray aside before relaxing her rotund elbows on bent knees. "Do you think Treva is okay?"

"I thought maybe we could talk about something interesting," Opaque sighed with dramatic exasperation. "Like the aura of rocks."

"I don't think she's okay, she looks really sick. Have you not noticed?"

He turned to her with a crooked face. "Are you kidding? How could I not notice? She's got a foot and two hands in the grave already! That girl is whacked, it doesn't surprise me at all. The nurse must've dropped her on her head."

Tamika laughed lightly.

"I'm not kidding!" he expelled with mock passion. "I've never seen someone so unable to resist temptation. She has no restraint, no discipline. It's pathetic, a real travesty."

"Aren't you the least bit concerned about her?" Tamika asked seriously.

"Oh, yeah...of course I am, but I'm not holding my breath. Who knows what will tickle her fancy next? Whatever she decides, I promise you she'll give in to it. Like I said, no restraint. I've never known a more compulsive person in all my life. Anyway, can we talk about something more interesting? How about the doll, let's talk about its clothes. It needs a new outfit, and that's something that I take very seriously. An improved wardrobe will enhance the aura of anything—even a rock."

73

She hoisted her hefty frame off the ground and looked out at the constant motion of traffic along Airport. Rain sprinkled from the sky, glistening the road with beads of water that reflected the sparse light of day like imprisoned rainbows. "Shall we start walking back before the rain picks up?"

He stood firmly upright, arching his back as he stretched the full extension of his gangly arms. His burnt orange hair streamed heavenward with black coils twisting through it. It looked like fire. He reached out for her hand, embracing her limp and stubby fingers. Linked together with intertwined knuckles, locked hand in hand, they strolled aimlessly to the road, waiting for a break in traffic. A red light opened a path between idle cars for them to cross to the other side.

"I think Treva's beautiful," Tamika said as they climbed over the train tracks. "And I think she has a great personality. She's always happy—it makes me envious. Makes me wish I knew her better."

"I don't agree," he confessed. "A smile doesn't correlate to a good intention. She smiles because she's insane. Big difference, you know."

"Maybe you're wrong, maybe if you knew her better, you'd decide she's not all that bad."

"I think she's completely selfish," he said with a straight face. "I don't like the way she treats my brother."

"I don't see her as selfish," Tamika challenged.

"I don't see her as anything else."

She thought a moment. "What if she's sick, what would we do? We couldn't take her to a doctor, none of us have any money."

"Sick?" he asked. "She's a junkie…and a whore. And she has my brother by the balls. My brother deserves better company than that."

She shrugged her shoulders in defiance of his statement.

"You don't know him," he told her sharply.

"That's true," she admitted, "I don't. Just like you don't know Treva."

"He's funny," he assured her calmly as he glanced into her deep, dark eyes. Her pupils were lost in the depth of her charcoal eyes. He could faintly see his purple lips smiling in their reflection. "On weekends when we were younger, we'd hang out in malls. He always tried to keep me entertained…he'd go up to strangers and ask what year it was—thinking about it now, I realize how young and stupid we must've been…"

Their pace quickened as the rain once again streamed from the miserably drab sky. They took cover under a weeping willow tree, watching the sky fall upon the saturated earth.

Opaque continued, "as soon as they'd tell him the year, he'd exclaim: My God, the machine worked, Louis is brilliant! Now, to find that android before it's too late." He looked up to see her smile. "Yeah, Jobie was funny. I suppose he still is, he just seems so serious these days." He thought a moment before laughing to himself. "One time, not too long ago, Jobie had this scheme to bring anarchy to Tacoma. He borrowed someone's car, some girl he was messing

74

around with at the time, and at four in the afternoon on Interstate 5 in downtown Tacoma, he straddled two lanes, put the car in Park, locked the keys inside, and just walked off. It was one of the worst days of traffic Tacoma had ever seen."

She giggled with a soft reserve.

"He used to always go to church parking lots, putting stickers on all the fancy cars. Pro-choice, Gay is the Way, Darwin...all the liberal stickers you can think of, and these cars would have their bumpers plastered with them. I can imagine they were on there for months—who looks at their bumpers?"

"Did you like Tacoma?" she asked him.

"I like Austin better. And you? No offense, but my mental image of that town—"

"It really isn't a town," she explained. "It's more a village of trailers, like a super trailer park from hell."

"The community motto being: *We Will Destroy What We Do Not Understand.*"

She laughed. "Yeah, basically. And that was me."

"They never destroyed you," Opaque corrected.

She raised her shoulders in silence as the rain splattered onto the pavement that surrounded them. The tree shrouded them like a green umbrella.

"You obviously had too much character to be a part of the in-crowd," he resolved. "I suppose it's safe to assume you weren't the Homecoming Queen?"

She shook her head with a faint smile.

"I always wanted to be the Homecoming Queen," he admitted. Her smile broadened to laughter, as he knew it would. "Tell me about the best day of your life."

"I don't think I've had it yet," she answered quickly. "The best night, I remember I was supposed to go out with Cindy, and she stood me up, as usual. I was furious, I chased all over everywhere looking for her. I remember feeling so alone that night, I have always been alone...then suddenly I realized as I sat in her gravel driveway waiting, wondering, worrying...that I was in love. The first time in my life. I can't explain it. But it meant everything to me."

He nodded respectfully.

"Are you ready to go?" she asked with a sudden tone of urgency.

He looked out at the somber neighborhood, through the wetness that made cake of the air. "It's still raining."

"Well," she said before stepping out from under the tree, surrendering to the weather's persistence, "I don't see it stopping. Let's just go." She stood in the downpour watching him shelter himself apprehensively under the hanging leaves.

"But my lovely hair," he groaned. "It'll be ruined."

"Come on, Queen..."

"Does it always rain like this here?" he asked as he stumbled reluctantly into the drizzle.

"No, not at all," she replied. "This is unusual."

They walked several blocks in silence, splashing one another with the water that collected in the cracked asphalt. Opaque's hair fell over his head like an orange hood, a drape over his ghoulishly white face.

"I think Jobie felt responsible for mom leaving," he suddenly revealed to her. "My strongest childhood memories are of Jobie on his bike, riding up and down the streets looking for evidence of her whereabouts. He'd be out there for hours."

"How long has it been since you've seen her?" she asked.

"I don't remember," he murmured. "I don't recall what she even looked like. For all I know, she died back then. To me, she basically did. Not for Jobie, though. He truly believed he could find her, and that she'd take us away from dad. Jobie was obsessed with finding her. He didn't give up for years, and when he did, he gave up on everything. Jobie wasn't always like he is now. Something must've happened when he was a kid, something I don't know about. Our home was not a happy one. Jobie and dad didn't get along at all. I'm so glad we're gone. So glad. I am eager to keep moving, I've never been to New Orleans. I can't wait to get there. But more importantly, my hair is ruined *now*. I'm horrified to be seen in public this way."

"I thought that was what you were shooting for anyway?"

He chuckled to himself, each breath pregnant with pride. "That's quite a compliment, thanks."

"No problem. So what inspired you to look as you do? See, I can look at you and appreciate the effort. I actually admire it quite a bit. But for me to choose to go through such effort every day as you do..."

"In your own way you focus on your physical self every second of the day. You think of what you would like to change about yourself. Well, I actually make those changes daily. The world is a stage and I am the star!" He paused to absorb his own bellowing confidence. "I feel that people seek identity in two different ways. There's the common type who try to meld into the world as part of the flock. These are the people who join social groups, maybe they go to church or are into sports teams that always win, or they are into a style of music that makes them feel part of a unit of something or other. They seek likeness in others, they want to feel that they are normal because they fear not being accepted by the masses, the Average Joes. The far less common types strive for individuality and pride themselves on the unique flavor their existence offers to a bland world. On one hand I really care what people think, yet on the other, I really don't care at all. Does that make sense?"

"Sure. So did you just start dressing odd, or was there some sort of revelation?"

"Ginger Trollop," he said dreamily. "Queen Ginger."

"Was this a band?"

"Nah, it was a friend, I suppose. Then again, more of an inspiration. Met her at Vogues some years ago in Seattle's Capitol Hill. She was about eight years older than me and had been dressing up since she had first laid eyes on Boy George in the eighties. She was elegant and classy and she schooled me on every aspect of the lifestyle. She taught me how to mesh the gender lines and how to shine with dignity and respect. She was my teacher."

"Don't be offended by this, but where does someone who *dresses up* work? How did Queen Ginger earn a living? Drugs? Sex?"

"You'd be surprised. You know the common types I had mentioned—the lemmings? They thirst for me—I break up the patterns in their mundane lives. You know the studio on the Drag where they shoot Austin City Limits? If I waited outside for all the tourists going to the show, I could make a killing just posing for Polaroids with their families. They can show the pictures to friends back in Ohio or wherever to prove they went somewhere exotic, I suppose. People like me belong on the other end of a camera. It's our lot in life. Like I said, you'd be surprised how willing the camera is to find me. I'm an artist, and the art is me. I'm worth a fortune."

5:27pm

Vengeful eyes peered through the dense foliage of shrubs that protected the university from the denizens of the Drag. Jobie shifted slightly, silently, angling for a better view of the traffic that crawled across the black asphalt of Guadalupe. The world moved ever so slowly around him, unaware of the eyes that preyed in secrecy.

The bruises were slowly fading on his body. His strength was returning. He had even gotten to where he could take a deep breath without feeling the sensation of needles throughout his back, kidneys, and stomach. His limp was also gone.

He took a deep breath of the sticky air that carried the scent of cold rain. Deep purple clouds were clumped on the distant horizon like a pile of grapes. They seemed to be rolling into Travis County with a booming roar of thunder to trumpet their approach.

Across the street on the corner of 22nd sat Dickhead chain-smoking cigarettes. Jobie studied every small detail, all the way down to which of his hands held the cigarette—right hand. Dickhead appeared bored, thoughtless, with his attention focused on a book of matches that he was wasting one by one. He abruptly stood, giving a quick glance to the violet sky before strutting down the Drag to a small gathering of Crusties. A band of Oogles stood nearby, honoring him with a whimsical flare.

Jobie glared, squinting, watching his steps, calculating each movement, formulating assumptions of weakness based solely on the hapless gait of his oblivious subject. He memorized the syncopated rhythm of his walk, the way it sounded like a slow beating heart. There was a casualness to his demeanor—a withdrawn lack of focus that opened up his surroundings. Vulnerable.

The moment was coming.

Saturday, September 26, 1998
10:47am

The Drag

Chasey held out her hand, admiring the way the gold ring looked on her creamy skin. The ring had a faint luster of cream, just a hint of flavor like vanilla. It went well with her complexion.

"Do you want it?" the old woman behind the stand asked with stale charm.

Chasey smiled, never taking her eyes from the shimmering band of gold. "Oh…I suppose not."

"I'm flexible with the price," the woman offered.

"I know, I know," Chasey told her as she slowly, unwillingly removed the ring. She placed it amongst the others that were submerged in a blue velvet showcase. "I just really can't justify it." What she meant was jewelry—especially rings—were ornaments of affection that were given out of love. She had only one ring, the one she received as a gift from her oldest sister years ago. Her jewelry, as sparse as it was, had no memory of men, only family. She'd rather things were different, but her social life never was much. People tended to make her very uncomfortable with their loose attitude on topics she deemed too sacred to even verbalize. Outside the church, she felt she spoke a different language entirely. "Sorry, not today."

"Maybe tomorrow," the woman said to her, familiar with this routine. She felt she should know Chasey on a first name basis by now, with as many times as she came by to admire the rings.

She stepped back from the stand, keeping her blue eyes on the gold ring. "Maybe." Could she find true love in a single day? Maybe what she meant to say was *hopefully*.

Love had been hit and miss in Chasey's life, though mostly miss. She was very active in the church's social circles and singles groups. All of her men were acquired there—she'd have it no other way. Each of the short romances ended with the man's intolerance of her sacred chastity.

Her first true love was a man named Ben. It was her freshman year, and he with his undetermined direction in life was acceptable at that early age. He was an avid rugby player, and Chasey became his eager audience. She never missed a game, owned a home jersey that she cherished too much to wear, and even had a sticker on her car that read *Give Blood, Play Rugby*. Every man thereafter was merely an attempt to recapture that magic she found with him. As with most first loves, she never fully got over him.

Skip was the follow-up, though almost too short a romance to even tally. He was a business major, three years her senior. His indifference was his appeal. She pursued him and his interests with zest, but by the time her first subscription to the Wall Street Journal had arrived, he was already out of her life.

Dusty was a web designer, and the upgraded modem connection she purchased for her computer nearly broke her at the time. Dusty was followed by Ray, the owner of a sporting goods store. In retrospect, she wasn't entirely sure if she was much more than a high-spending regular customer. At the time she saw it as support to her man, but she was left with little more than a closet full of jogging shoes and useless UT paraphernalia like giant orange foam hands extending a stiff index finger.

She roamed through the maze of stands that occupied the empty space between Bevo's bookstore and Texas French Bread. The Renaissance Market. Rows of long tables covered with burgundy and blue cloths displayed the wares of each vendor. Incense, crystals, beads, and jewelry covered the tables, luring the weekend traffic along the Drag. Large canopies hung over the tops of the tables, each a different color like enormous flowers. A mural depicting Texas culture and history covered the outside wall of Texas French Bread.

She would return next weekend, pandering to her own whimsically romantic dreams. The perfect suitor.

She strolled southward down the sidewalk, passing the horseshoe shaped rows of bike racks and the rusted street posts with all the colored fliers. Public announcements, music performances, roommates—one could live by the information posted on these poles.

"Spare some change?" the dull voices beckoned from atop the boxy newspaper stands.

"Sorry," she told them politely. "I can't."

"Bitch," one mumbled under his breath.

Case in point, she thought. Just how disrespectful and undignified our society had become. It appalled her. Her slow and fluid walk mutated into a disturbed stomp as she lumbered to the Bagel Shop. She had just about had it with the Drag. She knew she had long since outgrown her tolerance for the Dragworms.

"May I get a garlic bagel, please?" she asked the young girl behind the counter. "Is the owner Frank here?"

"The *owner?*" the girl asked with a smirk. Her know-it-all expression translated to: *I beg your pardon?* She wrapped the bagel in glossy tissue and passed it across the counter. "You mean the *manager?* Yes, he's out there," she said, pointing to the tall panes of glass.

Chasey looked over her shoulder before sacrificing some change to the metal counter. Outside on the narrow deck was Frank, sitting in solitude, huddling over a piece of paper. She had assumed he was the owner. Why did she feel disappointment in knowing differently?

"He's making the schedule," the girl told her. "He better give me next Saturday off. This is ridiculous working on a Saturday…I could be at Hippie Hollow right now with my friends."

Chasey walked to the side door, onto the deck. "Hello, Frank. Are you busy?"

He looked up with bloodshot eyes that appeared disoriented. His face lit up, and it was clear that he was happy to see her. "No, not at all…have a seat." He quickly cleared room at his table, placing his work in his lap before clasping his hands together over his belly. He let forth a deep and relaxed sigh. "How are you?"

She sat down opposite him and gracefully unwrapped the bagel. "Not too bad. Busy week."

He took a second to cap his fountain pen before forfeiting all his attention to her. "Deadlines?"

"No, although now that you mention it, our self-imposed deadlines aren't very practical. Vaughn is a work-horse."

"Vaughn?"

"Oh," she said quickly, "it's his project, I should've told you that. My boss, basically."

"I see." He wandered into her crystal blue eyes, hoping to retrieve her age or anything else he could excavate. He guessed she was somewhere in her mid-twenties, but he really wasn't sure. She had a style and sophistication that seemed very refined, yet her general physical appearance was quite youthful—deceptively so.

"At times I envy your work," she admitted. "Not that I don't love my research, but there is a constant, on-going issue of ethics involved in my area of study."

"I could see that," he replied casually. His words seemed to open up an awkward silence between them. He sensed a deeper implication hidden in her statement as if she was urging him to strip away her impersonal formalities to unveil a subtle meaning hiding between syllables. Like most women, she seemed to communicate on many levels. As a man, he spoke on a single level—the obvious, blatant one. "Do you feel that this project has an unethical basis?"

"It's not the project itself…maybe I shouldn't say."

"I'm just an ear," he reminded her. "I don't know these people."

She thought a moment as she nibbled on the tough skin of the bagel. She glanced quickly into his penetrative eyes. Did he find her attractive? "I don't know how to say…do you ever get that feeling in your gut about something or someone or somewhere? Where you feel that someone is a cheat, and you don't

81

know why…or that someplace is dangerous, and you don't know why? It's like God whispering a warning."

"A first impression is the purest insight," he told her as he admired her thick wet lips. "I know that whisper, yes."

She flipped her ponytail off her shoulder, watching as his eyes trailed its descent down her back. "Vaughn presented a report to me early in the week. It's leaps and bounds beyond our best findings. This report—I swear, he has to be testing this rudimentary formula on subjects already. The report lacked any sense of speculation, but that's not what concerns me. It's that he basically demanded four variations of the serum by this weekend, all with levels and properties that we haven't even discussed before. It's essentially the same composition, just that it seems…it seems he now *knows* what effects these combined chemicals are having on the body. It's as if he has moved beyond a rough draft."

Her intelligence both intimidated and intrigued him. Such an educated woman would surely disapprove of his past and all he sacrificed for a buried dream. So impractical. "What is the ethical problem? Should you wait to test this on people? I'm not familiar with the way these things work."

She wondered what kind of living he made as a manager of a bakery. Probably not a whole lot. "Okay, it's probably safe—God knows I can overreact. There's probably nothing to worry about, but when it comes to human testing, there are precautions that need to be addressed and taken very seriously. Large doses of this serum could cause adverse side-effects that we could never have imagined."

Their eyes remained linked, united with desire, though masked with mutual expressions of casual indifference. There was a giddy excitement between them regarding the outcome of unanswered questions pertaining to their compatibility.

"Do you need some type of permit to market genetically altered substances?" he asked.

"Not presently, no," she admitted. "You'd be amazed how many of the foods you eat have been genetically altered. There are no regulations against biological modifications of any kind in this country."

He shook his head in disappointment as his eyes glided over the faint freckles on her nose. "Is there any way you can find out if he is testing it on people? What if you just asked him?"

She could see his eyes roaming about her face, but his thoughts were hidden behind a straight and rigid face. He was the essence of self-control, she thought, yet surely his attentiveness would give some indication. She rubbed her nose to see his response. She was pleased to see his actions unknowingly mirror hers. Yes, she could safely assume that his entire world stretched no farther than her own fair skin. "Of course he'd deny it, and to be realistic, who would he find for this? Honestly, who would submit themselves to such a thing? Seems highly unlikely, and Vaughn is a very respectable and dignified person. I suppose I'm paranoid." She smiled suddenly, falsely. She felt guilty for saying too much, as if she had betrayed Vaughn's name and honor with her petty assumptions. "I'm very driven to do this work, don't get me wrong. I'm just paranoid."

Frank looked into her empty smile as though he was suddenly facing a closed door. He decided to change the subject, tempted by the hopes of unlocking whatever secrets she struggled to contain. "So where are you from?"

"Houston."

Immediately an image of a promising and stale neighborhood flashed in his mind. He found it interesting that that's where her personality seemed most suited. It most certainly wasn't the same for him. "I'm from Kansas."

"Kansas," she said, surprised. "Never known anyone from Kansas. Did you like it there?"

"Not enough to stay there, obviously. Did you like Houston?"

"Sure. Family, you know."

Her response wasn't one he had heard often. Most people he knew were very happy to get away from Houston's faceless sprawl. The city spread like an infection.

"Did you go to college in Kansas?" she asked.

He shook his head, feeling slightly uneasy. He knew his answer would disappoint her. He didn't even want to respond, everything had been going so well. "I've never been to college."

Her eyes widened. His response wasn't one she had heard often. Most everyone she knew had flourished in academics. What on earth had he been thinking?

"Did you go to college here at UT?" he asked.

"I went to graduate school here, but I got my undergraduate at Rice. So did you just decide to move to Austin after high school?" Her question was loaded. She was hoping he'd at least finished high school.

"No, I grew up in a small town, then I moved to Lawrence, Kansas and lived there for about six years before coming here."

He hadn't answered the question she intended, so she tried to be a bit more direct. Simple—the language of men. "Did you like high school?"

"No, I didn't," he said smugly. "In fact, I despised it. How about you?"

"Yes, I enjoyed it. Very much, actually."

He could've guessed as much. She seemed like the type of person who had a good thing to say about everything.

"I've always wanted to live in a small town," she said, "a nice little quaint place where you know your neighbors and everyone's friendly."

He laughed. "That's no small town I've ever seen."

"You didn't like the town, either?"

"No, not at all. I imagine that living in a small town is the closest thing someone can get to the reality of fame. Where everyone knows everything about you except who you really are as a person. They have a stigma of your personality, one that you either earned or inherited, and you never live that down. You will always be whatever makes for the most interesting conversation pieces because all you really are to those people is news. No, I didn't like living in a small town at all."

"You felt judged is what you're saying?" she asked.

His eyes began to wander over her shoulder, out to the street. "In all the wrong ways. I'm not against judgment. I think that the only people who fear judgment are the ones who wouldn't pass it very well. No, I'd want to be judged, personally. I'm a firm believer in judgment, it's the only real way to grow." He looked down at the crucifix that dangled from her neck. "The Catholics were very right about that."

She smiled with delight. "Yes, I agree. I, too, am a firm believer in judgment. I live responsibly and have nothing to hide. Are you Catholic?"

"No. Not at all, actually."

She was becoming frustrated with how his attention was straying from her. Her bright smile revealed nothing of this. "Oh…that's okay. What faith are you?"

"I'm not religious," he said. "Not at all." He could see that she was not satisfied with his answer, so he explained further: "I'm not one to believe that spiritualism is a group effort. I think it's something someone finds on their own or not, and though religion is an adequate vehicle for enlightenment, it's not for everyone."

"I don't agree," she finally snapped as her face straightened. "Christ died for our—"

"I've heard it," he returned swiftly. "I've been pitched before, I believe what I believe—I respect your interests, please respect mine."

"Of course," she said uncomfortably. "Look, I have to go, it's getting late, and I need to meet a friend…"

He considered telling her that lying is a sin in the eyes of her God, but he refrained. "Sure." His tongue held a question, one that he had been prepared to ask, but now seemed perfectly inappropriate. "I'll see you later."

3:33pm

Vaughn scribbled furiously, dictating the results of each combination of the serum on pale green graph paper. The edges of the paper were slightly warped from the humidity that thickened the artificially cool air. The prominent muscles of his forearms flexed with each pen stroke, rippling under the sleeves of his flecked kelly-green shirt. Rubber medical gloves helped to distance himself from his unruly subject, the girl who called herself Purty.

His brow seemed heavy, and his eyes narrow with deep concentration. Dark rings from fatigue had settled under his wildly ambitious eyes. His lips were locked together, tense and firm.

The porcelain sink was filled with discarded needles, each one moist with Treva's blood. Her skin was pasty and sweaty with tiny red bumps scaling her body. Her eyes were glazed and wandering. Her head lobbed from shoulder to shoulder as she drooled onto her vomit-stained tank-top.

He dropped the pen to the wooden floor and reached for one of two syringes resting on the edge of the bathtub. A thick orange liquid sloshed inside the narrow tube, clinging to the glass with a gritty film. He tapped the sides of the syringe while he pushed a few drops through the needle, allowing it to ooze down the metal shaft.

He grabbed her limp arm and rammed the needle through her delicate skin just over her wrist. He injected the orange fluid into her body, watching the skin instantly clear itself in a small circle around the point of entry.

"Reaction," he demanded as he glanced down upon his clipboard. "Tell me how it feels."

The room smelled of bodily waste. Her panties were yellowed from urine, and he could only imagine what she was sitting on against the flat wooden chair. He found it hard to even breathe in her presence. He loathed the very thought of her continuing existence.

"How does it feel?" he repeated with agitation. "Does it itch?"

She shook her head slowly.

"No itch at all?" He grabbed her splotchy face with his firm hand, forcing her eyes to recognize his own. Her face was covered with red blistering welts. The saliva that dripped from her scabbed chin dangled onto his firm healthy hand.

"No," she grunted as her eyes roamed back inside her head.

He noted her response quickly before administering the final injection. He tapped the syringe, clearing out the air bubbles as he placed it against one of the more festering blisters on her arm. He shoved it deep into the coarse lesion as a small amount of blood and pus foamed from the injection. The shiny needle penetrated deep into her skin as the white liquid streamed down the shaft of the needle into her bloodstream. Her body heaved violently, over and over, until orange bile spilled from her mouth onto her chest. Her head fell limply to the side as she breathed deeply and uneasily.

"I'll be back in an hour," he announced coldly.

3:34pm

The sign on the door read Jack S. Blanton Museum of Art. Its physical exterior, the Ransom building, was as visually stimulating as a cinder block. It was easy to miss it across from the Baptist church on the Drag. Its creamy walls were textured with the impressions of seashells, giving it the appearance of craters on a lunar landscape.

"I can't believe you've never seen fine art before," Opaque scorned Tamika playfully as they approached the front doors.

"I've seen art."

"I'm not talking about starving artist sales in motel lobbies, I'm talking art that speaks of generations—*fine* art. It's the difference between Pee-Wee baseball and the Major Leagues." He opened the door for her to enter a brand new world of culture, one she hadn't seen before. "You're about to see history."

She led the way through the small entry room, avoiding the smaller displays in glass cases to get to the more spacious interior rooms. The ceilings were tall, and the air was cool, dry, and comfortable. The soft lights washed upon the chalky white walls with numerous paintings drifting through time. Each work spoke of an era, an open window into a portion of history. Directly in front of the main entrance was a sort of shrine, the museum's prize possession—the Gutenberg Bible, one of five existing copies in the United States.

Tamika briefly glanced at the sealed glass display, and then continued forward, magnetically drawn to the eruptive instability of a nearby section, the abstract expressionism. The walls were alive with a static explosion of chaos, desperation, and angst.

She hovered over one painting in particular, Joan Mitchell's *Rock Bottom*. She looked closely at it, at the thickness of paint that gave a beveled inconsistency to the work. Under such harsh scrutinized viewing, its flawed human origin was clearly prevalent in the details. The paint seemed scraped and splattered, random and thoughtless. At a distance, it was timeless. "This sums up my life."

"Someday I will make art that will change the world," Opaque resolved with confidence.

Tamika turned to face him with narrowed eyes. She had no idea he harbored artistic motivations. "You paint?"

He laughed. It was a common assumption, though wrong. "No, I sculpt."

"With clay?"

"No, cat shit…what else would I use?" he scoffed as they moved onward through the museum. "Maybe someday I will make a mold of you."

"I don't know about that," she protested. "That amount of clay would cost you a fortune."

He smiled. "Whatever…my creations are abstract, you'd hardly even know it was a person. It'd be angelic. Yeah, you'd be a perfect subject." He paused briefly to examine a work by a man named Soyer. The painting was entitled *Transients*. "Lovely," he sighed with delight. "Such atmosphere, so dark, and yet so human and real. Look at those faces. That's some callused pride. If that expressionist one was you, this one is me."

She stared into the rough detail of the paint's application to affirm its humble hand. It was almost as if she needed proof that someone had in fact taken the time to bring it to life. The human error she sought would only bring her closer to the creator. "I took a photography class in school once. I think that's something I could do…*maybe*."

They wandered aimlessly, slowly through the maze of separating walls, passing through slivers of time.

"I bet you'd have a good eye for portraits," Opaque said.

"Funny, that was my favorite thing to do—stark portraits in black and white. Like the mood of this one." She focused on a painting called *The Old Model*, "this is what I would try to capture in photographs."

Opaque looked into the withered wisdom of the subject in the painting. Its aged expression was a vault of secrets hidden from the eye of the observer. The lure of it was not to know what the secrets were, but simply to know they were there, safely locked behind the glassy eyes. She would soon be taking them six feet underground.

"That's what I loved about photography," she told him, "the ability to capture the essence of an entire personality with one single picture." She backed away from the painting, deep in thought. "Maybe someday I'll get a camera…I did a photo essay for a class once that I loved. I went to funerals and took pictures of people giving regards to their dead loved ones. I called it *Suffering*. My teacher was appalled." She stopped at an impressionist work, a small painting of a woman wearing a white dress, looking away into the murky gray scenery. "I love this." She glanced at the name, Thomas Eakins' *The Opera Singer*.

"The thing about impressionism is that it's all mood," Opaque commented. "To look upon it for too long is to take away from it. It becomes nothing more than thick, random brushstrokes. It's like a photograph that's horribly out of focus. It's my favorite period of art."

She nodded, never taking her eyes from the painting.

"You do realize that by your own definition, we're wasting our time gawking at canvas that has been ruined with dried, clumpy paint," he noted.

"What do you mean?"

He grabbed her by the arm and pulled her into a nearby section of the museum. He stood her in front of a white marble bust of a woman. "A rock," he told her. "Nothing more."

She smiled.

87

"This is all that remains of the artist," he said. "This rock, and maybe another one in a different gallery somewhere. The creator of this was named Hiram Powers. In death his name is still spoken. What greater honor is there?"

She looked down at the name of the work. "*Eve Disconsolate.*"

"Someday, when I die, I hope my future artistic creations retire in a place like this. And people can look upon my work and say: *what was this person thinking?* They'll think they know me, but all that really matters is that they know my name."

She thought about how she didn't even *know* his real name. Did he mean for that?

"But we should just leave—why waste our time looking at this rock? You're right," he agreed sarcastically, "we can become no greater than what we were given at birth. That Bible is just paper, and these paintings are old canvas, and this rock..."

"Her hair looks wet," Tamika said of the white marble sculpture, ignoring his biting sarcasm. "No, it *was* wet, and it is now almost dry. Damp. I could dream about her lips." Her own fleshy lips smiled mischievously. "Maybe tonight I will."

"She has wonderful ears," Opaque added. "Does she hear me now?"

"That's not what's important," Tamika replied. "Does Hiram Powers hear his name being spoken?" She slowly angled her head to one side, catching the sparkles of light captured inside the granite. To imagine the bust as a rock was far more difficult than seeing the representation of a woman. Yes, she resolved, it had an aura of life to it. A piece of an artist's soul, still living, even in death.

Thursday, October 1, 1998
10:12pm

The Drag

The syncopated rhythm of footsteps echoed down 22nd Street. Fallen leaves rose from the blacktop, airborne with the cool wind that howled mercilessly. The air reeked of mulch and grease, aided by a thick humidity that trapped and nurtured the scents of decay. The trees shimmied to the nocturnal breeze, scattering the hard lights of the city across the concrete landscape.

Jobie peered through the black metal bars that held the church like a fortress. He was crouched among the shrubbery, dissolved in darkness, waiting. The footsteps amplified with each step—a single set without a voice. He squeezed the thick tree limb in his hands, feeling its mass, thriving on anger. He had spent many hours that afternoon searching west campus for the perfect stick, heavy and durable.

He looked to the ground, to the shadow that crept along the damp sidewalk. Just as the shadow's legs came into view, Jobie sprang from the darkness with the massive stick raised high over his head. In Dickhead's eyes he saw the horror he had known so well in his life. Before Dickhead could fully raise his arms to defend himself, the piece of wood smacked him across the lips with an explosion of blood and tree bark. Dickhead fell backward to the ground, practically in slow motion, as his hands shrouded his face in pure agonizing pain.

Jobie was quick to return with a second blow, much more calculated than the first. Pulling the stick far back over his head, he smashed it down against Dickhead's ribs with as much strength as he could muster. The impact sent a dull thud through the barren streets. Dickhead curled into a fetal position as his hands covered his face with blood oozing between his fingers, down his arms.

Jobie towered over him in silence, watching his body convulse and flounder—all the while relishing victory. He brought the bulky stick over his opposite shoulder, using his backhand strength to strike another blow to his defenseless head. It was a trick he learned from his dad many years ago, the old backhand finale. The impact seemed to peel away his skin, leaving a nice pinkish-white gouge before the blood surfaced. For that split second, it looked like salmon in a grocery window.

"I told you I'd see you again," Jobie reminded him before he crouched over his body and struck his head once again, peeling the skin, releasing the blood upon the pavement. He tore Dickhead's hands from his bloodied face. He seemed dazed, not completely coherent, yet riddled with fear and confusion. Jobie grabbed both ends of the stick and shoved the blunt end of it directly into Dickhead's nose. There was a loud crackle of bones smashing from the momentum. Blood was everywhere. It made Jobie laugh. He dropped the stick to the bloodstained cement and looked directly upward to the bleak sky, clenching his fists, savoring revenge.

He grabbed Dickhead's arm and dragged him down the sidewalk with strenuous effort and no resistance. Dickhead's feet slid along the cement, scraping the sidewalk like sandpaper with a trail of blood slithering behind them.

A group of young Dragworms were huddled on the corner of 22nd Street. Their menial conversations tapered off as Jobie delivered his prize for all to see. He dropped Dickhead in the middle of them and wiped his bloodied hands on his ripped Crass shirt. He leaned down and searched Dickhead's pockets, finding a couple of dollar bills and the treasure he sought, the butterfly knife. "You guys have a good night," he said as he waved them off before strutting down the street. "I'll see ya 'round."

10:29pm

"I'm just glad I'm not a girl." Opaque popped the lid off the top of his newly acquired black felt pen, allowing it to roll along the sidewalk in front of the Goodall-Wooten. He slowly brought the pen to the doll's lips, painting them black with a steady hand. Its precious nubile eyes peered optimistically up at him, feigning a wicked ferocity. "It's a man's world, sad but true."

Tamika observed his creative efforts over his shoulder, watching as he applied the felt pen to the doll's eyelids, giving it a thick caking of eyeliner. Its pale plastic skin looked morbidly ill in contrast. "I wouldn't necessarily call you a man."

"Not in the conventional sense. Do you see me lugging around tools, keeping tallies on sports? Still, I wouldn't want to be a woman, not in this country. Actually, not in any country." He held up the doll for her to view.

"What are you going to do about the hair?"

He turned the doll around to look into its face. "Leave it as it is?"

"Bald?"

"Sure," he decided spontaneously. "Bald."

"It kind of looks like you," she noted. "Is that intentional?"

90

"Hmm...more reason to keep it bald, I suppose. There can only be one of me."

"Now let's talk more about your opinion of women," she said. "What's your problem?"

"It's not a problem." He placed the doll in his lap and turned to face her. "It's more empathy. All those expectations, plus the lack of expectation. Were you raised to think you'd ever need to find a career?"

"I wasn't raised to expect much of anything."

"Most of the girls I have known, the thought never crossed their minds. They weren't raised to think that way. They played house, or in other words, their idea of a fun time was pretending they had bills to pay and meals to cook for bitchy little kids. You call that a good time? How can you trust someone who played like that as a child? That's psycho, if you ask me."

"Were you raised to think you'd need to find work someday?" she asked. She put the cap back on the felt marker.

"I suppose so. You know, most boys are asked if they want to grow up to be firemen or cops or astronauts, and all the while they tell the little girls to get used to seeing the kitchen. I mean, is that absurd or what?"

"The hardest part of being female," she figured, "other than monthly cramps, is the emphasis on looks. Not just weight issues, but the idea that women must always smile. If I had a dime for every single time a guy has asked me to smile...but I can't overlook the weight issue. All those magazines everywhere you look."

"That's not men," he corrected. "Those magazines are made for women's interests. Men's magazines show the exact opposite—voluptuous women with big asses. If women stopped buying their trashy magazines, they wouldn't exist. Maybe I'm wrong, but if you think of whose opinion you most fear—is it a man's, or a woman's? When a girl frets about getting a bad reputation, does she really think a guy cares? No, it's the women's opinion that threatens her. Women dress and act as they do because of other women, not because of men. They feel threatened or competitive with one another, it's not always the men who are at fault."

Tamika considered it, nodding. "I can see that. Men aren't innocent, though."

"Neither are women. That's my point. You know, it's perfectly fine for a woman to admit she only wants a man with money, but if a guy says he only wants a woman with large breasts, he's sexist. Now really, what's the difference? Both are typically shallow, yet one is not only accepted, it's considered cute or funny. Why?"

She shrugged her shoulders. "That stuff doesn't apply to me."

"Or me, but in general it's true. Women are taught to receive, men are taught to give."

"Don't date women, then," she said, trying to usher his sexual preference from him.

He smiled without a reply. Instead, he reached inside his brown paper bag and removed a sewing needle with some thick black thread. He lifted the doll to his lap, resting it on his crossed legs.

Tamika watched him sink the needle into the doll's lips, penetrating its fair plastic skin. "I always envied how men could spit," she told him. "Men spit really well. I guess their saliva is thicker, almost like a projectile. Every time I'd try to spit like that, it was like this mist. Never really worked well. I'm not even going to talk about the whole *standing to piss* thing."

"If you could change anything in your life, what would you change?" he asked. "The consistency of your saliva?"

She shrugged her shoulders, thinking of how much she wished she could be the thin glamorous waif that men seemed so driven toward. She knew how well he'd take that answer, though. "What would you change?"

"I'd change my look more often, but I don't have the money at this point in my life. I'm ready for a new look. Now, answer the question. I asked you first."

"I suppose my answer would be the same as yours, I'd change up my looks."

He paused briefly to finish stitching the doll's mouth shut. The black thread crisscrossed over its mouth like a zipper. "You look fine."

"Have you ever fantasized about your own funeral?"

He laughed. "I think everyone does that. Let me guess, really dramatic, tons of people who are painfully miserable to have you gone."

"Really dark and beautiful…"

"I think that's pretty common. People want respect, but moreover I believe we as a species have an overwhelming desire to be remembered after death. Most people pass and are probably forgotten in a year's time. What a curse…that to me would be hell."

Jobie strutted confidently down the sidewalk toward them, smiling with a pompous swagger. He plopped himself next to Opaque, stretching comfortably in the openness of the city's lights.

"Is something wrong?" Opaque asked him. "Why the smile? It's so not you."

He shook his head as he opened the metal butterfly knife. Its blade shimmered in the streetlights. "Everything is great."

Opaque raised a single eyebrow, revealing the elegantly blended colors of blue and purple over his blood-red eyes. He glanced at the unfamiliar new weapon. He had little trouble piecing together the rest of the story. "Do you feel vindicated now?"

Jobie smiled assuredly.

Opaque turned to Tamika. "It needs a leather dress now. I'll have to make it."

Tamika stared down at the doll, at the monstrosity he had produced with such care. It returned the gaze with haunting charisma as the wind chased the leaves down the street.

A shrill scream of a siren echoed in the distance, intensifying by the second. An ambulance turned onto Guadalupe with its red lights blazing throughout the street. Its sound was deafening. It parked on the corner of 22nd, pulling a stretcher from the rear door.

"I wonder what happened," Tamika pondered aloud.

Opaque looked disappointingly at Jobie's smile, exchanging an understanding that went well beyond words.

10:31pm

"These findings are absolutely stunning," Schtepp admitted as he placed Vaughn's report on his desk. It slid easily over the tops of disheveled paperwork. "So how did you come to these conclusions?"

"What conclusions?" Vaughn asked with a very calm reserve.

Schtepp smiled, making a perfectly round sphere of his head. "Don't kid me, you're working with a test subject, I can tell. Who is it? Why didn't you let me know?"

Vaughn shook his head with a devious grin. "I can't lie to you." He picked up the report and quickly thumbed through the pages, allowing it to fan in front of his face. "This is the fruit of my passion. What I have right here in my hands…this would've taken months, and yet here it is. The price for this was nominal, pocket change to a young girl with a bad skin condition."

"Who is she?" Schtepp asked. "Sounds rather sketchy, must you be reminded of the policies—"

"No, I need not," Vaughn interjected quickly, masking his disdain with an even smile. "Would you like to meet her?"

"I would. In fact, I insist."

"This weekend?" Vaughn suggested.

Schtepp grinned shamelessly. The question he had waited to hear for so long, and under these circumstances, his colleague owed him for this breach of trust. Vaughn had no choice, he was suddenly at his mercy, and it was a wondrous feeling. "What time?"

"How does two o'clock Saturday afternoon sound to you?"

"I'll make the time," Schtepp grudgingly replied. "I'll see you then. And this whole procedure better be on the level, otherwise…"

"Trust me," Vaughn ensured him. "Trust me."

3:10am

Bats fluttered over the Congress Bridge, visible only for a blink of the eye as they devoured the insects that swarmed under the streetlights. A dense haze thickened the atmosphere, making luminous halos over the artificial lights of the city. Treva glanced back over her shoulder, out the rear window of the Plymouth Fury. Beyond the shark-like fins of the sleek automobile she could see the waters of Town Lake. In the nocturnal shift of days, it looked like a river of black ink flooding the heart of the city.

She wanted to be high again. Her body ached for it. Coming down was hell, and she'd give anything to never have to return ever again.

She turned to face forward, to look out at the enormous state Capitol building at the end of Congress. There was a soft pink luster to it, an attribute of the type of granite used in its construction. Everything is bigger in Texas, and the Capitol was no exception. A perfect replica of the nation's Capitol, though slightly larger.

The electric blue lights from the Franklin Federal building reflected against Phaedra's naturally black hair as Talon steered the Fury down Congress. The street was relatively clear, though not unexpectedly, considering the hour.

There was a shine to Talon's bald head, almost as if it had been polished with wax. The snake tattoo slithered up his spine from beneath his black shirt, resting on the center of his head like a mohawk. Its tail was a rattle, a subtle homage to the state of Texas. Flathead nails pierced his earlobes.

"You're an attractive girl," Phaedra said to Treva as she counted the money that had recently been hers. "You'd earn a lot more money on South Congress than you would bumming change on the Drag."

Treva scowled at her, despising her and her audacious comments. Treva was powerless. She clenched her scaly hands together, feeling the roughness of her skin. She envied Phaedra's perfect complexion. She imagined herself peeling Phaedra's skin off with a knife and wearing it as her own.

"You can earn twenty dollars a blow-job on South Congress," Phaedra suggested as she tucked the money away. She looked after her clients, always quick to suggest more lucrative means of obtaining the steadiest fix. The more they earned, the more she would inevitably earn. "You can suck a lot of dick in one day."

Treva brought her attention to her own arms. The coarse texture of her skin looked like red sand. She hated the fact that she had nothing on Phaedra. She felt revolting and monstrous. It made her desperate for another fix. "How late are you going to be up?" she asked them.

There was no answer.

After a bit of thought, she realized she probably couldn't find the money at this hour anyway. "Where on South Congress?"

"Oltorf," Phaedra told her. "By the grocery store. Walk south a couple blocks, and then hang out at the bus stop. Someone will pull over, and they won't even care about how you look. They just want their dick sucked."

Treva ran Phaedra's words through her head: *they won't even care about how you look*. Yes, she hated Phaedra. She hated her for every word of truth that tumbled from her beautiful lips.

She covered her scaly arms in shame and pondered how she could get to South Congress on her own. She closed her eyes, savoring the darkness behind her eyelids. She wished herself dead. And why not? She had never truly been alive. She ran her fingers across the cold vinyl of the back seat. She didn't have to look at it to know it was black. She could feel that it was. In her silence, she could hear Talon changing the gears on the push button console as they sat at a red light.

She remembered the darkness of her basement and how mortified by it she was as a child. And yet now she felt so at home in it. She had spent many nights locked in the basement as punishment from her father. She would spend the entire night screaming and crying at the top of the stairs by the locked door, never once looking over her shoulder into the pool of darkness that contained her worst fears. The wooden steps sank into a bleak void that petrified her with fright. Horrific scenes plagued her imagination all throughout the sleepless nights. The fear gnawed on her until sunlight delivered a new day. She was only five years old at the time.

She feared Vaughn in the same way she had feared her father. His eyes contained the darkness of her past. That's why she refused to stop seeing him. Her willingness to participate in his experiment was a triumph of her own withered spirit. Of course, there was also the dilaudid.

Her body hungered for the venom. Her veins seemed empty, just a river of blood lacking the fountain of heaven found in a syringe. In her Eden, she had no fears or insecurities. She, like the rest of the world, was beautiful. Now the lights were out, and there was nothing. No life, no happiness, no reason to live.

She could feel the car turning corners, yanking her frail body from side to side with each change of direction. She felt like a limp doll—a hideous, lifeless doll. When she opened her eyes again, the University Tower peaked over Lavaca. It was bathed in orange light. The mist in the air gave it a majestic presence.

"Get out," Talon breathed softly as he pulled up to the curb on Martin Luther King.

Treva stepped down onto the street and closed the door behind her. They drove off without so much as a single word. She was a ghost to them, the breathing presence of death. Her life meant nothing to them.

As she dragged herself down the lonesome sidewalk, she noticed the black iron fence of the church. Rows of spear-like metal penetrated the earth to repel the evils of the world from its sacred grounds. Each thin shaft of wrought iron dug deeply inside the ground like needles. How she wished it was her arm instead, or her body, for that matter.

She climbed over the low wall of the Bagel Shop's outside deck where Opaque, Tamika, and Jobie were all quietly sleeping on the pebbled surface. She looked down at Jobie, at the stained kilt that fanned over his knobby knees. His legs were hairy and bony with long strips of muscle streaming down his calf under pasty skin.

She curled up next to him, staring at his face and how peaceful and content he appeared while sleeping. She could see the movement of his eyes and wondered what he dreamt. Was it of her? Did anyone other than Jobie dream of her? The web tattoos across his cheeks twitched slightly as she kissed him softly on the forehead. In his arms she felt safe, protected from the world and all the horrors that lurked in the darkness of her youth.

She closed her eyes and smiled. She was asleep within minutes.

Quack's on the Drag

Frank gazed up from his plate of beans and rice, bringing his attention to two men at a nearby table. He had been listening to their boisterous and pompous conversation, on and off, for the past ten minutes. It was abundantly clear that all of the city's software problems could be cured at the hands of these two long-haired, pony-tailed gentlemen. Frank felt he knew them well, having seen them in so many faces throughout his life. He fabricated the story of their social lives, starting with their early days as rabble-rousers in the user-friendly Heavy Metal scene, then onto the liberation of their college days in the Deadhead scene. It was apparent that they had only recently graduated into Austin's immense pseudo-intellectual scene.

Frank smirked, finding humor in the way the common majority so desperately seeks a social niche, jumping from one group to the next, never allowing themselves to grow into their own skin but rather a skin they'd like to see themselves wearing. He wondered what these two men saw in the mirror. Did they look into a stranger's eyes? Did they calibrate their happiness by how well they had assimilated into their chosen persona?

Frank took his last bite of beans and rice, ready to return to work when Chasey walked in the front door. He relaxed himself deep in his chair once again as he admired her from afar. He scoffed at her black sweater's satin Jack-O-Lantern stitched on the breast with the words *Happy Halloween* in white comical letters. He wasn't exactly sure what it was about her that moved him. She was typical of what he had come to expect from the world—faceless, lost, and searching—seeking answers in a centuries-old book when the real truth stared at her every morning from her bathroom mirror. To know oneself is to know God, he had always said.

When Chasey noticed Frank sitting at a table in the corner alone, her heart raced. Her emotional response took her aback somewhat. She was really happy to see him, but she wasn't sure why. She didn't even feel comfortable around him, yet it was the source of that discomfort that intrigued her. She sought to understand it. To understand others is to understand oneself, she always said. She smiled at him and waved politely.

97

Frank wasn't sure how to take the gesture. She would wave to a sworn enemy, he was certain. The truth was so evasive with her that by definition, it didn't even exist. There were merely the trimmings, the color of the wrapping paper. For her, a happy home would be one with an excellent lawn and a shade of paint that accented the lovely flowers that surrounded it. The interior could be rotting with death, a dumping ground for bio-hazardous waste. Face value, and nothing more.

They couldn't be more different.

She placed an order for a turkey sandwich and walked directly with it to Frank's table. "May I join you?"

"Of course," he told her as he slouched lazily in his chair.

She formally sat down at the seat facing him, her posture firmly erect. She felt awkwardly stiff in his presence, so she decided to open the conversation with a pessimistic slant to bridge the gap. "I just went to the bank next door, and that manager there is strange."

"First State Bank?"

She nodded. "That woman there, she seems really…inappropriate. I don't like her," she admitted passionately, "she makes me nervous. Her mind is in the gutter, and she makes all these subtle innuendoes about sex." Chasey considered it immoral to even speak of sex, let alone laugh about it. The way she said the word *sex*, it came out like profanity. She suddenly realized that her attempt at snide cynicism had just backfired—she felt more rigid than she did when she arrived. She smiled once again to lighten the air. "So how are you?"

"I'm okay."

"I didn't know you ever left the bagel place," she threw out as humor.

"Have to get away for a little while, even if it's just a block away. The beans and rice here are so cheap, and so good."

"And healthy," she added optimistically.

He nodded in compliance. "Good source of protein. Fuel for my daily swim."

"You swim?"

"At Deep Eddy," he told her flatly, hoping to not go into a discussion about the purity of exercise.

"Good for you," she tweaked positively. She looked into his rugged eyes and smiled. "Got news."

"Really?" He watched her healthy white fingers clutch the turkey sandwich. Her burgundy painted nails looked like the moist skin of plums. She sunk her teeth into the slices of bread, chewing slowly while a single hand covered her closed mouth. She had the most marvelous lips, he noted when she took her hand away. He wanted to kiss her, but more than that, he wanted her to let loose with the vile vocabulary of a trucker. Anything to summon the real human inside.

"So how about this weather?" she asked casually before taking another bite.

"Lots of rain," he mumbled, bored by her small talk.

"I've never known it to rain like this before. It's flooding all over. Have you seen Buda and Kyle? They're underwater. We're witnessing history here, the flood of ninety-eight they'll call it."

"I've seen the news," he said dully, staring deep into her blue eyes, wondering what was the most perverted or sinister thought she had ever conjured. "Quite a thing." He waited patiently for her to finish chewing so she could break whatever news she had.

Her facial expression suddenly fell dour. She leaned forward, edging closer to him. "Yesterday I was sitting on a bench near the corner of 24th and Speedway. I was reading a letter I had gotten in the mail when I saw this young girl pass on the opposite sidewalk. Her skin, let me tell you, she was a fright. I know that sounds rude, and I don't mean to be disrespectful, but she had the most wretched skin condition I have ever seen in my life. I felt pity. I felt for her, whoever she was. And to my shock, she walked to the corner and was picked up by Vaughn."

He wondered what she'd do if he would reach across the table and kiss her passionately. The desire rang with such sincerity because he knew he never would. "Vaughn...the professor?"

She nodded vehemently. "Well, that's all I needed to know. I'm very morally opposed to this apparent arrangement. I feel it's irresponsible and completely unprofessional and it's even deceitful to me as well as Doctor Schtepp. If something happens to that young girl...I'm quitting, Frank. I've decided."

His eyes widened for a moment. "Really?"

"That's the other thing I'm telling you," she began, "I got this letter from a company called GenetiTech, Inc., which is a subsidiary of a larger and older corporation called Hodges, Hull, and Brown Laboratories. I emailed them a few weeks ago, and they called me immediately. They liked my background in both computer and biological sciences, and seemed very eager to have me."

"What would you be doing?"

She hesitated to take another bite. "There is a quest going on right now that you may or may not be aware of, but many universities and private companies are currently working on making a map of the entire human genome, the blueprint of our species. Hodges, Hull, and Brown are one of the leading companies in the race. This will happen within five years, we'll be able to manipulate the chromosomes of our potential offspring to rid them of disease, enhance certain genetic attributes, and so on. That is what GenetiTech has been established to do, to conduct this research. Also, they're working on a software program that will be able to take the DNA of a living organism and by putting its code into the computer, be able to present a three-dimensional image of it. Imagine its use in crime-solving alone. We'd have an immediate picture of the guilty person."

"So you could take the DNA from a sample of hair from a supposed Bigfoot and know immediately whether or not it's some weird unknown species…"

"Or just a bear. Although if we did find something like that, a strand of hair that could prove some cryptozoological mystery, we could produce the creature itself. Instead of us finding it, we'd simply take the data God gave us, and reproduce it in our own labs."

"That's heavy," he replied uneasily. "Almost makes me uncomfortable."

"It shouldn't," she assured him. "Responsibility will accompany such knowledge. If we are to progress any further as a species, we need to accept scientific advancements. There needs to be trust, though."

"Why trust?" he asked.

"Then why not go back to living in caves?"

"I'm not a trusting person," he told her flatly. Could he provoke her to swear? Probably not. He glanced down at her neck lustfully, admiring her transparently soft skin that hid her bluish veins. He wanted desperately to bite her neck, if for any other reason than to tally her response. "Would you have to move for the job?"

"Yes, to Oregon. I will leave Austin at the onset of November."

He smiled politely, a bit disheartened for some reason unknown to himself. "Good luck."

1:59pm

Ronald W. Schtepp pulled up to the corner of 51st and Avenue F, yielding cautiously to pedestrians on inline skates as he coasted his sporty white BMW to the side of the curb. He stepped out onto the tarmac that was drowned in a veil of pecan tree leaves. He locked the car, checking it once again for any dents that he may have otherwise missed before climbing inside the vehicle not fifteen minutes earlier.

The brick walkway to Vaughn's front door was a mismatched trail of uneven limestone lined with yellow pansies. The yard was a dark shade of green, thick and healthy from all the rain.

The small house was nowhere near as well kept as his own, in fact, its untidy exterior made him slightly uncomfortable. The lawn was overgrown and rampant with weeds. Fire ant mounds protruded from the grass like zits on an adolescent boy's fuzzy face. The house's white paint was chipped in several locations with its gray and deteriorating wood somewhat visible beneath.

He knocked twice, then a belated third rap for good measure. The door thrust open, and there stood his colleague. He was wearing a green collared shirt with a pair of faded black pants. It was the most casual he had ever seen Vaughn. Then again, it was the first time he had ever seen him outside a professional environment. Schtepp was thrilled to bare witness to this virgin experience.

"Come in, old sport," Vaughn said casually. He held the door as Schtepp stumbled clumsily inside the house. "My home, welcome."

"It's nice," Schtepp stammered submissively.

The interior was far more pleasant than the exterior. The wooden walls seemed to meld into wooden floors, giving the room a very organic feel. Schtepp redecorated the place in his mind, possibly with some English ivy dangling from hanging pots, or even some Ansel Adams photographs to break up the mesmerizing pattern of wood grain.

There came a thumping on the door. The two looked to each other as Vaughn stepped forward to gaze through the side window.

"Ah, she's here," he announced comfortably. He opened the door and in walked Treva dressed in a baby blue summer dress, smelling of cheap perfume. They exchanged a knowing glance before Vaughn turned to Schtepp. "Ronald Schtepp, this is Purty. He's the mastermind."

Schtepp smiled at Treva, though his attention couldn't fully be drawn from the blistering boils that covered her frail, scrawny body. It almost looked as if she had leprosy. "Nice to meet you."

She stared at him with a seething cold glare. This was the doctor behind all this, she presumed. This is the person for whom Richter worked, and this was the person responsible for everything that had happened to her skin. She felt deep anger filter toward him. Her physical deterioration, it was by his rotund hand. Her bloodshot eyes were torched with rage. Her teeth gnashed together.

"I've been working with Purty since mid-September," Vaughn told him loosely. "I'm sorry, Ronald, did you want something to drink?"

"No thanks."

He didn't even think to offer anything to Treva, which Schtepp considered to be rather curious.

"I'm fairly pleased with how things are progressing," Vaughn resolved with confidence. "I anticipate a lot of changes soon. You'll be astounded at my discoveries."

"Can I get a copy of your notes?" Schtepp asked him.

"Of course," he said. "The itch seems to be completely remedied. It's the inflammation that's causing me the grief at this point."

"We may need to resort to conventional means," Schtepp told him casually. "The itch is the biggest problem, of course. We've achieved a milestone with that alone, if your findings prove to be correct."

"Oh, they are as accurate and concise as you'll ever find."

Schtepp smiled proudly. He needn't be told this. He had perfect faith in his colleague. "We're getting there."

Vaughn looked to Treva, who then looked to Schtepp.

"I haven't got a lot of time today," Treva said evenly, as if she was reading lines from a script.

"Oh, I see…" Vaughn replied swiftly. "I guess we'll need to get started. I would ask you to stay, Ronald, but it's not the most exciting practice, as you can well imagine."

"No, I don't mind staying, if you don't mind having me."

Vaughn looked to Treva, sending her another unspoken cue.

"I'd rather it be just Professor Richter." A rumble of hostility shook her words. "If you don't mind…"

"Oh…no, that's fine, that's fine," Schtepp resigned politely. "I suppose I have things to do, I won't keep you."

Vaughn pleasantly escorted him to the door as Treva's eyes tightened with annoyance. Ronald Schtepp, she ran his name over and over in her head. She wouldn't forget it.

"Nice to meet you, Purty," Schtepp said to her before leaving.

She stared evenly at him, mutilating his fat body inside her opulent imagination.

"Goodbye, I'll call you on Monday," Vaughn said as he leaned closer to the door. He resorted to a low whisper. "On the level?"

Schtepp smiled. "Perfectly."

"I figured as much," Vaughn declared confidently before shutting the door. He watched as Schtepp waddled out to his BMW, examining the entire body of the car before getting inside. "That wasn't exactly the most pleasant presentation," he told Treva. He reached inside his pocket and pulled out thirty dollars. He placed it in her hand and said, "You didn't earn this, I can't believe he was convinced of anything...I told you to act civil, and what was all that?"

She shook her head with a posture of fury. "I don't like that guy."

"I don't either," Vaughn told her. "Now get your clothes off and get in the bathroom. We have things to do."

4:10pm

A tremendous roar of car horns and angry screams made chaos of the Drag. The traffic was at a dead stop at 22nd, backed up as far as the eye could see in either direction. It was a curious thing—hundreds of pigeons had suddenly converged upon the intersection, making it impossible to drive without killing them by the dozens. The modern world, in this tiny microcosm, had suddenly halted. The system brought to its knees—not by violence, but by compassion for the living. The Drag was steaming with anger.

Jobie sat on the edge of an empty stone flower box in front of the Bagel Shop, watching the ruckus unfold. He was more than an observer—he was the orchestrator. It was just another experiment to validate the opinions expressed in his writings—that anarchy would not be a difficult thing if the legion of anarchists in the world gave one concentrated effort like this. *The Apolitical Manifesto* sat at his side, awaiting the addition of his latest experiment. He gripped a cup of sesame seeds he had acquired from the Bagel Shop's dumpster, watching the gray pigeons hammer their beaks at the pavement in a feeding frenzy. The birds would need more seed eventually, but for now, it was better to just watch and appreciate.

He dug his fingers inside the cup of sesame seeds, letting the tiny pellets slip between his fingers. A couple of Crusty punk kids wandered in front of him, staring at him with fearful curiosity as they whispered from ear to ear. Jobie had earned an immediate reputation by ridding the streets of Dickhead. He was a force to be reckoned with, and he loved the notoriety. He sat in silence as the Crusties continued onward down the sidewalk, keeping their distance.

He inhaled comfortably, feeling perfectly safe inside his new reputation. He felt such profound confidence knowing that his presence invoked such fear in strangers. If they only knew...

The thought of Treva crossed his mind once again. Every weekend she was nowhere to be found, and never once did she give any indication of her whereabouts. He felt frustration toward her. At times he wished that no one else existed in the world other than the two of them. She was so easily distracted, lured into depravation so easily. If there were no outside influence, she would simply be his.

He thought back to his journey from Los Angeles to San Diego, how they stayed on the beach in Encinitas for three days before heading into downtown San Diego. He recalled a memory that never happened, an event that took place before their introduction. He visualized Treva at his side, sitting on the north shore of Moonlight Beach. Together they watched the setting sun drift under an orange sky. The immense ocean spread before them like grapefruit juice, sending a chilling breeze. Wide open space, safe and alone.

He would take her back there someday.

The Drag

His name was Big Sanders. A native of Austin and still living with his grandparents, he was a regular face on the Drag. He was an avid collector of vintage comic books, and would spend weekends playing Magic with a small group of acquaintances at Dragon's Lair comic book shop.

Big Sanders was a bumbling oaf, a large and awkward man in his early twenties, heavy-set, but not necessarily obese. He was simply a large person in every respect. His ears on any other man would seem a gross mishap of nature. Thick glasses shielded his squinty eyes that looked like peas lodged in his thick skull. His black T-shirt had the word *Zombie* over a print of some ghastly beast from a campy horror movie.

He stumbled clumsily down the sidewalk of the Drag with a toothy grin of utter bliss pasted across his broad face. A small teenaged girl with bucked-teeth and a non-existent chin clung to his hand, sharing his happiness. Her profile resembled a turtle with no distinction between her neck and jaw.

They giggled through an aimlessly optimistic conversation of no relevance. Happiness spoke clearly through every useless word, defying the restrictions of concrete definitions.

In her eyes, he saw his future. Never before had he seen such a thing. All of his dreams, all of his hopes, materialized in the name of this one girl—Ruth. As they strolled down the street over the heads of the hopeless, he suddenly realized he had never had a happier moment in his life. Never before had he felt so wanted, so comfortable, and so free.

He had spent his life searching for a place, desperate for a sense of belonging. On the Drag, he had found that place. He had friends—he even had stolen the heart of a transient girl to whom he was prepared to devote his entire life. The Drag had given him life, taken him out of his bedroom and away from the comic shops to enter the world of the living. On the Drag he was someone. He was Big Sanders.

Likewise, Ruth had never known love. With a history crooked and shameful enough to boil holy water, she had found her place in his heart. He accepted her and she felt safe with him, protected by his bulldog posturing. It was something she regarded with grave importance based on her helpless past. On the Drag he was someone. She liked that.

His fingers glided along the cold panels of the parked cars as they passed the wrought iron fence that surrounded the Baptist church. Water collected on his immense hand, dripping off his palm.

He barely saw the wiry little body that jumped from behind a parked car. The fist that pulverized his nose wiped the leisure smile off his face. Blood gushed quickly from his flared nostrils as shock immobilized him. His hands rushed to his face as he stared with confusion, trying to understand what had happened. An angry young Crusty punk kid stood in his path with clenched fists and a bent expression. He recognized the webbed tattoos that spanned his hollow cheeks. Purple and yellow bruises covered his face, almost invisible, but still in the final stages of healing. There was rage in this person's eyes, rage like he had never seen before.

"Bad memory?" Jobie hissed. Before he could get a response, he threw a quick fake punch with his left, followed by a hard jab with his right hand straight into Big Sanders' mouth. His head jarred back as Ruth gasped in horror. Jobie threw a firm uppercut to his chin, knocking him back two steps. "Don't remember me?"

Ruth rushed at Jobie with black painted claws reaching for his hardened face. Jobie effortlessly deflected her flailing hands and forced her to the cement, pinning her neck with his duct-taped shoe.

"Stay out of this," Jobie warned her. He looked up at Big Sanders who was now as angry as he was confused. Blood seeped from his mouth and nose, coloring his lips a menacing red. Jobie pulled the butterfly knife out of his pocket, twirling it in a twisting motion that opened the shiny blade.

Big Sanders recognized the knife immediately. Dickhead was his closest friend. He stopped in his tracks, petrified with fear. Ruth curled into a ball, still under Jobie's shoe, with the knife swaying back and forth through the air over her innocent head.

"Please don't hurt him," she sobbed with mercy as tears streamed down her tired face. "Please…"

Jobie tensed his angry eyes that pierced Big Sanders' fleeting sensibility. "Step forward," Jobie insisted.

Big Sanders took a short step closer to the knife with fearful apprehension. There was a wildness to his attacker that he knew wasn't to be trusted. This person could maim him without a second thought, and he had grounds to do so, based on his own memory.

"What is keeping me from digging this knife into your fat gut?" Jobie asked, presenting the question more to himself than to Big Sanders. "I could rip out your entrails and not lose a minute's sleep. I really could. See, I don't care who you are. You're nothing to me, do you understand?"

Big Sanders nodded.

"Nothing at all," Jobie continued. "And this fucking *whore* of yours…I'd kill her, too. I don't ever want to see either of you down here again. Not while I'm in town. Next time, I'll kill you."

Big Sanders stood quietly as the blood trickled onto his *Zombie* T-shirt. He kept his eye on the shimmering blade.

"Do you remember beating my ass in the alley?" Jobie inquired. "Do you fucking remember pissing on me?"

He nodded regretfully.

"You are a worthless, pathetic coward," Jobie informed him. "Your obedience is blind, you're a big, stupid dog. Today is your lucky day—I'm going to spare you! I'm giving you the respect you never gave me…or yourself. I expect you to return it. Never come near me again. Are we clear on this?"

"Yes."

"Next time I will kill you," Jobie promised sincerely. "Don't think I'm kidding…"

"I can tell you're not."

"Good," Jobie said. "Get your fucking *slut* off the ground, that's no way to treat a lady." He stepped back, allowing them to gather each other in their arms. She was mortified and shaking uncontrollably, babbling like an infant. "Let's not forget this." The raw fear that stifled their movements brought a smile of pride to Jobie's face.

Ruth cried violently as she gurgled indistinguishable noises from deep inside her unhealthy body. Even in Big Sanders' arms, she looked suffocated and trapped. Little did Jobie realize that he was witnessing their final day together. Ruth would be gone in the morning, fleeing Austin forever.

Big Sanders dragged himself shamefully down the street, holding his lover as they carried themselves away from Jobie's domain, the Drag.

5:04pm

"Vaughn," Chasey muttered as he struggled with his green vinyl jacket. She caught him just before he gripped the handle of the office door to leave. "Before you go, I have to tell you something."

He stood at attention, facing her directly with his square and commanding presence.

"I'm moving to Oregon to work for a genetics company."

"Really," he replied evenly without a hint of surprise. "Which company?"

"GenetiTech."

He nodded affirmatively. "Producing good stocks, that company. A wise choice, congratulations."

"My first day is the second of November." She stammered briefly, feeling as though her untimely departure was an act of betrayal. "I, uh…I guess this is my notice. I'm sorry."

"I hate to see you go," he told her without any emotional inflection in his strong voice. "But I wouldn't want to keep you from pursuing a career. We'll discuss it further tomorrow. I'm sure we could renegotiate your contract with the university."

His apathy shook her, though she smiled. Had her involvement in the project really been this futile? All that time spent giving her best to this man, and this was the thank you?

"I'm sorry if I'm leaving you high and dry," she told him politely.

"You're not, we can take over from here, and your efforts have been appreciated." His tone was thick with insincerity. "I'd be more than willing to send you off with a glowing letter of recommendation."

"Thank you," she told him, covering her insult behind a friendly smile.

"Well," he said in a hollow tone, "I must be on my way, things to do."

"Of course," she agreed passively. "We'll talk tomorrow."

11:12pm

Broken glass crushed under the soles of Opaque's lime-green boots. Each creeping step sounded like the crunching of bones. He wearily trailed Tamika through a dark and dismal alley known for its sordid activities. They had been warned against ever going near it, let alone entering. "Why are we here?"

She turned to his ghostly white face, painted up like a Kabuki doll. He practically ran into her. "You know why we're here." Fear and annoyance teetered in her words. She would rather be anywhere else. Yet she lumbered forward into the haze, squinting into the dark crevices between old milk crates and used soda dispensers.

Opaque wrapped his fingers around Tamika's arm, clinging to her for safety. His silver metal claws were cold on her skin. "How do we know she's even out here?" His fiery red eyes peered through the shadows, beyond the torn and dismantled asphalt, searching for Treva amongst the waste. It seemed they were the only living creatures in the entire one-block stretch. That, of course, was what they hoped. "Maybe she's with those people in the black car again. You know how she's always leaving with them."

"Not for this long." She could feel the fear riding up her spine. It didn't help that he was closer to her than her own shadow. "I'm worried."

He didn't reply. The sentiment was too obvious to reiterate. He merely stood a step behind her, riding her coattail for support, gripping her arm tightly.

Tamika stopped dead in her tracks with a frightful gasp. She pointed forward to a slender pair of legs stretching out from behind the dumpster. She swallowed hard, fearing the worst.

"If she's dead..." His words trailed into oblivion. He could feel his heart thumping. He grabbed her shoulders, ready to climb up her back.

They cautiously advanced with numbing apprehension. Opaque peered over Tamika's shoulder, hiding behind her for protection. A dark fluid covered the bony legs. It looked like blood.

Tamika's heart raced wildly. She wanted to turn around and run, but she edged closer to the metal dumpster, leaning forward with wide eyes, anticipating the horror. The smell of decay soured the air. It smelled like death.

Holding onto the edges of the cold dumpster, she peeked around the corner, expecting a gruesome mutilation. To her relief, she got neither. It wasn't Treva. It was an Asian man, pant less yet alive, still wearing a polo shirt and a smile. He seemed happy to see them. He was immersed in a putrid stench, covered with a revoltingly foul fluid.

She let out a belated sigh as Opaque glanced safely around her shoulder to bare witness himself.

He had had enough. "This is ridiculous. Let's get out of here." He grabbed Tamika by the arm and continued forward with a brisk and confident pace, leading the way for a change. "She's not here."

Just as his words left his mouth, he spotted Treva's lifeless body. She was curled up on the other side of an industrial-sized air-conditioning unit. She was little more than a contorted ball of human limbs, perfectly immobile.

Her head was awkwardly lodged in the corner between the brick wall and the unit. A hypodermic needle dangled from her arm with streaks of blood dried around the point of injection. Her body was covered with scaly red blemishes that looked like third-degree burns. She barely looked alive.

Tamika rushed to her side, pulling the needle out of her arm and throwing it into the darkness. It ricocheted off the stone wall, falling to the asphalt—ready for another junkie to use. Tamika placed her hand on Treva's prominent ribcage to find a pulse. It was there, faintly.

"Treva," she said desperately. "Get up. Get up, Treva. It's me—it's Tamika. Please wake up."

There was a gravelly noise emanating from deep inside her throat. Dried vomit covered her face and neck.

"Treva, wake up!" Opaque demanded fiercely.

She moaned, almost euphorically. The contrasting nature seemed positively evil. The devil was in her.

Tamika gently put Treva's arm over her shoulder and hoisted her from the rubble. She was the weight of a bird. Opaque grabbed her other arm and together they dragged her to the street. The toes of her shoes scraped against the pavement, and her head bobbed from one shoulder to the next. Strings of mucus twirled from her large nostrils. She mumbled disconnected thoughts that seemed torn from her mind in an esoteric collage of utter nonsense. Then came the clearly enunciated: *daddy...hurt me.*

Opaque dreaded Jobie's reaction to the sight of this. He knew Jobie was at the Bagel Shop waiting, worrying. Months ago, he and Opaque had successfully escaped the turmoil of their home, traveled thousands of miles...only for this. The charm of the vagabond lifestyle had lost its luster. He wanted to be home, in his bed, in his known surroundings, comfortable and secure.

"She's dying," Opaque said.

"No," Tamika replied angrily. "That is *not* happening."

Far on the corner, Opaque could see Jobie perched up on the low wall of the Bagel Shop's deck. Even at such a distance, he could sense the hopelessness. When Jobie turned their direction, his eyes livened with charisma. He sprang from the deck, running with tense steps toward them. His fists were drawn into tightened balls, his face hard with eyes that seemed to be melting. He swept Treva up into his arms, tossing her around like a doll as he held her tightly, desperately.

"Where was she?" he asked as he buried his face in her dirty raspberry hair.

Opaque noticed what appeared to be bruises in the shape of someone's hands around her neck. He felt he could almost see the person's fingerprints lodged inside her skin. He backed away from her as Jobie lifted her in his arms, carrying her like a wounded child to the Bagel Shop. He was the unspoken pack leader, protecting his clan.

Tamika and Opaque followed behind him, watching him stagger and sway. Her limbs dangled flaccidly to the ground. Her fingernails scraped the pavement.

Jobie hoisted her over the edge of the outer deck with Opaque's help. Tamika stretched her out onto the pebbled floor as the three of them stood over her sprawled body. Her breathing was shallow, sickly and smelled of death. She looked as if her body had been skinned with only the bloody red muscle visible over brittle bones. Only in death could she weigh less.

Jobie sat in front of her, gently placing her head on his lap. The snot rolled down her hollow cheeks onto his kilt. He caressed her scaly skeletal face, staring longingly into her unresponsive eyes. Her skin seemed charred like a burn victim. The bones of her face protruded under her paper skin, almost ripping through. Her chapped lips were so dry that the cracks were marked with creases of dried blood. Her lips were otherwise white and flushed.

"Treva," Jobie whispered.

"What if she dies?" Opaque murmured hopelessly.

Tamika shot him a hard glance. "She is *not* going to die."

"She's on junk," Opaque told him. "She had a needle in her arm."

Jobie's lips clamped tensely together as his eyes blurred with teardrops. His calm presence crumbled—it wasn't supposed to end like this. He had plans…why hadn't they left town sooner? A tear rolled down his tattooed cheek, falling onto Treva's open and dry mouth. "Please, God…" he mumbled desperately. "Don't do this to me…*please*…"

Treva opened her mouth. Inhuman guttural noises swelled deep from within her throat. "*He…hurt…me.*"

Tamika leaned back against the wall of the narrow deck and slid into the corner. She wrapped her thick arms tightly around her legs and closed her eyes.

She wanted to be anywhere else. All of them wished to be gone, to already be on their way to New Orleans. The air was thick with malcontent.

2:11am

Chains rattled in the darkness, hidden behind veils of violet tapestries that hung from heaven like mist. The air that surrounded Tamika seemed to glow a deep thickened purple that filled her lungs like grape jelly. Voices whispered, blind scathing voices that were one with the dark, lacking a face or body. Menacing evil whispers.

She lugged forward, stepping through the density with forthright determination. The metal chains faded into the cries of desperation. Human voices, amplified in a ghostly realm.

"Tamika," a familiar voice whispered in her ear.

She was alone, stepping forward. A dark wooden box appeared in the distance, floating in the purple velvet air. Black silhouettes sat morbidly around the box, weeping. The box, she came to realize was a coffin. Her own coffin.

"Tamika," the whisper came once again.

This time she recognized the voice. It was her dead friend Cindy. Upon recognition, Cindy emerged through the coil of darkness. The apparition was a stark representation of her friend, as if she had been recreated with sticks and mud. Its mouth was as hard as a bird's beak. Tamika felt no comfort in her presence. In fact, she was horrified of this demonic beast.

"You promised, Tamika," the thing sobbed. It suddenly looked up at her with a twisted smile that was nothing short of evil. "But you did die, Tamika, you did die."

Tamika shook her head.

The thing nodded in disagreement. "You are dead."

"No, I'm not."

Suddenly the coffin was at her side—a dark shiny wooden box tightly closed.

"You're inside here," the monstrous specter told her. "I wouldn't lie to you."

"You always lied."

The shrieks of pain reverberated through the thick purple air. Cries of desperation. Human voices. Cindy evaporated before her eyes, dispersing into vapor. Tamika was suddenly all alone once again, rid of the presence of the hideous phantom posing as a link to her past.

"She wasn't good for you," a tiny voice rose from the floor.

She looked down to see the doll she had given Opaque. It sat cross-legged, smiling up at her with peaceful, knowing eyes.

"Time to stop running," it told her. Its eyes seemed to dig inside her brain, sweeping the dust from her redundant patterns of thought. "Time to wake up," it said. "Time to wake up."

112

She opened her eyes quickly, sucking down a deep breath. The doll was next to her, staring her in the eyes, yet perfectly lifeless. She had been dreaming.

A deafening scream of pain shocked her. She looked up to see Jobie and Treva cuddled soundly in the corner, fast asleep. At the opposite end of the narrow deck, Opaque was awake, peeking over the edge of the Bagel Shop's concrete deck. She could sense his fear. It matched her own. Their world, it seemed, was crumbling around them.

She crawled on her hands and knees across the pebbled cement next to him. Painful cries rang from the street corner, no more than twenty feet from where they slept.

"What's going on?" she whispered nervously to Opaque as the horrendously desperate pleas were met only with what sounded like a severe bludgeoning.

"Something bad," he replied softly. "Really bad."

She peeked over the edge of the wall, glimpsing the twisted bodies of several Crusties. They were sprawled on the corner, lying in their own blood, crying in fear and misery. Four mysterious figures with khaki Dockers, black Vans, and black hooded sweatshirts—each with a massive red X stitched on the back, stood over the mess of them, kicking and punching.

"Who are they?" Tamika whispered.

Opaque shook his head in confusion. "A gang?"

"That could've been us sleeping out there," she told him quietly. "We're lucky."

"So far," he replied. "Maybe they know we're here. Maybe we're next."

"Should we wake up Jobie?" she asked.

"He'd be fool enough to try to mix with them," he told her. "Let him sleep."

Tamika sat perfectly still. Her heart raced. "I don't want them to come up here."

"I don't either," Opaque whispered hoarsely.

"I can't deal with this anymore...I can't go to New Orleans," she decided quickly. "I'm sorry."

"Don't be sorry," Opaque mumbled.

"It's not you, I would never back out on you," she assured him. "You're my best friend."

"Trust me, I understand."

Tamika glanced over at Treva's lifeless body as the cries of pain and desperation echoed through the night. Their pleas went unanswered, unnoticed. She could hear the strange visitors walking away, leaving the Crusties in their own pain and misery.

She stared at Treva's wrecked body. It was evident that Jobie held a corpse in his arms.

"I'm changing my life," she told Opaque. "Starting tomorrow."

Saturday, October 10, 1998
2:31pm

The Drag

Tamika stood at the register of Urban Outfitters, admiring the ruby red dress that draped over the faux oxidized metal counter. Her dirty pillowcase lay at her side, bulky with keepsakes and coins. She had dedicated every day all week mooching change from sympathetic college students. At the end of each day, she checked up on the dress, making sure it hadn't already been purchased. By the weekend, the dress was not only still on the rack, it had been put on sale. Thirty dollars, a steal.

Tamika lifted her pillowcase onto the counter and lined up thirty stacks of quarters totaling a dollar each. The clerk raised a carefully plucked brow to insinuate the acknowledgement of either a joke or a nuisance. The expression worked both ways.

"Cash in full," Tamika said confidently. Her curly hair was free of the ties, boundless and exploding like a black dandelion.

With grievous exaggerated effort, the clerk scooted the piles of change to the edge of the counter. He released one labored sigh after another as he tore through the shelves, seeking a canister or cup to store all the coins. He rolled his eyes in defeat and left the change piled on the counter, turning his attention to finishing the transaction to be rid of her.

She felt so much joy that she could hardly contain herself. A broad smile of sheer delight radiated from her circular face. "Thank you," she announced proudly as the clerk placed the dress in a paper bag and gave her the receipt. She hoisted the pillowcase over her shoulder and walked to the door. Her hair teetered back and forth, swaying to the rhythm of each step.

The humidity was perfectly visible through the cracked glass of the front door. It made a mess of her frizzy hair.

She concealed her treasure under her arm as she strutted confidently down the Drag to 21st. Her mind was awash with newfound goals and aspirations. She would soon find her own place to live, somewhere in a quiet downtown neighborhood. She'd get a job and she'd take showers every day—sometimes even more frequently, if she wanted. She would be empowered to make her own choices. And after rent was paid, she'd buy another new dress, and eventually she'd buy a stereo and music. She'd buy candles, and eventually a camera. She'd get cornrows. In a matter of months, she'd be truly free. Truly free.

As she reached the massively towering Dobie building, she crossed the street and walked through campus to Speedway. Thunder roared from above, threatening to release the rain that would melt the weightlessness of her hair. The rain fell just as she climbed the steps to the largest dormitory in the United States, Jester Hall.

She walked through its inner corridors, finding her way to the east wing.

"I have an odd favor to ask," she politely told the athletic black man behind the front desk. His orange satin outfit looked like a billboard for Adidas. "I'm homeless, I've been staying on the Drag. I need to find a job, and I'm going to do that today...but I need a shower." She reached inside her pillowcase and grabbed a handful of silver change, mostly nickels and dimes. She held it out in her thick hand. "I'll give you this if you let me use the shower."

He wrinkled his brow, and then shot a quick glance up at her. "You stayin' on the Drag?"

She nodded.

"Damn...that must be hard!"

She smiled. "You ain't kiddin'."

He tensed his lips and shook his head. "Damn...on the Drag...I ain't takin' that money."

"No?"

"Nah...do me no good—go ahead and keep it." He picked up the telephone and quickly dialed a five-digit number. "Get down here," he demanded the person on the other end. "Why? I said so, that's why. Don't worry 'bout it. Get down here. I've got a girl down here, she's wanting to use the shower." He cupped the mouthpiece and held it out from his face. "My girlfriend," he told Tamika. "She talks more than anyone I know." He put the phone back to his thick puckered lips. "Because it'll keep your ass outta confession for a change, doin' a good deed...now how could I take her up there when I'm obviously at the desk—where's your head?" He listened to her talk a while, rolling his eyes, and then glancing up at Tamika. "Yeah, she's a sister. All right, then." He hung up the phone. "Damn, that bitch can talk...she'll be down in a minute, after her program ends. She'll take you 'round, get you fixed up, but this is a one-time deal."

"You got it," Tamika sighed with relief.

"Now put that money up before someone takes it...shit."

2:32pm

Treva ached for the injection. She fantasized that the needle had become part of her anatomy like a catheter with a constant stream of dilaudid filling her veins. She could no longer tolerate the sight of herself. She cowered from her own grotesque reflection. She had become an abomination, a revolting monstrosity of corrupted flesh.

She fought the desire to cry as Vaughn tied her passive hands to the chair once again. She felt no fear, even at the thought of death. She was already there. Only the needle could bring her life. That's why she returned, that's why she needed him so desperately.

Panic and anger suddenly ripped through her lifeless body. Her teeth gritted together as every muscle clenched. "What have you done to me?"

He squeezed the handkerchief into a knot, confining her for another weekend of testing. He ignored her accusation as he stood behind her, staring down at her filthy hair.

He could feel the arms of failure moving in to embrace him. The serum in all its variations was not working. In fact, it was a catalyst to the problem. At first glance, its application appeared to be a miracle of modern medicine. The results were virtually instantaneous, clearing away the affected area like biological alchemy. Then as the hours passed, the affliction would return with a vengeance, painlessly burning the flesh from within like battery acid. Vaughn was at a loss, and each calculated and educated guess was in vain. His failure greeted him weekly, staring up at him, bound to a wooden chair with hostile eyes. He wished to discard the evidence of his shortcomings, to abolish her existence altogether and work again from scratch. At the rate of her exodermic deterioration, her impending death was unavoidable.

"You made me this way on purpose, didn't you?" she seethed with rage. "You had no desire to help me. You ruined my body for your own little science project, didn't you?"

He looked down upon her with contemptuous eyes that formed a pair of crow's feet. "It's your soul surfacing." He wanted her dead.

Her eyelids narrowed into vengeful slits that revealed the red lesions of skin surrounding her cavernous eye sockets. Her skin had become translucently thin. Her red musculature was almost visible through her disappearing hide. "I will kill you."

He laughed as he reached to the display of syringes lined across the sink. The contents of each were a mystery to all but him. "How? Here you are bound to this chair, a hostage by your own request, I might add, threatening me. Preposterous! Does anyone even know where you are?"

She stared angrily. Her silence was an adequate response.

116

"I own you. If you died, no one would know."

"You're wrong," she said quickly. "There is someone out there who knows everything, and he'd kill you."

"Your little boyfriend...isn't that cute? Let me guess, he's on the streets, too? Hmm...what a surprise. What a threat! You can stare at me with all your hate, but you put yourself here, and you continue to do so every weekend...where is my mercy? I have none, to be frank. Oh, but you want this," he said as he shoved a syringe in front of her nose. Its dark fluid swirled inside the casing. "What you live for, that cheap thrill...don't worry, you'll get it."

He lowered it to her arm and shoved the needle into her balmy and pocked skin. He pushed the fluid into her veins, penetrating her body with his fleeting whims and curiosities. He looked into her eyes, seeing her disappointment with retaining her coherence. It wasn't the junk she needed.

"Thought that was it, didn't you?" he taunted. "What if I were to tell you that I just infected you with the AIDS virus? Would you care? Would you even know what just went into your body? Do you care? You are dying, can you not see this?"

"I will kill you," she repeated passionately. She meant every word, too. Once she got her life together. Once the cravings could be curbed by other means.

He laughed at her naiveté. He visualized her body burning to ash with all his missteps in theory vaporizing into non-existence. Nothing more than a bad memory, bad judgement. "I just might get you first. Sock drawer, it's loaded. I can kill you right now. No one would ever know." He stepped up to the oak medicine cabinets and removed a razor. He placed it in the porcelain sink as he grabbed a handful of her raspberry hair and forced her head back. Her volcanic-colored throat became vulnerable, unprotected from his well-contained rage. He picked up a syringe with his free hand and shoved the needle deep into her neck under her jaw. As his thumb pushed the fluid into her neck, he watched the clouds fall over her eyes as the contents of her stomach spilled from her mouth onto the floor. She smiled blissfully as her head floated atop her shoulders. Bits and pieces of her most recent meal slid from her chin to her neck, clinging to the syringe. "You are the most repulsive being I have ever encountered in my life."

He left the room a moment, returning with a pair of scissors. He grabbed her hair and lifted her face, watching her cough out a giggle from somewhere beyond. He opened the scissors and clasped her hair, cutting away clumps by the handful. Her dirty hair fell to the floor in dark fuscia piles. He then scraped the hair from her scalp with the razor, leaving only the sickly red skin, textured with blood.

"Vanity stripped," he commended himself to an otherwise silent room. He humored the idea of killing her right then, of strangling her to death and taking her body to be dumped in Town Lake later that night. Some random

Dragworm, no one would care, including himself. It probably wouldn't even make the papers.

He wrapped his strong hands around her neck as the vomit squished between his fingers. He squeezed tightly, watching her veins thicken from the pressure. Yes, he could kill her, and it would be so easy. No one would ever know. He squeezed tighter and tighter until he could feel the air restricting in her lungs. He was overwhelmed with a sense of strength—like nothing he'd ever felt in his life. He could own the hands of death. His body was vibrating with adrenaline, and his otherwise flaccid penis was uncharacteristically erect. He stared passionately into her dilated and bulging eyes. His were ravenous.

He then loosened his grip, watching her head drift to the side. Her breathing returned at a rapid and desperate rate. As he stood over her, watching her, he considered all the ways he could kill her and dispose of her. It'd be so easy. Too easy. He considered slicing her throat, watching the blood flow down her esophagus into her lungs, drowning her on her own lifeline. Of course, he could fill the tub and drown her in the conventional sense. In doing so, he would certainly have to bathe in her blood, just to see what life-giving properties it supposedly had on one's skin. Then there was the gun, although that would only provide the satisfaction of watching her head being ripped apart by the bullet. He would rather her death be administered by his own hands, by his own brutal strength. Therein lied the motivation. Owning the hands of death.

She had nothing to live for—it would be a mercy killing. He would be doing her a favor by ending her life. He thought of how the Nazis had acquired so much medical information by the experiments they performed on the Jews. He found himself in a similar situation with his own experiments, but in this case, no one cared. No one would be busting down his door to save her, she was merely someone else's accident from start to finish. Her only function as a living organism was obviously to be the pawn for a serum that would bare his name, not hers.

He looked down upon her as she sat idly limp, held up only by the fact that she was tied securely to the wooden chair that had become her weekend throne. His work was not quite done. Until then, she still retained a purpose to society. He would kill her, though. Possibly in a week, possibly longer, depending on her value to his research. After which she would be of no further use to the world.

Then he would kill her.

3:56pm

Tamika stepped up to the entrance of The Bagel Shop, dropping her pillowcase between her black loafers. She looked nervously upon the store

118

hours, feeding on the acceleration of her throbbing heart. She was thriving on both anxiety and anticipation. She had spent almost every night in Austin sleeping outside this place, yet now she approached it with different function and meaning. She dug inside her pillowcase, searching for scrunchies to tie her hair into orderly pigtails. She reached to the bottom, fumbling through coins and lint…and a cassette tape. She grabbed the cassette, the only one she had, The Jesus & Mary Chain's *Psychocandy*. So many memories of the life she had once lived. Her life before Austin claimed her as one of its own.

She looked up at her reflection in the storefront window. She could hardly recognize the classy image that stood in her place. The red dress shined, she looked marvelous. Her smile was bright and warm and full of self-confidence. Her hair was massive, exploding like lightning in all directions from her head. There were even traces of make-up on her round face.

She looked through the glass beyond her reflection, shocked to realize that she was being watched. A man stood behind the counter, bored, watching her watch herself. It was the manager, Frank. She picked up her pillowcase and walked inside, abandoning her quest for hair ties altogether. She stepped up to the metal counter and relaxed her hands on its cold surface. Smooth jazz filled the air.

"Can I get an application?" she requested politely.

He reached below the counter, staring at her, squinting in an effort to recollect where their paths had crossed. "How do I know you?" He seemed leery of her presence, pestered by a vague and somewhat negative memory. He couldn't place it, though.

She shrugged her shoulders casually. "Hard to say…"

He placed an application on the counter, staring into her dark eyes when suddenly he snapped his fingers. "No, wait, you're one of these kids that hang out on the streets. You're always asleep on the deck every morning when I come in."

She looked at him, then down at the application. Her smile washed away with his realization. She had hoped to begin her new life with a clean slate. She felt like turning around and leaving, giving up entirely on the whole idea.

"Am I wrong?" he asked suspiciously.

"I don't currently have a place to live," she admitted sheepishly. Her eyes shot upward as determination overwhelmed her once again. She clenched her fists on the counter and looked him squarely in the eyes. "Please give me a chance."

"There really aren't a lot of positions…"

"I'll take anything."

He looked at her shaggy hair. It was a frightful mess, though it was clean. That was an improvement, at least. A second glance at her stylish outfit gave room for doubt. She was entirely overdressed, especially for such a laborious job. It did seem out of character for a Dragworm, her behavior. She seemed desperate.

"Where'd you get the dress?" he asked.

"Saved money all week," she responded proudly. "I wanted to make sure that when I went looking for work, the people would know I was serious about it."

He raised his brow, genuinely impressed. "That's a lot of spare change."

"I was determined."

"Where are you from originally?" he questioned. "I mean, when you *did* have a home."

"Kyle, Texas. Where the floods are right now."

"Why do you feel I can trust that you won't be feeding all your friends on the Drag when I'm not here?" he asked.

"I don't have many friends."

"I take it you're trying to get off the streets now? Why?"

She thought a moment, realizing that honesty was probably the best approach. "After my best friend killed herself, I ran away to Austin. I had nothing left, nothing to live for...I don't mean to sound so heavy...it's the truth, though. I think I did the right thing, but out there," she paused to point at the large pane windows, "I've seen a lot of really bad things. I now know where I don't want to be. I know what I want from life, I know what matters to me."

They stood facing one another without expression. There was a short silence as they determined the size of one another.

"The only shift available is a night baking position," he told her. "That would be to arrive at work at midnight and bake until eight o'clock in the morning. It's not easy. Most people can't handle it. It's not hard to understand why."

"I'll take it," she insisted confidently. "Please. I won't let you down."

He looked straight into her black eyes with a decidedly firm glare. "You better not let me down. I'm giving you only *one* chance—tonight at midnight. One minute late, don't even bother."

She was eager to take him up on his challenge. "I'll be here."

The Drag

Jobie stared at his brother, needling his red eyes, perturbed. The air between them was icy and dissonant, full of static.

"Not *going*?" Jobie mumbled again to himself. "What do you mean?"

"Just that. I'm staying."

Jobie's eyes squinted hard, tense like his lips. His hands clutched themselves, resistant to the emptiness that now shrouded him like a frozen glove. "How? Why?"

"What do you mean? How…I'll get a job somewhere. Why…we're not traveling, Jobie—we're running. We are so fearful of the past catching us that we haven't a clue as to where we are in life right now. Jobie, we're sleeping on cement every night in the cold. It's only going to get colder, and I know it's only going to get harder. This isn't living. Freedom is control. I need to take *control* of my life."

Jobie was stunned, speechless. He wanted to tell him he couldn't fathom leaving without him, to be on his adventure alone… "Whatever you want."

Opaque nodded. "How will we keep in touch?"

Jobie shook his head with deep dissatisfaction. "That's the deal, now, isn't it? We won't. So the family ends here because you're too fucking scared—"

Opaque laughed sardonically. "I'm not afraid, Jobie, you're the one who is running scared. And you hide behind this Hercules front…give me a month to get a phone, then call me collect from wherever you are. I'll give you my address and all you need to know. I expect to see you on my doorstep at Christmas."

Jobie scowled, grinding the toe of his shoe into the ground.

"This isn't the end, Jobie," Opaque told him. "It's the beginning…it's where our lives start. Who knows what will happen? Might be good, might be bad, but I *know* that now I am holding the wheel. I'll be a free man." He smiled to himself, at the thought.

"Me, too," Jobie scoffed. "I'll be a free man when I drive out of this miserable town *alone*."

"Don't give me that—you have Treva."

Jobie bit his lip with a quick nod. "Yeah…yeah."

"I'm sorry," Opaque offered. "I can't leave, I can't keep running. You can stay—stay with me. We'll get a place together."

Jobie turned to walk away. "Not a chance." He threw his hand in the air as if to discard his presence entirely. "Not a chance..."

11:47pm

The Bagel Shop

Frank's complexion was ghostly white. He lowered the letter to the table, holding it with shaky hands as the broken streams of streetlights striped the paper with luminescence. His best friend was dying. It was a secret that had been kept from him for years, since they were still in high school back in Iola, Kansas. His friend had been ravaged with rheumatic fever five times in his childhood—none of which Frank ever knew. It had weakened his heart. The doctors didn't expect he'd survive into his twenties. Now they were absolutely certain he wouldn't make it to his thirties. Things had recently turned for the worse.

Frank thought back on all his assumptions of his friend from their past together. He had always thought that his friend lacked the confidence to ever leave Iola to pursue college. Now it was all clear. He was determined to die where he lived, living each day as though his last. Even his friend's wife knew of his declining health. He suddenly felt as if he had never really known him, as if the past they shared was a lie.

There came a gentle tapping at the glass door. He looked up to see Tamika standing with a smile—bright, alert, and ready to bake. She was wearing a thick black shirt and long pink sweatpants. Her hair was teased into a massive afro.

He stood up uneasily to unlock the door. "How are you?"

"Very good, thanks. And you?"

"I've been better," he admitted gravely.

She looked up at him with concern. "Is something wrong?"

"I'd rather not say," he told her abjectly. "Are you ready for another shift?"

She nodded confidently.

"Good, I'm ready to go home."

"How am I doing so far?" she asked.

"Very good, very dependable." There was a lifeless quality to his voice. It was very unlike him.

"Great," she replied, unsure if his mood had anything to do with her.

122

They walked to the back of the bakery together, stopping in front of the massive silver boiler. The clear water stewed like lava.

"Do you have questions?" he asked.

"None," she replied swiftly.

"You have to be fast at pulling them out of the boiling water," he told her. "That's where you'd lose a lot of time."

"Not a problem. When the morning driver arrives—"

"He'll be in here at five in the morning..."

She smiled. "It will all be done."

His eyes narrowed with uneasiness. "Okay. I'm going to leave...you have my number."

She nodded.

He apprehensively walked to the door. "Call me with any questions."

"I will."

"Okay...goodnight."

She watched him stumble away, groveling in despair. He grabbed a piece of paper from one of the tables and entered the darkness, locking the door behind him.

She glanced up at the bake-list, double-checking her rack of bagel dough. The enormous kettle of water bubbled and steamed to her left as the oven rumbled in front of her with each rack inside rotating like a carnival ride. Blue flames burned brightly behind the racks.

She stepped over to the jambox, fumbling through her pillowcase for music. She grabbed a cassette, the only one she owned—*Psychocandy*. She examined the worn cover, how most of the words had been scratched away from excessive use. She loved this album, though she suddenly realized that she felt nothing toward it, or the past that was intertwined. Those days were gone— in fact, she liked her distance from them. A new day would emerge with the sun at the end of her shift. She was now a creature of the night, hiding from the world, earning an honest living.

She smiled happily as she tossed the cassette in the trash.

11:48pm

"Tell me a story," Treva whispered as she lay at Jobie's side on the Bagel Shop's deck. Her voice was raspy and weak. Her shaved head was no more than a red skull with eyes.

Jobie fell back into reflection, digging deep into his memory. "I caught my dad cheating on my mom once. I was young. I told my mom about it, and the next thing I knew, she was gone. I never saw her again." His voice trembled slightly as he paused to regain some control. "I felt responsible. I felt as though it was my fault. I think my dad felt the same as I did. I don't ever remember getting along with my dad, but I do know that things got much worse after that incident." He turned to face her, resting his cobwebbed cheek against the cold stone surface. "I have never told anyone this, not even my brother."

"That wasn't really a story," she grumbled with disappointment.

"You're right," he said. "That was more of a secret than a story."

"I'm on the inside now, huh?"

"Yeah, you can't say a word." He raised his head from the pebbled cement, looking inside the bakery to catch a glimpse of Tamika working. He felt safer knowing she was in there. He reclined against the hard floor once again. "Let's trade secrets."

"I have no secrets."

"Really?" he challenged. "Then where have you been going every weekend?"

She was silent.

"I want to help you," he told her. "You need to trust me."

She turned her bald head away with disregard. Her scalp was coarse with nicks and scrapes. "I don't need help."

He pulled the butterfly knife from his sporran and placed it in her feeble hand. "I want you to take it, you may need it someday, who knows?"

Her red, scaly fingers glided along the length of it before opening it up to reveal the shiny blade. She squinted as the streetlights ricocheted from the metal into her tired eyes.

"Where have you been going on weekends?" he repeated with a more tenacious tone.

She closed the knife and shoved it inside her deep pocket. "You wouldn't believe me."

"Try me."

"Well," she began as she scratched her enflamed and hairless head with her fingernails. Droplets of blood surfaced on her dry scalp, following a trail from her dirty nails. "I've been getting help from a doctor. He's been looking at my skin." Even as the words escaped her mouth, she knew it sounded absurd. It was apparent that her health had worsened progressively with each visit.

He was somewhat startled, expecting anything but the truth. Was this just a strange affliction that would soon be cured? He could only hope, for his hormone's sake.

Suddenly she burst into tears. "I'm dying…" she sobbed. "And I'm hideous."

His face briefly lit with an empowering smile. Her weakened spirit harmonized with his insurmountable interest. The deeper she slid into despair, the closer he felt to her. "No, you're not."

"Yes, I am. I don't know what he's done to me…and now I can't stop seeing him…"

"Why?"

"Because he's supposed to be curing it. And the money…I need money."

"What money?" The desperation in her voice irritated him. Her submissive dependence infuriated him further. "He pays you?"

"Yes," she replied with a passive sniffle.

"Is he rich?"

"I don't know…"

His face clenched with anger. He felt insecurity about her reliance upon this person's charity. It enraged him to know that a stranger offered something to her that he never could. "I hate rich people. I want you to stop seeing him."

She silently wept. "I can't."

"Why? Is he the person who cut off your hair? I thought you loved your hair…"

"Leave me alone," she replied angrily.

His eyes tightened with hostility. "Where does he live? Are you fucking him?"

"No, and if I was, it's not your business." She sat upright, leveraging herself with her palms. She felt weak and dizzy. Her head seemed to be floating over her shoulders, practically blind and numb to her surroundings.

"It *is* my business," he concluded aggressively. "*You* are my business. Do you not realize what I have done for you?"

The truth of his statement besieged her with guilt. "You've done nothing. You think I need you?"

He remained still, deflecting the threat with silence.

"I won't stop seeing him," she insisted. "Not until my skin is normal."

"You honestly believe he will cure you?"

She knew he wouldn't, or it would already have been done. "Yes," she belied hastily, deceiving only herself.

"You make it very hard to give a shit about you," he admitted. "You depend on all these people, but who are they? They control your life."

"Shut up," she hissed. Again, the truth was too venomous for her to handle. She imagined the needle penetrating her skin, sending her far away. That's all she really wanted. "You don't know."

"I think I *do* know—I know better than you do."

She thought a while, maintaining an awkward silence. When she spoke again, her voice was as soft as a child's. "Let's leave Austin. Let's go to New Orleans. Let's go tonight."

"You're too sick to leave."

"I'm not either," she declared with a recognizable exhaustion. "I'm ready to go, I'm ready now. Let's do it, let's leave."

"Not yet."

She scoffed aloud. "I need to go, there's nothing more I want than that. Please, Jobie, let's leave town tonight—*right now*."

"You need to sever all your ties here, at whatever cost," he told her. "*At whatever cost.* Trust me, I want to leave as badly as you do. I want it so badly I can taste it. In fact, I can't think of anything I want more. I can feel the walls of this town closing in on me. I see it in the way these people look at me. They want me dead, but they're too afraid to even look at me..."

"All that we need to do to leave is to stand up and start walking. We can leave all this behind us right now. It'd be just you and me. You and me."

The idea of it wasn't short of appeal. He weighed the possibilities before realizing how futile it was to even consider. It frustrated him how unaware she seemed of the circumstances. Her circumstances became his burden, and he begrudged her for it. "Not until you get well again."

She sat quietly a moment, thinking to herself. The thought of everyone she had met in Austin filled her with resentment. "I'll get them out of my life." Her rage simmered inside her, waiting to explode. "I know what I'm going to do. I will need your help."

He sat up, eager to listen, eager to help. "Let's hear it."

She laid out her plan in all its brutality. As she had suspected, he was willing to participate in her nefarious scheme. They immediately began plotting the details of her revenge.

Saturday, October 31, 1998
10:17pm

Sixth Street

Chasey edged her way down Sixth Street alone, admiring the elaborate costumes of the thousands who packed the notoriously renowned spectacle. It was her last night in Austin. Halloween. She would have preferred to spend it with anyone other than only herself, but her options were few and far between. She hoped that a higher level of morality existed where she was going, because Austin had proven itself to be nothing more than a thoroughfare for marauders and sinners.

A couple passed—the male wearing a crown of thorns with a white robe, while the female was clearly the Virgin Mary.

"Forgive them for their sins, Father," she whispered under her breath. "They mock you in vain, forgive them."

No, she wouldn't be missing much by leaving this town. She would be leaving as she arrived, hopeful and empty-handed.

Her attention quickly strayed to a young couple standing on the curb watching the mob of ghouls and hooligans flaunt their pageantry. She recognized the young girl, her horrendous skin infliction made her stand out as one of the most hideous monsters on the street. On a night like this she would mix well with the crowd, just another vile island in a sea of atrocity.

"Have mercy on her," Chasey whispered to the cool air that blew through the crowded streets. She turned to walk down a side street with one last glimpse of the wild extravaganza she would soon be leaving behind. "Goodbye, Austin."

10:32pm

The black Fury drifted through a veil of fog down a vacant alley. The headlights sliced the haze of cold humidity as its rubber tires splashed through potholes of stagnant water. The brick walls were glazed with a slippery sheen from all the rain. The city was waterlogged.

127

Phaedra glanced into the rearview mirror, into her own reflection. Her almond-shaped eyes looked upon themselves with deep satisfaction. Her black hair was clean and straight, shining like her latex corset and skirt. It made her soft skin seem pale in contrast. She was looking her best, ready for the performance of the year, the annual S&M Ball at the Voodoo Lounge. She was to be on stage within the hour, submitting her flesh to the whip.

Her savagely beautiful eyes caught sight of Treva standing by the alleyway entrance to the Voodoo Lounge. Early as expected. When Treva turned to face the Fury, Phaedra gasped. Her skin appeared to be melting off her malnourished muscles and bones. Her face looked like a skull covered in red wax with shifty, volatile eyes. She had the eyes of death, as though her life had been stripped, leaving only a mobile skeletal corpse in its place. Her clothes draped her bony frame as if to mock her rapid decline. They were designed to accent the body, not flaunt its deterioration. She was a walking disease.

She nudged forward with the grace and fluidity of an insect as the Fury rolled to a stop. She perched her weight on the car's black hood to support her languid body. Her flesh began to burn with envy as Phaedra's beauty ate her like cancer. She missed her own haystack hair. In fact, there wasn't much she didn't miss, including her sanity. "Do you have it?" Her voice was raspy and weak.

Phaedra opened the car door, leaving the engine running with the headlights ablaze. She placed her latex knee-high boot onto the sticky blacktop, standing upright from the driver seat. She held the leather pouch in her smooth hands. "Money?"

Treva hunched over the hood, barely holding herself vertical as she tilted her ghastly head to seek the darkness. "Away from sight."

Jobie stood at the end of the alley, secretly watching the exchange through a blanket of fog. He scanned Trinity to the police barricades at Fifth, relishing the macabre atmosphere of Austin's traditional Halloween celebration. Superheroes and legendary monsters emerged from back streets, filing into the herd that revolved in a massive circle up and down Sixth. Loud music sprang from every bar along the old street, meshing into a thick fuzzy noise of sporadic rhythms. It sounded better as one conglomerate mess, a hodgepodge of American pop culture in all its faceless glory.

He watched Treva hobble to the dark space behind the dumpster. Phaedra followed a few steps behind as though she were pacing herself with an elderly woman. Treva turned to her, just out of the way of the Fury's headlights. No one was around.

"Let's make this fast," Phaedra demanded. Her tight black latex outfit stretched provocatively over her supple skin. It devoured light like a black hole. It made Treva furious. "I need to meet Talon right now." She looked at the scabs that covered Treva's poorly shaved scalp. She made a foul face of repulsion. "You look like rotting hamburger meat."

Treva didn't reply. Instead, she mentally carved the flesh off Phaedra's flawless body. Her mind was a scrambled mess of fantastical murder and mutilation—it brought a warm smile to her wretched face, only to fade into a hateful scowl. She could barely focus her thoughts over the muddled sounds of digitized music throbbing in the distance on Sixth Street. She looked down at the lethal hand that served her death in a syringe. She wanted to skin her alive. Given the opportunity, she'd do it, too.

"Where's the money?" Phaedra repeated.

Treva reached into her back pocket as she glanced down the alley through the rolling fog. She gripped the cold metal butterfly knife in her hand, opening it inside her deep pocket. She could feel the blade's length in her pants as it became fully extended, yet hidden from view. Just as Phaedra's attention went to her leather pouch, Treva lunged forward, thrusting the blade inside her chest. She felt it cracking through bone and cartilage before piercing the softer organs.

Phaedra's beautiful eyes widened with horror, unable to even react defensively. She instinctively grabbed at the knife, clasping onto Treva's grotesquely scaly hand. No words or noises escaped her mouth, only panic melting the transparent beauty of her face. Treva covered Phaedra's gaping mouth with a cold, claw-like hand while slowly pushing her back against the moist brick. The blood trickled down the black latex, over her bronzed muscular legs, to the beer-stained ground. Before there could be a struggle, it was over. Phaedra slid down the wall to the blacktop, dead. Her body twitched.

Treva smiled with wild excitement as footsteps raced down the alley toward her.

Jobie rushed to Treva's side, staring at the bloody body that stared back like a wax mannequin. He shook his head, smiling. "Ain't nothing but a damn thing."

Treva trembled with delight. She fell to her knees, running her fingers through the blood that seeped from the wound. She brought her fingers to her mouth, licking them clean. She rubbed her victim's blood on her own hollow cheeks, painting her face with fresh death. She was alive once again.

"Come on," Jobie demanded uneasily as he pulled Treva away from the bloody body. "Let's get her out of here."

He reached down and lifted Phaedra's limp body, leaving the knife deep inside her chest. He dragged her back to the Fury, opening the passenger door just as the alleyway entrance of the Voodoo Lounge opened. Jobie dropped Phaedra to the pavement as three costumed gladiators stopped to witness.

"Holy shit, that looks real," one said excitedly.

"Totally," the other replied. "You should've had the bartender cut her off an hour ago." He glanced at Treva's skin, how it seemed to be dripping off her body. "You guys should work in Hollywood...except those tattoos on your face, they don't look real at all. No one tattoos their face." They continued onward to Sixth Street, seeking more costumes and facades to criticize.

Jobie lifted Phaedra into the car, shoving her limp and bloody body into the backseat.

The black Fury disappeared into the dark haze.

11:59pm

Treva dragged the corpse from the car, pulling it through the dark open country. The sky was a dull pink from the nearby city lights, and the air was alive with the strident sounds of cars racing down the Capital of Texas highway. She propped the body up on a rock as Jobie stood at her side drinking Everclear from the bottle.

"Purty," she said to him as she coddled the dead body like an infant. A cigarette burned in her chapped lips. "That's her name. Her name is Purty, the little cock-socket slut."

Jobie took a quick gulp to squelch his thoughts. The alcohol burned his throat like petrol. He was eager to leave Austin. It was coming so soon, he could taste it. He wanted nothing more than to stare out at a dark and lonely highway facing an open future. He watched Treva strip the corpse of its stylish clothes, setting them in a neat pile at her side. The corpse's head lolled to its shoulder.

"Shut up, Purty," Treva lambasted the corpse as though it had smarted off. "No one wants to hear you talk. You're just pussy." She caressed the corpse's breasts with her fulsome hands, pinching its nipples. She ran her hands down its smooth stomach over the leopard spot tattoos. She spread the corpse's legs, airing its shaved genitalia. The labia were pierced in several places with silver barbells tapering from the hood of the clitoris. Treva shoved a finger inside its vagina as she said, "You're a whore, Purty...you're a fucking whore." Her childish voice was exacerbated. "No one likes you when your legs are closed."

"Treeeva," Jobie slurred with a kowtow, "maybe you need...a drink." He held out his bottle to her. "We need to get ridda this fuggin' body."

"I want to keep it," she insisted as she grabbed the bottle and took a sip. She exhaled the fumes with a gasp. "It's me. She's mine because now she's me. I want to keep her." She poured the contents of the bottle all over the corpse, dousing its black hair, covering its shapely body with the stench of alcohol. Treva hugged the corpse tightly, affectionately.

Jobie rolled his eyes, mildly humored by her daftly capricious behavior.

Treva dropped her cigarette into its lap and watched it smolder. No effect. She took out her lighter and lit its hair on fire. The alcohol caught the fire and pulled it down over the body like a shroud. The flames ate at the skin, blanching it before it flowered into a shade of damask.

The pupils of Jobie's eyes receded in the heat as he watched Treva slink and careen around the body, giggling as the beauty of the corpse boiled hairless. He only wished she hadn't wasted all his liquor on this crazed spectacle. The flames dispersed as quickly as they spread, leaving its skin covered with red abrasions and boils. It bore a stark resemblance to Treva.

"Isn't she pretty?" she asked him. "See, she's me now."

"Yeah," he mumbled nonchalantly. There was an irrefutable similarity. "She's pretty, all right."

"She's me," Treva declared with sheer delight. "Do you want to touch her pussy before I skin her?"

Monday, November 2, 1998
2:10pm

Hyde Park

Sunlight streamed through the open window, following a refreshingly dry breeze. The sky was vast and open, a solid shade of clear blue with tumbling white clouds sparsely spanning the horizons. The saturated land was suddenly alive once again. The world shined green.

Tamika sat in the center of her bare studio apartment, savoring the tranquility of an easy afternoon. The sunlight covered her body, warming her mocha skin with its surplus of vitality. On the floor next to her was the twelve-month lease for her new efficiency. Her bold signature was scratched at the bottom of the lengthy contract.

She hadn't budged an inch in hours. There was no place to be and nothing to do other than what she was already doing. Of course, she could run down to the nearby Fresh Plus grocery to stop the growling in her stomach, but that would require so much effort...

She had taken the time earlier in the day to absorb her new surroundings. She had stared at the walls, correlating the glossy sheen of the creamy paint with tasty peach pudding. She familiarized herself with the ceiling's bumpy white buttermilk texture. Silver glitter clung to its surface for some sort of starry effect when struck with light. The carpet on which she reclined was soft and gray. Stone gray. Much like the sky had been. The door was the same color as the walls, easy for it to disappear if not for the bronze doorknob. In its reflection she could see herself lounging in an empty room. Her room.

In the corner of the efficiency was her pillowcase with all her clothing spilling onto the floor. Her new red dress had the contrasting luminosity of a fiery Phoenix rising from the ashen carpet. One picture hung from the glossy wall—her Christmas picture taken years ago. She finally recognized that giddy smile. It was her own.

A gentle rapping came to the door.

She rose to her feet, excited to receive her first guest. She was stiff from immobility. It was a nice feeling, one she hadn't felt enough of lately.

Opaque stood in the doorway, his black lips grinning as he held his morose doll like a docile infant. His dour facial paint didn't mix well with the brightness

132

of the day. The straps that connected his black bondage pants seemed restrictive, and his black chiffon shirt was a bit too snug for comfort. He seemed stiff and colorless, contrary to his trademark regality. The pink crepe myrtles along the street easily stole his limelight.

"Come in," she beckoned hospitably.

He entered with rigid steps, slightly uncomfortable with what seemed a formality, as he browsed the room. He felt like a stranger. Moreover, he felt like the train had left without him, leaving him alone on an empty avenue without many options. "Nice."

She closed the door behind him, trapping them both inside the comfortable little shell. She teased her frayed hair into a relatively presentable shape. Her gestures were free and easy, naturally uninhibited by his presence. "Do you really like it?"

"I do."

"It was cheap," she said. "I'll be able to afford it without any problem."

He walked over to the one picture on the wall. "That's you."

"Yes, it is." She dropped herself back on the carpet in the center of the unfurnished room. "Please sit down, relax…my place is yours."

He did as she requested, sliding down the wall, stretching his legs across the floor. "I love the Victorians in this neighborhood. Someday I want to live in one."

"Hyde Park," she said. "Gotta love it. The yards out here are like art. All the flowers, the trees, the new paint on the old houses…the apartments aren't quite up to scale, though. An eyesore, really, in a neighborhood like this. Students. All their balconies are used as a storage space for odds and ends. It wouldn't be hard to fill this tiny space, though."

"You can almost get a sense of your neighbors just by the contents of their balconies."

She nodded. "Bikes they never use."

"This is great," he suddenly exclaimed, capturing his sudden realization. "Your own apartment. How vogue you are now."

"No more sleeping on the Drag," she gloated. "I'm going to buy a bed with my next paycheck. Do you want to have a slumber party when I get it?"

"If you fall asleep, you know I'll put your fingers in warm water so you'll piss yourself."

"Any time you want," she told him seriously, "the place is yours."

"Watch your offers…I'll become a nuisance really fast."

"No," she said quite simply, "trust me, I know—I wouldn't go back to that pavement for another second. Speaking of, have you talked with Jobie and Treva about leaving for New Orleans?"

"I have no idea where they are. Haven't seen them in days."

"Let me ask you a question," she proposed uneasily. "You may decline, but I must ask. How would you feel about being my roommate? I mean, we could buy twin beds—the place is small, but the rent is cheap, we'd pull ahead in no time. You'd be off the streets, too. I will worry about you now, you know."

He looked up at her, linking the gaze of his red eyes with her deeply sensitive black eyes. There existed a mutual depth of understanding between them. More so than even she knew. "I would love to."

"Really?"

"Yes. We could save money and travel in style, no jumping cargo trains, or sleeping on the streets…we could sleep in motels if we chose to travel again."

She smiled gleefully like a child. Like the photograph on the wall. "I'm so happy to hear that."

"I'm so happy you asked," he admitted, "and I promise I'll find work so that I can keep up my end of rent. Hell, if I have to cut my hair and go New Romantic, then I will." His stiff posture became elastic. "Where would my bed go?"

"Wherever you want," she replied. "It'd be your place, too."

He studied the room, gauging the amount of space he'd require, which wasn't much. Though it was small and boxy and would inevitably be far too cramped for two people to share for very long, its potential for freedom was immense and boundless.

"Do you mind if I take a shower *right now?*" he pleaded. "I can't even remember how long it's been."

"It's your place," she reminded him. She really liked that, the sound of her own generosity. It was nice to finally have something to offer. "Have at it."

He stood eagerly, rushing into the bathroom that was roughly the size of a walk-in closet. He shut the door, closing off the entire world. There was a sense of privacy he hadn't felt since he left Washington. He twisted the plastic knobs of the faucet and watched the water swirl down the drain. The rest of his afternoon disappeared with it as the clock ticked in the company of deaf ears. The air-conditioner exhaled its pleasantly cool breath upon him, relaxing his hardened senses as he focused on the sound of water, allowing his mind to drift to thoughtlessness. He collapsed to the floor without a care in the world. It was one of the most exciting moments of his life.

Tamika was almost asleep by the time he had actually bathed. She rubbed her tired eyes with thick knuckles, only to open them to an unfamiliar young man wrapped in a towel. His lips were a nice skin-tone, and his eyes were a warm shade of brown. She never knew. His skin was clean and cosmetic-free— he looked very male, and quite attractive. His orange and black hair was clean and slicked back over his well-sculpted head.

"True euphoria," he remarked on his showering experience. His voice was calm and mellow, gruff and gravelly. "I feel like a new woman."

Her lips stretched briefly into a smile as she remained fixed on the face of a friend she had never actually seen before. Why had she never acknowledged this mask?

He was quick to realize her thoughts through her awe-struck expression. "My real name is Rik," he told her. "Rik Wallace. Have I ever told you that?"

She shook her head, comforting herself with his unexpected handsome masculinity. It was the most extreme change she had yet seen with him.

"Nice to meet you, Rik," she told him sarcastically. "Are you hungry? I'm famished. I have some extra money from my paycheck, maybe we should order a pizza..."

He laughed as he took a seat by the door, sprawling comfortably on the floor. "We don't have a phone."

"We'll have to put that on the list of things to get...a phone...to order pizzas." She looked up at him and smiled. "I'm so glad you're here."

He inhaled deeply, followed with a rich sigh of relief. "Glad to be here. I have a home again." He closed his eyes, basking in the serenity. His face was strong and firm, perfectly male. Their genders had suddenly split from one another for the very first time. "Home," he murmured before falling into a deep and peaceful slumber. It was almost as though he had never used the word.

2:11pm

Jobie savored the rush of attention that unwittingly tended him from across Sound Exchange. His eyes remained low, seemingly focused on the stacks of seven-inch vinyl records in the sale bin, flipping through them with dirty fingers. His presence was calm and unimposing, though the overbearing sense of caution amplified his blood pressure like a drum. His peripheral vision kept the observers in check—two Oogles who had been trailing him for over an hour. Inconspicuously so, but not in Jobie's eyes—he was very aware of them. A brief glance revealed their interest was not fueled by respect. Dickhead loyalists, typical Oogles vying for acceptance in the dregs, begging to have a semblance of an identity as lowly disheveled vagabonds.

Jobie pulled out a record of a band called Lower Class Brats and brought it to the counter. As he stood before the cash register, he felt the presence of the two Oogles closing in on him. The hardcore music that played throughout the store put him somewhat at ease, despite the fact that another confrontation seemed imminent. It had been so long since he had heard *good* music—it was just the boost he needed. To him, the greatest invention of mankind wasn't the wheel. It was music. Hardcore music, specifically. Fuel for the fire.

Without saying a word, he placed the exact change on the counter and walked outside into the dimming light of day. As he passed around the corner of 21st, he caught sight of the two Oogles following relatively close behind with hard, rugged steps. He walked calmly to the alley, away from the safety of the public eye. The butterfly knife, his only weapon, was in the possession of Treva—he was defenseless.

He pulled the record from the sleeve, focusing on the circular grooves in the black vinyl before breaking it into two serrated pieces.

As he turned the corner to walk into the alley, he slipped behind the wall with his lethal shard of vinyl poised in his hand, waiting to strike. Within seconds, he could hear the kicking of rocks from aggravated steps as they rounded the corner. He sprang from behind the wall, thrusting the jagged vinyl into the throat of his nearest opponent. It penetrated the flesh beneath his chin with a gush of blood streaming down the black vinyl. The broken piece of record dangled from his chin before he pulled it free in a panic. It let loose the flow of blood as though a cork had been popped.

Jobie grabbed the clean Misfits T-shirt of the other Oogle and shoved him backward against the brick wall. His shoulders impacted with a dull thud that loosened the corner bricks of the crumbling wall. Jobie held him tightly by the collar, staring wildly into his eyes with biting anger. He kneed him in the groin and pulled him to the ground amongst the rubble, pinning him with his foot. Jobie stood over him, staring down at his unknown opponent as his crony gripped his own bleeding neck, wandering in frantic circles. Jobie picked up one of the loosened bricks and smacked it over the downed Oogle's head, leaving him limp and still.

"What do you want?" Jobie asked his bleeding comrade.

The Oogle stared with wide eyes that swelled with tears.

"You're a coward," Jobie told him as he stood toe to toe. "You want me to leave town, huh?"

"I don't care," the Oogle whimpered.

"You cared enough to follow me, what did you plan to do?"

"I don't know," he cried.

Jobie shook his head, enraged by the Oogle's passive nature. He smacked him upside the head with the brick, sending his perpetrator straight to the ground. Jobie kicked him once in the stomach as he dropped the brick onto his head. He stood alone over two twisted bodies whose blood streamed to the center of the alley.

He nodded. It was in fact time to leave Austin.

Hyde Park

Treva's eyes bulged from the pressure of Vaughn's grip on her neck. His powerful hands clamped her throat viciously, digging deep into the elasticity of her shedding skin. She could feel the darkness penetrating her as she stared into his maniacally twisted eyes. Never before had she seen him so passionate, so alive. Never before had she craved death with such conviction. It was the ultimate sacrifice to her oppressor. Her eyes stared into his, fearless and submissive.

Her larynx felt as if it were collapsing. Her last breath was fading, trapped inside her lungs. The darkness was overwhelming. She looked from side to side, trying to focus on the world that was disappearing in a veil of black fog. She could see the still water in the bathtub behind him. She knew that her dead body would soon be bled into it for his sadistic pleasure. She also knew that her corpse would be tied with bricks and dumped into Town Lake, never to be found.

She hadn't believed him. She didn't think he would actually kill her. Now it was too late.

The day began routinely enough, the clipboard, the notes, the handkerchiefs and the wooden chair…she had watched him turn the porcelain knobs, releasing a steady flow of frosty cold water into the old, deep bathtub. She had noticed there were no syringes anywhere. Her intuition throbbed of danger as he bound her hands for the last time.

She watched him stare at his clipboard, at the disorganized mess of notes on green graph paper. His eyes were glassy, almost rueful. His bearded face was hardened from defeat. She didn't expect him to suddenly tear the notes from the clipboard and discard them into the clear bath water. They floated atop its surface like algae before slowly sinking to the bottom.

He looked down upon Treva, at her rotting flesh. Her skin had tiny rips that ran the length of her body like veins. He had failed. Failed miserably. The serum had taken a life of its own, feeding on the very thing it was designed to save. She would soon be dead, but not soon enough. His failure had eyes, and

137

for as long as she lived, it wasn't merely his secret burden. He shared the cold truth of his declination with his subservient little guinea pig. "You're dying."

"I thought you were going to help me," she sobbed disparagingly. She struggled to free herself. She could feel her skin giving with the tension, tearing like paper. She dissolved her futile efforts immediately. "What are you going to do about this? How can you help me?"

"I can't. I'm simply going to destroy you."

"You already have," she cried.

His empathy singed his stoic mien. He needed her dead, aborted completely from his life. His efforts were a disgrace to his father's name, and it left him emotionally eroded. He couldn't stand to witness his failings. "I will give you the choice of your demise. Consider it merciful. The worst for you is yet to come. I'm offering you a less gruesome death than what lurks in the near future for you. How would you rather die?"

His tart statement was received stolidly, free of panic from its dire implications—she was too dispirited to care anymore. She gave her immediate thoughts: "I want to overdose. Pump me full of dilaudid. I want to die in heaven. Especially since you put me in the hell I'm in. You *owe* it to me."

His compassion quickly crumbled under his steel composure, fueled by the vexing qualities of her insolent personality. "I will drown you, or I will strangle you." He sloshed his hand through the icy bath water. "I want you to die," he confessed with harsh sentiment. "I really do. I want to take your life, I want to finish what I started. I really want that. Quite frankly, I need that."

"You failed, didn't you?" she asked dejectedly. "Your potion poisoned me."

His face tightened with humility and anger. How true her words.

"Cure me," she pleaded. "You will never have to see me again, I'll leave town right now. Right now. I promise."

He sighed. It was beyond his ability and he knew it. He had failed. The realization was catastrophic to the once sturdy foundation of his ego. The fragility of his collapsing spirit was too much for him to bear. "Let's get this over with so I can forget it ever happened." He hovered over her like a vulture, gripping his hands intently. He was ready for the kill.

"That doctor—Doctor Schtepp...this is his fault, isn't it? If I could slaughter that son of a bitch...it's his fault, he did this, didn't he?!"

Richter smiled. He nodded his head, and oh how he wished it were true. "Choose your death."

Tears swelled in her eyes. The ghosts of her past were beating her into a horrified exhaustion, from which there was no escape. She was a little girl trapped inside a cage with the cruelest of demons. They violated her body, wearing the guise of her father's face. Her soul was exhausted, and she was tired of running. No matter the distance, the brutal nightmares were always waiting to ravage her in sleep. She desperately craved the dilaudid, anything to hush the voices in her head. Her mind was crumbling from the pressure. Her flesh was peeling from her weakened body. Death surrounded her.

"Strangle me," she told him.

Thus was her fate. The darkness consumed her, and the lights faded at the mercy of his hands.

He watched her body fall limp. What clear skin remained on her face had turned a pale shade of blue. He loosened his grip on her neck, watching her body give way to gravity. Lifeless. It appeared that her color was shifting slowly again, returning to pink, but he really couldn't tell—not with the rash that covered her face like a mask of clay. Her lungs appeared to expand slightly, or was it a convulsion deep inside her chest from the organs resisting death?

His posture stiffened. His stomach turned, he felt himself rile from the morbidity of the situation. He couldn't look at her another second. He buttoned his satin emerald shirt to the collar and stepped away from her body. She was like furnishings, no more alive than the chair on which she sat. He walked to the door, grabbing his keys as he left the house to gather his thoughts and to figure out a way to dispose of the body. He walked to his car uneasily. He had done it. He had actually taken her life. Yet he felt nothing. It was a mere fact. He unlocked his car door, letting the thought slip from his mind as he backed the car into the street. A black Plymouth Fury sat by the curb like a topless hearse. Vaughn didn't even notice it, or the raging eyes that peered from within.

6:37pm

Vaughn returned home just as he had left, cold and uninspired. The lingering death was internal.

He threw open the bathroom door where her fleshless body was swathed to the chair. The room was dark, and her figure was little more than a silhouette, but the details were clear enough. There was a foul odor in the air, morbid and grotesque. She seemed to be in an advanced state of decomposition, but with what had happened to her body, he didn't know what to expect. This was death, he concluded, this truly was death. A corpse…there was no rich pool of blood with a warm body—this was death in all its cold grandeur. A stiff, lifeless, rotting corpse.

His heart raced, he felt ill. He stumbled out of the bathroom and to the nearest phone, calling his colleague, the only man he could remotely trust.

"Ronald, I need you!" he exclaimed desperately, breaking the silence of the cold wooden room. "I need to speak with you—now. Please call me immediately. She's dead. Purty's dead. I've killed her… I don't know what to do…"

He collapsed to the bed, slouching nervously. The thought of leaving the room mortified him. He stared forward, almost catatonic. Hours seemed to pass as he sat in cold silence.

The phone rang. He let it ring once, twice…the caller ID showed it to be a cell-phone, but it wasn't Ronald Schtepp's. It was his own. He picked it up without saying a word as he breathed uneasily into the mouthpiece. He could almost feel the tips of bony fingers grazing his spine as the voice of a ghost spoke into his ear: "Surprise…it's me…it's Purty."

He trembled, barely able to hold the phone, shocked and horrified. He visualized her dead body standing in the bathroom, holding his cell phone to her lifeless face. He could see her eyes, glassy and covered with a white film. Practically skinless.

"The doctor is dead—I killed the bastard with your gun, it's at the crime scene."

Disorientation made a swirling mess of his comprehension. He considered all the notes in his laboratory pinning him to a crime he didn't commit. "Who is in the bathroom?" His bark was unnaturally weak. "Who is she?"

Her voice sang out breathy and insipid. "Phaedra."

Flashes of red lights danced down the street to the distant shrill of sirens.

She chuckled innocuously. "I listened to your confession on the doctor's answering machine. You've made this all too easy…"

"Someday…" he snarled. "I will catch and kill you."

"No, you'll never see me again," she corrected him before hanging up.

The flashing lights of police cars surrounded his house. He stood slowly, firmly erect as he gazed across the room to the front window. Several officers apprehensively approached his quiet domain. He stood alone in darkness, watching his life fizzle and sputter before him. The death he had brought on was his own.

This was the finale of his father's legacy.

11:01pm

Jobie stared out at the lonesome highway as the black Fury raced eastward across the Texas border into Louisiana. For all its lofty anticipation, New Orleans was short of a breath away. His hand dangled over the steering wheel as he veered onto the exit ramp into a tiny town named Vinton.

"Where are we going?" Treva wheezed as she scraped her bony fingers along her skeletal cheek. Her speech had worsened. Her bottom lip seemed to be falling from her face.

Jobie pointed straight into the windshield, into the bleak darkness to which they sped. "This way. To get me a rock from Louisiana." He pulled off alongside the ditch some distance off the interstate.

The breeze was algid and moist with the slightest scent of the ocean. Treva inhaled the air deeply in her failing lungs, struggling to accept the death that nipped her heels. She watched Jobie wander into the dark and fumble clumsily, feeling for the perfect stone on the near-frozen earth.

"Jobie," she croaked weakly. "Do you remember when you said that every rock you have reminds you of me?"

His reply was deliberately slow. "Uh-huh." He wandered back to the Fury where he looked down upon her frailty with concern.

"Will you remember this night forever if I ask you to?"

He held out a dark and smooth stone. "You don't even need to ask."

"Jobie…I do know what you've done for me—you once asked if I knew all the things you've done. I do know. I do…I lied to you, though, Jobie. I'm not going to survive this. I'm not going to miraculously heal. I can feel it. My body is dying."

His expression remained fixed like a statue.

"Do you love me?" she exhaled listlessly.

His head slowly lowered, then raised quickly, suddenly. It was more or less a nod.

"Do you?" she repeated, demanding a more absolute response.

"Yeah…"

She smiled peacefully with lips torn like paper. "If I could live my life over again… No one has ever loved me, Jobie, not like you do. Of all the people out there, you chose me. No one has ever done that before." She closed her eyes in serenity while breathing deeply, stumbling into memory. "I loved the sound of rain in the morning while lying in bed. I loved standing in an empty field of snow in the middle of the night—have you ever been in snow?"

He shook his head.

"It's so quiet. You can't imagine. So quiet and peaceful. The snow rolls out like eternity and it collects all sound and light…it glows in the night. It actually glows."

He smiled and listened.

"I loved the smell of chocolate chip cookies when they came out of the oven, and I loved the way my dog looked at me like I was the most amazing creature on the planet. I love the way you look at me, and listen to me. You're the last person I will see in my life, Jobie."

"No," he muttered. "No…you're not dying."

"Silly boy, look at me. I'm falling apart. I once had great skin, and now I don't even have skin! If I was to list my favorite things in life, I'd have to say you were one of them…where were you taking me?"

"We're going to New Orleans. And to the ocean, you're going to sit on the beach with me."

"Oh, I'd love to go…" Her voice sounded ancient and fatigued. "When you go, just know that I'll be there with you. I wouldn't miss it for the world."

"You're not dying, Treva."

"If I ask you to do something for me, would you do it?" she asked.

"Of course."

"The last wish of a dying girl…"

"Don't say that."

"Make love to me, Jobie, please. I've never been loved, I want to know how it feels before I die."

He exhaled deeply and slowly, giving no answer as he clenched his fists in solemn desperation.

"Help me with my pants," she requested.

He knelt beside her, unfastening her loose jeans and pulling them from her body. Her flesh was red and glossy like meat in a butcher's window. She reached up to his face and pulled him down upon her by his ears. He fell on top of her slippery body and nuzzled his face into her slick-textured neck. He closed his eyes and imagined her riding on the freight train that carried them through the desert to Texas. He could see the sun burning over her shoulder like a fiery plum, blending purely with her once beautiful hair. She pulled his kilt up to his waist as he squeezed his eyes tightly together. She spread her legs and he slipped inside her easily, gracefully as if they were an old feeble couple. He could feel the resistance of her flesh, shredding and tearing and unifying. He held her tightly, holding her gently as she breathed heavily into his ear, "Kill me." She grabbed his hips to keep him from stopping. "This is how I want to die, with you inside me. Please, I'll be dead soon…I'll die miserable and alone, but to die like this—do you understand? What better way to go?"

"I can't kill you."

"If you love me—if you *truly* love me, you will kill me."

He hesitated, feeling the cold clamoring of his senses.

142

"You won't be alone," she assured him with stunted breath. "I'll never leave you. We'll live forever. We were meant to." She looked into his eyes, bleeding the peace into him. "It'd be the best gift you could give me. I'm not afraid. I'm ready to go. I *want* to go…I'm tired, Jobie. I'm so tired. Help me. Please."

"I'm not ready for you to go."

"I'm dying, I have no choice. It'd be a mercy killing, it'd be out of love." She reached into the pocket of her pants that lie at her side on the floorboard. She pulled out the blade and placed it in his hands. He clutched it in the faint light, staring at its smooth metal surface. "Cum inside me," she beckoned. "Then kill me."

He pushed his cock deep inside her, thrusting quickly with vigor as his heart froze in his chest. The loneliness overwhelmed him. He could feel his heart beating furiously in his chest as he savored their final togetherness. It was better than any moment in his life, the beginning and the end. The best and worst wrapped in one single stroke of the brush.

His body quaked violently as he exploded inside her like a fountain. He raised his hands to his head as he gripped the knife firmly in his gaunt hands. He visualized the sun and the desert and the train…and the knife collapsed through her chest, into her heart. The blood spilled onto the floorboard as she gasped desperately, "Don't forget me." He could taste the blood on her lips, and he could feel the convulsing muscles quake inside her vagina as she fell slowly to silence, succumbing to death.

He sat at her side for hours, talking to her body and crying, sharing his life until the sun lit the sky like cold grape juice. As he drove his love to New Orleans, his body felt like glass—fragile and transparent. Her head rested on his lap peacefully as he imagined her spirit following high overhead in the stars, watching him, protecting him. As he drove into the darkness, he knew he would never be alone again.

Talon

Tuesday, August 31, 1999
11:45pm

Venice, California

"Timmy," Josephine Ott's voice trembled helplessly from the backseat floorboard. "Timmy...please answer...*please.*"

The car's engine purred through the silence.

"Timmy, dammit, answer me!" she repeated desperately to her brother.

She could smell the gun smoke, and she could smell the blood. His blood.

Her copper-toned cheeks were streaked with tears that fell from deeply set, swollen eyes. Her heart thumped wildly inside her chest. Images of her brother as a doe-eyed child flashed painfully in her memory. A sad and lonely child in full-body green pajamas, up late, waiting for mama.

Her mind stumbled back to the chaotic furor of the moment. She clenched her fists frantically over slivers of glass moistened with blood splatter. "Timmy...*please.* Talk to me, tell me you're *still alive.*"

Silence.

She held her staggering breath as she shuddered with terror. She visualized merciless killers prowling outside the car, waiting for her to surface for target practice. The gunmen were the faceless enemy she had grown to fear throughout her seventeen years of life—the rival faction, the Marvin Crips of Venice.

In the passenger seat, Timmy's friend AK-Jay had taken the first bullet, as she remembered. A direct hit to the face and spine, she had no doubt that he had perished. Instinctively, she had dropped to the floor as the gunfire first spilled upon the car. She had somehow evaded the shower of bullets, but her brother in the driver's seat—she was the only one who could help him.

She gazed blankly into the shards of glass scattered over the clear plastic floor mats as reason melted into dread. Her copy of Hemingway's *To Have and Have Not* was speckled with thick droplets of blood—the blood of her own kin. The sight of it disabled her judgment. Her hand trembled as she once again imagined the barrel of a gun peeking through the broken windows, housing the bullet that would end the life of her negligent mother's only daughter. Her morbid thoughts dissipated like fog into deeper confusion. Had hours passed? Minutes, or merely seconds?

She cautiously lifted herself from the floorboard into the light. The distant streetlights of Venice Boulevard were blinding in intensity. The car's windows were broken out in jagged strips like shark's teeth. With one apprehensive glance into the front seat, she saw what she feared most—Timmy had not survived.

Her slender body convulsed as she slid into the darkness once again, immobilized like a fetus inside a frozen womb. Her tongue burned with the acidic bite of vomit.

Her caretaker and nurturer was now nothing more than a gang-related casualty. *MANSFIELD CRIPS PERISH IN DRIVE-BY SHOOTING*, a low-profile headline would read the following day.

Timothy Ott was an unlikely role model, especially for an honor student awarded the dubious title by her classmates, Most Likely to Run for Office. Timothy's reputation was distinctly in contrast to hers. He was a high school dropout and notorious gang member deeply imbedded in Venice drug trafficking. Cold-blooded and fearsome by those who knew of him. But to Josephine, he was still the little boy with the green full-body pajamas. The boy whom forced chastity upon her by frightening any potential love interest from ever speaking her name again. The boy that fed her voracious appetite of the written word with random and frequent gifts that could fill a library. The boy whom insisted she attend church in his years of absence. The brother whom cared for her as a father. Warm and protective and openly opposed to her being even remotely involved in the thug lifestyle. He was intent on a different direction for her. One of education, prominence, and stability. She was to go to college, and Timmy would make sure of it. Although her education would be funded by the lucrative profits of the narcotics trade, his best intentions outweighed common sense. He wanted his sister to have what he felt he never could.

She slowly surfaced into the light once again, upright and still, choking on her own breath.

Lincoln Boulevard was unusually inactive. No sirens were heard in the vicinity or in the distance. She considered running to a nearby phone, but dismissed the thought as quickly as it came. There was no help to provide. The casualties of the shooting would end up in some office that would calculate statistics to suggest strategic placement for law enforcement. Ultimately resulting in just another vain attempt to shut down an operation that paid the way for all parties involved, including the police.

Josephine looked down in the front seat at AK-Jay, at his blood soaked, black fingers that clutched tightly to a plump leather bag. She had always resisted crime, always. Yet she could swear that her brother was pushing her to take it. She looked over at him to confirm her delusion. The sight of his disassembled face horrified her, blasting her into motion across the seats. She ripped the purse from AK-Jay's hands and opened the door, racing madly into the darkness of night. She clutched her book tightly between her thin ebony fingers as she scrambled desperately for cover, managing the purse in her other fist with the utmost importance. She had no idea how much money was inside, but she was very aware that it was from the hands of lost lives, broken families, and overall misery. The money was cursed, she resolved, but it was now hers. If only for what she felt could be the final moments of her life.

She dodged the streetlights as she sidled through the dark crevices along Lincoln Boulevard, southward past Washington, following the flight of jumbo jets overhead. Sweat accumulated on her tall and prominent forehead, trickling down over her ridged brow. Her small cornrows acted as drainage for perspiration that dripped down the length of long and black braided extensions that bounced with each footfall. Large golden loop earrings banged lightly against her neck in rhythm with her steps. Her hazel eyes were bloodshot and burning.

Her white leather Adidas bounded effortlessly across the pavement with fear and confusion fueling her long and thin muscles. Her long, red fingernails dug deeply into the leather bag, leaving deep impressions in its smooth surface. The air was warm and stuffy with the scent of city pollutants. The planes intensified in volume as she raced with burning lungs down the street, hiding from traffic, fleeing the pedestrians.

"Timmy, Timmy, Timmy..." she mumbled with shortened breath as she sprinted down the sidewalk.

She ran for what felt like hours, losing only thirty-five minutes. In the distance she could see Westchester Playground just beyond Manchester Boulevard. Behind her, far in the distance the sirens had come and gone. By now her mother had been notified, if they could find her. Were they searching for a third person, or did they know the details at all? Did they care? Their lack of interest in pursuing the crime was expected, and equally her only hope in surviving. That said nothing about the Mansfield Crips, though. With so much of their money missing, their threat was far more severe than merely serving time in prison.

She was a criminal now. Wanted by more than one organization in the city.

As she reached the bright lights of the Los Angeles airport, she collapsed on the sidewalk momentarily, clicking her nervous red nails on the pavement. It took less than a minute to gather her breath as well as her thoughts. She had to leave the city. There was no other choice. She could not stay, not now. She saw no other option than to flee the country. Her irrational thoughts and panic lifted her from the pavement, carrying her to the LAX terminal.

"What have I done?" she mumbled to herself between panting breaths as she staggered forward with uncertainty. Her aching muscles felt as though battery acid had replaced her bloodstream. "Clearly, think clearly...this is nuts."

She assumed the police were very likely on her trail, possibly searching the airport at the moment. She had to be calm, had to appear like any other, yet she had to move quickly—no time to gather her composure.

Once inside the airport, she retreated to a bathroom to clean up and develop a plan. She knew she needed to leave Los Angeles, but she had no idea where to arrive. She realized that a young girl of her ethnicity would raise far too much suspicion by paying cash for an airline ticket…unless it was to a nearby city.

Her reflection on the pane glass windows sobered her. She appeared crazed and desperate, much as she remembered of Timmy's clientele. She took several deep breaths and focused on her surroundings. Her white Team USA pullover and black vinyl sweatpants were not the classiest outfit, but they were not rags, either. She hoped to blend with the pedestrians that filled the airport on a busy Wednesday evening. She mopped the faint blood speckles from her face with a paper towel, removing any evidence of the recent events. She removed her pullover and tied it around her waist. Her black sports bra was stained with sweat. Her coppery skin glistened like melted caramel.

She stepped into a bathroom stall and locked herself inside to regain her composure in silence. The privacy of the confining stall was the perfect anti-stimulus. She closed her almond-shaped eyes and envisioned a beach setting at dusk. Eventually her breathing slowed and her tears dried as she maintained the thought. Her life depended on it.

As she opened her eyes, she looked down into her lap at the lecherous leather bag. She slowly unzipped it…then panic overwhelmed her. She felt suffocated when she suddenly realized that she had left her dead brother on a city street for the police to find. Her heart raced as she struggled to contain herself.

"There was nothing I could do," she mumbled under her unsteady breath. "There was nothing…"

She eased herself once again, closing her eyes and focusing on that warm tropical beach. She had to remain calm—her life depended on it. With her eyes still closed, she reached inside the bag, clasping onto a pack of Marlboro cigarettes resting on top of a mound of bills. She pulled the money out of the bag with both hands. At the bottom of the bag was a plastic bag with several rocks of crack and two small bundles of cocaine. She immediately flushed the contents into the toilet, ridding herself of anything that would incriminate her.

Then she started counting the money. The process took several minutes despite the fact that it was entirely comprised of large denominations. Lying in her lap was eleven thousand dollars. She stuffed the money back inside the bag and tucked it under her arm as she exited the stall.

With a deep breath to hold her composure steady, she left the restroom and made her way to the ticket counter. She casually toted the bag as though its contents were meaningless to hinder suspicion. One would easily believe that her book was far more cherished. She cradled it like an infant as she waited patiently in line.

"I would like to go to San Diego as soon as possible," she spoke with a shaky voice, her English perfectly unaffected by ebonic inflections.

"Round trip?"

She thought a moment, and then nodded. "Yes, I would like to return Saturday," she fibbed as her voice trailed to tears. "My grandmother is in the hospital, I need to be at her side…"

"I'm sorry to hear that," the woman behind the counter offered politely. She quickly keyed up several flight options on her computer. "I have a flight here that leaves really soon, how quickly can you run?" She glanced at her athletic attire and smiled. "I think you can make it. How will you pay?"

"Cash."

"Okay," the woman said without a second thought as she rang up the total.

The transaction was a blur. It was as though she was watching it all on television, removed from her own reactions. She vaguely remembered finding the gate, forfeiting the boarding pass, and waiting in the seat, staring out the window at the darkened runways.

Each new face entering the plane strickened her with paranoia. She imagined each an undercover agent following her trail. When the plane was sealed and the crew prepared for the flight, it occurred to her that the authorities probably had no idea a third person was in that car. And they were very unlikely to investigate further, following the assumption that the money had become property of crooked cops.

Her muscles eased with the thought that there was likely no one tracking her. Nonetheless, she was in possession of a considerable amount of stolen money. If that was her only crime, it was still a crime. Caution would be her ally.

Watching the city shrink below the airplane gave her the clarity she had lost on Lincoln Boulevard. At least some of it. She tucked the return trip ticket into her pocket where it would remain unused. Leaving Los Angeles was the hard part. In San Diego, she would purchase travelers checks to dissolve her trail. She knew that taking large steps was not the answer. Short flights, quick destinations. Getting away from southern California was more important to her than preserving the enormous amount of money she carried.

She looked at the cover of her book as a distant memory stole her train of thought. She recalled her childhood, no more than five years old. Timmy, her only sibling, had tucked her into her single bed and was coaxing her to sleep, to no avail. He presented a small picture book, offering to read to her until she fell asleep. Unwilling to be shown up by her older brother, she snatched the book from his hands and began telling the story to him, using the pictures rather than the words. The more he laughed, the more she embellished as she flipped through the pages, browsing over the text that meant nothing to her. It was the birth of a ritual that persisted until she actually learned to read. Each night she'd sit upright in bed, back arched, one finger jabbing the air as she unraveled new tales from the same old book. Sometimes the pace was slow with luxurious detailed embellishments. Other times her invigorated pace was so brisk that she would choke on her own saliva. Eventually the words on the pages took meaning as she learned to understand them, diminishing the value of the book that served as a well for her creativity. Both she and her brother agreed that many of her interpretations were far more captivating than a book about a dog running up and down a street.

As the plane descended into San Diego, she plotted an eastbound route using a traveler's periodical stuffed in the pouch with the safety diagrams. San Diego to Albuquerque to Texas...as far as she could make it until money or land ran out. It would take a while to arrive wherever she was going, but lacking a plan opened the door for spontaneity and revisions. In time she would make a plan, a real plan.

Wednesday, September 1, 1999
1:12am

Austin, Texas

Geeks, Freaks, and Legendary Scars.
Didi Hammond gazed wondrously at those magnificent words, marveling at the grand scale of the tour bus parked along Sixth Street in front of the posh Driskill Hotel. The exterior of the bus acted as a giant marquee for the most renowned shock troupe in the entertainment industry—The Czars of Scar. Caricatures of each member covered the sides of the bus like a twisted carnival nightmare. Felina, the Mysterious Cat Woman. Koz-Mo, the Known Universe. X, the Unknown Factor. Each drawing maintained perfect likeness, capturing their macabre appeal in a reproduction that would lend itself comfortably to Saturday morning cartoons. In fact, rumors of such a show were purportedly in production, along with action figures, video games, and comic books.

Didi stood apprehensively on the curb with the rain trickling onto her well-fed body. Her dark makeup ran down her high cheekbones, streaking her acne-scarred skin. Black curls of wet hair clung to her softly feminine shoulders. Her arms were scarified and branded with Celtic symbols, each one raised slightly from the skin like permanent blisters. Behind a sorrowful, pitiful expression masked by cosmetics, she was radiantly beautiful. But the reflection she saw in the rearview mirrors of the bus was preposterously hideous, a deplorable trick by the blurry vision of her self-deprecating mind's eye.

The pouring rain cascaded down the side of the bus like dripping wax. The curtains were drawn, revealing the silhouettes of what appeared to be unearthly demons nestled safety inside. Horns could be seen on an individual leaning against the window, while another bore the image of a cat with clipped ears and whiskers.

Decades ago, freaks were born into their trade. Aside from knife-swallowers and geeks, it was an exclusive market for those cursed with deformations and rare genetic disorders. The technological revolution forever changed the dynamics of the industry, making it possible for anyone with the desire to become outlandish to do so through cosmetic surgery, a process known as Body Modification. The Czars of Scar were nothing more than a group of well-trained performers born of healthy stock, drawn to the trade by choice.

Didi raised her left fist to the door, hesitating to knock as the voices inside rumbled with the exchange of pleasantries. The streets that surrounded her were unusually quiet. Only the rain.

She sheepishly tapped on the cold metal door.

No answer.

She spread her fingers out to loosen the tension caused by so much apprehension. Two of her digits were missing—her pinky finger was entirely removed, and her ring finger was down to the last knuckle. The swollen end of her ring finger was red and tender, still recovering from a recent and deliberate removal.

She hammered at the door once again, making a much larger racket. Calm footsteps moved through the bus. Didi stood perfectly still, her heart pounding from inhibition and insecurity as the rain splattered against her head, drenching her Christian Death T-shirt and blue jean skirt. When the door crept open, she nearly gasped. It was Koz-Mo himself. The Legend. The television personality. The most famous member of The Czars of Scar, towering over her in divine exaltation.

He gazed down upon her with indifference, and grunted, "You Talon's girl?"

She nodded her head anxiously, speechless in his eminent presence. Koz-Mo was an icon to her and many others who shared her subversive interests. He was the host of *Far Out*, a television show featuring cutting edge music and extreme sporting competitions. His body was thick and bulky and stripped of all hair, including his eyelashes. He was covered head to toe with tiny tattoos of stars, suns, moons, and ringed planets. There was a cartoon-like simplicity to the uniform style of his celestial motif. His eyes were dark and menacing. He watched her, studied her, gauging her presence by the control of her eyes. She had very little.

"Come in," he instructed with forced hospitality. "Wait." He held out a firm hand, keeping her in the rain a few seconds longer. He gazed down Sixth Street, and then back toward Congress Avenue. "Are you alone?"

"Yes," she replied timidly.

He lowered his hand, granting her entrance into the glorious lair of The Czars of Scar. It was the greatest moment in her life.

"Have a seat," Koz-Mo temperamentally insisted.

She coyly took a seat, careful not to interrupt the flow of conversation.

A group of three reclined on the plush couches, toasting champagne. There was no need explaining the significance, it was clear—they had just completed the last leg of the North American summer tour. Winter would fulfill independent contracts for each of them—efforts to make ends meet in the off-season of touring.

Of the three on the couch, only one was familiar to Didi on a personal level. Talon. Her lover. The perfect lines of his face mesmerized her. The definition of his musculature made him hazardously irresistible. Simply making eye contact was enough to frighten away the inner demons that dragged her down into self-hatred. He gave her hope and meaning. Without him, she was nothing. At least in her own tormented mind.

Talon's black leather pants were skin tight with matching boots that breached the knee, fastened tightly with shiny silver buckles. He was shirtless with black satin armbands that hugged his muscular biceps. His head was shaved with a meandering tattoo of a snake slithering over the top of his skull. Its forked tongue splayed at his widow's peak. Its beady eyes were green and sinister.

Sitting opposite Talon was X, the Unknown Factor. X had been the new feature attraction during the tour, taking over Koz-Mo's spotlight since the troupe's inception eight years earlier. Puncture wounds with dried specks of blood gave his occupation away. Suspension was his forte, but this tour brought forth a few new tricks, from walking on machetes to electrocution. The act he was most known for was the one that earned him fame through a television commercial selling light bulbs. Inserting a light bulb into his mouth and a live wire through his nose, the two are joined deep inside his throat, illuminating every orifice on his face while creating a subtle glow in his neck.

X's body was covered with tattoos of circuitry and strategically placed computer chips. A barcode spanned the length of his forehead, resting atop his thick eyebrows. His five o'clock shadow concealed the intricate tattoos of fine colored wires that seemed to give function to his prominent mandibles. Two horns emerged from each temple, the product of subdermal teflon implants. Tattoo work gave them the appearance of stubby antenna. His tongue was bifurcated, or split like a reptile.

Next to Talon was the troupe's infamous founder, Felina, the Cat Woman. Didi was surprised to realize that Felina was pregnant, possibly even beyond second term. She somehow had not noticed during their performance. Felina was dressed in a tight brown velvet body suit, which accentuated her pregnancy. She still appeared wildly savage. Her ears were clipped and pointed with countless rows of silver loop earrings. Her teeth were filed into fangs and her top lip was split from the center to her nose, giving her three lips, much like a cat. Artificially implanted whiskers bloomed from her cheeks. A pair of phony contact lenses turned her pupils into narrow slits. Charcoal-colored tattoos of tiger stripes stretched across her back and down her legs. Her Gravity Act— lifting bricks and weights with the piercings in her nipples, tongue, and clitoris— had always been the show-stopping, crowd-pleasing finale.

Over the years, Koz-Mo's duty with the troupe had transformed with his celebrity as the Dark Master of Ceremony. Contractual obligations kept him with the company, though the limelight inevitably replaced his interests of hooks and whips with microphones and autographs.

Didi smiled proudly at Talon, eager to join the celebration of his soon-to-be new career as Felina's permanent replacement.

"This is your girlfriend?" Koz-Mo asked without regard to her presence.

Talon directed his sights to Didi, sending his cold gaze through her. She recoiled nervously into the cushions. She feared his answer. She already knew what it was despite his disregard of the question altogether.

X and Felina seemed perfectly unaware of her presence as they focused on Talon, having received only abrupt responses from him to their barrage of questions. Felina and X exchanged glances with subtle, approving nods.

"Welcome aboard," Felina told Talon as she motioned to the signed contract lying next to the vase of flowers and potpourri on the coffee table. "Welcome to the circus life." She stared at him with her yellow reptilian eyes. "And now I retire to raise our child." She looked happily to X, the father, as all eyes fell upon her belly. Attention was no stranger. "Give me your hand," she demanded of Talon.

Talon leaned forward with a determined and natural fluidity as he placed his hand in hers. She ran her fingers across his palm, scraping his delicate skin gently with her long, black pointed nails. She closed her eyes and tilted her head back ever so slight.

"What have you lost?" she asked calmly.

The entire mood of the room altered with her soothing tone of voice.

He was quick to respond. "My love."

"She died a gruesome death," Felina picked from the air.

Talon's silence urged her to continue.

"The wrong man was pinned to her murder, and you seek…"

They all waited.

"And you seek…" She took a deep breath. "Something else. What is it?"

Talon was quiet. His face was rigid, his eyes hollow. "My father's Fury," he hissed with a raspy breath.

"A gift from deceased family…is there a connection?" she asked, her eyes still closed.

"Yes." His response fell from his lips without enthusiasm as if riding on a sigh. His feelings were masked under a brilliant pokerface.

Felina caressed the palm of his hand and gently said, "The Child of the Sun makes his home in the Fury. To get to the Key, you must go to the Key. The Child of the Sun is one with night—the storm will be your warning. Caution be with you."

Talon's face crinkled slightly. "If I find them," his words escaped with his breath, "I will kill them."

"Do not jeopardize your career with us," X stated with deep conviction, uncertain if he was overreacting to a bluff or a deeply rooted premonition. "Your reputation and choices in life are now linked to us. What you do will reflect on this company."

Felina gracefully stood, extending her hand for X to arise at her side. "Fate will be."

X stood and offered his hand to Talon. Talon reached up to embrace it with his own, gripping it firmly.

"Good to have you," X told him. "We'll be talking more in the future."

X escorted Felina to the door, helping her through the rain to the Driskill Hotel.

Didi looked up at Koz-Mo, who was staring at her unshaved legs. She crossed her legs uncomfortably, though loving the attention.

"I'll need to be in Los Angeles in two weeks to start shooting the next season of *Far Out*," Koz-Mo announced. "If you have nothing better going on, I wouldn't mind spending some downtime."

Talon tipped his head slightly in acceptance of the offer. He could see that Koz-Mo had taken a sudden interest in Didi.

"Take off your shirt, Didi," Talon demanded. His voice was edged with intensity.

Her eyes widened as she exchanged an awkward glance with Koz-Mo. She apprehensively reached down and grabbed the wet fabric, clutching it with her incomplete set of digits. She reluctantly lifted her shirt over her head as her wet hair draped her bare shoulders.

"All of it," Talon insisted.

She looked into his eyes and all that she knew of herself melted away. There was only Talon. She unfastened the bra and let it fall to her lap. Her small perky breasts were still moist from the rain, her dark nipples firm.

"Take her," Talon offered to Koz-Mo. "She's yours tonight."

12:10pm

Key West, Florida

"Skin," a little boy mumbled under his breath, reading the fresh tattoos on the knuckles of a fellow tourist. He looked over to her left hand, noticing four more letters, each claiming a single knuckle just like the right hand. "Head."

Sharon Kern stood at attention before the large buoy-shaped monument marking the Southernmost Point of the continental United States. In the distance was the Atlantic Ocean, a sight that she still had not grown to accept as mere scenery. Children surrounded her, hoping to figure out her gender while admiring the new tattoos on her powerfully androgynous hands. Throughout her twenty years of life she had grown accustomed to the gawking stares of strangers, though she never welcomed it. At six foot three with an unusually husky build, she naturally attracted unwanted attention. She was without a doubt a peculiar sight. Far more interesting than the popular landmark that preoccupied her attention.

She grazed her fingers gently across the patch of the American flag on the breast of her burgundy flight jacket. The ground on which she stood was the closest she had ever come to leaving the United States. Just beyond the horizon was an undiscovered world that she felt certain she would never experience. Or would desire to experience. Being so far away from home made her realize her weakness for simplicity and familiarity.

She squinted in the light of the midday sun as sweat dripped from her shaved head down her fair temples. Her dull, strawberry blond hair earned her the nickname Rusty, which she much preferred to her real name. Sharon, she felt, was the name of some farm girl from the boondocks of southern Illinois. She had already earned that identity. She ached for change.

"S...H...A...R...P," one of the little children spelled aloud, reading the inscription stitched across the back of her flight jacket. She looked like a soldier to them, one designed in a Top Secret military laboratory, an experimental killing machine posing as a female human. Their imaginations ran wild with the possibilities. "Sharp," the same voice whispered under breath.

She turned to face the child, inadvertently frightening him into a retreat to his camera-wielding parents. She identified the little boy as similar in appearance to a particular sitcom actor, but could not place the name. She squinted at him with one open eye through a thin wisp of hair that curled over her freckled forehead. Her eyelids were puffy and sagged slightly over subtle cheekbones, giving a lazy mien that even her tense lips could not flatter. Her eyebrows were so slight that they were practically transparent. Her chin was the only petite feature on her body, which did not bode well with the rest of her appearance. She had heard herself described many ways. *Pretty* was not one of them.

She reached into the pocket of her flight jacket for her disposable camera. The monument was exactly the type of thing she wanted her mother to see. No one had ever cherished her as her mother did. Rusty strove to make her proud, pushing herself to find the confidence and courage that so inspired the woman who had brought her into the world. Two weeks earlier on the day she left for Florida, her mother was beside herself with excitement and envy. Rusty was doing what her mother never dared, she was about to brave the boundaries of southern Illinois on her own. To appease her mother's curiosity, Rusty had schemed an entire photo collection to show what her mother had given up to start a family at such a cruelly young age.

Rusty shooed away the peddlers offering to take her picture. In her solid presence, they abided without a second consideration. She centered the shot with the monument in all its glory and graffiti, making sure the Atlantic Ocean was clearly visible behind it before she snapped the picture. She could not wait to share her experience with her mother as a retrospect.

She stuffed the camera back inside her jacket and crossed her thick arms. She smiled. She had never been in the tropics until earlier that week and her enthusiasm had not faltered since her arrival.

In the back pocket of her hard denim jeans were two fliers, both of which she would eventually add to the Florida trip photo album. One flier was for the upcoming Drag Show, the "Queen of the Keys" annual pageant. The other, the disciples of Reverend Strickland, the notorious racist homophobe who found international fame with the slogan "The Lord Hates Queers." In the underground network of anti-racist skinheads, it was commonly known that the proceeds from all his media campaigns were funding a group of racial purists known as the National Reclamation Front, or the NRF. Anonymously founded in the late eighties, the ultimate objective of the NRF was a simple one—Racial Holy War.

Over the course of roughly one year, Rusty had familiarized herself once again with old college buddies who were members of the order known as SHARP, or Skinheads Against Racial Prejudice. The group kept a close watch on the NRF and all their activities. When the Gainesville SHARPs sent her a personal invitation to be present at a NRF protest in Key West, Rusty found her calling. She left three weeks later.

Several days were spent in Gainesville in the apartment of a charismatic drunk known as Smitty, listening to records and drinking beer. A bold new life experience was discovered on her very first night—sexual intercourse. Smitty, a professional drinker and talker, was equal her weight and half her height. When serviced with enough alcohol, she learned, he became quite frisky and flirtatious. If she was able to keep him from passing out, she found herself in the arms of another human being. As hollow and cold as the experience was, it was unlike anything she had ever known before. For the first time in her life, she felt desired.

As she turned to walk down South Street to the Southernmost Motel, she imagined her new comrades sitting in their room drinking cheap beer, slurring the words to *The Worst Day Since Yesterday* by Flogging Molly. The thought made her smile. She could not wait to join them.

With each step her wispy bangs swung across her knobby nose like a curly fry. It swayed back and forth, lapping at her pale, sweaty skin. She squinted into the sun-drenched stretch of road before her, wishing she had remembered to bring sunglasses. She was surprised her mother had not thought of it, either.

She recollected the evening she decided to take the trip. Her mother was sitting at the dinner table, working on a crossword puzzle as her older brother stared over his dinner plate with mischievous shifty eyes—a sign that a practical joke was in progress.

"Ma," Rusty announced across the table, dragging her mother away from her beloved puzzles. "I'm taking a trip to Florida."

Ma raised her head, revealing her widened eyes. She was flabbergasted. "What?" She placed her pen diagonally across the page as she reached nervously for her pack of Camels. She pulled out the last remaining cigarette and placed it in her creased lips. "How?" she asked as the cigarette danced in her mouth with each word.

"The usual way," Rusty began as she watched her mother strike a match, "an airplane."

Her mother raised a beleaguered brow and lit the cigarette, unmoved by her daughter's sarcasm. "Where are you getting the money?" Ma asked in an exhalation of gray smoke. She knew the answer before she asked, but felt obligated to throw in an objection regardless.

"Savings. What else can I do with my money? I just sit here day in and day out, wasting away."

Her mother narrowed her wrinkled brow and took a deep drag off the cigarette. The cherry burned a bright orange when suddenly its tip sizzled in a plume of smoke and yellow flame.

"J. R. Kern!" Ma scorned lightly as she coughed into her feeble hand. She pointed an accusing finger across the table at her mammoth son.

His deep and throaty giggle gave away his guilt. He rubbed his bearded chin and shook with laughter. Over the years, his growth was determined only by his size. His level of maturity, like most men, was stunted in pre-adolescence. "The old match head in the cigarette!" he announced proudly. "You always fall for that one."

Ma extinguished the cigarette in the ashtray on the windowsill as she shook her head and chuckled under her smoky breath.

"Florida?" Ma asked again, this time more calmly.

"Yeah," Rusty told her as she wrapped her thumbs around the straps of her Big Smith overalls. She quickly thought of her old wardrobe from college, the Docs, the braces, the flight jacket—all the things she never wore on the farm and had not worn in over a year, since she dropped out of school. "I'd first go to Gainesville to meet some people I met online. Then onto to Key West for a week, maybe longer."

Ma's eyes lit like a match head, though her face was calm and stoic. She shook her head and sighed. "Dear, that's so far away."

Rusty shrugged her shoulders. "What else do I have to do? Except waste away…"

Ma dared not argue. The answer was clear. Nothing, other than assist her brother on the farm, as she did day after day, year after year.

"I'm not asking for permission, Ma," Rusty told her in a soft voice. "I'm twenty, I can make these choices on my own."

"It'll be a great time," J. R. threw in as he gnawed on a piece of steak. "There ain't nothin' needin' to be done 'til then. I can handle it."

Ma crinkled her lips, clearly retaining a smile she did not want to wear. It was no use. She was very excited. "Florida, huh?"

Rusty gazed over her left shoulder down Duval Street into the bustling activity of Key West's main thoroughfare. "Yeah, Florida," she proudly whispered to the air.

3:42pm

Houston, Texas

Josephine studied a map of the continental United States that was spread on the table before her, establishing potential destinations. Her red fingernails scraped across the paper, running a trail from west to east, onward to land's end in Florida. She squinted as her eyes headed to the southern tip, searching for the farthest stretch of land—one that she had learned about in a Hemingway novel. Her red nails followed down the speckled islands of the Florida Keys to the last one. Key West.

She took a deep breath and looked up from the map, spying the empty and overpriced Houston Hobby airport diner where she had spent the entire evening without sleep. *Betty's World Famous Apple Pie*. She had never traveled so far from home. In fact, she had never left the state of California before.

She glanced over at the clock on the wall. It was a little past eight in the morning, and the terminal was slowly gaining its momentum. Outside, she could see the landscape of runways. Inside, an adolescent girl with bad acne and an even less appealing sense of fashion waited at the counter, watching the *Jerry Springer Show*. Her face was drawn into a complacent scowl that lightened only when the incestuous prostitutes came to blows. She smiled, finding comfort in their pain. It made her feel normal, average. It made her skin fit more comfortably. Most importantly, it strengthened her faith in mediocrity. Her transparent eyes gave this away. Josephine imagined her thoughts as she stood at the job that sapped her life: *this is as good as it gets...* There were no other occupants inside the diner.

Josephine quickly folded her map and stepped up at once, grabbing her foam cup half-filled with Pepsi as she stepped into the busy terminal. From the window, the world seemed immense. It did not look that way the day before. When her brother was alive.

160

Friday, September 3, 1999
7:10pm

Key West, Florida

The air of Mallory Square on Sunset Pier was as sweet as candy. Key West, with its coastal atmosphere and stylishly trendy shops reminded Josephine of the Third Street Promenade in Santa Monica, California, merely miles from her Venice home. She felt strangely at home there.

She followed her nose to a single wooden cart where the aroma of sweet roasted almonds brought to life the pier's distinct smell. Carts and card tables lined the pier, selling anything from shark and Megaladon teeth to coconut postcards and seashells. Palm readers dispelled fortunes of prosperity and romance while others savored a fifteen-minute shoulder massage, waiting on the picturesque sunset.

Josephine worked her way through the crowd, finding the dock labeled *Restricted Area, US Customs* and leaned her face between the gate's metal frame. The sky was vibrantly orange, topped with pink clouds that were pierced by the sun's prickly rays. The water itself mirrored the sky, coloring it a warm shade of pink lemonade with an orange juice undercurrent. The sun was setting over a tiny island covered with the silhouettes of dream homes. Jet-skis raced through the otherwise still water.

She was slightly disappointed that the sun did not actually set over the water as it does in California, but she could not complain. The atmosphere in Key West carried a peace she had never imagined. The rest of the world was a façade to the island of Key West, nothing more than a validation for its thriving existence. She felt right at home on the tropical island, almost allowing her to leave her concerns and worries on the distant mainland. Almost.

The audience cheered when the sun disappeared altogether. Josephine turned to face the spectators, playing with large golden loop earrings as she watched the crowd. Whereas drugs dominated the freelance market in her Venice neighborhood, henna temporary tattoos and freshly squeezed lemonade dominated the trade on Sunset Pier. Several tourists wore another local product—hats made from the leaves of banana trees. Not the type of thing one would even think to wear in public upon returning home.

161

Her brother Timmy used to love the performers on Santa Monica's Third Street Promenade. He would often tell her that someday he would join the circus and leave everything behind. Everything except her. Together they would sit in forts made of pillow cushions and blankets and discuss the schematics of what they would do. Timmy would be a knife-swallower, and she would do the flying trapeze. Looking back, she wondered why they never considered the flawed logistics of a flying trapeze in a street performance. Nonetheless, it offered hope. Many hours were spent imagining the onlookers of pleased pedestrians in distant cities fillings jars with generous tips.

Then Renny would enter the room—mother's friend, the next-door neighbor. When mother had fallen asleep, he would stumble into the room and take Timmy away with him kicking and screaming, reaching out at Josephine with horrified eyes. She would hide deep in the fort, petrified with guilt for not helping him, remaining perfectly still, hastily planning their escape into circus life to save them both.

A cool Atlantic breeze rushed passed her, bringing her attention to a dark cloud that seemed to be connected to the ocean through a thick curtain of rain. It looked like a broad chef's hat resting on the horizon. Many of the vendors were already packing their gear, preparing for the storm that crept ominously toward the island.

Josephine proceeded across the brick that was laid out like plaid—red with white and gray crisscrossing stripes. Unicyclists weaved through the crowd that seemed to swarm around the street performers. Trained dogs charmed the easily amused tourists. Some watched the jugglers while others sought a blinking eye or twitching lip on the human mannequins—one a silver deity, the other a white angel. As the sky darkened, the crowd thinned. The gaslight-styled street lamps came ablaze, giving the atmosphere a distinct timelessness.

Josephine wandered to the largest entanglement of tourists located under three flags—the United States, Florida, and the Conch Republic. Beyond the riveted onlookers was a single male, spidery and lean, his skin painted red, his face yellow, and his hair dyed a bright orange. His entire color scheme correlated to his trade, a fire-eater. He spoke no words to the crowd, which was unlike any of the other performers, yet his performance was enough to keep his hat overflowing with dollar bills.

Droplets of warm rain began to speckle the brick, chasing away the few remaining tourists. As the occupants of the pier quickly retreated for cover, Josephine stood her ground, allowing the sprinkles of water to bathe her coppery black skin. The raindrops collected between her cornrows and dripped down her long braided extensions.

She watched the fire-eater gather his money hastily, and then she suddenly realized she was alone on the pier with him. He looked up at her and paused momentarily. His eyes were a faint blue, so clear that his pupils appeared as tiny magnets, pulling her attention. The paint on his face began to drip down his body over his red shoulders. A second passed as they held each other's attention. Two seconds passed. He nodded with cold indifference as he gathered his few belongings and splashed through the rain alongside the Conch Republic Cigar Factory.

She can do this, she decided as she stood alone in the rain. On this island, somewhere, somehow she could manage to survive through catering to tourism. Others, like the fire-eater, had learned to do it. She could as well. She smiled as she looked out over the vacant Sunset Pier, her new home.

She followed the fire-eater casually through the rain, keeping a safe distance. Suddenly she noticed something about him that had somehow evaded her moments ago. The paint on his skin was not running, or even fading. It remained a crisp red, almost like a sunburn, but too evenly dispersed and luminous. He was, from her vantage point, naturally red. Red as a cherry. Red as fire.

11:57pm

Austin, Texas

Speckles of sweat spotted the skin of Talon's back, reflecting the red stage lights that painted the club's smoky air like blood. A large wooden prop in the shape of a cross loomed in dark abstraction before a black curtain. Talon's arms were bound to the structure with leather straps, his back to the audience, his bare chest mashed against the massive wooden icon. His left cheek rested against the wood, giving the audience a view of his profile. They were there to see the pain, to watch his resolve crumble.

They would be let down.

Didi closed her right eye to aim the dart at Talon's soft flesh—flesh that she craved with every fiber of her being. She released it into the air as the audience gasped with bewilderment. The shiny metal tip penetrated deep inside the tissue of skin and muscle. It dangled at the base of his spine as a tiny droplet of blood trickled from the punctured skin, melding with the red lights that bathed his moist salty skin.

The audience applauded. Some held their stomachs while others covered their eyes. Despite the random objections, no one could resist the gruesome spectacle. Talon's performances had made the rounds of many water cooler discussions throughout the city. Many were there to verify the claims. Disappointment was scarce.

Didi presented another dart to the crowd. Smiles of enthusiasm combined with encouraging words. Their eyes lit with deeply rooted instincts of bloodlust. They hungered for the pain. His tolerance of it both perplexed and disappointed them.

Taking aim, she tossed the second dart. It struck a reasonable distance from the first, far up near his shoulder. His muscles flexed from a softened state, making the darts ascend erect.

The disjointed sighs from the audience were female. The awkward chuckles were from men struggling to make sense of their primal urges. For those unfamiliar with the performances, there was confusion. Confusion on the nature of sexual impulse, and why the venue was so thick with erotic tension that only vanity kept them safely clothed. Baring witness made them feel safe. Safe from the immoral acts that carried a deeper resonance of commonplace than their own denominational religious faith.

To the relief of the audience, Didi presented the third and final dart. Aiming carefully, delaying the throw as long as she possibly could to increase the sadistic needs of the crowd, she sent it to its destination. It impacted his spine with a thud, holding itself in his skin for a moment before falling to the stage floor. It left a thin trail of blood down his back.

Didi motioned to Talon for applause, which the audience generously gave.

"As many of you know, Talon has now joined the world famous Czars of Scar," she proudly announced. "This was the final performance in Austin for some time to come. Thank you."

She moved forward to release Talon as opinions of excitement and revulsion mixed through the audience. She gently removed both darts from his tender skin before unfastening the leather straps.

"You missed one," he scolded with a raspy whisper. "For that…" He waited until she had released both hands to finish. "…the show is not over." He stepped forward to the edge of the stage, standing over the audience that was slowly dispersing. "We're not done."

The crowd turned to him, greeting his comment with awkward silence.

He turned away from the blank and lustful faces. "Do you love me, Didi?"

Her eyes lit up, so rare was his affection, and never without some recourse.

"Didi is going to remove an entire finger," he revealed to the spectators.

There was silence and confusion. Surely not. Too far, too much, and too perfectly wrong.

"Yes," he replied, turning to her once again, trading his attention between her and the crowd. "Yes."

Her face was flushed. The mob's collective stares begged that she reveal the sick joke, while others hoped it be true.

"Yes," Talon repeated as he slowly placed the microphone on the stage. He left the stage momentarily, returning with a bag of small props—a chopping block, a rubber band, and a chisel. He picked up the microphone once again. "Yes."

She had done it before. Three times before, each time provoked by Talon. Never had she done it publicly. It was a fetish of his, a weakness. He had admitted to her that there was no stronger act of devotion and submission. Therein lied the union of souls, he told her. Complete and irreversible sacrifice.

She stared into the crowd, into the faces of the skeptics. She held up her right hand with all its digits perfectly intact. With only seconds to choose the unlucky piggy, she twisted the rubber band around the base of her right pinky. Tighter and tighter until the blood swelled in her finger, and then the sensation of touch resided to numbness.

She placed her hand on the chopping block as Talon hovered over her feeble posturing. He handed her the chisel. The crowd was silent. Slowly, calmly, remorsefully she held the chisel firmly in her left hand while placing its sharpened end between the bones of her hand and pinky finger.

Screams of terror followed the act. A mass exodus of the venue ensued.

Koz-Mo stood in the venue's shadows with his arms crossed, smiling shamelessly as the club personnel rushed the stage with mops and towels.

Key West, Florida

Josephine stared blankly at the television set, watching another repeat of *Far Out* as she painted and repainted her nails. Her room at the Merlinn Inn was like an enormous wooden box, perfect for one person. The bed stood far off the floor with thick pillars of wooden posts at each corner. The blankets were in disarray, and the pillows were stacked in a mound against the wall behind her back.

Stacks of twenties covered the wooden nightstand at her side. Alongside the loot was AK-Jay's pack of cigarettes, opened. All afternoon she placed and replaced a cigarette between her lips, humoring the thought of a new hobby. One that would relieve her stress.

She had hoped to find a television show that could take her mind off Timmy's death. Nothing could maintain her attention. Instead, she chased one memory after another, threading their history in uneven spurts of recollection. She faded into another...

She was a child, creeping through the darkness following Timmy's lead, holding onto the belt loop of Shasta, their next door neighbor. They cautiously approached a door outlined in faint yellow light, its entrance cracked with a thin thread of visibility in the dark hallway. Josephine trembled, fearful of what lie beyond the door. She clutched tightly to Shasta's curvaceous hips, staring into the darkness with wondrous and hopeful eyes.

Shasta was an only-child, Renny's child. She was tall and gangly with skin the color of bronze. Her kinky hair had a natural red tint to it, and without hair products, had a tendency to frizz into dry, chaotic spirals. She was a year older than Timmy, four years older than Josephine. She had matured quickly. In fact, Josephine had no memory of Shasta possessing a child's body.

Josephine did not really know Shasta, but they shared a history that surpassed her memory. She had always been there. History, so often mistaken for depth, bound them like sisters. Timmy, on the other hand, had a different concept of Shasta. One that Josephine would learn in time. Josephine hoped that someday they would all become one family, sharing a single house, having barbecues on the weekends and decorating the house for holidays. With

166

Josephine's mother and Shasta's father becoming so close, she felt it was just a matter of time before her dream would come true.

Timmy and Shasta slowly moved into the strain of yellow light slipping from inside the bedroom door. Josephine knelt on the ground below them. Her pupils shrank as the strip of soft light lined her dark face. She was eager to witness for herself, to verify Shasta's claim that their parents were making a baby. That is why Renny visited so often, they wanted to start a family of their own. Josephine was elated.

At first, all Josephine could see was the corner of the bed with its sheets horribly disheveled. Then she saw feet hanging over the edge—Renny's large, callused feet. Her mother's distinctly large hairdo emerged from the sheets, rising upright from the bed. Josephine instinctively backed herself from the light, but quickly realized that somehow their cover had not been blown. If it had, there would have been hell to pay.

Her mother put a short glass tube up to her robust burgundy lips. The end of the tube was charred and apparently clogged with a dark, uneven stone. She flicked a lighter several times, all the while staring down at the end of the makeshift pipe with crossed eyes. A tiny flame emerged from the lighter, and her mother eagerly placed the pipe up to the dancing fire, sucking it hard through the pipe. Her lip quivered as the muscles in her face lost all tenacity. She fell back to the pillow, out of view, as a trail of smoke rose to fill the space she had just fallen from.

Josephine backed away from the door, confused. She had never known her mother to smoke.

"Yeh, they makin' bay-bees," Shasta whispered happily.

9:54pm

Rusty sat in silence at Mallory Square, listening to the waves break. The sky was dark overhead and the pier was quiet. The flags rippled with the calm nocturnal breeze, gently tossing the nation's colors with the wind.

A group of homeless kids were huddled near the water, sharing a can of baked beans and a two-liter of generic cola. Their numbers had grown as the night progressed. Thinking back on the small collection that founded the group, only then did she realize how long she had been there. Alone, but not vulnerable. She never felt vulnerable.

The time spent was well worth it. The sights and sounds were fresh and new, so unlike those she had previously known. The sand, the air, the rocks, the vegetation, the old Victorian houses…it was like something out of a dream.

What she loved most about it was how familiar it all was to her. For all its eccentricities, Key West was unquestionably American. Part of the same fabric from which she was cut. She need not look up to know which flag claimed the ground in which she sat.

She could hear the homeless kids criticizing the United States. It angered her. During her brief stint of college, she had grown very intolerant of the liberals and anarchists that tended the same social gatherings. One group she grew to despise was the Crusties, the homeless anarchistic punk kids. Much like the ones sharing their generic cola and stolen can of baked beans.

She listened to them criticize every aspect of her homeland, glamorizing other countries for their history or for their more casual approach to living. They exchanged opinions on global politics and how the United States fit in, as if they had any real idea. No matter the subject, there was a conspiracy hiding the truth—a truth they somehow knew.

Armchair Critics, Rusty thought as she listened and chuckled under her breath. She lumped them with so many others, guilty of their own badgering, an askew perception brought on by the spoils of living in such a great land.

She felt that they confused history for culture, as so many do. She listened to them talk of the real culture that exists in Europe. Europe, with all its extensive history, kept alive by tourism. But the modern center of culture had not changed since the onset of the modern age. From ragtime to Big Band to jazz to rock to rap, the culture of the twentieth century was predominantly rooted on American soil.

Rusty found their opinions to be a strange irony. Today's counterculture is tomorrow's mainstream, eventually defining the era in years to come. All movements start on the fringe. Like most Americans, their mixed ancestry resulted in an identity crisis. Whereas their descendants found sanctuary in people with similar heredity, they found theirs in modern Western subculture. Rusty felt that someday those subcultures would define Western culture. Those setting the standard of what could someday become general American culture were also those so sharply against everything it stood for. Trends die, yet subcultures can potentially persist until its values are seamlessly integrated into society. With their subculture of interest being older than themselves, Rusty felt it was a strong candidate for eventual assimilation into the society they ironically scorned.

She leaned back and looked up at the American flag fluttering in the wind. In the grand scheme of things, the twentieth century will be remembered as a time of recovery from the shame and scorn of the Victorian era. Each counterculture movement was a small step away from the rigidity of the nineteenth century. Feminism and fashion had led the way, taking hold of the very essence of human evolution. When scholars look back upon the twentieth century, they will recall a century of war, and also the emergence of women. Yet society still recovers.

Monday, September 6, 1999
8:11pm

Key West, Florida

"This is it?" Reverend Strickland grumbled to himself as the Ford Escort coasted to the curb on Eaton Street. His paranoid and beady black eyes wandered the empty, wet streets. There were absolutely no pedestrians, let alone mobs of angry protestors. His sense of self-worth slumped like his bony shoulders. "I guess this is it," he sighed with disappointment. He thrived in opposition, and sank without it.

The brash melodies of Wagner pulsated vigorously through the tiny car speakers, firing their passions like the drumming presence of war. Brother John gripped the wheel with white knuckles while staring at the Reverend in the rearview mirror. He chewed his bubble gum in silence as he had the entire journey from Atlanta, frequently glancing at the Reverend with deep admiration. He felt graced in his presence, honored to be with the man who would cleanse the western world. A true patriot—a hero for the common blue-collar American. In the presence of the Reverend, his life had meaning. Pureness. His eyes followed the length of the Reverend's large, knobby nose to the black goatee that withheld his lips. His beard matched the receding hair on his narrow head.

The four occupants of the car absorbed the stillness, sharing a quiet discouragement over the lack of fanfare to greet their arrival. Without bringing it to words, it was clear that each of them feared the protest would be a dismal failure. Their efforts were pointless without the opposition to lend them credibility.

"What do you think, Reverend?" Kinsman Torben Kale belted gruffly. Aside from the Reverend, Kinsman Kale carried the seniority as the chairman of the Southeast Division of the National Reclamation Front. He gazed out the window into the quiet street, searching for movement. "Trouble?"

Reverend Strickland shook his head slowly, steadying his entourage with a calm ease. "No. This town feels...funny. Much like how New Orleans...just kind of funny." His accent was unmistakably Southern.

"Brother John and Brother Paul," Kinsman Kale barked to the occupants of the front seat, "get the motel room, and make sure everything is safe for the Reverend."

The two quickly obliged with their voices united as one, sharing a strong sense of purpose as they placed their right fists over their hearts and grunted: "Ra-Ho-Wa." The United States would soon understand their broken syllables and its meaning—the Racial Holy War, or Rahowa. Kinsman Kale and the Reverend sat quietly in the backseat as they watched the two matching skinheads march up the steps of the Artist's House Inn.

Kinsman Kale loosened the top button of his black Ben Sherman, revealing a thick tuft of dark chest hair. His shaved head was spotted and streaked with scars that prevented further hair growth in thin lines, leaving his squared skull scuffed like a ratty old baseball. Abrasions covered his face from a life of quarrel, with several years of it spent in prison. His firm facial features seemed to have been drawn with a ruler and a T-Square. His lips were so thin that they seemed to be one solid horizontal line. His nose was perfectly triangular with ridges that extended from the edges of his nostrils down to the corners of his mouth, creating a larger triangle with the inclusion of his linear mouth. His brow was prominent and heavy, seemingly falling over his deep-set brown eyes.

He reached down to his briefcase and pulled out some brochures from the Chamber of Commerce along with a few odds and ends he had gathered from the Internet.

Reverend Strickland never stopped scanning the street with his overly cautious eyes. "The muds couldn't survive here, Brother," he said, referring to the natives who once inhabited Key West. "When the Europeans settled here, all they found were bones. *Cayo Hueso* is what they called this land, translated as the Island of Bones. Eventually they Americanized the name from *Cayo Hueso* to Key West. The muds couldn't handle it. But look what we've done with it."

Kinsman Kale nodded as he looked out at the peacefully somber neighborhood. "The white man will reclaim, Reverend."

Reverend Strickland glanced over his shoulder at the Club Chameleon, responding to an unsettling sensation like a breath on his neck. In the shadows of the palms next to the building, he glimpsed what appeared to be an image of a demon staring back at him. Its maniacal eyes seemed to be surrounded by flames as red as the stripes on the American flag. Upon second glance, the specter's face evaporated into the foliage. He rubbed his eyes, certain he was delirious from fatigue. "I don't like that building."

"It's haunted," Kinsman Kale reported matter-of-factly with a voice like gravel. "That's what it said on the Internet. I looked into the history of this island, especially this street. For safety. Children were burned inside. The building caught fire." He flipped through his papers, searching for the print that would back his claim.

Reverend Strickland shrugged his shoulders, skeptical of anything mystical or supernatural. That was the folly of the muds, faith in hocus-pocus. The white man was better than that, he resolved. Holy, pure as Chernobyl snow.

Brother John and Brother Paul returned with a triumphant march, claiming victory over the empty street. Their matching green flight jackets, military fatigues, and shaved heads made them appear as a covert faction, which is exactly what they believed to be. Brother John opened the door for Reverend Strickland and escorted him to the inn like a humorously feeble and inadequate bodyguard. As Kinsman Kale and Brother Paul watched them safely enter the house, Kinsman Kale put his arm firmly on his counterpart's shoulder. It was an endearing, though macho gesture.

"How about a drink at Sloppy Joe's Bar?" Kinsman Kale suggested. "Long trip. Nice to unwind with a beer, what say?"

"Sure," Brother Paul replied, looking up at Kinsman Kale who was easily half a foot taller and fifty pounds heavier.

As the two stomped forcefully down the sidewalk away from the Artist's House Inn, they unwittingly strolled past the palms of the haunted theater. The fiery red face with the piercing eyes stared from the shadows.

The face, unlike the legend, was flesh and blood.

8:12pm

Steam rose from the shower, warming the salty air like summer. Josephine found her mind adrift as she watched the water curl inside the drain, racing into the darkness. The sound of the water soothed her, dragging her inward with it.

She felt as though she had been tossed a handful of daggers—thrust into adulthood without the knowledge of even the simplest of tasks like balancing a checkbook. All the plans, all the romantic notions, all the dreams—all would be unfulfilled.

As she swabbed her fingernails with an acrid polish remover, she realized suddenly that her brother possessed no attribute stronger than any of her own. He sought to strengthen her with wisdom and sensibilities, and in doing so she easily outgrew the humble nest he had created. A rift was imminent. Tension between them had accelerated continually over the past two years. She had always hoped he would come to his senses and flee his lifestyle before it was too late. In retrospect, it all seemed too unreal, too sensational. But she knew it happened. Just as she always thought it would.

She placed the polish remover on the sink and stretched her tense body. Her legs felt heavy and restricted, as though she had been treading uneasily through miles of mud. The brown hardwood made her look twice.

As she stepped inside the shower, safely concealed in a steamy fog, her tense muscles loosened. The water descended down her braided extensions, trickling over her dark skin. Her self-condemnation had become its own burden, a self-imposed cabin fever of sorts. She suddenly felt summoned by the outside world, drawn into the night for reasons unknown.

She considered her limited wardrobe, contemplating the most appropriate colors to wear in such a drab state of being. The thought offered a pleasurable escape from her self-consuming misery. She would be eager to leave.

8:13pm

Rusty stared into her reflection in the bathroom mirror, looking down her crinkled nose while flossing her crooked teeth. Her gums were prominent and pink like cotton candy. The soft white light seemed to powder her clean shiny skin, accentuating each freckle like flecks of bronze. Seeing herself with her old Devilock hairstyle from her freshman year of college psychologically reduced her age and opened a newfound sense of freedom. It was an even trade for the shoulder-length hair she had shaved the night before she left for Florida. All that remained were her bangs that tended to cling to the perspiration on her sloping forehead, sticking to her subtle and nearly transparent eyebrows.

For years her mother had begged her to pencil her eyebrows, but she adamantly refused. She felt makeup made women look like clowns, and was certain that cosmetics would only soften her bristly soul, forcing her to care about things she knew she should not. She cringed at the thought of becoming a frazzled woman with running makeup, crying without control like an audience on *Oprah*.

She looked at the lines etched into her face. The crow's feet and the crinkled brow. She wondered how her face would appear if the world had less annoying people. She attributed this to her early aging, genetics not withstanding.

She glanced up at the single lighting fixture over the mirror and thought back to the first few seconds of the year. As she watched the ball drop in Times Square that New Year's Eve, she immediately marched into her closet with a felt marker, unscrewed the light bulb, and wrote across its glass surface: "Change Your Life!" She screwed it back in and went straight to bed. Many months later in August when she went to replace it, she received her old forgotten message. She immediately logged onto the Internet, searching the chat rooms for an excuse to get away from the rut of her existence. *Stop the NRF in Key West* caught her attention in one of the skinhead chat rooms.

172

She smiled at her reflection, happy in her surroundings. Happy to be anywhere other than Olney, Illinois.

A mutual tube of toothpaste on the sink provoked thoughts of mischief. A measly dab of jalapeno juice mixed into the top portion of toothpaste...but she was certain the gag would not be appreciated by her new comrades. Not as her brother would appreciate it. It suddenly occurred to her how uncomfortable and unnatural she felt in their presence. To them, life was beer, brawls, babes, and a lot of boasting about the three. Not once did they ask a question about her— where she lived, what she loved, or what she believed. She was one of them in their eyes. Just another number to validate their choices in life.

She found herself chuckling at all the wrong moments in their presence, drifting in a split second to the memories of her brother's wild antics. She never felt they had ever been close. They shared little more than laughter, but their ongoing goofy shenanigans were some of the most important moments in her life.

She thought back on the lonesome summer nights where the two of them giggled hysterically over watermelon seed spitting contests. She was certain that he had rigged his victories somehow, though she never could prove it.

Then there was the time they had ventured to the nearby highway with a shallow cardboard box, five stuffed beanie kittens, catsup, and the guts from turkey dinner. During breaks in traffic they rushed the items out to the center yellow line to initiate the gag they called "Accidental Roadkill". The words *Free Kittens* were scrawled in bold black letters across the front of the box that straddled the centerline. The stuffed kittens were scattered over the road in a staged bloodbath. They spent the afternoon on the bluff with binoculars, trying to determine the best facial expressions on unsuspecting motorists. The school bus won, hands down.

As they aged into more mature bodies, their lowbrow humor reflected their level of physical maturity. For instance, the time they covered the mailbox with packed snow, transforming it into a seven-foot erect penis—still operable as a mailbox in the process. Freezing rain solidified it into ice later that evening, making any attempts to dismantle it an effort in vain. Since it did not hinder the collection of mail, it remained a fixture for over a week. They were both grounded through the duration.

Usually Rusty was merely J. R.'s accomplice, sharing only the laughs and the blame. Anything that would take Ma away from her mystery books and crossword puzzles was punishable enough on principle alone. But there were those other times when the gags were aimed at one another. Like the time J. R. put petroleum jelly on her truck's wiper blades just before a hard rain. There were also the ones that backfired, like the time Ma opened the door to a bucket of trash falling at her feet from a can tipped mysteriously against the back door. Rusty's favorite gag was one of retaliation, and the source of immense personal pride that lasted years.

It all started one weekend afternoon when J. R. stumbled in from their cattle farm, tired and hungry from a long day's work. He found Rusty in the kitchen sporting one of Ma's aprons.

"Yer pooch took a dump on the floor!" he informed her as he stood over the heaping pile of poop.

"I know." She pulled a sheet of chocolate cookies from the oven, fanning them with the hot pad. "That money on the counter is what I owed you."

"If you knew the dawg dropped a load indoors, why didn't you clean it up? Wait—what money?"

She stomped across the wooden kitchen floor with brisk, nettled steps to pick up the little brown turds. "You have a bad memory."

He picked up the coins and dropped them just as quickly. He yelped frantically with shock, squeezing his hand into a disabled fist. His face was flushed with shock, his eyes wide with confusion. "What did you do? You had those coins in the oven, didn't you?"

Without a moment's hesitation, she shoved the dog turds into his face, smearing it from cheek to chin. He was speechless and appalled.

"It's cookie dough, J. R.," she admitted. "It's not dog poop."

With his burnt fingers shoved in his mouth, he smiled his mischievous and crooked smile. "That's good, real good. Just remember," he threatened as he scooted to the kitchen sink to relieve his burnt fingers, "paybacks will be hell."

He stuck his injured fingers under the faucet and twisted the chrome knob, releasing an unexpected cold shower straight at him from the sink sprayer. The sprayer nozzle had been wrapped with rubber bands and strategically aimed just for his arrival. He scrambled to turn it off, batting wildly at the stream of water in the process. He turned to face her with faux turds and water dripping from his face.

She released her victory laugh with a triumphant fist clenched at her side.

He smiled, always the fan of a good gag. "Like I said, paybacks will be hell. Do I dare open the freezer for some ice?" He speculated the possibilities as he wrung out his sopping wet shirt. "There's a bucket of water propped inside the freezer door, waiting to fall on me, isn't there? You knew I'd go for ice once I burnt my fingers, huh? Just like you knew I'd go to the sink…"

She opened the fridge to reveal no booby traps, much to his dismay. She snickered as she handed him a piece of ice from the freezer.

He shook his head, unamused. "You better watch your back. Fair warning…"

He took a handful of piping hot cookies and retreated to his bedroom, hiding his insult behind a closed door. He did not stay long, though. The laxative cookies awarded him a sleepless night that was spent mostly in the bathroom.

"Rusty," a sour voice declared beyond the bathroom door. "Are you almost done in there?"

She stared into the mirror and wiped the warm smile from her face. "Almost."

10:24pm

A deep foreboding lingered in the crisply warm air. By day Key West was a quaint tropical paradise, but as night fell, the town was blanketed with an eerie, otherworldly ambiance. It was almost as if the *Island of Bones*, with its extensive and scarred history, was somehow self-aware with the eyes of the dead lurking in every shadow, around every corner. The spooky little town of Key West, as best as Josephine could tell, was in itself spiritually alive.

It was the perfect atmosphere for hide and seek. Just like she used to play with Timmy and Shasta when their parents smoked their glass pipes and continually tried without success to make babies. Josephine remembered stumbling in on Timmy and Shasta once during a game, finding them naked and intertwined in an animalistic passion that startled her. She exploded with anger, screeching, "Renny did this! It's all his fault!" She never understood the root of her claim, but somehow seemed perfectly appropriate. She always assumed Renny had done to his daughter what she knew he had done to Timmy.

She tightened her fists into tense balls of hatred as she glided down the quiet street. Her bright red fingernails dug into her palms. Then she released them, forcing her entire body to relax as she drifted forward like an apparition, a ghost of whom she once had been. It was all behind her now. She had to keep it there.

She suddenly felt the unsettling sensation of eyes preying upon her. The hair on her arm stood erect as she hastily returned to the Merlinn Inn. She glanced frequently over her shoulder to a vacant neighborhood along Simonton Street. It was almost as though the air was *too* still. She had yet to become accustomed to the inactivity of such a small community. Especially a tourist town in off-season.

Her white leather Adidas bounded effortlessly across the pavement, stealthy and quiet. The only sound she could hear was her own breathing and the fabric of her slick black sweatpants as they met with each deliberate step. Her brand new white Florida Keys T-shirt appeared as a reflector to the sparse traffic at such a late hour.

Then she heard whispers. Faint whispers coming from the darkness. She peered over her shoulder to find only an empty street.

Silence resumed.

She held her breath and listened, but there was nothing to hear. A bit shaken, though paranoid, she increased her pace, keeping her senses on full alert. She nervously played with her large golden hoop earrings in an effort to ease her mind. As she reached the corner of a dark intersection, she cautiously reached down into the dense shrubbery to find a large stick for protection.

"Lookin' fer sumptun?" a male's voice slurred from around the corner, beyond her field of vision.

She stepped forward to find two skinheads merely footsteps away. Kinsman Kale and Brother Paul. Kale stood before the other, dressed completely in black and wearing a cocky, drunken smirk on his stone-like face. They were close enough for her to see their angry bloodshot eyes. She stumbled backward as she grasped the thick shrubbery for balance. Kinsman Kale lunged wildly, grabbing her by the collar and forcing her to the ground. His black Doc Martens boot stepped on her veiny throat to keep her down. Her braided extensions seemed to spill from her head onto the concrete.

"I'm feelin' horny," Brother Paul announced with excitement.

Kinsman Kale jerked his head quickly, angrily. "We don't screw the coloreds," he stated with near sobriety. "Give me your pocketknife, Brother Paul."

Josephine stared up in terror as he fumbled for the knife in the pockets of his stiff denim jeans. He fished out a small pocketknife and clumsily opened the shiny blade. Giggling fiendishly, he placed it in Kinsman Kale's eager hands.

Josephine prayed silently for mercy as Kinsman Kale focused his blind rage on her. He clutched the knife with a determined grip, holding it over her with a threatening posture. She could not believe that this would be her fate, after all that she had endured.

Suddenly a bright flash of light exploded from the shrubbery. Flames from an unknown source engulfed Brother Paul's face, igniting his eyebrows and hair. He frantically stumbled down the street, screaming, tripping haphazardly without direction as smoke rose from his singed hair.

When the inferno vanished, a thick and rusted chain emerged from the dense foliage in its place, wrapping around Kinsman Kale's neck, yanking him partially into the shrubbery.

Josephine scampered backward to safety, convinced beyond any doubt that Timmy was actually still alive, protecting her as he always had.

To her surprise, a ghastly red figure slithered from the darkness like a beast from hell. It held tightly to the ends of the chain, squeezing the breath from Kinsman Kale. Then it looked upon her with its devilishly piercing eyes, and she immediately recognized him—the fire-eater from Sunset Pier.

Kale gasped desperately for air as he descended to his knees. He struggled helplessly as the red assailant very calmly whispered in his ear, "If you don't leave town, I will kill each of you."

The Kinsman awkwardly reached up with the small pocketknife and slashed at his oppressor's hands, opening his radiant flesh with a crooked gash. The flow of blood was darker than, but nicely complimenting his unusual skin tone. It dripped onto Kinsman Kale's face as the chain compressed his neck like a vice. Then he lost consciousness.

The fire-eater dropped him to the pavement, carefully reassembling the rusted chain over his own shoulder as Kale slowly began to breathe again.

Josephine watched with terror as the fire-eater advanced toward her with a face so menacing and expressionless that it rendered her perfectly immobile. He towered over her trembling body and gently lowered his hand to her, calmly and patiently.

"My name is Jobie Wallace," he told her as he helped her to her feet.

She stood next to him, roughly the same height, easily the same build. Kinsman Kale, twice his size, lay in a pathetic heap. She was stunned.

"Josephine Ott," she told him flatly, still trying to make sense of things. "How did you know…"

"HammerSkins," he replied matter-of-factly. His hair was bright orange, cut short to reveal the bright contrast of his brilliantly red skin. Cobweb tattoos spanned his hollow cheeks. His plain black T-shirt melded into the night. His green/blue plaid bondage pants worked as camouflage against the green groundcover. An unusual dark strap linked his pants at the knee. "They're with the NRF. In town for a couple days, you should watch walking these streets alone. Normally it's safe out here, but not with them in town, not this week." He started walking forward, the direction she was originally heading. "This way?"

"Are we safe?" she asked. She noticed that his combat boots were so dilapidated that they were bound with duct tape to keep them intact. She looked back at Kinsman Kale lying perfectly still on the sidewalk behind them. Brother Paul was nowhere in sight.

"We're never safe," he responded gravely. Blood dripped continuously down his fingers. His nails were painted black—a devious contrast to his strangely red complexion. "This way?" he repeated casually.

"Your hand," she spoke to the wind as she rushed to pursue him. "We need to get you to a doctor."

"No." His voice was dry and insistent with a trace of paranoia. "No doctors. I can take care of it, but we need a safe place, somewhere they can't find when they come looking."

"My room is only a few blocks away…" her voice trailed with concern and confusion as she struggled to keep up with his brisk pace. "You must be in pain."

"No, I'm not. I'll explain." He pointed down the street with a stiff red finger as the chain rattled over his shoulder. "This way?" He could sense her uneasiness with her apprehensive gait. "I told you I'll explain…"

To say the least, she thought as she sprinted to his side. He had quite a bit to explain.

They entered the Merlinn Inn property through the side gate. It was as if they had stumbled upon another world safely concealed within a secluded courtyard—invisible from the street merely steps away. Josephine led him to the small swimming pool nestled under the soft lights that were scattered throughout the courtyard's abundant greenery.

Jobie sat on the edge of the pool and dipped his arm into the clear, chlorinated water. His blood swirled to the surface before dispersing. He reached inside his pocket to retrieve a roll of dental floss. A tiny needle was stuck inside the plastic container.

"In case I tear my clothes," he explained as he threaded the needle with floss. "Or my skin."

Her eyes widened with disbelief. Before she could verify his seriousness, he began stitching his injury, pulling it tightly together while washing it clean in the pool water. She gasped and covered her eyes.

"It's not as bad as it looks," he told her evenly. His demeanor was icy cold. "I have lost my sense of touch."

Her face scrunched, befuddled. "Why? Or...how?"

"It's a disease, I think. I got it while making love to my girlfriend. It killed her, but I only lost the sensation of touch...and now I look like an apple." He laughed to himself. "Soon after she died, my ability to feel anything went the wayside."

"Are you going to die from it?"

"Haven't yet. It's been a year. No...I don't think so. Seems to have only ruined the nerves in my skin. Funny thing about losing your sense of touch, you begin to learn how the body works together to understand the world around you. One sense feeds off another. For instance, you can smell heat and you can smell cold. I know it sounds weird, but you can actually taste the temperature. It's only when you lose your sense of feeling that you realize this is true."

She thought a moment as she watched the final stitch. His wound was sewn together like a rag doll. This was not the first time he had enacted such a procedure, she decided, as she carefully inspected his flaming red skin from a safe distance. His arms were streaked with scars, some still sewn together. He tied a knot at the end of the new stitch and bit off the excess.

"I don't mean to sound rude, but is it contagious?" she asked sheepishly. "It must be, based on what you have said."

"Only through sex," he replied bluntly.

"I hope you aren't sleeping with someone now."

He belted out a short burst of unexpected laughter. His face then quickly fell straight as he dipped his hand into the pool once again. This time no blood emerged from his injury. "Where do you live?" he asked.

She raised her brow, caught between answers, unsure of her own residency. "I guess...here."

"Here?"

She nodded. "Right here."

"At this place?"

"For now," she confirmed.

"Where are you from?"

She thought a moment. "I don't know if I should say."

He did not question her further, honoring her wish for privacy. "I'm from all over. I've been everywhere, I have a collection of rocks from each state I've been through to prove it." He paused to gauge her reaction. She had none. "I'm originally from the Pacific Northwest, in Washington."

"How long have you lived here?"

"Since May. I lived in New Orleans for several months. I don't remember much of it, though. When I heard that Florida gave disability checks to people with facial tattoos, I decided to come here. Haven't looked back since."

"Where did you learn to...what would you call it...blow the fire out of your mouth?"

"It's easier than it looks," he confided. "Easy money, tourists are such suckers. I make a killing off them."

She smiled.

"I'm not kidding."

"I believe you," she told him. "Do you save it?"

He looked up at her skeptically. "Yes, but not in a bank. No way, never."

She laughed at his paranoid caution. It seemed strikingly similar to her own reserve. Aside from momentary lapses of reason, such as foolishly walking alone at night. "I don't blame you." She considered the stash of money underneath her mattress. "Do you live far from here?"

"Maybe." He lifted a single brown. "Can't say."

"Can't say, or won't say?" she asked.

"Will never say."

"You're a very secretive person," she observed aloud.

"If you were me," he said as he stood and brushed himself off, "you would be too."

"Are you leaving?"

He nodded affirmatively.

"Well, hold on," she said as she rushed to her feet. "I haven't even thanked you."

"No need," he replied flippantly.

"No...please, let me pay you."

"Civic duty," he shrugged. "All in a day's work."

She laughed. "Okay, whatever you say. Will I see you again? Down at Mallory Square maybe?"

"No," he told her as he edged closer to the gate. "I think I may take some time off until this passes. It could get messy down there. One more performance just to pad my pocket, and that's it for quite a while."

"I understand."

"Maybe we can go for a ride in my car," he suggested. "Plymouth Fury. It's as black as night."

"Black as me?" she joked lightly.

His smile was a small victory on her part.

"Even darker," he returned. He set his cold gaze upon her, freezing her like a deer in headlights. "I'll pick you up the day after tomorrow, an hour after sundown. Out front of this place on Simonton, be ready."

"Okay," she complied as he strolled to the gate, disappearing into the darkness from whence he came.

**Tuesday, September 7, 1999
12:31am**

Austin, Texas

"Tell me your name," Talon whispered in Didi's ear.

His breath on her skin caused her teeth to chatter. Her writhing hips urged penetration. The handcuffs locking her wrists to opposite corners of the bedpost were tight, cutting her soft flesh as she squirmed with desire. She loved the pain—she ached for her body to ache. A large chunk of ice dangled from a chain off the bedpost, dripping frozen water onto her hand. She could feel it with her few remaining fingertips.

"What is your name?" Talon whispered once again. His voice was cold and distant.

Didi closed her eyes, breathing deeply. Her pale complexion was further washed out with ghostly white makeup like a China doll. Her lips were painted red, and her eyes were lined and narrowed with eyeliner for an Asian appearance. The latex outfit that Talon had chosen for her to wear was made for someone two sizes smaller.

As he licked the ridge of her ear, her breathing trembled with euphoria. She struggled to part her legs, but her ankles were secured to the lower bedposts, rendering her immobile. She imagined him climbing on top of her, owning her, using her. She wanted him to release his seed inside of her. His lack of regard seemed so strong and powerful, she wished for him to father her children, and to father her as well.

"Who are you?" he asked her.

She opened her eyes to see his face over hers, floating in the darkness. His aura mixed seamlessly with the shadows. When he looked upon her, she felt as though he were summoning demons. More specifically, a dead woman named Phaedra Lin. The woman whose clothes she was wearing.

Didi was very familiar with the legacy and tragic demise of Phaedra Lin. In life she was Talon's lover and sidekick in a shock performance duo known as The Skin Ensemble. Phaedra Lin's beauty was legendary to her and everyone she knew.

"Tell me," Talon whispered again.

She knew what he wanted to hear. It pained her to know. This was not intimacy as she so wished. This was a game. A sick and twisted mental game to deepen their mutual anguish.

"Phaedra Lin?" Didi asked him. The cold water dripped down her hand from the block of ice that dangled from the chain like a gruesome decapitation.

"Yes," he breathed in her ear as he backed into ebon like a wisp of smoke. "But you know that isn't true. You could never be her."

"I would be her, if it would make you happy," she pleaded as he stood over her helpless body.

She despised her body and its inability to fit the clothing she so desperately wished to fulfill for him. She closed her eyes tightly, wishing she could remove herself from the world. She gnashed her teeth with frustration, grinding them together with a clenched jaw. She wanted to puke, wishing that she could expel twenty-five pounds or more from her body.

Her arms pulled violently, knocking the block of ice as the cuffs grated against her wrists, breaking the skin. The pain filled her with meaning. She wanted more. There was no better satisfaction.

"I have saved all your gifts," he whispered to her.

She knew what he meant. Her face softened immediately. Her heart fluttered with hope.

"I've kept them in a box," he informed her. "I plan to make a necklace of your bones. I will wear them forever."

She smiled with her entire being.

He tenderly stroked her right wrist. "I need more." His fingers encircled her soft skin, and then squeezed firmly below the cuff. "This hand," he whispered, "I want this hand."

She visualized him on stage with The Czars of Scar, wearing her bones like affection. She felt close to him once again, she felt needed and desired. But Phaedra Lin's latex outfit chafed her, squeezing her ribcage like a black claw.

"Okay," she told him eagerly. "Take me, please."

He stepped further away from the bed, submerging deeper into the shadows. "I must go."

"Where?"

"Away," he sighed without reservation. "On vacation with Koz-Mo…before we start working on the new act, and before Koz-Mo begins dubbing the cartoon."

"What about me?"

His response was as cold as the block of ice that dangled over her hand. "What about you?"

She raised her eyebrows in fear. Would he dare leave her to perish as a prisoner of her own fragile will? She imagined her starved and lifeless body still chained to the bed when he returned.

"The key to unlock the cuffs is attached to the end of the chain, frozen inside the ice. By the time it has melted, I will be long gone."

Her screams echoed through the dark and empty room hours after he left.

11:12am

Key West, Florida

Sunshine and sandcastles. This was everything Rusty had hoped for. She remained fixed in a permanent location under the shade of the palm trees along Smathers Beach. An extensive smile lit her face like the sun-drenched tropical world on which she was perched. Her pale skin was covered with a creamy film of suntan lotion, which was a rather effective glue for loose sand. Her eyes squinted wondrously at the crystal blue seascape.

A capped pen weighted the pages of the partially finished crossword puzzle resting at her side. It had nearly become buried in the sand after hours of neglect. She was enduring a brief hiatus from it sparked by the painful realization that she had become her own mother. She was unaware that a transformation had even begun to take place. It made perfect sense, though. Inactivity in such obscure quarters could certainly propel the mind to straightjacket fits. Crossword puzzles kept Ma out of the funny farm. She hoped it would serve her just as well in the dire and lonely years ahead as the family's Old Maid.

She leaned back against the sand with her arms stretched high over her head, perfectly relaxed under a canopy of palms. She shut her dry eyes and let her mind drift aimlessly like the sea gulls overhead.

"Follow me," J. R. beckoned in memory. "I want you to see this."

"See what?"

"Come on," he persuaded her with a mischievous grin. His juvenile face was covered with adolescent peach fuzz. He had spent his life dreaming of owning a full beard like those worn by ancestry in old sepia photographs. Facial hair had suddenly made a man of him, and he was eager to fully realize his masculine prowess—beginning with the mastery of power tools. "You'll see. In the barn, come on."

Reluctantly though curious, she followed him into the backyard. Darkness had blinded her, but after a lifetime on the farm, she knew exactly when to duck to miss clotheslines and tree branches. She knew the yard better than she knew herself. The cool and moist grass was soft under her bare feet, with individual blades being yanked from the earth by her clenching toes. A cool late spring breeze swept through the yard, stirring the budding leaves on the trees. The air was rich with life.

He shushed her as they arrived at the barn entrance. "Don't let Ma and Pa know we're out here. Be quiet."

"Okay."

Together they unlatched the barn doors and quietly opened each squeaky door. The barn was dark and cold and musty. It always gave her the creeps, though she would never admit such a thing to him. He fearlessly entered the darkness, leaving her alone at the door. She checked over her shoulder more than once, a reaction to all the ghost stories he had convinced her were true throughout her young life. And every story took place in and around the barn. She had no doubt that their barn was the most haunted building in all creation. He swore by it, though she had never seen or experienced anything personally.

A burst of light bloomed from a kerosene lantern. Rusty raised a defensive hand to shield her eyes. When she opened them, she found herself staring directly into the face of a horrendous monster. A four-foot vulture created by a conglomeration of scrap metal and spare parts from old machinery. Its beak was a hook from a log chain. Its wings were strips of steel while the feathers were forks and spoons and butter knives. Its claws were chain derailers off old bicycles. Each part came together to form one ghastly beast.

"Like it?" he asked. "Took all weekend. Bet you didn't even know I was out here working on something, did you?"

Her face contorted into a smug scowl. "I'll have nightmares of this thing."

He laughed proudly. "Great!"

"Why is this a secret? Ma would love this thing. If you show her in the daytime, that is. She loves everything you do."

"I have this idea," he began enthusiastically, "something fun we can do now that it's summer."

"Yeah, and what will that be?" she asked.

He took a seat on the riding lawn mower and smiled that old devious smile of his. "You know how the *Olney Register* newspaper has started that anonymous editorial section for people too afraid to take credit for their opinions? Well, see the markings on its belly?"

She looked down its Harley Davidson gas tank torso at three unusual symbols. The top one was a crescent moon with an arrow through it, the middle one a simplistic flame, and the bottom one a circle with a ring over the top of it like a halo.

"What does it mean?" she asked.

"You tell me!" he laughed while smacking his muscular thigh. "But I reckon this town will figure out some meaning in it, especially after they read the anonymous editorial from The Secret Society of Satanists—warning of doom!" He slapped his knee as he chuckled. "We'll tell them that our numbers are

184

strong, from city officials to firemen to the old lady next door! Satanists everywhere, waiting for that omen to be delivered from the bowels of hell!"

Rusty scratched her chin as her face slowly lit. She was definitely intrigued with the possibilities.

The editorial ran two days later, introducing a cryptic and sinister premonition of evil lurking behind their neighbor's pleasant smiles. J. R. spent several afternoons at the feed store that week, discussing with townsfolk the hypotheticals while spreading rumors he had heard from unnamed sources—people in the "know". For lack of better news, his information was never questioned. The intrigue was too valuable to the quiet little town. Each day the story gained new embellishments as it raced around town and back to the feed store the following morning for J. R. to throw them another curveball—something new he had heard from undisclosed sources. By Thursday, he had dropped the almighty bomb on them—something big would happen that weekend.

"Dear Lord," Ma mumbled to herself from behind the newspaper on Sunday morning. She lowered it to peer over the top with eyes like fire. A wicked smile painted her face like a child. "Kids, you won't believe this!"

She turned the paper around to show the front-page story. *IRON VULTURE LANDS IN OLNEY!* The photograph showed several firemen carrying the magnificent metal bird away from a group of newspaper carriers struck with awe.

J. R. shot a quick glance to Rusty.

"What is it?" Rusty asked Ma, bemused by her own faux innocence.

"I trust you kids are smart enough not to be devil-worshippers," she lectured them. The thrill of the news prevented a response. "I didn't believe it, but it's true. There are devil-worshippers in Olney! Last night this…Iron Vulture was actually welded to the flagpole in front of the *Olney Register* offices."

J. R. laughed aloud. "How cool!"

Rusty struggled to contain her composure.

"What's more," Ma said eagerly, "it has a secret encryption on it." She gave them both a toothy smile. "Well, who better to crack this code?"

J. R. rolled his eyes. "Ah, Ma…"

"Don't you '*ah, ma*' me, son," she boasted, "am I not the perfect candidate for this type of detective work? I have spent years honing my skills on crosswords, game shows, puzzles, Agatha Christie books…I can figure this out. Those symbols mean something, and by God, I'm going to solve this riddle!"

"Then what?" Rusty asked.

She shrugged her shoulders, still gleaming with wild energy as she fumbled for her pack of cigarettes. She steadied the ashtray on the kitchen table with nervous hands. "They took it down to the police station where they plan to analyze the symbols. Old man Peterson will let me in there, I just know it."

"You're going down there to look at this thing?" J. R. asked uneasily.

Ma seemed genuinely confused. She struck a match to light a cigarette while shooting her son a mean eye. "Do you not realize how much fun this can be?"

"Oh, I do," J. R. assured her, his words layered with meaning. "Trust me, I do."

"Then you'll come with me?" Ma asked with an exhalation of smoke.

Rusty and J. R. glanced apprehensively at one another, and then back to Ma, simultaneously responding, "No."

"Too busy today," J. R. added.

"Yeah, lots to do," Rusty agreed.

"Someone needs to protect the livestock from the Satanists," J. R. told her. "I suppose that'll be me."

Ma shrugged with a smug disregard. "Your loss." She stood up and went straight for her purse. Her quick movements stirred the smoke that lingered over the kitchen table. "I'll be back this afternoon."

Rusty and J. R. watched the car race into the horizon with a trail of dust. They sat silently together, flabbergasted.

"I've never seen her so excited," Rusty finally said, flipping her thin red hair behind her ear. "What should we do?"

"What can we do?"

"Should we stop?" she asked.

He shook his head defiantly. "Why would we stop? We couldn't pay to have this much fun."

"We could get in such trouble!"

"How?" he challenged. "Setting up fake metal birds in the middle of the night is hardly a crime. Besides, you said it yourself. We can do it for Ma. I mean, look at her. She probably hasn't been this excited since Prom night. And look at the faces of the people in that photograph. They love this!" He stared down at the table, deep in thought. "This could be the greatest moment of my life." His face slowly lightened into an excursive grin. "This is my moment of glory—my twisted sense of humor is headline news! My fifteen minutes of fame, right there on the front page! We've got to make another one. If not for me, then for Ma."

Hours later, Ma came rolling up the driveway with a dust storm in hot pursuit. She burst from the car with a hearty grin, stepping through the dusty haze to find Rusty sitting on the porch, staring at the barn.

"Where's your brother?" Ma asked eagerly.

Rusty glanced to the barn. Through the crack in the door she caught a glimpse of welding sparks dancing across the stone floor. Their new monstrosity was slowly and secretly taking life.

"He's working on something or other out there," she forfeited without sentiment. "Leave him be."

"I wanted to share my findings," Ma bragged as she took a seat next to her daughter. "I wanted to show you kids how clever your ol' Ma is." She handed

Rusty a sheet of paper with the familiar symbols sketched in pen. Several random words were written below each symbol. "I think I know what it means. I've broken the code."

"Really?" Rusty asked, truly surprised.

"Yeah, it's simple. It's a warning. Something big is going to happen next Wednesday night."

Rusty cocked a perplexed brow. "Why do you say?" She was veritably intrigued.

Ma chuckled confidently. "I'm not a novice at this type of thing, you know."

"Oh, I know. But how did you…"

"The crescent moon with the arrow through it, it's a date. The next crescent moon on the calendar is next Wednesday night. I think they're going to burn a church."

"Why do you think that, Ma? That's crazy…"

"The fire over the halo, dear, it's obvious."

"Oh. I see. It wasn't obvious to me."

Ma quickly stood. "I've got to get going on my kitchen work. Stay out of churches until Thursday." She walked inside, leaving Rusty alone on the porch.

Rusty chuckled to herself while rising to her feet. She lumbered across the yard, laughing aloud while at the same time, impressed with Ma's reasoning. She pulled open the barn door and caught a glimpse of the new vulture, more menacing and evil than the original.

"Ma has it all figured out," she told J. R.

He stood quickly, flipping back his welding shield. His face was flushed with disappointment. "She does?"

"She *thinks* she does. Can you have this thing ready by Wednesday?"

J. R. looked down at the beast, staring deep into its ball-baring eyeball. "Easily."

"That's the night we need to take it out."

The following Thursday morning, Rusty was awakened an hour before sunrise.

"Wake up," Ma whispered as she jabbed her shoulder with a stiff finger. "It happened again."

Rusty cracked an eye, squinting in the early morning light at her mother's toothy grin. The world was bathed in a warm shade of violet. Ma seemed luminous in its glow.

"There's another one of them damned metal birds," Ma told her, hoping her excitement would be contagious. "Wake up, we can go look at it if we hurry up."

"I was up late, Ma…" Rusty muttered, and then caught herself before giving up too much information. "Couldn't sleep."

"I already woke up your brother," Ma said before making a noisy exit into the hallway. "Now get up."

The discovery of the second Iron Vulture was made by Hubert Nelson, the city parks maintenance engineer. The day had started like any other, with a routine so practiced and rehearsed that each day seemed a copy of the previous one. At exactly twenty minutes after five in the morning he arrived at the baseball fields to start the sprinkler system in preparation for the evening games. To his bewilderment, he was not alone. A hideous beast of partially rusted steel towered over the pitcher's mound, staring into the darkened sky with enormous outstretched wings. He cautiously stepped backward from the monster, retreating to his old Ford truck. He notified the authorities at once.

THE IRON VULTURE RETURNS read the headline of the newspaper.

Rusty read through the lengthy and paranoid newspaper editorials as Ma raced her two children to the site.

"I can't believe how this town is reacting to all this," Rusty said as she threw the newspaper on the floorboard.

"You can't?" J. R. jeered. "We're talking about Olney here, sis."

"The paper is full of hysterical letters to the editor—"

"Look at this," Ma interrupted as they rounded the corner to the baseball diamond.

The dirt parking lot was full, and the field itself was littered with onlookers. It was a major event, like a livestock show or a hog roast.

"I can't believe this," J. R. murmured in monotone. "My fifteen minutes…"

Ma steered anxiously to the nearest parking spot, waving at old familiar faces as she passed. Each person present was vertiginous with excitement, overwhelmed with the thrill of mystery and intrigue. They found themselves participants, yet safely at a distance from harm's way. Of course, there were those who had written lengthy letters to the editor warning of the apocalypse, but the vast assembly at the diamond that morning was none of the like. It was the next best thing to a traveling carnival.

Ma led her two burly children through the crowds. Whispers circulated, each a question posed to the listener and themselves alike. To understand this phenomenon," one said to another, "to find its meaning, is to find it in ourselves." Their individual interpretations mirrored their own hopes and fears. Never before had Rusty heard such deep and introspective conversations in the town of Olney. All because of some randomly placed scraps of metal.

Ma carved a path to the pitcher's mound where the sinister abomination seemed to be screeching at the rising summer sun. Children surrounded it, climbed on it while fancying all its movable parts. Eager mothers snapped pictures with disposable cameras—photographs for grandma's fridge.

Ma leaned over to Rusty and dispelled her first discovery, "An upside down cross." She pointed to the engraving on the beast's chest. "I was hoping there'd be more of a riddle."

"Maybe they weren't clever enough to come up with any clues," Rusty suggested. "I'm sure they tried."

"Hmph," Ma grumbled.

"Maybe you aren't looking close enough," J. R. threw in, clearly disappointed. "What are those markings on either side of the cross?"

"I can't really see," Ma said as she squinted in the harsh morning sunlight. "Oh, yes. It's a gavel. Or a flyswatter. And the other side, it's a house." She pressed her lips tightly together as her two children watched her intently for her conclusion. "That's easy."

"Really?" J. R. asked, discouraged.

"They're burning down the courthouse."

Rusty blew a sigh of relief as J. R. chuckled to himself.

"I was right about the day, wasn't I?" Ma asked as they retreated back to the car, leaving the hordes of onlookers. "I said something would happen Wednesday night, and it did. I'm a sleuth, kids. You don't give your ol' Ma enough credit." She thought a moment as she dug through her purse for her cigarettes. "You know what, though…this could also mean that the Satanists are actually…Judge Pinkerton and Mayor Windell. Dear Lord…"

In the days to come, the editorials were rampant with speculation. A supplemental page had to be added to the circulation just to accommodate the volume of mail on the subject of Satan. Rusty meticulously composed a letter to the editor, informing readers that the third and final Messenger of Satan would soon arrive. The editorial claimed that the Messenger would open the gates of hell in Olney. The Order would be exposed in all its glory. Names would be named. The secrecy would end. The days of communal serenity would soon be of the past. Doom would befall the people of Olney…

The night of the final delivery, Rusty sat up with Ma, waiting for her to retire to bed. For the first time in years, the crossword puzzles were closed. She sat quietly in the deep leather recliner where she composed her thousand-piece puzzles on card tables. Her calloused fingers raised and lowered newspaper clippings to her thick bifocals. Her lips were tense, her brow slumped, her eyes tired though terse.

"Ma, shouldn't you be going to bed?" Rusty asked. "You look really tired."

"I'm not tired."

"You need to give it a rest, you've become obsessed with all this," Rusty insisted.

"You kids seem far less concerned about how I spend my time when I'm putting puzzles together or working on crosswords. Besides, I've figured this out," she confessed boldly as Rusty perked up attentively. "I'm just admiring the work they did on these damned birds—hideous creatures, nothing I'd want on my lawn, but well made. The *Order of Satanists* are pretty handy with the welder." She removed her bifocals and rubbed her eyes with white knuckles. "I want to see the last bird. It must be a doozy."

"Well, they say it's coming—"

"No, I want to go out to the barn to see it. You kids act like I crawled from a cave just yesterday, as if I haven't spent the past two decades raising you hoodlums, being the straight guy in all your shenanigans. Order of Satanists, pshaw! You kids…"

Rusty was suddenly distraught, though equally excited. "How did you know?"

"It wasn't in the clues, it was in the *style*. Like I said, after twenty years…if it looks like a duck, and sounds like a duck…it's probably one of my kids in a damned duck suit."

Rusty smiled proudly. "I knew you'd solve it."

"You don't give your old Ma enough credit! Now, let's see that last bird." She stood from her comfortable chair and walked with her daughter to the screen door. "You're taking it to the courthouse lawn tonight, aren't you?"

"After you go to sleep," Rusty admitted as they walked out onto the porch together. "But now that you know, we probably won't. You were so excited about all this, that's why we kept it up. We never intended all this to be so big."

Ma stopped at the top of the old wooden steps of the porch and gave her daughter a stern glare. "You're taking that thing down there. I insist. I'd like to think if I taught you anything, it's to follow through with things…no matter how bizarre. Otherwise, you'll leave everyone hanging."

Rusty looked up at her, solid as a statue. "Come on," she beckoned lightly. "Come see it. It's the best one yet."

"This must remain a secret," Ma demanded as they crept across the thick green lawn smothered in dim moonlight. The cicadas screeched all around them. "No one is to ever know."

"No one wants to know, really," Rusty told her. Sparks could be seen flashing through the barn's open loft like the machinations of Victor Frankenstein. "They want a secret Satanist society to worry about, not pranksters."

Ma edged closer to the barn door with the eagerness of a child. She reached out to the cold metal door handle and gripped it firmly with anticipation. "Will it give me nightmares?"

"No more than anything else we've done before."

Ma took a moment to face her daughter with a smile that she tried to contain. Her desired expression was one of authority, which her voice tried to convey despite her countenance. "There's going to come a point to where you kids need to act like adults. You keep me on my toes, child. Both of you." She shook her head and smiled lightly. "There's never a dull moment around here…let's see this thing." She pulled the door open, bringing a dusty wall of light upon them.

J. R. was working on minor details in the trim, unaware that his space was now shared. The "Messenger of Satan" had taken over a week to create, a work of art in its own right—an iron nest with a vicious mother vulture feeding on its own young.

"Lord have mercy," Ma groaned aloud.

J. R. disengaged the weld and quickly threw back his welder's shield. His face was awash with disappointment. "Ma, what are you doing in here?"

"She figured it out," Rusty boasted on her behalf. "She knows."

Ma tiptoed across the dusty stone floor to the beast's nest. She circled it slowly, examining each subtle detail.

"Well...what do you think?" he asked her.

Ma shrugged her shoulders and smiled. "It's horrid, absolutely evil. But also a very fine work of art, son." She looked him square in the eyes and said, "I'm helping you take it to the courthouse."

"What?!" he protested. "No way—hell no."

"You act as though this will be a dangerous mission," Ma told him lightly with a slight twinkle in her eye. "Let's get it going, I have a busy day tomorrow."

"It rolls," Rusty told her. "We won't need to lift it."

"Is this truly the last one?" Ma asked with a subtle threat.

"Yes," Rusty assured her.

"Good. Okay, what are we waiting for? Let's move it."

J. R. folded his arms and shook his head. He could not believe it had become a family affair.

"Bring up the truck, then, Ma," Rusty instructed as she stepped behind the nest and started wheeling it to the doors.

It loaded just as conveniently as they had speculated, and when covered with an old military tarp, it was perfectly inconspicuous.

Downtown Olney was perfectly inactive, a ghost town by any definition. Ma sat nervously behind the wheel of the parked getaway truck, scanning the empty streets for witnesses while Rusty and J. R. rolled the nest off the trailer and along the sidewalk to its destination. J. R. had loaded two sheets of plywood into the back of the truck so they could wheel it off the sidewalk and onto the lawn. The process was slow, pushing it over the flat surface of one sheet of plywood onto the other, and then moving the back sheet to the front and so on. When they had decided on the best location for it, they pulled the plywood from underneath it, leaving it on the grass with no clear trail to indicate how it had arrived at its destination.

The Iron Vultures were the biggest attraction in all Richland County that summer. People from as far away as Effingham and Vicennes came to see the Olney Vultures. Old man Wooley carved miniature wooden replicas for sale, while Harriett Stark's old secret chilidog recipe was renamed *Vulture Dogs* and sold from a folding table covered in gingham. Any connotation with Satanism was quickly dismissed for favorable tourism to boost the dry summer economy. The identity of the culprits was never discovered, which aided the mystique.

Eventually the metal birds were placed in winter storage where they would remain, forgotten within two years by the fickle residents of Olney.

8:23pm

"What's going on?"

Jobie looked up from the crisscrossing bricks that surrounded him on the Sunset Pier. His flammables and face-paint were at his side. He counted his earnings for the evening, which would be the last for quite a while. People were slowly beginning to clear away, leaving him alone with only the usual vagabonds that crowded the shores late at night.

"Not much," he said, acknowledging a familiar face. "About to leave."

She had been on the streets long before he had arrived in Key West. She was a cute little runaway from Boston. She had taken a fancy with him, sometimes luring him with the prospect of beer and late-night company. He never got her name, and never really cared to, although he was not against her other offers from time to time.

"Can I help you with all this?" she asked politely, bending down to offer a hand.

He quickly pulled his tip jar into his ribcage and shot her a furious scowl. "Don't touch my stuff!"

She backed off apprehensively, yet grinning with lust. She found him as strange as he was alluring.

"I was hoping you'd maybe want to come by later..." she mumbled as she flipped her ratty brown hair over her shoulder. When she did, the stench of her sweaty armpits filled the ocean air that surrounded her. "We could drink a few. What say?"

He gathered his belongings and stood up to her, still not eye to eye with her. He looked up her nose with a forceful glare. "Not tonight."

"Well," she continued, following him alongside the cigar factory walls, "how about tomorrow?"

He looked her up and down, unsure what to say.

"My place or yours?" she joked.

He glanced over her shoulder at *her place*—the Sunset Pier. It was as good as any to drink.

"Maybe," he told her bluntly as he continued walking, "I'll let you know."

192

Wednesday, September 8, 1999
10:10pm

A single cinnamon-scented candle radiated from the peak of stacked red milk crates, illuminating the tiny decrepit wooden shed. The candle had succumbed to tropical heat over time with its slender shaft melted into a disproportionate curlicue, burning limply at an angle. The harsh light of the summer sun seeped through the shed's shanty framework, held intact with rusted nails and layers of white paint, peeling from neglect.

A shrine of rocks labeled with the names of states was displayed inside the lid of a shoebox atop a stack of milk crates. On lower tiers of milk crates rested a jar of red M&Ms that he deemed poisonous, and a small container of very few marbles that equaled the estimated number of years left in his life. Empty beer cans cluttered the dirty floor. An adjoining stack of milk crates contained toiletries for his infrequent hygienic practices. The air inside the shack was thick with the odor of grime and decay.

Jobie ran his ruby-colored fingers down the back of his quiet bed partner. Sweat dripped down his temples to the razor stubble that covered his tense jawbone. The black cobweb tattoos that spanned his hollow cheeks had recently been professionally retouched and shaded. They were a perfect contrast to his vibrantly red skin. He scratched his scalp with his chipped black fingernails while wiping the sweat from his greasy orange hair.

In his lap was his journal of anarchistic viewpoints, his reason for living, *The Apolitical Manifesto*. Papers of various sizes spilled from the cheap cardboard binder, each dictated from a train of thought as they arose, wherever they arose. His inspiration had an uncanny sense of untimeliness, pushing the bounds of his resourcefulness. Some notes were scratched on napkins while others were written across leaves once green, now a crispy brown. Someday he would neatly transcribe all his notes into a single readable manuscript with solid thought processes and a focused initiative for order. Or disorder.

He paused a moment to relax his hand and recap his writing. On the top line of the notebook paper in bold black letters were the words *Enemies of Progress*, a new installment in his body of work and a new direction of focus. Those who had made the list so far were lined up in a column, each addressed with its crime against humanity.

The Maxx shoe corporation had made the list for depending solely on third world countries to make their products at slave labor wages. Working against the good of mankind in order to make a higher profit margin on an already profitable product.

The Perico Food Corporation earned their rank with the deforestation of innumerable acres of Amazon rainforest to raise cattle ranches. Villages were destroyed, thousands of species of plant and animal life driven to extinction. All for the profit of a handful of people.

The Happy Camper Hardware stores were notorious for opening chains in small communities with the sole purpose of owning a regional monopoly, all the while brandishing nationalistic advertisements to fever any well-earned misgivings of the general public.

GenetiTech with all their genetic research on everything from stem cells to modified crops.

The Sentinal Trading Group, a secretive operation purportedly headquartered in Israel, consisting of an established American family immersed in both politics and oil, and a Saudi Arabian family with unparalleled wealth in the buildings trade. With unscrupulous dealings in the highest levels of global economics and represented by the villainous World Trade Organization, Jobie equated them to global cancer. The type of illness that can devour its host and suck the life from it without ever making its presence known.

Only one name on the list was a single person, a one-man brigade of hatred—Reverend Strickland. Or as Jobie endearingly referred to as *The Stickler*.

Reverend Strickland was a relatively obscure name in mass media, but Jobie considered his entourage a growing national threat. His army of minions maintained a vastly circulated newsletter that clearly laid out its intentions of a second Civil War within the United States. His campaigns and protests of homosexual activities in the country had made him a favorite on daytime talk shows, earning him notoriety, credibility, and a sizable income that funded his lesser-known operations—the preparations for the coming Racial Holy War.

Enemies of Progress

The root of subordination is fear. Christians have practiced this form of terrorism for years, watering down the gospel with revisions designed to terrorize the masses into submission. Rewritten for the human agenda, much as history has been. In 1933, the German Parliament was burned to the ground by an unknown arsonist. Less than a month later, fear provoked the Parliament to grant Hitler's wish to pass the "Enabling Act" which was the springboard for Hitler's dictatorship. Books were burned, guns were confiscated. History would point the finger at Goering as the arsonist—terrorism to gain power as the motive. In ancient times, Nero burned Rome, blamed his enemies, and became the dictator. It is only a matter of time before the United States will fall under a deplorable terrorist attack. The finger will be pointed at a known enemy, a scapegoat to set the wheels in motion. Enabling Acts, under the guise of patriotic acts, will be instated to preserve security and "rid" the nation of the terrorism that was in reality schemed secretly on our shores against our own citizens. We will become accustomed to seeing armed soldiers occupying our streets, offering the safety we will undoubtedly sacrifice for security. Anyone brave enough to come forward with the truth will be persecuted for speaking the unthinkable, that our trusted leaders

194

could be responsible for such atrocities. That is why the Enemies of Progress must be taken out before they are capable of taking power.

"Must be taken out," he grumbled under his breath, his voice shaking with passion.

A rustling noise outdoors stirred in the silence, the stealthy movements of the neighborhood alley cats. Quicker than he could decipher their harmless movements, his senses came alive with crippling fear. His heart pounded inside his chest as adrenaline shot through his thin body. He tried to calm his irregular breathing. A panic attack, nothing more, no harm, no threat, he told himself over and over. No harm, no threat. He sat in the silent little shack with wide eyes that just as well looked down the barrel of a gun. He did not fear death, not in the way he feared the panic attacks.

No harm, no threat.

He scowled at the names of evildoers as he slammed shut *The Apolitical Manifesto* and blew out the candle. In the darkness of his living quarters he kissed his silent lover with quivering lips on the nape of her neck as he snuggled closely against her body. His own shook with unnatural fear.

11:03pm

Smitty's breath was like that of a dragon, so fueled with the burn of alcohol that Rusty felt she could get drunk by simply breathing the same air. Sweat covered her naked body—not her sweat, but his, descending from his large naked body that pounded on her like a drill. A small, ineffective drill. She placed her arms around his neck, feeling the clenching of his muscles as he penetrated her, claiming her as a conquest just as she claimed him as the next best thing to love. Underneath him she felt pretty and loveable.

In the other room, her new friends laughed, reminiscing meager triumphs over the edgy and proud songs of Cock Sparrer. She could hear them joking about Smitty's beer goggles, but she did not care. She refused to allow the truth to detract from the moment.

Her labia had grown numb from the friction, but she was there by choice. She had spent the entire evening steering the events to this moment, as she had done several times since her arrival in Florida. She felt a bit of shame when she thought how much money she had spent on beer that she had not even drank. It all went to Smitty, just as she had planned.

As she reached up to kiss him, he moved his head away and gruffly slurred an unintelligible protest. She put her head down on the pillow and watched his face, the determination in his closed eyes, and the tension of his lips. She wondered who he was thinking of, what was her name, how did she look?

His hands clutched the sheets as he climaxed inside her. He rolled off her quickly, acquiring his clothes without saying a word as he left her in silence, alone.

She closed her eyes and imagined him lying next to her, loving her. His juices filled her, seeking the egg that she desperately hoped they would never find. She felt angry with herself for not being prepared, for not using protection, but she was caught in the moment, lost in the dream of being someone's entire reason for living.

In a distant field in rural Illinois, her mother watched out her kitchen window in the darkness, hoping that her daughter was having the time of her life in the Florida Keys.

11:13pm

The world outside was frozen, as far as Josephine could tell. She crept the blankets up to her chin as she stared into the faint reflection of artificial light cast upon the walls. Her room had become a cave in the silent darkness, though strangely comforting. There were no words to be heard, no cars, and no reason to believe another soul existed. Only the palm trees rustling in the calm oceanic breeze.

Her future seemed to exist in an abstract haze of confusion. More than anything, she wanted control of her destiny. First item of business was to find a place to live. Suspicion would soon be raised about her extended stay at the inn. She had evaded skepticism of the staff by planning her stay two days in advance. Prepaying the first week with traveler's checks, she secured the room without a second consideration. But each day stripped away at her cover. There was nothing more frightening. The lure of independence dangled before her, tipping the scales toward optimism.

She opened the pack of cigarettes and placed one between her full lips. She struck a match and lit the cigarette, her third one of the day. The nicotine seemed to calm her nerves better than anything else she could imagine. She closed her eyes and let her mind wander through recollection as her tense lips tightly held the cigarette. A birthday party, video games at the arcade, skipping rope, a bubble bath, awkward sexual encounters…and the shatter of trust in Shasta. Looking back, Josephine laughed at the futility of it all.

She visualized the moment once again, staring out the window late at night, her hair in rollers, her tiny body draped in a pink nightgown. On the porch, covered in sweat and shadows were Shasta and Timmy. Their lips were locked and their hands were free and natural with one another. The moment lacked discomfort—this was not an isolated occasion. In that moment she remembered herself seething with rage, overwhelmed with betrayal. In that moment she hated Shasta. The temptress, the wrecker of trust. That one kiss had capsized their collective youth and innocence. Things would never be the same.

Time had diminished the intensity, and Josephine laughed aloud, filling the void of silence in her empty world. In retrospect, she actually wished that the moment had endured, that they could have found the will to stay together and become lovers. Instead, they drifted over the course of the next two years.

Josephine smiled at the thought of what could have been. Timmy would still be alive, she was certain.

She took a deep drag from the cigarette before snubbing it out in the ashtray. She forced herself to reflect on the more favorable memories. One very odd and random memory immediately came to mind involving Timmy's old dog Boomer. He had been taken to the vet for an apparent discomfort in his hind region.

"It's an infection," the vet told him. "Yeah...these glands need to be emptied...it's the anal sacks, just like I thought."

Timmy suddenly became alert, feeling pressured into some sort of sick confession. "Anal sex? That's what's wrong with him?"

"Yeah," the vet responded calmly. "Anal sacks. He's full of fluid, poor little guy. It happens, it's really not that unusual. Definitely not something that will cause any permanent damage."

Timmy appeared awestruck. He seemed openly shocked at the vet's deadpan attitude toward such an atrocity. It was as if he was to be convinced that this type of thing was normal. It was difficult to imagine what type of heathen would be the perpetrator. The thought clearly repulsed him.

Later that evening he broke the news to Josephine that something very sinister was going on with Boomer late at night when everyone else was asleep. Alone in the yard, hiding in his doghouse from some sicko—they both agreed that Boomer would become an indoor dog from that day forward. It took years for them to realize the misunderstanding. By that time, Boomer had already met his maker by natural causes.

Josephine smiled to herself as she rolled over and fell fast asleep.

Thursday, September 9, 1999
10:48pm

Josephine relaxed her slender arm out the passenger window of Jobie's Plymouth Fury, allowing the warm ocean air to crawl the length of her smooth ebony skin. The sleek black car coasted through the hub of Key West, chasing a trail of artificial light and sound through a virtual ant farm of tourism and no-repeat business. She had never experienced service as poor as she had found in Florida, specifically on Duval Street. It made no difference to the staff or the storeowners—a new face would replace the dissatisfied customer in a matter of minutes. Like so much cattle.

She found it unusually comforting to be immersed in such a homogenous atmosphere. The absence of black culture along the busy thoroughfare actually put her frazzled mind at ease. She dreaded the thought of spotting a familiar face from Venice. Such an interaction could potentially trigger catastrophic consequences.

The Fury's rancid odor forced her to hold her breath at each stoplight. Its cushioned seats smelled like rotten meat. She immediately opened a pack of cigarettes to combat the repulsive stench of decay. "Care if I smoke?"

Jobie shrugged his shoulders with a simple, yet admissive nod. His limp wrist dangled casually over the fur-covered steering wheel as he squinted through his dark sunglasses into the nocturnal surroundings. His cobweb tattoos seemed to connect the cheap sunglasses to his gaunt cheekbones.

She offered him a cigarette before striking a match. "Do you smoke?"

"No."

"This is a smooth ride." She lit her cigarette and tossed the smoldering match out the window. "Where did you get it?"

"Austin," he responded with intentional ambiguity.

She blew a breath of smoke into the warm, tropical air without a second thought of delving deeper into his statement. "To answer your question...Venice."

"What question?"

"You asked me last night where I was from. Venice, California."

"What brought you here?"

She sat in silence with slumped shoulders, taking a long hearty drag from her cigarette. "Can we talk about anything else? Like, anything *but* that?"

He removed his sunglasses and gingerly placed them on the floorboard. He then turned the Fury onto Truman Avenue. "Seems we're at a stalemate."

"Huh?" Her thinly striped eyebrows creased inward as she scanned the bright and busy street to understand his statement. "What do you mean?"

"We have nothing to share, obviously."

His abrasive earnestness made her unreasonably defensive. "Maybe not," she replied coldly.

He raised a single brow. Her sharpness of tone unsettled him in return, sparking his short temper. "I guess I should take you home, then."

She took a quick and final drag off the cigarette before mashing it into the ashtray. "You're asking too many personal questions that I am *not* ready to answer. Just…chill out, will you?"

"Are you telling me how to act?" he threatened lightly with a straight and rigid face.

She raised a firm and flat palm up to his face. Her lips were pinched tightly together, which made her speech strenuous and labored. "You can stop right there." Each word was clearly enunciated.

He released a shrill cackle of laughter with a playful nudge on the steering wheel. "Sassy! I like it!" His wildly erratic smile quickly melted away. "Okay…how old are you?"

"Eighteen," she replied deceitfully, adding a year to her life. She decided that at that moment and for many years to come she would be eighteen, so it wasn't a complete lie. "And you?"

"Nineteen," he replied truthfully as he turned toward the White Street Pier. He shoved his long, bony finger her direction out the passenger window to the modest buildings along White Street. "Cuban food, great place to eat if you want to get away from the overpriced tourist traps."

"I'll remember that."

"Any brothers or sisters?" he asked.

She suddenly burst into tears, shocking both of them. They sat together in awkward silence as she sobbed with a pathetic wailing lament.

He watched her out of his peripheral vision. His chest tightened as she covered her face from the world, her fingers clutching her temples fiercely. Her black braids trickled over her shoulders like a veil.

"I'm okay." She exhaled passionately as she looked up, her eyes swelling with tears. The vast stretch of ocean was suddenly in front of her, black and seemingly distant, though she could taste it in the air. Salty, organic, and alive. She sighed slowly and repeated, "I'm okay."

"We couldn't be doing this on the west coast," he told her as he idled the car to the side of the street. "It'd be far too cold at this hour."

She smiled. It was her thought as well. Suddenly this stranger seemed intimately closer. More than that, she realized at the moment he was all she had. A potential confidant, if anything else. "I thought you were from Texas?"

"No," he corrected her, "the car is from Texas, I'm from Puyallup, Washington. My brother lives in Austin."

"My brother died," she revealed boldly with a sniffle. "That's why I came here."

He gave her a moment of respectful silence as she sobbed into her hands.

"I understand perfectly what you are going through," he confessed. "When my girlfriend Treva died, I went to New Orleans and stayed there throughout the winter. I honestly don't remember much of it." He recounted his memories with discomfort. It made him happy to be where he was, but it would take years to recover from those days, he thought to himself. "I had to live in this car the entire time I was in the French Quarter. I eventually became desperate for money...I had to live outside the law to get by." He tightened his lips and squinted his eyes. "Treva was a junky, I wasn't going to go there. I kept clean, but I couldn't handle being without her. I would wake up at night in a cold sweat. I became convinced that the Masonic Temple was acting on behalf of the FBI. They wanted to get me. I saw them everywhere, all over the French Quarter, there was no safe place for me. I felt myself slipping more and more, seeing the Devil staring from the darkness, all the while losing touch with myself entirely."

"Were people really out to get you?" Her tears dried as she listened intently to his tale.

He shrugged his shoulders, still uncertain. "Late at night as I would return to the car from another night of hell, I would catch a glimpse of this face. Just when I wasn't looking, there it was, the Devil."

"The Devil?" she questioned.

"The Devil. His face was desperate, though my glimpses were rare, I would see his face and run in terror."

"I can imagine."

"One day I saw him. I looked into his eyes. I will never forget that face, that expression. Imagine the face of your worst nightmare, a maniac. The Devil himself. Now imagine the horror when you realized that you were staring into a plate glass window at yourself. A virtual stranger of pure evil. I've had a hard time adjusting to that identity."

She sat quietly as the ocean breeze lapped at the idle Fury.

"That face haunts me at night," he added grievously. "It hides in the recesses of my mind. It is *me*."

"What about the Masonic Temple?" she asked. "Do they follow you still?"

"Always." He turned a sharp left onto South Street. His demeanor suddenly lightened as they switched directions. "Do you want to see my mailbox?"

She smiled. "Sure."

He drove down Whitehead, past Hemingway's House, past the Lighthouse Museum. He pulled up to the curb next to a business called From The Ruins.

"See the gingerbread in the picket fence?" he asked.

She looked closely at the fence, at the way that it was cut and placed together. Before she could focus, the images of wine bottles and hearts emerged from the patterns like a negative.

"They did that for prohibition. It was a subtle way of letting people know that this was a speakeasy back in the day." He pointed to the enormous tree growing at the edge of a stone wall. "There is a tin can underneath a rock at the root of that tree. If you want to reach me, leave me a note there. Otherwise, you won't find me anywhere, even if you try. This is my only connection to the world."

"Doesn't look very...legit."

"I don't get a lot of mail," he admitted. "In fact, I've never gotten any before. And I don't live anywhere near here, either. But it's where I get mail, if I get any mail. Just remember, okay?"

"Sure. Why not a real mailbox, though?"

He veered back into traffic. "To my home? I haven't got a real home. It's an old shack."

"Is it a secret? If you have a bunch of weapons stashed away, or drugs...I know more about that stuff than you might think."

His expression was coy, yet devious. "Some things are best left unknown."

His hard lips broke slightly into a smile, the guilty pleasure of secrecy. "Have you had any Key Lime Pie yet?"

"Not yet." She chuckled under her breath, entertained by his curious nature.

"Well, you need to try some Blonde Giraffe pie," he insisted. "Want to try some?"

She smiled comfortably, feeling her troubles evaporate into the warm summer air.

11:31pm

Reverend Strickland peered down his knobby nose at his subservient comrades, bouncing his sights from one to the next, across the bar. Their alcohol consumption had been under strict scrutiny since their careless confrontation. His tendril fingers scratched his coarse beard with a scowl smeared across his face. His entourage was intended to be an example to back his message, and he despised the one they had set. He was ashamed to stand in their ranks. For the first time in many years, he was happy that his presence in public was met with minimal attention.

Modest and fickle applause trailed each lengthy song performed by the house band. They merged standard blues over reggae rhythms to cater to the region's demographics. Conversations in the smoky den swelled to compensate the volume of their performance.

Kinsman Kale tilted his head back, allowing the Guinness to flow down his scratchy throat as his eyes shifted between the house band and the busy traffic along Duval Street. His neck was marked with a swirl of bruises and minor scrapes from the attack. More irritating than his injuries was Strickland's skepticism of his description of the assailant. Red. Not sun burnt, but red. Rose red. He may as well have told him that he was accosted by Martians.

Brother John stared into an untouched bottle of beer. His white face was flushed from the burden of turning from predator to potential prey. He was edged with dread and discomfort, and his youthful vigor seemed to have vanished overnight. He raised his sights from the foam in his beer to Kinsman Kale's neck, and then to Brother Paul's burnt and hairless face. It could have been him, he reminded himself repeatedly. To make matters worse, he was convinced that retaliation was inevitable. As his anger disbursed into fear, his ideology on race and history crumbled along with it. He felt a stranger in his company, and it was a refreshing feeling. He could not wait to return home, to return to anonymity.

Kinsman Kale avoided any eye contact with Strickland. He was certain that his attacker would be at the protest, which would validate his outlandish claim. He peered out into the street where his rented Vespa sat curbside. A black Plymouth Fury was waiting at the stoplight, idling alongside his scooter. The light turned green and the Fury rolled into the intersection along with the rest of the traffic. He scowled at the slender ebony arm dangling from the passenger window, and though he did not immediately recognize her, the driver's appearance threw him into shock. The bottle of Guinness slipped from his hand, falling to the floor unbroken, spilling onto the stained floor. He jumped to his feet and pointed without saying a word. His firm and angular build had tightened into a defensive posture as he watched the Fury move further down Duval Street.

Strickland was stunned. Though the car was nearly clear from view, there was no mistaking the unusual skin tone of the driver. Being a self-proclaimed authority on race and heredity, he was at a loss. He had never seen anything like it before. He looked up at the Kinsman as he towered over them, his black attire creating a dark wall to the street beyond the bar. He was preparing to break into a wild sprint. The Reverend quickly grabbed his flight jacket, holding him in place.

"Listen to me, Kinsman," Strickland spoke articulately. "Stop and listen."

He turned with a vigilant scowl. His linear facial patterns were bending with anger. "Have you lost your mind? That's him!"

Strickland motioned his hand down to silence him. "Not until after the protest. Follow at a distance, and find out where he lives. We must be smart, calculated. Blind rage will do nothing but bring more trouble. Once we know how to find him, he is as good as dead."

Kinsman Kale's face contorted into a sinister smirk as he quickly bowed his head in compliance.

"Payback will be hell," Strickland said with a sneer.

The Kinsman placed his right hand over his heart. "Ra-Ho-Wa, Reverend."

The Reverend copied the gesture, adding, "Victory will be ours."

He raced to the curb in a flash of black clothing. He quickly mounted the Vespa and threaded through the dense traffic. Two blocks away he could see the Fury turn off Duval toward Simonton. He signaled to follow, turning down a quiet street that grew darker and quieter with each second. At the intersection he stopped and waited, scanning the street to find the Fury. As it turned the corner toward him, he steered into the shadows, allowing it to pass quietly down the street. He stepped off the Vespa and crept to the corner where he crouched behind a row of parked cars.

The black Fury sat by the curb in the distance. There was little movement inside the car. The brake lights blazed in the darkness, partially concealing the two in its glow. Then the passenger door opened. He could see her bidding farewell before walking across the street. She steadied a plate in her hand, seemingly containing a single piece of pie. The Fury swept onto Truman, mixing with traffic and vanishing from sight.

Kinsman Kale quickly returned to the scooter and rode down Simonton toward the scene they had just left. He passed slowly, watching Josephine enter a gate on the side street. He committed the name of the establishment to memory—The Merlinn Inn.

He smiled fiendishly all the way back to the company of his colleagues. They shared a toast over conversations of revenge.

Friday, September 10, 1999
3:13pm

Rusty strolled along Duval Street, window-shopping the displays of countless gift shops. She was discouraged with the lack of variation although she had grown to expect such a thing. For a land built on diversity and freedom of choice, she was always amazed how her countrymen were so drawn to banality. The faces of America passed her without a second glance, each of them thrill-seekers with no span of attention, soft to the touch. She looked out at a society burdened by political correctness, of self-proclaimed victims obsessed with the hardships of living in the safest land during the most prosperous and comfortable time in known history. She believed political correctness to be a form of social cancer, a modern McCarthyism. She held firmly to her belief in the significance of inequality. Equality, in her eyes, would be the pitfall of human evolution, the pure assimilation of mediocrity.

A blend of cultural backgrounds brought color to Duval's concrete landscape—Italian-Americans, Asian-Americans, Irish-Americans, African-Americans. She wondered what the United States would be like if there were only Americans. How unified and strong the nation would be if its citizens were to claim it without regard to a third or fourth generation that immigrated from a land and heritage they personally had never known.

As she looked out at the passersby, she was shocked to find a unique yet familiar face floating in the crowd. She gasped with sheer delight, practically choking on her own saliva. Her face stretched into a fanciful smile that put her prominent gums and overbite on display. She lumbered anxiously down the sidewalk, following the trail of young tourists who had noticed the same infamous oddity—Koz-Mo, the host of the cable television show *Far Out*.

She scurried up to the mob of fans with her heart racing wildly. She had never seen a celebrity in all her life. She dug through her few belongings, searching for a keepsake that could bare his signature. She found the perfect item in a postcard purchased minutes earlier for her mother. Like a ravenous bull, she plowed her way to the inner core of the gathering where people shoved papers in his tattooed face, begging for his signature or asking him to pose with them in a photograph. She held her postcard up over the crowd, shaking from an overwhelming sense of joy. She found herself drawn to the imperfections that would humanize him—his large ears, his yellow teeth, the trace acne scars

204

on his cheeks. She preferred the other Koz-Mo, the televised version with the biting wit, stylish clothing, and perfect lighting.

She heard a sinister whisper boil from the crowd. "Leeches." She looked to her side to trace the source. She found herself staring down onto a wickedly evil tattoo of a snake with malicious green eyes slithering over the top of a pale and shiny pate. The serpent's tongue split over a face of tight muscles and prominent bones. His skin seemed unnaturally stretched and fiendishly white. Black sunglasses covered his eyes, giving him the appearance of an insect. His build was lean and strong, efficient and streamlined. Tight satin clothes flattered his powerful physique. His aura tasted of salt and venom.

"Fans, Talon," Koz-Mo corrected his comrade over the ruckus of the crowd. Koz-Mo's smile was soft and sedate, as it so often was in the company of those enthralled by his presence. He lived for the inconveniencing requests and demands of strangers. He could scarcely imagine a time when it didn't mean the world to him. "You'll soon have them," he assured Talon.

Rusty's eyes widened. She contemplated getting this mysterious man's autograph as well, wondering if he was to be the next Big Thing somewhere for some reason. Just as the thought came to fruition, Talon spit out a growl of disdain. Rusty shuddered back as she watched Koz-Mo's smile diminish slightly.

"They don't see you," Talon hissed. "They see a cartoon."

Koz-Mo's eyes tightened, hardening his superficially smooth expression. The lines of his face naturally formed a grimace—lines of wear and tear that predated his fame. "Show business," he explained to Talon.

"You've sold your soul," Talon snarled with a voice as sturdy as concrete, though soft as smoke. "You've lost your edge."

Koz-Mo's smile disappeared altogether. It was a highly sensitive subject that had haunted him for years. His real identity, former class clown and High School wrestling champion Paul Jeffries existed only as a distant memory. He found it perplexing how the general public had grown to accept his bizarre form of shock entertainment with such open arms. At times he felt the Koz-Mo persona was perceived as nothing more than a modern Bozo the Clown. The most difficult part was the knowledge that it was his choice to back away from shock entertainment when it stopped being a financial necessity. It was his choice to cash in his act of physical endurance and pain tolerance to become a spokesperson for extreme sporting events. Years in the spotlight had turned him into an impressionist of his own design, a mere shadow of the edgy performer who had tirelessly carved his own unusual niche in the ever-elusive entertainment industry. There was no longer a need for struggle in his life. The comforts of success guided him toward a path of least resistance, with his confidence coming not through accomplishment, but rather from the complimentary words of strangers. He worshiped his fan's euphoric gaze—he was addicted to them. The pleasure was much more his than theirs, and it horrified him.

Rusty pushed her postcard into his face, begging that he autograph it for her mother. He signed it with a scowl, suddenly annoyed and short of patience. His signature, with the O's cleverly crossed like planetary rings, had become his trademark. It had never appeared so sticky sweet to him as it did at that moment. He winked passively and insincerely at her when he handed it back, causing the hair on her arm to rise at attention.

As the crowd expelled her like refuse, she coughed out a sheepish giggle while clutching the postcard tightly with both hands. She scanned the street for a mailbox, all the while speculating on the possibility of another unexpected encounter—one that would allow enough time and solitude to forge a meaningful relationship. She humored the idea of becoming his friend and trusted ally, of long phone conversations and Thanksgiving dinners at the farm.

Her mind ran wild with the possibilities.

9:38pm

Josephine sat in the center of her bed with crossed legs, sorting through a plastic bag filled with nail polish of varying shades, from blood red to raspberry cocoa. Contemplating a new day's nail color kept her mind off other, more pressing issues. Black corded braids rested on her clean and bare shoulders. Her thick lips were unusually relaxed, possibly from an unprecedented amount of nicotine in her bloodstream. Plumes of smoke clung to the wooden ceiling, the product of a pack of cigarettes that had quickly become a collection of butts in her glass ashtray. She lit her last one as she chose two potential color candidates. Savage Rose and Vintage Plum. Following a deep and slow drag, she dropped the Savage Rose back inside the plastic bag while shaking the Vintage Plum with her other hand. The noxious fumes of the polish mixed with the smoke to create a foul, but comforting odor to her.

She placed the cigarette on the edge of the overflowing ashtray before carefully painting each lengthy nail with a steady finesse. She could practically see her own reflection in its delicately dark sheen. As she admired her flawless work, she considered a career as a manicurist, though she was not entirely convinced she could handle a lifetime of such tedious labor. In any case, she was aware of the urgency in finding employment, whether Key West or another settlement yet to be discovered.

She found herself trapped by circumstance. She knew she had to become self-sufficient in order to survive, and yet the very realistic threat of the Mansfield Crips was constantly breathing down her thin neck. Then on the other hand, she knew that there existed the very strong possibility that they had no idea she was even present at the scene of the crime. For all they likely knew or even could have presumed, the money had been pocketed by the city's crooked police officers. One thing was certain—Shasta would know.

Josephine contemplated a quick phone call to her old childhood friend to end all the nerve-racking guesswork—or begin a new reign of terror. It had been years since she had spoken to Shasta. In fact, she had become a perfect stranger of the years, one that shared no resemblance to the little girl raised in the same backyard. It was quite a stretch from the gangster she eventually became. Josephine was not entirely sure she could even trust Shasta anymore. She knew firsthand what Shasta had endured to join their ranks. The abuse, the violent gang rape by the men she sought as loyal brethren. To Josephine it was a horror story, one she would never conceive putting herself through for any supposed allegiance. But as she grew older, she developed a better understanding. The process earned them respect, and it became their order, their pride, and their sense of being. It was better than any of their own broken homes. In many ways, it helped Timmy…until it killed him. By witnessing their choices firsthand with all the ramifications to follow, Josephine knew exactly how *not* to live her life.

Without warning, her body convulsed with a tremor of anxiety. She was suddenly struck once again by the fact that her only brother had actually perished in a shooting. Her heart raced inside her shallow ribcage, and she wondered how many times she would rediscover the gruesome fact before it simply became common knowledge. She felt vulnerable and cold and isolated from the living world. In a sense, she had died along with him. He had sheltered her from so much…and the money—the horribly tainted money scraped from so much misery and misfortune, it was poison. It was corrupt and cursed, and it was hers—overflowing from a black leather bag on the nightstand.

She felt compelled to call Shasta, to confess what had happened, to urge her to leave town and live on the stolen money until they could start new lives together. She desperately wanted a friend, a companion—someone to trust. Someone to care for her. She shook the thought immediately.

Shasta was now the enemy.

Josephine hugged her folded knees while squinting her eyes to combat the tears. She was immersed in a loneliness she could not have dared to comprehend in her youth. She felt defenseless and vulnerable to a vicious world she did not completely understand.

"Timmy," she whispered with a shaky voice, "please help me…send someone, anyone to *help me.*"

11:50pm

Jobie sat in his quiet quarters, surrounded by comforting darkness. He peered down at the page in the clutches of his red claws. The words were barely visible in the streaks of light cast from the cracks in the dilapidated shed. His old ballpoint pen raced across the page, a new entry into the growing volumes of *The Apolitical Manifesto*.

Commercialized Blindness
I am astray from the path of my fellow Americans. I do not seek the house with the picket fence, nor do I aspire to find power in the workforce. I live out of necessity rather than luxury. I own nothing, and therefore nothing owns me. I live by my own means. My will makes me strong. It is who I am, it is all I am. There is only myself. I see weakness in the eyes that steal my breath. They are junkies—addicts of their own flimsy will. Their need for the cosmetics of life is in constant evolution with the media telling them who and what they are, what they feel and what they should believe. The path they follow is owned by the pushers of their dependencies, yet they are blind. Triviality keeps them in motion. Pettiness keeps their attention away from the bigger picture. In their need for acceptance on their eternal quest for normalcy, they sacrifice the only thing they truly own—their identity.

Jobie closed *The Apolitical Manifesto* and pulled it tightly to his chest. To him, his writing was priceless, which principally made it so. He slowly fell back onto his makeshift bed, smiling in the shadows, scheming the details of the coming attack.

11:59pm

Austin, Texas

Didi could no longer feel the heat of the bathtub water. It looked like cranberry juice, thick and red. She shivered, freezing as the room's bright lights began to fade in and out. She tried to focus on the room, but she couldn't. Everything blurred. The towels on the floor, trailed with a stream of blood, were Talon's towels. She convinced herself that he would understand, he would appreciate how much she loved him.

Her body quivered in short spurts, freezing. Yet steam drifted across the hot, murky water.

She felt tired. Her head bobbed from fatigue. The cold should have kept her awake, but instead it pushed her toward sleep. She felt exhausted, drained. Her body was going numb, which helped against the strange sensation of frostbite that ravaged her body.

Light blurred, teasing her tenses. She felt thirsty. Painfully thirsty. She tried to open her eyes, to raise herself from the tub to quench the unbearable thirst. But she could not. She could not move. Panic overwhelmed her as she gasped for air. Her mind drifted, and she stopped breathing, stopped caring, and stopped fighting. The world faded. The blackness she had been fighting had released her spirit from the body she so desperately despised.

Her dead body sunk into the bloody water.

On the porcelain counter by the sink, resting on a pillow for Talon to find upon his return was the gift he had requested.

Her right hand.

Saturday, September 11, 1999
6:51pm

Rusty focused her attention on the name Jeremy Sands as she clinched her fists and stomped angrily down Duval Street. She had first met Jeremy Sands in kindergarten, though her strongest memories came less than a year later on the school playground. Jeremy's persistent badgering of her looks and size had turned into a trend that lasted beyond High School. Few people were as pivotal in her development as Jeremy Sands, and therefore he became one of the most important persons in her life—for all the wrong reasons. Her eternal hatred toward him was a perpetual source of negative inspiration, pure and raw.

She gnawed her crooked teeth and furled her brow with rage, unaware that the Gainesville Skins were following her lead, yet lacking her emotional charge. She visualized her mother's shoulder, her blouse wet with her tears of humiliation and self-defeat.

"Someday...you will make a difference," her mother tried to soothe her desperate sobbing. "You will help a lot of people...and he will have to eat his words."

She felt that day had arrived. Each step brought her closer to that destiny. She was certain that by nightfall, she would be a hero.

Reverend Strickland's ranting could be heard over a block away, even without a microphone. She rumbled across a busy intersection, catching her first glimpse of the protest with no more than two-dozen onlookers. A few Drag Queens stood out front of Diva's, mocking their cause and taking advantage of the opportunity to promote the "Queen of the Keys" pageant. Two police officers stood apathetically between the NRF and the few disinterested pedestrians.

Rusty felt her blood boiling as she visualized the distinct face of her own life's tormentors. In spirit they would be here with their fellow bigots, she resolved. Her trimmed nails indented the palms of her curled and tattooed fists. Each step gained thicker momentum and longer strides until her heavy gait had mutated into a heated jog. The salty oceanic air burned her lungs. Her breathing intensified with exhalations that seemed to explode with angry grunts. Her new enemies were a stone's throw away, closing the gap to redemption she had blindly sought for so many years.

A sect of racist skinheads known as HammerSkins stood guard over the Reverend, each with crossed arms and fixed militant expressions. A crowd buffered them, fencing them off from the world. Rusty had only seen Strickland in pictures, and was surprised at the discrepancies in her own mental image. He was much more frail than she would have assumed. Taller and thinner, with a thin head to match. His hair was receding and his dark little eyes screamed malice and envy of the world. His mouth moved invisibly behind a thick black goatee.

"...and this is why our country has fallen from grace with the Almighty, the downfall of the white man has been his tolerance..." he declared with enthusiasm.

She wanted him dead.

She slowly paced back and forth behind the crowd, scowling blankly into the ground as she listened to his speech with utter disdain. She prowled the perimeter of the spectators, contemplating her course of action. She felt a product of her own design, an iron vulture with a lascivious urge for destruction of ignorance. She was convinced she had found the perfect target. She was also convinced that Jeremy Sands could easily have grown up to be someone very much like Reverend Strickland. She took a moment to gather her breath and thoughts as she listened to his sermon of hate.

Standing beside the Reverend was a HammerSkin that looked like well-groomed roadkill. His face was hard and angled, his eyes nothing more than reflectors that concealed his thoughts with perfect precision. His stocky frame was clearly visible under a tight black Ben Sherman shirt and black jeans. The only color in his wardrobe was the red laces of his black Doc Martens boots and red braces that suspended his hard jeans. Tattoos of crucified skins, crossed hammers, and American flags ran the length of his forearms. His neck was thick and muscular with a row of bruises that circled his collar from an apparent strangulation attempt.

The two skinheads that flanked opposite sides appeared as clones of one another with their military fatigues and green flight jackets. Their black Doc Martens were new and shiny with white laces that signified their rank as "babyskins". The one on the right was completely hairless, as though his face had been waxed or burned. It added to the rigid composure he so desperately sought.

Rusty stood with crossed arms, watching them with a scrunched face when she suddenly realized that this event was it—the entire basis of her trip. Yet there she stood watching, doing nothing. The Gainesville Skins stood quietly at her side with stiff postures and angry snarls. She knew they had no further intentions other than making their presence known and possibly defending their honor, should the opportunity open itself readily. It became clear to her that the day would be an uneventful one, much like any other...unless she did something rash.

She charged without restraint, knocking down two unsuspecting tourists that were gawking at the absurdity of the demonstration—the type they thought only existed on daytime television. The police moved effortlessly to apprehend her, grabbing her burgundy flight jacket and dragging her away as she thrashed and screamed, "Die, Sands! Die!" The HammerSkins bravely stood their ground, watching the police protection at work. They were smiling. It was exactly what they had hoped for.

The officers pulled her against the wall and made firm warnings that amounted to nothing more than hollow threats. Their words drifted into the warm coastal breeze, never making it as far as her thick ears. She stared blankly at the meager crowd, feeling like a perfect failure. She bowed her head with humiliation, wishing she had never left home.

She watched curiosity seekers come and go, dedicating very little attention to the spectacle. A strange and pitiful vagabond drifted through the crowd under a makeshift cloak of old, tattered beach towels. It looked like a Halloween costume of a ghost gone terribly wrong. A bipolar gypsy wandering harmlessly toward the source of attention, she presumed.

"Have we made ourselves clear, ma'am?" one of the officers asked her as the other glared up her nostrils with a sour face.

She nodded her head indifferently as she watched a red claw reach out toward the NRF from beneath the piecemeal cloak, releasing a handful of fire like pixie dust. The flames seemed to drift to the concrete like autumn leaves, bringing forth an explosion of blinding white light that engulfed the unsuspecting protestors. A pillow of black smoke shrouded them in temporary darkness as the fires scattered harmlessly to their feet.

The disoriented officers rushed through the panicked crowd, pushing people aside only to find a scant puddle of flames carpeting the pavement. Reverend Strickland, though badly shaken, stood unscathed yet petrified with shock.

Rusty stepped forward from the wall, searching for the perpetrator.

7:12pm

It was the smell of turpentine that initially tipped off Kinsman Kale. Its fumes burned his nostrils, putting his senses on high alert. He quickly scanned the crowd, bouncing from face to face, searching for that perfect balance of cunning and forthrightness that could potentially spell danger. Complacent stares of disinterest surrounded him, each chuckling at the words fervently spoken by Reverend Strickland—the words that he believed in with all his heart.

Then he saw him. Beneath the discarded beach towels thinned from years of use, a mismatched quilt of browns and grays and spoiled whites. His strange attire had yielded the suspicion, but it was that quick glimpse of skin tone that gave him away. The color of a fire engine, and impossible to forget. Like a demon or an exotic bird's feathers, he appeared perfectly inhuman and unquestionably evil.

The bruised skin of Kale's neck seemed to flare at the sight of him. With the cops restraining a misled skinhead girl cursed with hideous genes, there would be no holding back his wrath. He waited patiently, watching the cloaked figure step to the front, unknowingly walking into a regretful mistake. He took a firm step forward to intercept the hooded bandit just as turpentine spilled from the sleeve of the cloak, dowsing the ground on which he stood. He did not see the match fall, only the blinding flame that scorched his vision and enveloped him in unbearable heat.

The fire retreated quickly to the concrete like a blanket of flames. It clung to their pant legs and danced in the fumes, eating away at the fabric of their jeans. Black smoke rose from the sidewalk. Kale stamped out the fire while gathering his thoughts into a quick and effective counter assault. Seeing that Reverend Strickland and his entourage were unharmed, he raced wildly down Duval Street in pursuit of the mysterious arsonist.

He strode with weightless steps, bounding his steel-toed boots in flight over the sidewalk, closing in quickly on his aggressor. He kept his sights locked on the tapestry of terrycloth as it threaded through pedestrians and around corners. Each step paced him closer and closer to vengeance.

He pursued Jobie across Simonton Street, so hot on his heels that he could smell him in all his putrid vileness. He swatted at him with his outstretched hand, all the while sprinting wildly in pursuit. He lurched forward and caught a fluttering strip of disheveled towel, reeling Jobie in like a fish on a line. The handmade cloak ripped from the tension, tripping both of them in a collision of unbridled ferocity. They skidded across the pavement, landing against the curb with Kinsman Kale pinning Jobie to the concrete like an insect. Kale cocked his powerful fist, preparing to strike—then his vision went black.

7:22pm

Jobie stared fearlessly from beneath the weight of his racist oppressor. He watched the fist pull back beyond Kale's shaved head, anticipating the impact that would tear his face like construction paper. Even if he had been given the chance to stand against him, the confrontation would have been brutal and short-lived, not in his favor. He could see the scars on Kale's squared head, evident even in his expansive pupils that calibrated the most efficient attack. He appeared to have been bred strictly for hand-to-hand combat.

The weight suddenly lifted, stripped away with a crackling thud that echoed through the somber neighborhood. Jobie raised his head, certain that the impact he heard was his own bones breaking from the first destructive blow.

He was mistaken.

He looked up to see that Kinsman Kale had been knocked onto the street, curled like a fetus under a shower of blows from a gigantic skinhead girl. Rusty. Jobie propped himself on his pointy elbows, dumbstruck by the sight of this stranger kicking and punching Kale until there was no more movement left in his thick and muscular body. She was seething with a blind and deadly rage that seemed to have no bounds.

"Bastard Sands," she gurgled angrily to herself during the bludgeoning.

Sirens echoed in the distance down Truman. The chaos of the fire's aftermath could still be heard nearby. It was only a matter of seconds before the authorities would be on their trail.

Jobie sprung to his feet and approached her quickly, though with caution. His foul odor peeled her attention away from Kale, sobering her angst. He tugged on her powerful arm, but there was no budging her.

"Come on!" he beckoned passionately, staring at her with his wildly fierce eyes. "I can help you get to cover." The remains of the cloak draped over his shoulders, hanging from his thin body like strips of flesh.

She stood in awe at the mess she had made of the Kinsman. It was the most violent act of her life, and it opened an overwhelming sense of liberation.

Kale coughed desperately, blowing spouts of blood onto his face like the eruption of a volcano. He was barely conscious.

Jobie yanked on her arm and growled with a tense sharpness, "I'm leaving…you can follow me to safety—if you want."

She looked beyond his strange appearance and into his fiendish eyes. They were as captivating as they were frightening. He was wise beyond his years, a byproduct of vagrancy, she presumed. He clearly was not a novice squatter. It saddened her to see the spark of compassion that unwittingly fueled his overbearing rage. She felt compelled to tame him, to show him a better way. His nerves were taut. She could see the blood pumping through the veins protruding from his temples.

As the sirens intensified in the distance, she stepped forward with unyielding trust. Her actions seemed surprising even to her, yet she felt completely sure of herself. It defied reason, but it was a comfortable defiance. She clasped his clammy hand and followed fate. They raced down the street as one, arriving quickly at a nearby inn. They stepped inside its front gate just moments before the ambulances raced to the aid of Kinsman Kale's severely beaten body.

Together they stood safely in the shade sharing hard and heavy breaths. She glanced uncomfortably at him, finally seeing him with post-adrenaline clarity. He was a ghastly sight, a savage and heinous monster from a living nightmare. His ghoulishly red skin seemed prematurely aged with creases, scars, and wrinkles. Despite its coloration, his skin seemed more fitting of a man twice his age. His clear blue eyes seemed rabid though strangely childish.

She questioned her judgment, but masked it behind an awkward smile. She looked up to see a modest blue swimming pool nestled in a quiet little garden. Trickling water could be heard from fountains, and the air smelled like a tropical jungle.

He looked up at her while nervously running his fingers through his short and messy orange hair. It seemed to blaze like a candle's wick. "Thanks." He kicked at the wood chips awkwardly, uncomfortably. He stuck out his hand and said, "My name is Jobie."

She sighed, feeling a resurgence of trust. "No problem. I'm Rusty." She shook his skeletal red hand and smiled as she added, "you look kind of rusty yourself...or *rusted.*" She hoped that there was a choice in his malevolent appearance. To her delight, he flashed a brief, though sincere smile that faded quicker than a breath.

"It's not contagious."

Her face fell flat. "I'm sorry...did I offend you? I just thought—"

"Offend me...I don't think so," he grumbled as he let loose her hand and walked further into the greenery.

She followed.

They passed between the trees and shrubbery, walking along the wood chip path. A pay phone to the left, the laundry rooms to the right...into a small courtyard with a hammock hemmed to two magnificent palm trees. A young black girl dozed with a calm and systematic snore, gently swaying with the calm breeze. She was wrapped only with a thick white bathrobe like an oversized straightjacket. A baby blue shower cap, puffy and thin like a parachute, covered her braided hair. Her properly manicured fingers were wedged in the center of a book that rested on her flat belly.

"Josephine," Jobie whispered in her ear.

Her eyes sprung open with sheer terror as every muscle in her body clenched. She was suddenly on the verge of tears with her breathing labored and short. Her panic dramatically receded at the sight of him. She placed a hand over her heart to calm herself. She began to speak, but her voice trailed into a muttering of confusion. Jobie's unusual attire sidetracked her attention, which she regarded with a sour expression of disapproval. She took a deep breath and snapped at him, "What the hell did you do that for?"

"Can you help me?" His tone of voice was more of a demand than a request. He pointed at Rusty's large tattooed hands. "She needs help."

Rusty raised her hands, shocked to find that her thick knuckles were covered with blood. Kale's blood.

Josephine was suddenly alarmed once again. "Was there an accident? Are you okay?"

215

Rusty nodded calmly. "I'm fine, ma'am. It's not what—"

"Can we use your bathroom?" Jobie barked.

"What happened?" Josephine inquired with a tart firmness that Jobie could not challenge.

"I just had another run-in with those guys," Jobie explained. He jarred his head toward Rusty as if pointing at her with his nose. "She saved me."

"What guys?" Josephine asked. Her eyebrows raised and her mouth formed a perfect O. "You mean *those* guys from the other night?"

Rusty stood at his side, speechless and confused.

"Yeah, those guys," he hissed. "Can we wait in your room until things cool down out there?"

Josephine swayed off the hammock, rising to her long and narrow bare feet. She looked up at Rusty, staring in awe.

"Damn!" Josephine belted out. "You are one tall woman, you know that?"

"I know that," Rusty replied coyly.

"That's cool," she assured her. "My room is messy, don't look at my underwear on the floor." She tiptoed across the wood chips and bounded up on the porch as she fumbled for her keys in the pocket of her bathrobe.

7:50pm

Jobie tinkered incessantly with the remote control, playing with it like a profligate child. He flipped from one channel to the next, criticizing the hairstyles and fashion of the actors and newscasters. His own tangerine hair was an uncontrollably frightful mess by comparison. The remains of his cloak looked like a peeling banana, revealing his weathered red skin. He eventually became bored with his own banter and shut off the television, placing the remote control at his side. He stretched out across the wooden floor and gazed around the room with irresolution. He was perfectly relaxed despite the fact that police officers were combing the neighborhood searching for him.

Josephine sat at the foot of the bed, painting her toenails. She had begun to question her decision to stow them inside her room. She was unaware at the time that they were the instigators of the confrontation, not the victims. She was now a partner in their crime, whether she liked it or not. Biting her own lip, she focused on her task at hand—painting her nails. The room was silent with only the sound of the shower running in the bathroom. She imagined Rusty using her soap and shampoo to wash away the blood of a man they had probably hospitalized. The thought of it enraged her enough to vocalize her brooding thoughts.

"What's the deal?" she demanded of Jobie.

He looked up at her, at the blue shower cap that blossomed over her head like a flower. He truly did not understand her question or the anger that backed it. "What?"

She rolled her eyes, and then moved her head from side to side with the accent of each word, "Who is in my shower, what really happened out there, and why did you bring your problems to my room, of all places?"

"I don't know who is in your shower," he responded shortly. "I just met her. I don't even remember her name." He paused a moment to escalate the tension. "Those skinheads that were going to carve you up, they were this close to doing that to me." He held his finger over his thumb to sell his case. A book of matches could have fit in the gap. "That girl in your shower came to my rescue."

Josephine raised a condescending brow. "Their plans of attacking helpless strangers sure do get foiled often, now don't they?" Her tone of disbelief was thick and venomous. "How is it that you seem to always be there?"

The water had shut off in the bathroom, bringing perfect silence between them.

He shrugged his shoulders and let out a deep sigh. "I thought I could depend on you now. I thought you would return the favor. I guess not."

She took a deep breath and leaned against a stack of pillows. "Look, Jobie," she began with a more reserved tone of voice. "This is all kind of...weird for me. Getting arrested in Key West really does not fit with my plans." She struggled to keep her voice down in the silence. "I should not even be in this town." Her eyes began to mist with tears. She stumbled for words that would explain her erratic behavior, but even she did not understand. She took a moment to sniffle back the tears before mumbling an apology. "I watched my brother die." Her uneven voice lowered into a raspy whisper. "I took some money. Dirty money—drug money...from a gang."

Jobie's eyes widened with the burden of such a revelation. Suddenly it was *him* second-guessing his involvement with her. But that was short-lived. The prospect of such perilous intrigue made him all the more interested in befriending her.

She wiped away her tears, careful not to streak her fresh nail polish. "I think I made a big mistake."

"No," Jobie protested, softening his voice to match hers. "This is exactly where you should be right now. Your brother would've wanted it this way." He looked up at her, finding a persistent stare that ravished his clumsy statement with hunger. He gave her a mischievous smile. "Lots of money?"

She nodded. "Oh yeah."

He laughed. "You did the right thing."

The bathroom door opened and Rusty walked out wearing the same bloodstained clothes. She lumbered inside the quiet room, killing all conversation while consuming their attention. Josephine was still astounded by

217

her enormous presence. She thought she had dated some stocky men in the past, but none could compare to the build of this woman. She looked like a lumberjack. In fact, she felt that it would appear perfectly ordinary for her to carry a sledgehammer over her shoulder in public to mock her massive proportion. She also believed such a thing would fit her personality as well.

Rusty plodded over to the corner and slid down the wall onto the floor. She stared into the wood grain with her shaved scalp shining in the soft light. Her wispy strawberry blond bangs dangled in curls over her shiny clean face. Her large hands sat limply on the hardwoods with her long fingers stretched out like thick tree branches. Old English letters claimed each knuckle of both hands, forming together the word *skinhead.*

Josephine scowled. She had not noticed it underneath the blood when she was awakened by their turmoil. She did not like the word and all its racist connotations.

"What do you plan to do now?" Josephine asked Jobie, her voice edged with hostility once again. She hoped to hear that they would soon be leaving.

Jobie looked up at her with his piercing eyes. "It's not safe for us to leave here right now."

"Thank you for this," Rusty said softly to Josephine. Her voice was warm with sincerity. "I understand that you're putting yourself on a limb for our well-being, and I truly appreciate it. My name is…well, my friends call me Rusty."

"I'm Josephine," she said with a forced smile. "In case you haven't caught his name, he's Jobie."

"We exchanged words briefly on the way here," Rusty said with a slight drawl. Her voice was serene and pleasant. "How did ya'll meet?"

"Boneheads jumped her," Jobie replied coarsely, pointing his gnarled finger at Josephine. "I just happened to be casing them on that particular night."

"He really helped me out," Josephine clarified.

"That's good to hear." Rusty shook her head with a smile that displayed all her crooked teeth, and even more gums.

"Aren't you a skinhead?" Josephine squinted at her with narrowed eyes. "I mean, the tattoos on your hands…"

Rusty looked up at her—the first time she had made eye contact—and cocked her head with confusion. "Don't you know skinheads ain't all bad? I mean, there are those guys that you met under unfavorable conditions, and then there are the *other* types of skinheads. I'm no racist, not me, no way. Not all skinheads are racist. In fact, the vast minority of skinheads are racist, not the other way around."

"Why be a skinhead then?" Josephine asked as she adjusted her shower cap. "There's a stigma that you'll never live down. Just seems pointless."

"There's a unity that you never live down, either," she responded plainly. "That's why."

"More of that brotherhood stuff—I've heard it before." Josephine began to lean back against the pillows, and then stopped. "Did you want a pillow?" Before she could get a response, she threw each of them their own. "Okay, I get it. You guys need a place to stay, don't you?"

Jobie nodded.

"It would suit us best," Rusty replied. "If you don't mind."

"You'll have to sleep on the floor," Josephine told them without remorse. "I know that won't be comfortable, but I refuse to share my bed with anyone."

"That's fine," Rusty complied. "Perfect. Thank you. I will have to return the favor sometime."

Jobie stretched himself over the cool hardwood floor with his colorful head lying comfortably on the pillow. The coolness of the room was something foreign to him. Within minutes he was deeply asleep, snoring loudly.

7:50am

Rusty opened her eyes slowly, squinting in the light of the morning sun. The blinds had been pulled closed the night before, but the warmth of a new day seemed to burst from the world hidden beyond.

She rolled over, her back sore from the sleeping arrangements. Jobie lay next to her snoring like a swine, blanketed in peace. Total peace. The room was full of it. The light had washed away all the concerns of the night before.

She extended herself upright with slow gestures, cautious to not arouse anyone's slumber. As she passed the bed on her way to the bathroom, she stopped in mid-stride. Josephine was strewn across the bed so comfortably that she seemed to have melded with the sheets. Her bathrobe was partially open, revealing a loose white shirt and skimpy underwear. Looking at her body, she could not help but feel envious. Her black skin looked soft and silky, and her limbs were so docile and petite, yet muscular and lean. Her full cheeks were like a baby's, and her lips were so dark and full. She wondered how nice they would feel against her own. She had never known herself to think lustful thoughts toward her own gender before, and she knew that it was not the type of thing she would ever choose to act upon. It was merely the admission of beauty. Josephine, with her soft and lengthy lashes and tiny little ears, was beautiful to her. More than beauty, she sensed her intelligence, even in sleep. A solid foundation—a young life budding with profound insight.

As she stood over her, she realized it was the closest she had ever been to a different race. She had defended the civil rights of her race, yet this was as close as she had ever personally been. She found it strangely exciting.

She tiptoed into the dark bathroom that was still sour from the acetone. Little hard cotton balls filled the sink, all with different colors of fingernail polish, ranging from bright red to a thick burgundy. She felt eagerness toward her new acquaintances, more than she had felt with the Gainesville Skins. With them she was constantly concerned about her image, not only as a skinhead, but as a human being. Her concerns were left at the door when she first walked into the room, washed away like blood down the drain.

When she returned from the bathroom, she noticed a pack of cigarettes freshly opened, and a book of matches on the bed stand. Acting on a wild and inexplicable impulse, she instigated her brother's old *match head in the cigarette* trick that her mother had so frequently fallen for. She returned to the floor with sheer delight, certain that her gag would be well received.

She could not wait to begin a new day, to share it with her new friends.

Monday, September 13, 1999
9:00am

Reverend Strickland dropped his bag at his feet, allowing Brother John to carry it to the car. Strickland kept close to his two bodyguards, Brother John and Brother Paul. His cautious eyes wandered the sticky moist street in front of the Artist's House inn. His thin and receding dark hair shifted with the soft ocean breeze as he trailed his comrades within arm's reach. He trained his sights for the color red, which was not difficult—skin tone was the core of every man, he had always figured. It was the first and last thing on his mind with any man he had ever met.

Heritage defines whom we are, not our life experiences, his writings told. In essence he viewed each person trapped in a shell, their fate forever dominated by genetics their ancestors developed to survive and conquer their surroundings. He was so far removed from the progress of evolution that his perception was no more pliant than the concrete that shielded him from a reality long since forgotten in society. He was perfectly incapable of understanding that the ancestry of all humankind had a hand in creating the vast privileges of the modern world that awarded his freedom to speak against it.

Strickland's head swiveled from side to side, checking his blind spots for Jobie. His tense lips were hidden in the thickness of his goatee. The biggest shock came when they reached their Ford Escort without incident. He imagined a bomb hidden inside, or a trap waiting unexpectedly down the road. He imagined his knobby nose centered in the sights of a rifle. Worst of all, he imagined none of this was true, that this ominous new nemesis did not care enough to even show up for one last confrontation.

Brother Paul opened the rear passenger door for Strickland as Brother John packed their bags inside the trunk. As Strickland slid into the safety of the backseat, he took a close look at the minor burns on Brother Paul's face. His brow furled with aggravation as he struggled with a peculiar emotional response of envy.

Brother John took the driver's seat once again as Brother Paul manned the front passenger seat. They left town just as they had arrived, in humdrum silence.

"What of Kinsman Kale?" Brother Paul asked after nearly an hour of exhaustive silence.

221

Strickland kept his gaze out the window, staring into the turquoise water that surrounded the Florida Keys. His face was awash with anguish that neither of them could understand. "His bills have already been claimed, probably family," he grunted without any real concern. "He can fly back to Atlanta when they release him."

"He never spoke of family," Brother Paul muttered to himself. "Other than us."

Brother John kept his eyes on the road. He chewed his gum as his scope on the world expanded beyond the confines of the bitterness so present in the Escort. He did not agree with their treatment of their most loyal member, Kinsman Kale. His heart went out to his comrade in the hospital bed, alone in Key West with his only known friends driving away, their superficial mission fulfilled. It was not how he envisioned the loyalty of brethren. Never again would he refer to another man as a *Brother* based solely on face value.

Strickland stared blankly out the backseat window, haunted by the fact that no one cared to hinder his group's departure. He felt like a common man. Like all the rest. He sunk into his seat, shuddering in the solitude of the Ford Escort as they continued down the stretch of highway, just another car on another highway. Equal. Like all the rest.

8:45pm

Koz-Mo stared unflinchingly at the tattoo needle as it hammered into his skin, bringing a brand new blue rocket ship to life. Tiny droplets of his blood accumulated like dew on the spacecraft's cylindrical hull. It appeared ready to burst like a bottle rocket on a collision course with a yellowish comet under his left armpit. Very little skin on his body remained untouched by needle and ink. He estimated three more years would completely cover his skin with cartoon space debris. Little by little, Paul Jeffries slid into the shadows, lost in space, and destroyed by Koz-Mo.

Two apprentices watched over the shoulder of the tattoo artist, eager to witness a new and rather insignificant addition to a celebrity's permanent physical portfolio. It was a high profile job, and only the best would do, despite the comical simplicity of the work itself. Koz-Mo chose the most renowned tattoo parlor in Key West, The Ink Spot. The appointment was made a week in advance. The staff was all present, eager to shake hands for pictures that would be added to the wall and preserved for years to come.

Talon stood unnoticed in the waiting room, looking at all the colorful flash of potential tattoos that would be taken to the grave by future senior citizens. They were the same works of art as in any tattoo shop in the Western

Hemisphere. Tribal designs, flags, eagles, unicorns, dolphins, naked women, and ancient or foreign symbols to personify some sort of belief or worldliness. The symbols themselves were usually so far removed from their origin that their function in history tended to be completely forgotten. Their new purpose became a promotion of individualism in an overpopulated world—a unique voice chosen from an array of drawings on a tattoo parlor's wall, each a potential calling card for the person to identify themselves. It's meaning would make no difference to anyone other than themselves—much like a personal lifelong inside joke.

Talon slowly moved onward to a display of photographs of in-house work featuring retouches, cover-ups, and complicated designs to demonstrate skill to potential clients. The contrasting colors of the fresh tattoos were so vibrant and glossy that they partially reflected the flashbulb in each shot. Specks of blood were still visible in each picture—except for one. One in particular that had caught his eye. One where the blood somehow perfectly matched the skin. The picture was of a touchup of black spider-webs spanning grotesquely hollow cheeks. An intricacy had transformed the old jailhouse style design with shading and blending that stretched from the subject's ears to his jawbone.

Talon ripped the photograph from the wall, examining it closer as he drifted back to Koz-Mo's shrine of stargazers. The weathered texture of the subject's red complexion was as disturbing as its inhuman coloration. It had a very sickly appearance. Though his memory was of a relatively healthy male with pasty white skin, he was absolutely certain that he knew the person. The eyes alone were unmistakable, and the tattoo was a dead giveaway.

He crept up to the mob that surrounded Koz-Mo and pushed the picture into the tattoo artist's face. "Who is this?"

The artist glanced briefly, hesitant to pull his attention away from the career-enhancing job at hand. He shrugged his shoulders. "Beats me."

Talon continued holding it up in his line of view, perfectly unwilling to accept his lackadaisical response. "When was this?"

"Look," the tattoo artist challenged him. "I have no—"

"He lives here," one of the apprentices interrupted. "Yeah, I see him around town. He's always up and down this street, you can't miss him."

Talon turned to the apprentice, redirecting his menacing prowess. His disruptive posturing demanded that she divulge everything she could. She recoiled defensively, though struggling to maintain her composure. It was a struggle she practiced daily in her line of work.

"Do you know him?" he hissed.

"No."

"When did you last see him?"

"Recently," she revealed. "Driving up and down the street in that car."

Talon's face became as hard as granite. "What car?"

"That old black car, he's always driving it around. That's where I see him the most. Just driving around."

Talon's seething anger conflicted with his excitement to finally avenge his beloved Phaedra. Although the evidence in the case pointed elsewhere, he was certain that this person was the one who had mutilated her dead body and stolen his car.

He would kill him.

"His name was Jobie, I remember that," the apprentice told him. "Do you know him?"

Talon stared at her, giving no indication. "Yes...yes. Jobie, it was. Where can I find him?"

She shrugged her shoulders apathetically, already losing interest as she returned her attention to the final touches of Koz-Mo's tattoo. "Hard to say where it is." She double-checked her camera, making sure the new film had been properly loaded. She would be devastated to not capture such a momentous event.

Talon stuffed the photograph into his pocket while retreating to the front door. He stepped into the open air where hordes of people strolled up and down Duval Street. The warm ocean breeze blew across his hard and expressionless face. He stood motionless underneath the artificial lights, glaring down the active thoroughfare. Those who passed along the busy sidewalk shot him a second glance, hesitating as they kept their distance from his naturally disarming presence.

He would find this man with the cardinal skin. He would find him and slowly dismember him, one appendage at a time.

8:50pm

Jobie's tiny hidden shack concealed a war of light and darkness. The flickering candlelight chased the shadows across deteriorating wooden walls while he scribbled his thoughts passionately in *The Apolitical Manifesto*. The modest domain was a labyrinth of upturned red milk crates that sent shadows of right angles crisscrossing through the barren dwelling, painting the walls with shadows like black crosses.

Or like a prison cell.

The remains of his dinner, a stack of half-eaten pancakes shaped like a crescent moon rested on a nearby milk crate at the foot of his makeshift bed. Pancakes were his delicacy, a nightly dish that was extremely affordable and required only an open flame. With fire being the tool of his trade, he had much to spare.

In the corner by the bed, blanketed in darkness, was a stack of shoeboxes that contained his earnings as a street performer. Each was overflowing dollar bills, stuffed beyond capacity. He was too frugal to tap into the savings, and rarely did. As he basked in his peasantry, his savings from tourist hospitality reached into the thousands, and grew nightly.

He kept his loot and keepsakes in a corner of the shed deemed sacred. He felt his money was safe there, guarded by the graces of good fortune and life. He called the corner *The Compass Needle* simply because if it were the head of an arrow, it would face directly north. North to life, south to death, he theorized. Where he lived, there was no south—not for those living on land. There was no way to go but north. North to life, south to death.

He slept with his head closest to *The Compass Needle*, facing the rickety wall of life—facing north.

A thin shadow danced across the sheet of notebook paper, following the lead of each furious pen stroke. His eyes tensed and widened as though speaking the words dictating silently to the page. His bright pupils stared intently at the soft blue lines that would soon carry his thoughts. His pupils seemed to explode with determination, as if his soul was a combustible swirling mass of heat and flame.

He paused to run his claw-like fingers across his red skin as he read the words he had just written.

> *War, What Is It Good For? Evolution.*
> *I have never lived in times of a full-blown war. My generation has been deprived of war's natural selection. I am not a proponent of violence, but a religious war is exactly what the world needs. Not through the draft. By choice. Any fool willing to take arms against another religious zealot for differences of opinion should die. They both deserve their fate, and the world will be a better place. Let the fanatics provoke Middle Eastern intervention. Let the gun-toting cretins join the United States military so that I will live in a brighter nation in their absence. Let their folly reveal their ignorance in future history books. Let war wipe out the ignorant that choose to partake of its futile cause. Let their lives be spent on cheaper prices at the gas pump. Thin the herd.*

Jobie smiled proudly to himself. He placed *The Apolitical Manifesto* on the edge of the bed and stood to stretch. His wiry frame twisted and quaked with the loosening of his frail musculature. He took a deep breath, inhaling the foul stench of his surroundings, as well as his own revolting odor. He looked over at the crescent shape of dry pancakes lying on the upturned milk crate.

It would be breakfast.

He reached down to blow out the candle, turning briefly away from *The Compass Needle* toward the south corner of the shed. *The Dry Fixins*, as he called it.

He blew out the candle, bringing a blanket of darkness over his devious grin.

Wednesday, September 15, 1999
8:14pm

Jobie stared up over his cards, contemplating his next move. By the rules of their game, not only was it his turn, he was obligated to reveal one personal item of information. He pulled a two of spades from his hand and placed it on the wooden table. Rusty and Josephine watched intently, though equally disarmed by his foul odor. His distinct stench tainted the clean, organic air of the Merlinn Inn's small courtyard.

"I prefer vanilla," he confessed. "Vanilla is not plain, you know. Everyone thinks it's plain. It's not."

"And..." Josephine grumbled.

"What?"

"That's it?" she protested as she rearranged her hand. "You really have no secrets to share? No skeletons in your closet?" Her glassy candy apple fingernails shimmered in the evening light. "Do you not get the objective of this game?"

"I think it actually says a *lot* about me," he argued. "When I eat hamburgers, I eat them only with mustard and pickles. Chinese food—chicken with broccoli. A lot of people throw in other things like those little corn on the cobs, or carrots and celery, but I don't need all that crap. I don't think more is better. Most people think more is better, but I don't. People also think that new is better, that something new is worth more than something old, no matter what it is. I don't think that way. That not only says something about me, it says *everything* about me. That's more about me than if I were to tell you that my first dog's name was Edgar, the first girl I kissed was named Frances, or that I masturbate daily—sometimes even more."

Josephine looked up from her cards suspiciously. "You do?"

He shrugged his frail shoulders casually. "Depends on how busy I am."

"Is that a lot?" Josephine asked with a guilty whisper. "That seems excessive."

"I don't think so," Rusty replied. "But I grew up on a dairy farm, and there wasn't a whole lot to do."

"You too?" Josephine gasped with wide eyes.

"Me too what?"

"You masturbate that often?"

"Did I say I did?" Rusty returned defensively. "Go—it's your turn."

Josephine raised her brow, fishing through her hand to choose a card to play. She laid down a three of diamonds and said, "I'm into firemen. Now, I don't have the hormones you both seem to have, but if I was to do such a thing..."

"Masturbate," Jobie said, filling in her shameful thought.

"Right," she agreed, picking up where she left off, "a fireman would rescue my ass every damn night. That's my fantasy, to be rescued by the fireman. Don't even get me started. Go, Rusty, it's your turn now..." She opened her pack of cigarettes and anxiously prepared her match.

Rusty watched her light the cigarette, hoping it was one that she had sabotaged with the match head. "You really should quit smoking. It's a dirty habit."

"You mind your own stuff, now, don't be up my ass like that," Josephine said as she took the first hearty drag. It was not the trick cigarette, to Rusty's dismay. "It's your turn Rusty—didn't I already say?"

Rusty placed her card onto the deck, eager to unveil her predetermined revelation. "I'm really afraid to turn out like my Ma. But I'm more afraid that I haven't got a choice. I mean, don't get me wrong, I love my Ma, of course. She just seems to be more excited about my pathetic life than her own. She has no friends, she doesn't do anything but crossword puzzles and smokes all day."

"From all that you've said," Josephine told her as she held the cigarette with a limp wrist that displayed her perfectly manicured fingernails, "your Ma, as you say, sounds cool. Maybe that wouldn't be a bad thing to be like her. I'd rather end up like your mother than like mine."

Rusty let out an exasperated sigh. "I love my Ma, I really do. I just don't know where my life is going. I don't see any real future for me. I know what I'm going to do—the same thing. Same damn thing, the rest of my life." She scratched her head with the force of a bear and confidence of a lamb. "Jobie, it's your turn."

He laid down his card and told them, "I've made a lot of enemies in my life."

"Like who?" Rusty asked.

"Like...well," he thought to himself, wondering which name to reveal. "The Freemasons, for one."

Rusty nodded her head in a coddling sort of way, airing her disbelief. "Why would the Freemasons care about you? That's nonsense. You're just being paranoid."

He scrunched his brow at her and snarled, "They know what I'm writing." He threw a determined jagged index finger into the air to drive his point.

"What is it?" Rusty asked. "A journal? A book?"

"Words that will change the world," he boasted.

"You don't even like people," Rusty noted aloud, "so why would you care to give the effort?"

He prepared to challenge her, and then stopped. A perplexed fog seemed to cover him momentarily as he sat silently, stewing the logic.

Josephine cleared her throat as she placed a five of diamonds down onto the table. "My only brother died three weeks ago."

Rusty gasped. "How?"

"Drive-by." She impatiently pointed to Rusty before anyone could present further questioning. "Your turn, Rusty."

Rusty shook her head, hungry for more details, but respectful of her wishes. "Lordy..." She dropped a six of clubs. "My brother owns the farm."

Jobie stared at her with his ominous eyes, unsure if it was a figure of speech or literal truth. "*Owns the farm?* What the hell does that mean?"

"Well, not right yet," she clarified. "But he will. He's older, more abled, and more interested in the livestock trade."

"What do you raise on your farm?" Josephine politely asked. The cigarette dangled between her full, plum-shaded lips.

"Pinzgauer cattle," she told her. "Four hundred forty acres, two hundred head."

Josephine browsed her cards, rearranging them for strategy. "Where is this farm?"

"Olney, Illinois," she responded with a certain amount of pride. "Well, somewhat near there. Actually, somewhat near nothing." She took two cards from her hand and replaced them at the front. "It's triangularly between St. Louis, Indianapolis, and Louisville. About an hour and a half outside of Terre Haute and two hours from Evansville. Out in the sticks. Farms, and not a whole lot more."

Josephine selected her card, and then paused to ask another question. "When you say that your brother has the farm, you mean it will someday be his?"

"Yes," Rusty told her.

"What about you, then?" Josephine asked as she gently tapped her shiny red nails on the wooden table.

"What about me?"

"Do you not get any of it?"

She shook her head indifferently. "Not enough to go around, my parents have needed other sources of income from time to time. I'm not certain my brother will be able to handle it without their help. Besides, I don't want to live on a farm. I know my mother hates it, she acts like she doesn't, but I know better. I know her."

"How did you end up in Key West?" Jobie asked.

"Plane," she replied dryly, waiting to see if they caught her humor. They did not. "That was a joke...I came for the protest outside the queer bar."

"You came all the way across the country to watch a couple of idiots rant for twenty minutes?" Josephine asked snidely. "You must have had a lot of time on your hands."

Rusty shrugged her meaty shoulders. "It's something I happen to stand for."

"Funny thing about white people," Josephine snickered, "either you hate minorities, or you go far out of your way to show that you aren't racist. Seems very few of you simply accept and let it go at that. Racist, anti-racist...one side or the other. How about just *being*? How about not even noticing race? That's one step beyond it all."

"I just be," Rusty replied defensively. "My daddy is a racist, I've never liked it."

"I never even met my dad," Josephine admitted.

"I wish I'd never met my dad," Jobie added.

"That's why I say," Rusty explained. "With a little education and tolerance, we won't have to be as our parents were."

"Is it my turn?" Jobie grumbled impatiently. He lowered a seven of clubs to the wooden table. "I miss my dead girlfriend." His eyes remained fixed on the air before him, caught in a memory that brought an unusually warm smile to his face. "Sometimes when I wake up in the middle of the night, I see her standing over me, talking to me...but I can't hear what she is saying. It lasts a few seconds before she fades and reality sets in."

"I completely understand," Josephine comforted him. "It's happened with me, though only in dreams."

He sighed with a casual and confident resignation.

Josephine shook her head, in an attempt to shake the thought. She shifted her attention once again to Rusty's non-existent future. "So how about going back to college?"

"Once is enough," she told her. "After three semesters at Indiana, I didn't like it much. I was far from home, and I missed my Ma—not because she's my mother, but because she's my best friend. I met some good folks at Bloomington, you know...but they ended up being more into their issues and causes than they were into me as a friend. I tried to make it work out, but it just didn't click. I left college, I kind of felt abandoned after a while."

"They must not have been very good friends, then," Josephine insisted.

"Don't know," she replied indeterminately.

"True friendship is a funny thing. It isn't a pretty flower, it's a weed," Josephine told them as she took the last drag from her cigarette. She mashed it into the ashtray and continued. "Flowers bloom only in season. The rest of the year you're working to keep it going, forcing it to bloom for your personal interest. A weed exists out of freedom, it exists because it can, because it will. It's pure. You don't tend to it, and usually you can't do anything other than feed it and observe it. It doesn't require maintenance, it just grows. If you give it *too much* attention, you can kill it. Friendship isn't a flower, it's a dandelion."

"I think friendship is a selfish thing, personally," Rusty said. "We choose our friends for how they make us feel about ourselves, and what attributes they cultivate inside us. When someone dies, we don't mourn their death so much as we mourn that part of ourselves that will never live again."

"Yeah," Josephine said, "you really haven't had a good friend, have you?"

"That's where you met other skinheads, isn't it?" Jobie asked. "In Bloomington, at college. I doubt there are many skinheads in…wherever you're from."

"Just one," she corrected him. "Me."

"When did you get the tattoos on your knuckles?" Josephine asked her.

Rusty laid her palms on the wooden table with her thick fingers spread like rolls of coins. "Gainesville. And when my Ma sees this, she will come unglued."

"I still can't believe you came all the way from Illinois just to start a fight with some racists," Josephine laughed. "That's some serious boredom there." She placed a three of hearts onto the accumulating pile. "My brother was in a street gang," she offered up.

"A gang?" Rusty asked with sheer delight. "Like Bloods?"

"No, like Crips. A Mansfield Crip, if you want the truth."

"Your brother got shot by a Blood…" Rusty resolved with a gasp.

"No, by a Marvin Crip."

"I thought that all the Crips…" Rusty speculated under her breath, a bit confused.

"And I thought all skinheads were racist, too," Josephine told her lightly. "No, things are different nowadays. After the LA Riots, a lot of the gangs formed treaties of no violence with one another. It's all about commerce. Drugs, whores…whatever brings the money. The territory control is based on where the market is. The bigger the money in an area, the stronger the struggle among the gangs. If you hang out by the Civic Center, when you hear the whistles blow, it's dope time. The pushers signal each other with whistles. When you hear the whistle, you know the dope is there—open market. More organized and structured than you'd ever know. Passing strangers have no idea."

Rusty stared in awe, her mind working to tie this information to that which she always thought she had known. "On all those songs from the gangster rap groups, I always thought there were only Crips and Bloods."

"There are so many gangs in Los Angeles, you wouldn't believe it. No neighborhood is truly free of gangs in that city. Besides, Hispanic gangs like Mara Salvatrucha and 18th Street pretty much dominate the city. What you become involved with depends on where you're from and what you were raised around."

"You ever mess with gangs?" Jobie asked her.

"No," she asserted forcefully. "Never. Watching my brother get sucked into it like he did, I saw that there had to be a better way. Now I know it. I mean, I'd be lying if I would say right now that I was never around it. Obviously I was. Makes me want to never have my own kids, if that's what I can expect of them."

"No," Rusty objected, "don't say that. You'd make a great mother."

Josephine chuckled at the thought. "That's the furthest thing from my mind right now."

"I personally can't see it happening for me," Rusty revealed. "It'd require a dad, of course…and you know, I really don't like most people, so odds are extremely high that my kid would qualify as *most people*. I'd end up hating my kids, and that wouldn't be good. What about you, Jobie?"

He grunted an indistinguishable remark and rearranged himself in his seat. "No thanks. Whose turn is it?"

"I don't remember," Rusty said.

An unsettling silence followed as they tried to figure it out.

Jobie placed his cards on the table and quickly stood with an aggravated posture. "I don't care about this game anymore, let's get some beer."

Rusty and Josephine placed their cards on the table, forfeiting their hands for him at the mercy of his wildly erratic mood swings and darkly secretive nature. Rusty watched him pace back and forth, uneasy in his presence. From her limited experience with Crusties on the streets of Kirkwood in Bloomington, she developed very little respect for them. Jobie's fleeting attention and hot temper did not dissuade her opinion.

"Are we getting drunk or what?" he asked them.

Rusty and Josephine looked at one another, and then Josephine said, "Not me."

Rusty raised her brow, signaling her interest. She was eager to get to the bottom of him, to learn what made him tick. Her lack of knowledge and prejudice was all the more reason to find out. "Sure."

"Come on, then," Jobie beckoned as he stomped to the side gate beyond the courtyard. "You paying?"

"Why me?" she asked, hot on his trail.

"Why not?"

Rusty turned to Josephine and waved. "I'll see you later, Josephine. If it's okay with you, I'll drop by tomorrow maybe?"

"Sure. That'd be really nice."

"Okay…well," Rusty muttered as she tugged her head toward the gate, "I guess I better catch up." She placed her hands around her mouth as if to share a secret. "I'm going to get the scoop on him, I'll share my findings tomorrow."

"Okay," Josephine told her with a warm smile of reassurance. "Bye."

Rusty gave a pernicious grin as she chased after Jobie, leaving Josephine to gather the cards in solitude once again.

8:15pm

Talon crept like a phantom through the mob of pedestrians scattered across Sunset Pier. His black leather attire rubbed against soft cotton, striking sensations of hard, cold flesh. The tourist's faces were drawn with soft lines, their expressions carved with a dull and lackluster blade. His presence was cut and criminal by contrast. He threaded through them like a wispy shadow—the breath of sin itself—tainting their sterile auras.

The tattered photograph of Jobie was clamped between his strong flaxen fingers—the only resource he possessed to avenge the past. He continued his futile search for that unusual skin tone, and the cobwebs tattooed over emaciated cheeks. Jobie had proven to be extremely elusive to his hunt. So much so that he began to question whether or not he remained in Key West.

At the furthest corner of Mallory Square, he turned to face the crowd once again. His sights crossed many people's curious gaze. They glanced away in discomfort, broken by the strength of his ominous presence. Children gave a second glance when he passed, only to see him vanish deeper into the crowd.

He found the street performers along the pier to be a condemnation of his own sacred ritualistic art. They treated it as a formality, a bold contradiction to the inherent edginess of the form, perfectly lacking any risk of danger. He scoffed at them—they held nothing to his deviance. Sword-swallowers, fire-eaters, jugglers…all paled in his shadow.

He continued onward through Mallory Square, finding his way to a row of benches occupied by drunks and vagrants. A newspaper covered the face of one passed out man, rekindling Talon's hope of trapping his nemesis red-handed. As he reached out to the crumbled page, a headline caught his eye: *RIOT!* He uncovered the bum's unshaven elderly face, reading the newspaper caption. *'SCARLET' PERPETRATOR STILL AT LARGE, ONE MAN HOSPITALIZED.*

11:13pm

"The only people that are truly free," Jobie told Rusty as they shared a bottle of cheap beer on the curb of the Southernmost Inn, "are the homeless."

"How do you figure?" she challenged with an inebriated slur.

He took a quick swig before answering. "You aren't truly free in this country, don't kid yourself. The land you think you own, you actually are renting it from the government. Except it's not called rent, it's called property tax."

She snatched the bottle from his wiry fingers.

233

"Don't believe me?" he snarled defensively. "Try living in this society without having a job. You can't. Do you think homeless people apply to statistics? Of course not, we aren't civilians, we're a burden on society. The only people that matter are the ones who pay, the ones who fund the government. Not me."

"I do see your point," she admitted. She took one last drink before handing him the beer. "But I'd rather pay taxes and enjoy a decent standard of living. I think you make a great point, it's very noble...and very unrealistic."

"In your opinion," he snapped.

"Yes, in my opinion. Even if you could convince forty-nine percent of the population to live as you do, you'd still be the minority. Change can only occur on the inside. That's the beauty of our government, by the people, for the people."

He grumbled his dissent. He tipped his head under the bottle and took a quick gulp. "You are living a lie, my friend. You're living a lie. It's the illusion of freedom—freedom by name, not by definition."

She scoffed with an accidental snort.

"Someday, you'll see!"

"Yeah, what are you going to do?"

"Mark my words," he promised, "I will bust the cap off tyranny."

"How?"

He raised a finger to his lips. "I've got plans, you'll see. Enemies of progress, they will perish."

"Are you going to become an assassin? That's not a very passive approach. Aren't you all about peace?"

"Who said I was passive?" He took a quick swallow of beer, wiping his lips with the back of his hand. "You have the wrong guy in mind, Rusty."

She took the beer from his hands and finished it in one big gulp that inflated her cheeks like balloons.

"Have you ever wondered why there has never been an attempted takeover in this country?" he surmised. "With all this power, why has no one even tried? Doesn't that seem odd?"

"Maybe they have and we don't know about it. Maybe it was successful. Maybe they were not seeking a takeover as much as they were seeking a different outcome of world affairs. For instance, Kennedy's assassination was followed with an entirely different political direction with Johnson. Lincoln's assassination also affected the Reconstruction very differently. And FDR's New Deal..."

"I'm talking about these days, right now," he barked with drunken confidence. "We are the world power now. Why would no one ever attempt to take this over? Think of the Roman Empire and all the attempts of controlling that power from within."

"Okay, okay" she replied diffusely, "go ahead and tell me why it hasn't happened."

"I think it *is* happening," he told her bluntly. "It's been happening for a while. Wait and see. Something will happen that will cause America to choose patriotism over freedom. The symbols of freedom will matter more than freedom itself, you just wait. A terrorist attack—one that will be blamed on an enemy that probably doesn't even exist. And the walls will close in because we will choose to have them close in on us as we wave our flags."

"You've got quite an imagination...and a lot of paranoia. That's the thing with conspiracy theorists like you, everything is a secret plot."

"Everything *is* a secret plot!" he insisted with a clenched fist that jabbed at the air.

"What if something like that happened, say a police state would try to take things over, and then what?"

"You don't know the rest? Martial law, that's it. Then we labor for the New World Order. That's why NATO was set up. That's their role in the big picture. The New World Order will be the former NATO. That's the sole reason it was set up in the first place, to control the world. And that's what it has done, gaining more and more power."

"The problem with your theory," Rusty said, "and all theories like it, is that you are from the city. If you leave the city, you'll find that the people living in the areas you would call *the sticks* would be a real problem in terms of this theory. They know their territory well, they are well armed and know how to use their arsenal, and they are spread sparsely throughout this country, taking up the majority of the land. You call them rednecks, but they would fight for the same principles as you would. You'd be surprised. Taking the cities would be one thing, but to truly take this country, it'd be a much more difficult task than you think. If you don't believe me, travel to rural Illinois or Arkansas or Indiana and stay for a while. People in the cities haven't got a clue what it's like living in *the sticks*. But country folk watch city life every day on the television. Your limited scope could benefit a great deal by truly knowing the people you claim you are hoping to save. They would likely end up being the ones saving you."

He shook his head in contempt. He refused to even argue her points. He remained silent with his body language screaming objections.

"Who are you going to assassinate?" she asked. "You can tell me."

"I had my chance and blew it."

"Strickland?"

"He's an evil man," he told her with drunken candidness. "He's a lawyer, you know. That's why he protests the funerals of AIDS victims, picketing the service. He's trying to provoke people to confront him, and when they do, he takes them to court and runs them over the coals in court costs. He's an evil man. He doesn't respect the living, so why would anyone respect him in death? It'd be a public improvement—"

"An enemy of progress, you got that right," she said, nodding. "Good luck. So what of this book, or whatever it is? What's it called?"

"It's called *The Apolitical Manifesto*. I would like for you to look at it."

"I would like to look at it," she told him.

"I'll bring it to you, but you can't keep it. It's all I live for." He reached out and grabbed her limp hand, raising it in the light. His red skin was cold to the touch and clammy like a frog. "Any other tattoos?"

"Yeah, I have one on my back. My mother has never seen it. She would kill me if she knew."

"What is it?"

"It's Big Bird."

He laughed.

"No, really. I used to always be called that, all throughout school. I guess I look like Big Bird! Anyway, it's Big Bird wearing a black flight jacket, braces, Docs, bleach splattered jeans, and the feathers over her big round eyes are shaped like a fringe. She's a skinhead like me, get it?"

He chuckled to himself, unimpressed. "Yeah, I get it."

"I know that you are on this crusade for peace," she began, "but don't you think it's unnatural to our species? I mean, come on—be realistic. We seek conflict. We can't get enough of it, not in our movies, in our books—we crave chaos and destruction. If you're reading a book, you want to know that the ending will be packed with all kinds of drama and chaos. Good news is no news at all. We want mass destruction. It's who we are."

"We can become more. It's in us, we can imagine, and we can live it. Violence is no more real than evolution—it's in us to destroy, and it's in us to evolve toward greatness."

She stood clumsily, her entire demeanor withdrawn and morose. She stumbled forward, catching the rail with a firm left hand. "It's getting late, I need to get to bed." She retreated awkwardly to her room, waving her hand politely over her shoulder at him. "Good luck with the assassination, man...and bring your writing by, maybe tomorrow," she muttered politely. "We'll have to do this again, it was fun."

Thursday, September 16, 1999
10:21am

Jobie unraveled the garden hose, dragging it across Miss Reinbrandt's tiny fenced backyard to his paltry rented shed. Long vertical boards comprised the walls of his domain with the entire structure kept intact with horizontal boards nailed to each panel for backup. The ramshackle fortress was covered with a thick coating of white paint for adhesive purposes rather than aesthetics.

He kept his eye on the wasp nest in the snug upper corner of the shed as he pulled the hose to its full extension. He held the hose limply in his red hand as the cool water sprayed down his leg. He could not feel a drop of it.

Wasps swarmed around the roof where the paint was already beginning to peel, leaving the gray wood exposed to the elements. A very ingenious plot by the Freemasons, he thought as his face spread in a devious smile. He was quick to their ploys, always keen with their surveillance. It was a simple plan, really, as most of their schemes tended to be. The wasps were genetically modified in some Top Secret research lab, and each stinger carried a deadly man-made virus. With his skin unable to detect an attack, he would die a slow immobilized death.

He partially covered the end of the hose to intensify the force of the stream as he sprayed the nest and the small swarm that surrounded it. One by one the wasps fell to the ground, delirious. One by one he crushed them with the heel of his shoe, flattening the dizzy carriers of death. Eventually the nest was overtaken and ripped from the wooden frame, later to be sacrificed with fire.

He smiled as he brought the hose back up to the house. It amazed him how incompetent his non-existent oppressors were. The simplest task—getting inside his shed—proved impossible to them.

He had gone through considerable lengths to keep the contents of his shed safe from outsiders. First, he had paid two years of dirt-cheap rent on it, cash in advance. Miss Reinbrandt, an elderly woman with no known family had little interest in what he intended to do with it as long as he was quiet and kept it clean. Considering that he personally maintained her lawn, he was certain that no one else had access to the fenced yard that guarded his fortress.

The fence was padlocked and booby-trapped with razor wire to keep strangers from entering the yard. The shed itself was barricaded and secured with a barrage of padlocks and chains.

He had gone to considerable effort to keep the whereabouts of the shed known only to him. Despite his delusions of secret government agencies seeking to cease his personal anarchistic writings and undermine his plots to overthrow the system, he had substantial reasons to maintain his privacy, a true sentiment of his unquestionable lunacy.

He walked back to the shed and disarmed each lock and chain. The door creaked open slowly, bringing light to the hideously foul confines of his fortress. The light of the summer sun burst into the sparse quarters as though it were a dank and mysterious dungeon. Dust swirled in the air like carcinogens, lifting from his makeshift bed, covering the single-unit stove he purchased from the junk dealer in Marathon. Negligence and filth covered his writing material and empty boxes of pancake mix. His eyes squinted proudly upon his insidiously creative work in all its deplorable glory.

10:21am

Kinsman Kale woke to the voice of the Devil once again. It was a soft whisper—different than before—soothing, though icy cold.

"Who did this to you?"

"I know where he is," Kinsman Kale gasped incoherently.

"Tell me."

Kale wet his lips and swallowed uneasily. What he really wanted was for the doctor to bring more painkillers. The doctor's African ethnicity made little difference to him, not under such circumstances. "Who are you?"

"I told you all you need to know."

"Are you here to take me home?"

The Kinsman partially opened his swollen eyes, seeing nothing out of the ordinary. The same white sterility of his small hospital room. For as far as he could tell, he was alone.

"Who did this to you?" the whisper came once again, this time from over his shoulder.

He struggled to turn, but his body still had not recovered enough for such mobility. He clinched with discomfort.

"Who is there?" Kinsman Kale asked gravely. He closed his eyes as his head fell to his left shoulder. He could feel someone's warm breath on his face. "Reverend…is that you?"

"No," the voice whispered. "I'm here to find the man who did this to you."

Kinsman Kale cracked open his right eye to see the green eyes of a tattooed serpent staring back. He closed his eyes in recourse. The room carried a faint smell of warm leather.

"I am here to help you," the voice whispered once again. "Tell me. Where is he?"

"Merlinn Inn," Kinsman Kale revealed with a gravelly whisper. "Simonton."

"Good boy," the voice muttered as it drifted away.

Kinsman Kale listened to the faint footsteps leave his room as he lie perfectly still with closed eyes and furled brow. He was asleep again in minutes.

10:21pm

Josephine closed her eyes as she listened to the gentle waves lapping up against the White Street Pier. The darkness of night transformed the clear blue water of the Atlantic Ocean to a disembodied void that became one with the sky. There was nothing to see, only to hear.

"This is how it is on the farm," Rusty whispered as she lay quietly on the dock. "Dark as coal."

"This isn't what I'm used to," Josephine purred with delight as her bare feet dangled off the pier, swaying ever so slowly with the soft breeze. She removed her mesh Raiders jersey and placed it at her side. Her gray sports bra was slightly damp from perspiration with small granules of sand stuck to her moist skin. She reclined against the pier with her arms splayed in opposing directions across its cool surface. The salty breeze crept inside her black satin shorts, giving the material lift parachutes. "I could stay here forever."

"I think I'm going to take off my boots," Rusty said as she sat cross-legged, staring out into the dark ocean. She remained still as if waiting for a response.

"Go ahead," Josephine mumbled.

She quickly began unlacing her Docs with the vigor of a child. "I wonder if there are any sharks out there."

"Of course there are," Josephine told her.

"I've never seen a real shark before," she marveled as she plopped a heavy boot at her side. She yanked on the other, pulling it off with the pressure of a corked bottle. "Have you?"

"At the Aquarium."

"I should go to the Aquarium," Rusty decided as she sprawled across the dock, assuming much the same position as Josephine. "I want to take your picture for my photo album. My Ma will want to see what you look like." She smiled in the darkness, comfortable in its invisibility. "I know when I get back to Illinois that I'll be talking about you a lot. We'll have to exchange addresses. Maybe you could even visit. You'd like my Ma."

Josephine smiled. "I wish I had a relationship with my mother like you have with yours."

"Yeah, she's cool," Rusty decided. "I talked to her last night on the phone, I was a little drunk...Jobie's a bad influence...but I told her about you and him. She wants to see pictures. I can tell she wishes she were here. I told her about all the chickens that walk all over town. She can't believe they can just walk around town like that. That's not how things work on a farm!"

Josephine gave a slight chuckle. "How many rolls have you shot?"

"Three or four." She looked up at the starless sky. "Josephine...um...can I ask you an odd question?"

"Sure."

"Are you a virgin?"

Josephine chuckled. "No."

"Have you slept with a lot of people?"

"Three guys." She yawned casually and stretched her lanky limbs. "The first one just to get it out of the way. It wasn't good at all. So I figured it was the guy rather than the experience. Had sex with a different guy and learned it was the experience after all. I kept away from any such thing for a while. Then I met this guy named Sean a few months before I left. I really started to like him. We had sex three times and I actually enjoyed it quite a bit."

"Did he love you?" Rusty asked.

"I guess so. I mean, he said he did, but you know how guys are."

"How was that?"

"How was what?"

"You know," Rusty said without continuing the thought.

"No," Josephine finally said, "I don't. I'm not sure what you mean."

"I lost my virginity recently," she revealed. "One of the Gainesville Skins. We didn't like each other. Well, I didn't know him, but maybe I would've liked him. I don't even think he knew my real name." She was silent for a long stretch. "I hope I'm not pregnant."

"Did you use any protection?"

Her question was met with silence.

"No, you can't do that," Josephine scolded her. "You can't ever do that again."

"I know, I know...I just thought maybe if I asked him to put on a condom, he'd think it was too much effort, and it isn't like they're breaking down my door."

"It makes me sad just to hear you say that, Rusty. You should have more self-respect than that."

"I know, I know."

"Don't do it again." Josephine said. "*Ever.*"

Rusty remained silent, listening to her own breathing while secretly fantasizing about raising a child that would depend on her, need her, and love her. Deep down, she wished she carried his child in her womb. "I know this sounds dumb, but I miss my cow. Cleo. I have a cow, have I told you that?"

Josephine laughed. "In all my life, I have never seen a real cow."

"She's an Ayrshire, we milk her. She isn't much use commercially, but she supplies the milk for the family. I love that cow. I want you to meet her someday."

"I'd love to meet her."

"Really?"

"Of course."

They watched the sparse and gray clouds drift over the dark sky as the waves lapped quietly against the shore. The stillness of the atmosphere absorbed them seamlessly into the setting.

"You're not very angry, Rusty," Josephine said, cracking the extended silence. "I expected a skinhead to have a lot of anger. You don't seem that angry to me."

"I guess I'll take that as a compliment," she responded quickly as though she had already come to the same conclusion on her own. "That's what I liked most about the punk kids I had met in Bloomington when I went to college. They weren't all that angry. Not like I thought they'd be. I know this sounds weird, but I decided that since they were into an art form that allowed them to express anger and aggression, they didn't bottle up their anger. It wasn't a part of them because they allowed themselves the release under controlled circumstances. But the Catholics and the do-gooders, they keep it inside because they're afraid of it. When you scream at the world, you end up feeling a whole lot better afterward."

Josephine smiled. "That makes sense."

"That was the best time of my life, living in Bloomington. I never felt comfortable in Olney, but at college I really felt I had found my place. You know when you'd go to the High School football games and you'd walk by the bleachers of the other school and there were all those unfamiliar faces with those other school colors? You'd see your school on the other side and you couldn't wait to get over there where you belonged. I never really knew that feeling until I made friends in Bloomington. Whenever I see skinheads, I feel like I have kin, like we are part of the same team."

Josephine crinkled her face in dismay. "That's gang talk right there, sister."

"Oh no, it's not a gang."

"You really think skinheads aren't a gang?" Josephine asked. "You're fooling yourself."

"Well, maybe. I guess you'd know, having been around it your whole life."

"But then what?" Josephine asked. "What do you do down the road a ways?"

"I see it as a cocoon," Rusty assured her. "It's not a lifetime commitment. I feel that—speaking for myself—teenagers have an inherent identity crisis. Feeling so much absence in my life, I stumbled upon a counter-culture that had everything I sought in life, from what I knew of life at that point. Their style was absolutely alien yet so cool to me, and I was so drawn to its unity. I felt that my entire presentation expressed exactly whom I was when I walked out into public. I got respect, and the fear that I saw in people's eyes while in my presence, I have to admit, it was a rush. I felt like someone—someone to fear. Eventually I started picking up on the fact that I dressed just like everyone else that I hung out with, mimicking someone else's wardrobe from years and years ago. But to me, it was all mine. Because that was my limited perception. But it defined who I was, and eventually in a few years I know I will outgrow it and hang up the boots in favor of shoes that fit more comfortably. I know some people who are certain they will live the lifestyle their entire life, and what once gave them wings will become their shackles in time. They never grow, they stay in that small pond and stagnate. This applies for any group. It's a cocoon, and to think it's anything more is fooling yourself. It's the person that comes out on the other end of it that has the chance to make all the difference, or live in stagnation."

"I can see that," Josephine agreed. "Then there are those like me who never needed the guise of a clique to find themselves."

"And that's great. More power to you, but I wouldn't take back any of it. I'm not ready to hang up my Docs, I'll always have my heart involved, but I know that I will grow as a person, too."

"Of course."

"People tend to separate punk kids and hippie kids, but they are the same thing, for the most part. Means to the same end. Punks are drawn to having firm boundaries—they are the *no* subculture for middle class white kids. The hippies are the *yes* subculture, they want to open their boundaries and expand their horizons. But both subcultures have the same function on the soul, defining oneself and the role of self in a world of billions."

"That's pretty heavy, Rusty."

Rusty laughed with all her heart, gums, and crooked teeth. "I have a lot of time to think these things through on the farm. Not much else going on." She stared up at the night sky, devouring the soft ocean breeze with all her senses. "I'm glad to be here. At this moment, in this very second…I'm knee-deep in joy. These are the best days of my life."

"Simply because you took a trip away from the farm?"

"Maybe," Rusty acknowledged.

"Well, then…move away! Why stay there?"

"Oh, no," Rusty said with certainty, "I could never do that."

"When are you going back, then?"

"I don't know. The people I came here with, they're leaving in the morning. But you know, I think I'm going to stay an extra couple of days. The skins I came here with, they aren't what I thought. The girls don't like me much, and the guys, they think I'm one of the guys. We drink beer together, and that's great, but they don't care about who I am. We're all part of some cause, supposedly, but I can tell it's something to do, an identity. They don't stand for it as strongly as I do. It's just this sense of self-importance that they seek. They just like to fight."

Josephine shook her head in disapproval. "Let them be, then. I'm glad you're not leaving with them. And you can stay away from that guy, what's his name?"

"Which guy?"

"The one you had sex with."

"Oh," Rusty said, "that one. Smitty. That's what they called him."

"What was his real name?"

"Who cares?" Rusty said with a distinctly confident snarl.

"Good answer."

"What do you think of Jobie?"

Josephine raised her hands in the air as if weighing the scales. "He's troubled."

"Yeah," Rusty agreed quickly.

"He has a pure heart, he means well. I would say that he is as he is for that exact reason. He has some issues to deal with, but he saved me from a horrible incident that could've been a nightmare. How can I say anything bad about him? What I can say is that he is loyal through and through and seems he'd go out of his way to help a friend. He considers us friends. I take comfort in that, I consider him a friend as well. Even if some of his stories are a bit...unbelievable."

"Like how he got his red skin from his girlfriend?" Rusty asked skeptically.

"And that she died."

"Yeah, but who knows? Maybe it's all true."

"Even if," Josephine said, "there's still something going on with him. He told me so. Gave me the creeps. I can only imagine, coming from a terrorist-minded wacko like he is." She laughed aloud, reinforcing her jesting comments.

"And how secretive he is about where he lives," Rusty added. "I think he's building something. I don't know, but something strange is going on there, whatever it is."

10:23pm

Koz-Mo stood in the shadowy entryway, silently watching Talon meditate in the center of five black candles. Darkness surrounded Talon, feeding on his space—leaving hungry. His muscles were tense and bulging, even while at rest. Sweat glistened on his hairless pale skin. The light of the candles bathed him in a comforting tangerine glow, casting harsh shadows over the surface of his lineless face. His eyes were submerged in a veil of dark, impenetrable shadows.

Koz-Mo felt drawn to Talon's unyielding aura. He sought to understand the allure that disarmed his caution. His natural instincts urged retaliation. He resisted himself, choosing to learn from Talon what he had unlearned in the spotlight.

To Talon, there was only the moment. Only the tenacity of his own beating heart. He existed in a calm tranquility, purely accepting himself. There was no sin, only the risk of making no sacrifice. He pushed his endurance and will to the brink, it was routine to him. It magnetized his soul with the power of a black hole. In its presence, Koz-Mo watched his own lustrous glow dissipate. His energy was drawn, tapped to a faint pulse.

Yet it was for his very own salvation, Koz-Mo decided. Once, not too long ago when he was much leaner, he was like an amplifier of raw intensity. He yearned for the sins of nature, when he had danced so fearlessly close to the open flame. He stood against the elements invincible. And the world stood in awe. The mighty Koz-Mo. The once great Koz-Mo.

Each flashbulb exchanged his spark for a more superficial one. He now understood the theory of film capturing one's soul. It was not a literal interpretation, rather one of vanity. Each accolade stripped away his fire as if plucking the mane of Samson. His image was carried on lunchboxes, cheap paper stickers—even plastic action figures. The only concern in his life was dubbing the lines for the new *Scars* Saturday morning cartoon.

Throughout Koz-Mo's young life, he had always been a rebel. The first facial tattoos he had ever seen were his own, years ago. The sight of him once instilled fear in strangers like a repellent of triteness. Now children woke up early to see him as the new *Scooby-Doo*. Much had changed for him in five years. Through example of daily routine, Talon revealed to him the curse of it all.

Koz-Mo watched the candlelight flicker over Talon's strong body. The light painted him red like a chili. His muscular control was captivating. Watching him, Koz-Mo realized there was much to regain, and Talon would show him the way.

Koz-Mo smiled deviously to himself, flexing his largely stout body, proud of his impressive physical stature. He ached to bring his soul to the grindstone, to lace his aura with arsenic. He ached to bring the monster alive once again. The monster behind his own eyes. The monster once known in select small circles as Koz-Mo.

Jobie yanked his shirt up to his left armpit, revealing a long jagged scar that zigzagged across his waxy red skin like a bolt of lightning. Josephine's toes curled at the sight, making a ripple of waves across the swimming pool from where her feet dangled in the deep end. Rusty leaned forward, examining it curiously with squinting eyes.

"This one is called Governor Nicholls," he told them as he ran his finger down his ribcage, following the scar's uneven trail. It had grown together disproportionately by means of his own shoddy stitch-work. "It's named after the street in New Orleans where I got it. Brawl with two other guys, kind of a territory thing…they lost." He trailed into a sinister laugh. "You should've seen the other guys, though. This is nothing."

Rusty rolled up her sleeve and laid her forearm flat into the scattered light. There appeared to have once been a tear across her pale skin. A short, thick scar remained—unusually white. "Hay bailing wire. I was ten years old…but I never named it—I never thought to name a scar." She looked over to Josephine and smiled politely with her profound gums glistening in the evening light. "How about you? Any scars?"

Josephine opened her pack of cigarettes and gently placed one between her thick red lips. "No." She struck a match and lit it while gently sucking its smoke into her lungs. Her face softened as the nicotine entered her body. To Rusty's disappointment, it was not the sabotaged cigarette with the match head.

"Look at this one," Jobie tempted them as he placed his left leg forward across the wooden deck surrounding the swimming pool. He raised the pant leg of his ripped and stained black jeans up to his knobby knee. A circular scar covered the bone. "The Geyser, from the stairs of my old house. Dad was drunk—he knocked me down just as I was about to run away up the steps. It was a mess, blood all over. It's not a big scar, but it sure bled a lot. It's the coolest looking scar I have. It's one big swirl."

Josephine raised the short sleeve of her Mile Zero T-shirt, pampering a faint bruise on her coppery shoulder. "It isn't a scar, but it's new." She tapped her cigarette over the pool, allowing the ash to drift into the naturally salty water. "Sleepwalking. I've never done it before, but last night was the second time it's happened since I've been in Key West. Except it's not sleep*walking*, it's more sleep*running*. A crazy mad dash into a wall."

245

"What were you dreaming?" Rusty begged with concern.

"It's weird," she giggled. "I was in a submarine that was sinking. Water was coming in through the walls and I had to get out of there, so I took off running. I woke up after I had smashed into the door of my room. I was in shock—still partially stuck in my dream—thinking I had been thrown into the wall of the submarine, waiting for my death."

"I have those types of dreams all the time," Jobie told her dismissively. "It's a stress thing."

Josephine scoffed as she threw her braids over her shoulder. "It's a painful thing, is what it is." She reached for her nail polish and shook it up. With a slow twist of the cap, she removed it and took a whiff of the contents, raising her brow as she did. "Stress, huh…I suppose I need a vacation."

"You're in just the right place," Rusty quipped. "Have I told you about my Ma's dream?"

Josephine shook her head as she slowly began to apply the red polish to her long fingernails.

"It's kind of weird, but it's about me, she thinks." She stammered from insecurity, and then picked up once again on the trail of her breath. "She had the dream when she was pregnant with me. She was certain it was about her unborn child."

"Well, what was it?" Jobie demanded impatiently.

She released a stuttered sigh. "That I would grow up to be someone special. Someone that helped the people in some way."

"Do you not believe it?" Josephine asked.

"I think that my mother has made me believe it. That's part of why I came here to the protest, to be honest. I had this crazy idea that that's what it would be—my calling."

"You don't need to do something great to have an impact on the world, Rusty," Josephine said.

"It doesn't hurt, though," Jobie interjected. "Being a good mother in the suburbs is nice and all, but it will take more than that to fix things."

"Why are you so convinced they're broken in the first place?" Josephine challenged him. "You keep talking about all the bad things in the world…what about the good things? Do you ever think of those things?"

"Not usually, no." He turned to Rusty and said, "I brought my writing for you to check out. You can't borrow it, though. I want you to read it and give it right back—I can't afford to lose it."

Rusty smiled. "I'm eager to read it…but your comment…I do think that a good mother in the suburbs can change the world. I also think a bad mother in the same position can also change the world—in all the wrong ways." She nervously rearranged her burgundy flight jacket as she watched Josephine paint her nails. She was impressed with her refined skill, something she clearly enjoyed to do very often. "Anyway, I have my rolls of film right here." She raised a plastic bag over her head, and then lowered it to the wooden planks that surrounded her. "Do either of you have any stamps for a postcard?"

There was no answer.

"I guess I can get some tomorrow," she decided aloud.

"I may have some," Josephine offered, knowing very well that she did not. "I'll have to look. Just leave them here with me. I'll take care of it."

"Thank you," Rusty replied with deep sincerity. "I probably won't be staying in town much longer. The Gainesville Skins left today." She looked toward Josephine and said, "I didn't even see them off."

"Good for you," Josephine threw in unexpectedly.

Rusty smiled proudly, though unsure for what reason. "This may sound really weird because I feel I've just gotten to know both of you, but I'll really miss you guys when I go back home."

"We'll keep in touch," Josephine assured her, prying on her confidence. "I'm going to meet your cow, remember? What was its name?"

"Cleo," Rusty sang optimistically.

"Right. Someday I'll visit the farm, meet your Ma and the rest of the family."

"Well, I for one don't plan to visit no cows on a farm, but you both have been really cool," Jobie threw out with his distinctively cold tone. "I feel that either of you would lend a hand for me, and...I want you to know that I would, too."

Josephine stopped cold, staring in awe as she reached out for her cigarette. She was speechless.

"I want to keep in touch with you, Jobie," Rusty pleaded. "Will you give me an address?"

"I have a mailbox," he informed her.

Josephine rolled her eyes. "She meant a *real* mailbox."

"It is real. You can put things in it, can't you? Well, see then...it's a mailbox."

"Will you give me the address?" Rusty repeated.

"I'll show it to you before you leave."

"It's not a real mailbox," Josephine told her.

"It is, too!" he snarled.

"Okay...okay...show it to me before I leave, Jobie," Rusty said in a soothing tone. Then she remembered what she had intended to tell him. "Did you see the newspaper? You're in it."

"I'm in the paper?" he asked, dumbfounded.

"Well, *you* aren't," Rusty corrected as she reached into her bag to retrieve the clipped article. She held it up for them to see. "*He* is." She tapped her thick finger against the thin paper, pointing to the small picture of the Kinsman lying in his hospital bed covered in blankets and bruises.

Jobie snickered at the headline, reading it aloud, "*The Scarlet Perpetrator!*"

"You know, I probably shouldn't say this, but I will," Josephine began with a quick drag from her cigarette. "He's sexy. Big brute of a white man."

Rusty turned the clipping around and examined his photograph. "He could be a fireman."

"He could be!"

"He's not," Jobie growled. "He's a bigot. He's part of the reason this world sucks."

Josephine rolled her eyes and sighed. "Oh great, here we go again…"

"If he wasn't good looking, they wouldn't have printed his picture, you know." Rusty resolved. "Have you ever noticed that when attractive people die, it's a shame, but when the ugly ones kick the bucket—well, they probably deserved it, right?" She made a sour face. "I hate that. I doubt I'd even make the back page of the *Olney Register.*"

"Is it printed on a piece of notebook paper, one-sided?" Jobie questioned facetiously with a condescending grunt.

"If it was, I guess I wouldn't get the back page, then, would I?" she snapped back at him. "Anyway…when the poodle gets ran over, it's a crime. But when the pit bull is flogged to death, it's better off dead, isn't it?"

Josephine quietly tended to her nails, realizing that all of Rusty's theories had never been tested on an audience. She gave her the floor without interruption.

"You know, Jobie, I like your bad attitude," Rusty decided.

Josephine laughed.

"No, really…I do. Seriously." She turned to face him, greeting his defensive gaze. "You're an asshole, but you know who and what you are. That's the thing with bitches or assholes—I usually like them. They tend to be people who are keenly aware of themselves and have very little tolerance of other people's lack of character. Tolerance is another thing that's overrated. Intolerance is the way our culture *should* be. We are way too forgiving."

Jobie smiled. "I couldn't agree with you more. In fact, I think you're going to like *The Apolitical Manifesto.*"

"I'm eager to read it," she assured him once again.

"I'm not a bitch…" Josephine murmured as she capped her polish and blew on her red nails to dry them. "Okay, maybe sometimes." She dipped the tip of her cigarette into the pool where it fizzled into a charred nub. She pulled it up to look into its black remains, staring at it with crossed eyes.

"Are you going to stay in Key West…bitch?" Jobie asked Josephine.

"I don't know, you asshole." She flicked the cigarette butt into the trash container by the pool. "I may stay a while. May get a place to live, stay through winter. I don't know. I feel I *should* know, but I don't." She kicked her feet in the water, creating waves that dispersed the ash she had dropped into the pool.

"I like living here," Jobie stated matter-of-factly.

"I'll need an income," she realized. "How did you come up with the idea to be a fire-breathing performer?"

Jobie reflected briefly before staring into the rippling water, responding with a methodical delivery. "When I first arrived in Key West, I would often crash by the front doors of the Club Chameleon. Rain couldn't penetrate, it was close to the center of town…but I had bad dreams there every night. Burning, screaming children trapped inside a church. On more than one occasion a small boy would enter into my dreams, turning them into nightmares. His skin was burnt and crispy. In one dream, the very last one I had with him, he had a handful of fire. He reached out to me, trying to hand it to me. I felt obligated, as though I had no choice. I took it from him, and suddenly woke up in a state of peace and understanding. That dream changed my life."

"How?" Josephine beckoned.

He smirked at her, edgy with confidence. "That was the last night I slept at the Club Chameleon," he replied, ignoring her question.

"Where do you sleep now?" Rusty asked.

His face fell straight and cold. He shook his head in an effort to shake the question. "No comment."

"Why? Does it have anything to do with this anarchist journal you keep?" Josephine asked, following a notion.

"You mock me," he responded with a threatening tone.

"No, not at all," she assured him. "I'm just asking."

He thought a moment. "Possibly. And then again…maybe not. I won't say. So don't ask."

"It has to do with fire, doesn't it?" Rusty assumed. "The fire and the journal. I see." She shot him a mischievous smile. "You're too easy, you damn terrorist! What have you got planned?"

There followed an extended and awkward silence. Josephine and Rusty shared a glance of concern as they each imagined a dark room filled with explosives and guns and potential political targets on the wall.

"Let's get some beer," Jobie suggested.

"Yeah," Rusty anxiously replied, eager to step beyond their current discomfort.

"No," Josephine countered shortly and assuredly. "You'll have to count me out. One of those lingering things from my brother's life. When he went *drinking*, it meant knocking off liquor stores and 7-11's in Palms. I always equate it with trouble. I'll stay here where it's safe."

"I understand," Rusty sided quickly.

Jobie stood and slipped inside his disheveled combat boots. "We'll tell you how much fun we have, then." He turned to Rusty and handed her the notebook of overflowing loose papers—*The Apolitical Manifesto*. "I want you to read it."

Rusty scrunched her face, not yet ready to step away from Josephine or her relaxing atmosphere.

"We'll hang out tomorrow," Josephine promised her, sensing Rusty's apprehension. "And I'll mail your postcard in the morning. You can leave your bag with me if you want, so you don't have to lug it around."

Rusty shrugged with a sigh as she pulled herself to her feet. She placed the bag by Josephine's fingernail polish on the boarded deck. "Thanks. I'll call first thing in the morning."

"See you later, Josephine," Jobie barked as he retreated to the gate without a lingering formal farewell.

Rusty put her hand on Josephine's thin shoulder and said, "Sleep well, and don't run into the walls again tonight."

"I'll try." She stood and followed Rusty to the gate where Jobie waited in the shadows. She watched them walk down the quiet street, drifting toward Duval Street. "Be safe. Both of you." She waved until they stepped out of sight around the corner.

As she returned to her room, she dug through Rusty's bag to retrieve the postcard. It was buried under several black canisters of film. One canister alone was labeled "Key West chickens."

She pulled out the postcard and—acting on an impulse—flipped it over to read the brief note on the backside. It was to Rusty's Ma, telling her that she has had the best week of her life with her great new friend, a black girl named Josephine. She smiled and dropped the postcard alongside the plastic bag on the bed.

There came a light tapping at the door. She rushed to it with a smile, expecting to see her two comrades. Instead, she opened the door to a stranger.

He was compact and lean with menacing eyes and a twitching lip. Black leather covered his alabaster skin. A dark and scaly snake with evil green eyes was tattooed over the crest of his hairless head, slithering in a thin line down his scalp. Its tongue split at the point where his hairline should have began.

"Can I help you?" she asked him cautiously.

11:43pm

"Listen, Rusty," Jobie slurred as the two of them stumbled down Whitehead Street past Hemingway's House. He paused to look up at the white lighthouse museum poking up through the palm trees. "I've got this plan, see." He pitched his empty beer bottle over the wall that concealed Hemingway's House. It landed in the thick brush with scarcely a thud. "The time is coming for me to take political action…"

"Against who?" Rusty asked with a more distinctly sober voice. Her swaying gait and lethargic strut proved that her investment of Guinness beer earlier that evening was not poorly spent. "What are you gonna do?"

He pointed his finger at her with rigid determination. "Whatever it takes. Certain people are better off dead. Better for our world."

"Do you really think..." she took a breath as she made sure it was safe to cross the street. Her joints were still stiff from sitting on the curb out front of her motel's parking lot for several hours. It was very late, and the effect of the alcohol was slowly beginning to wear off. "Do you really think you could kill somebody?"

"I already have." His words trailed with uncompromising panic. He had given himself away. Then he smiled as the alcohol burned away his paranoia. "I killed Treva."

"Your girlfriend?"

"Yeah, that's her. I did it because I loved her."

Rusty threw her hand to the air. "Pshaw! I don't believe you. I don't believe you killed your girlfriend, and I don't believe you'll kill...whomever you said."

"I didn't say."

Rusty laughed at him, tickled by his bulldog front. "I don't agree with all your political stuff, but I really liked your writing. I think you're onto something. You need to present it to the public—get it out there and make a *real* difference in the world."

"Of course you don't agree with it," he slurred as his stumbling swagger became more determined. "You have no reason to."

"What does that mean?"

"On your farm with all your pigs and cows and...chickens...what reason do you have to be mad at the system? I'm on the streets, I have a reason to be mad."

"You *choose* to live on the streets."

"Blah, blah, blah..."

"You want to know what I think?" she asked, speaking much louder than necessary on the quiet back street. She did not wait for an answer. "We, as a species, have no direction." She waited to be interrupted, and was surprised when he—the political know-it-all—kept quiet for a change. "The whole reason we do what we do on a day to day basis is beyond us. You never hear about why we do what we do, or where this is all heading. We industrialize the world to make things easier on us. Soon our industry will control itself. Machines will be able to perform all labor for us. Then what? Isn't that the goal? Hasn't that been the goal all along?"

"It's one of those big picture things that no one ever notices or mentions."

"Exactly! So tell me, Jobie...why is your skin red?" She was shocked that she had asked him so bluntly. It was the alcohol speaking, giving her tactlessly loose lips.

"It's the disease that was killing Treva. I got it from her."

She clinched her lips in frustration. "I never know what to believe with you. One minute you claim to have killed her, the next she had died from some skin disease."

"Did you think it was one huge tattoo?" he joked lightly with a muffled slur. "I've made myself clear on everything, I feel."

"I wasn't sure…just seemed so odd. Sorry if that offended you, man."

"Offend me…hell, no way."

"Good, I wouldn't want to make you mad. You're a good friend." She smiled to herself as she followed him down the street, carrying *The Apolitical Manifesto* under her arm for him. "So…where are we going?"

"We're coming up to my mailbox," he told her. "Didn't you want to see it?"

"Sure," she said brightly. "Do you live up here?"

"No."

"You don't?"

"No."

"Why do you have a mailbox up here?" she asked.

"It's not really a mailbox. I mean…not *really*. I don't get any real mail in it."

"Then what is it?"

He sighed as the two of them continued down Whitehead Street alone. "It's a tin can. I keep a low profile, you won't find me anywhere, even if you try."

"And why not?" she asked, somewhat offended. "You wanna know what I think? I think you're afraid to live in society, you're afraid of failure."

He chaffed with underlying malice. "You keep telling yourself that."

"Who are you going to kill?" she asked him again.

"When?"

"When you do it," she clarified.

"You'll find out."

"All for anarchism?"

He did not respond.

"Don't get me wrong, Jobie. You and I are very similar. I don't want the picket fence dream, either. Really, I don't even know what I *do* want. The thought of it scares me, I feel so lost. It's like I'm driving without headlights. All that I know, what I want more than anything is to do something good. I don't know…that sounds so simple. But you're the same way, aren't you? You'd go to the ends of the known world to defend those you love, wouldn't you?"

He kept silent, just walking forward with fierce momentum.

"I think we're very similar," she mumbled with less confidence.

When he spoke, it was with biting passion. "Someday the people of the streets will rise to my words and avenge themselves against tyranny…that's my dream. To lead that cause."

"I know you better than you think, Jobie," she assured him. "So tell me, how long has it been since you spoke with your brother? Do you know where he is? How long has it been since you've been around someone that really cared about your well-being?"

He stepped up to a large Ficus tree. It was settled comfortably behind a stone and brick wall. Several of the thick leaves had initials scratched into them.

"This is it," he told her. "My mailbox."

She watched him bend down to uncover a pile of rocks. "You have got to be kidding. I almost take this as an insult. You expect me to send mail to a stack of rocks?"

"Wow," he roared joyously as he pulled a note from the top layer of rocks. "There's mail!" He lifted the scrap of paper up to his nose and began reading aloud, "*Bring the Plymouth Fury to Smathers Beach Sunday at noon. No games.*" His heart raced with panic, it was the Freemasons, he knew it—they had finally tracked him down. "That's tomorrow..." His brow crinkled with curiosity as he tossed the remaining rocks aside and shook the tin can in the dim light. His inquisitiveness turned to dread. "Something is in here." He emptied the contents onto the pavement.

Josephine's severed pinky finger rolled between them on the ground. The red paint on the fingernail shimmered under the streetlight.

2:12am

Koz-Mo stood in the center of the living room, blanketed in darkness. He watched the soft light coming from underneath the bathroom door. He wanted to hear shrieks of terror coming from the poor soul hog-tied in the bathtub. Yet there was only silence. A morbid and restless silence. One that spoke ghastly atrocities.

He smiled to himself as he envisioned a bloodbath beyond the door. Of severed limbs and terror-inflicted dementia. He visualized a stream of blood oozing from a lifeless body.

His breathing was unsteady, quivering with ecstasy from his morbid imagination.

He closed his eyes and placed himself in the bathtub, witnessing the death of the celebrity that took his name and betrayed his honor. He envisioned Talon dismembering his limbs with a crude set of tools, working toward eventual and total disembodiment. In life, he had fallen into a trap of luxury and simplicity. He was certain that only Talon could spring the trap for him, to release him from the prison he had willingly made his home.

Total disembodiment. Salvation from the public eye.

Sobriety came quicker than words. In fact, Rusty and Jobie had not spoken a word the entire frantic journey back to Rusty's motel room. Jobie plopped himself onto the foot of the bed, staring into the wall as Rusty paced anxiously back and forth across the length of the room. She gripped her temples with her fingertips, grunting incoherently as she smashed her fist into her open hand.

"That isn't going to help," he told her, still keeping his eyes aimed directly at the wall. His vision was focused at a considerable distance, though the wall was a mere three feet away. "Sit down."

Rusty turned to him, her eyes wild with rage. The words that came from her knotted face were strained with control. "What…is…happening?"

"I don't know."

She leaned down into his face. "What do you mean, you don't know?"

He could smell her alcohol breath—she was so close—yet he never once looked away from the wall. "I don't know."

"It's your car! It is *yours*, isn't it?"

He nodded positively.

"Where did you get it?"

"I told you," he responded evenly. "I got it in Austin, Texas."

She stood silently, unable to draw any realistic conclusions. Even if he had obtained the vehicle by unruly means, the odds seemed very unlikely that the circumstances could have followed him.

"Besides," he added, still looking into the wall. "Think about what has happened. Josephine has been taken as a captive, and I am to show up with the car to meet a stranger."

"Strickland!" she exclaimed. "The NRF!"

He nodded with a maddening sneer. "Yes."

"They are seeking us for what we did, aren't they?" she resolved boldly.

"Why else would they take Josephine and do what they did?"

She rammed her fist into her palm once again. "Damn!" There was silence as she paced the room twice. Jobie's line of vision never changed as she crossed his path. "We've got to stop them," she announced with conviction.

"*We?*"

"Yes, *we*," she insisted as she rammed a stiff finger into his chest. "*We* are in this together."

"In what together?"

"That's why I'm here," she reminded him. "To stop these people, to put them to rest."

"You want to kill them?" he asked her, turning away from the wall to face her.

She was silent for a moment as she stared deeply into his eyes. "Yes, I do."

"Good," he said coldly. "Then you understand why we cannot contact the authorities over this?"

She thought a moment, running her tattooed fingers across her freckled scalp.

"Josephine is on the lam," he reminded her. "We put that guy in the hospital...and I have some skeletons in the closet myself." He collected his thoughts a moment with tense eyes. "The authorities would rather have us than them."

She nodded. "So what are we going to do?"

"We're going to meet them. We're going to show up exactly when they want. They want something from us, and it's not just the car. We're going to find out what that is."

Sunday, September 19, 1999
11:14am

Koz-Mo stood in the doorway of his room, listening to the helpless pleas of Talon's captive. He did not understand why she fought, why she struggled so hard against it. He presumed that her soul was strengthening by the minute under their care—he felt that she should be thankful. He laughed at her anguish, pleasured by the cries for mercy. Her hoarse voice was considerably stifled by the gag in her mouth and the space between the thick old walls of the inn. One could almost think it was another tenant lost in ecstasy rather than experiencing grueling, dehumanizing pain. Koz-Mo was not sure there was a difference between the two.

He strutted across the room to examine his wardrobe. What would he wear on such a day, with such an encounter? He fished through his outfits, pulling out a black mesh muscle shirt and black satin pants with silver studs running along the seam.

He quickly assembled his attire, dressing himself while posing in front of the mirror. Most of his characteristic tattoos were hidden beneath his clothing, though his arms were covered with quasars, satellites, and flying saucers. His face was lean and strong, revealing every firm muscle that locked like porcelain when he clenched his jaw. Two rockets shot toward his short black hair on either side of his thick eyebrows.

He imagined his actions making headlines, tainting his sanitary reputation with deviancy. He sat down on the bed, smiling. His knees knocked together in impatience. He glanced over at the clock, forty-five minutes short of noon.

He slipped his feet into his steel-toed black Tredair shoes and wiggled his toes for optimum comfort. He hated shoes.

He placed his hands on his knees and sat quietly with closed eyes. He felt vile and wicked. Alive once again. He had not felt it in years.

Sunlight crept through the cracks of Jobie's tiny shack. It was as if the walls were lit with pinstripes. Dust floated in the still air, catching thin rays of light to create a series of luminous bars throughout the shanty quarters.

He was covered in sweat, sitting on the edge of his sleeping post. The heat of the day was unbearable in his little hovel, and the stench was far worse. Even he could barely tolerate it, despite how used to it he was.

His makeshift terrycloth cloak was sprawled flat at his side, its dingy material already seasoned with the blood of his opponent. He had revised its design, adding hidden internal pockets and loops fitted to hold unseen weaponry. It was battle ready, as was he.

He stood up—faint from the heat—and threw the cloak over his head. All its hidden compartments were lined up perfectly for quick reflexes. He made some test runs, practicing his draw with each secret "holster". His swift movements stirred the dusty air, dismantling the strips of light that penetrated the many cracks in his modest dwelling. He was very pleased with the results of his work. Strickland and the boys would not even see it coming, he was certain.

He sat down on the bed once again, reaching for a ratty brown paper bag housed inside a red milk crate. He emptied the contents on the bed—a rusted chain, pepper spray, and a butterfly knife. He tucked the pepper spray inside the secret internal pocket and took the butterfly knife in hand, leaving the chain on the bed.

He sprang to his feet and bounced to the door, careful to disassemble the booby traps. The battery acid poised to spill by opening the door. The razor blades set up to slice the shins. The netting that would fall from the ceiling onto any unwanted intruder. He was not in the habit of accepting company. In fact, he would never dare. His future depended on it.

His pupils collapsed into tiny pinpricks as he stepped into the bright daylight. He took a moment to reassemble his lethally external traps—his self-made security system that would protect his labyrinth of dark secrets. He walked calmly through the yard under the cover of his thick and heavy beach towel cloak. By the fence, hidden from view, was his old moped, which he had named Ol' Bessie. It was covered with rust and chipped red paint, barely road-worthy and nowhere near meeting safety standards. Yet transportation nonetheless. He pulled it out of the gate and into the road alongside the Plymouth Fury, which was hidden underneath a pale blue tarp. He did not give a second glance as he sped off down the street on Ol' Bessie, leaving the Fury alongside the curb.

It was forty minutes before noon.

Rusty waited in the parking lot of her motel, balancing herself over the drain, searching for Jobie. She wanted to be able to see him approaching, yet at the same time she did not want to be perfectly visible in case the NRF would happen to find her first.

She looked down the street once again. No black Plymouth Fury in sight. She grew uneasy, twiddling her thumbs on her belt loops with her hands partially tucked inside her pockets. Sweat covered her brow, speckling her fair skin. She reached up to wipe her forehead with the back of her hand, checking her watch again before tucking her hand back inside her pocket. It was thirty minutes before the hour of noon. She lunged forward onto the toes of her oxblood Doc Martens, and then rocked back to her heels. Back and forth, waiting, sweating.

She could hear what sounded like a gnat buzzing in her ear. It grew louder and louder, irritating in its unhealthy sputter. She leaned forward, catching a glimpse of an old weathered motorized scooter heading toward her down Whitehead Street. A trail of thick cloth fluttered in the wind behind the shanty contraption, rippling in the breeze like a flame on a wick. He pulled up alongside her as the scooter coughed in discontinuity.

"There's room for two," he told her as he edged forward.

"You're kidding," she protested, not budging an inch as she squinted in the harsh sunlight.

He pulled his head out of the cloak to greet her with his piercing eyes. His skin, though normally appearing as a severe sunburn, was practically luminous in natural light. His complexion radiated like a string of red Christmas lights. It somehow looked perfectly natural.

"They wanted the car," she reminded him frantically. "We need to bring them the car!"

"I'm not giving them my car," he grumbled with a disturbing rile as if her suggestion was utterly absurd. "They aren't walking away in one piece today. I don't know what you were expecting…"

"I was expecting that your car would matter less to you than Josephine's safety."

"They aren't bringing her today," he informed her. "That's a ploy to get us there. There's more to this than we presently know."

Rusty stomped her foot forcefully on the ground, clenching her fists into tight balls that shook in front of her. "I'm not interested in getting even with them, I want Josephine back safely."

"It'll happen," he told her casually. "Get on. And don't underestimate me."

11:44am

Talon knelt before a single purple candle. His eyes were closed, his body covered only with darkness. His hands were crossed over his chest with his palms flat against his collarbones. All his muscles were deeply relaxed, his mind at ease.

He could visualize his deceased lover Phaedra. He summoned her image in his mind, keeping her alive in memory. With deep focus, he could feel her presence. Tortured, confused, and unavenged. He could smell her perspiration. He could feel her restless spirit clamoring in a realm akin to vapor. He reached out to her with his mind, calling on her for guidance.

I have found the man who killed you, he verbalized in his mind to her. *Soon, justice.*

His fingertips pressed firmly against his skin. He bowed his head with his eyes partially closed. He could feel her—she was there. And she was pleased. As he knew she would be.

His knees trembled against the hardwood floor, yet he remained still—focused on a reality outside his own. Her reality.

He could sense the swell of anger. Every warm memory of her felt like a shower of brimstone on his soul. The rage had been contained deep inside, waiting to someday explode.

Today was that day.

He raised his head and opened his eyes, looking straight into darkness. The candle was no longer lit, just a smoking stem with a glowing orange tip. There was no draft, no air currents. Yet he was not surprised. She was there with him—he had not bullied his own emotions.

He stood, stretching his arms out like a weathervane. He envisioned her body pressed against his. He put a foot forward, stepping loosely, dancing somberly in the darkness with the dead.

He was stirred by muffled screams of pain. He stood still, listening. It was his captive. Gagged and hog-tied in the bathtub.

He walked through the darkened bedroom to the clothes hanging on the closet door. Black, skin-tight cotton pants, white cotton shirt, and a loose black coat with tails, styled after nineteenth century apparel. Tucked inside the pocket of his coat was a chisel still covered in blood, and a gift for Jobie.

He sunk his feet inside black leather Gripfast shoes and walked into the well-lit living quarters. Koz-Mo sat impatiently on the divan gazing at the clock. Fifteen minutes before noon.

Koz-Mo stood eagerly to greet him. "Shall I get the girl?"

Talon shook his head slowly with steady calculation. "No."

Koz-Mo raised a single bushy eyebrow. "Aren't we taking her down—"

259

"No," Talon repeated in a soft, raspy breath. "She stays."

Koz-Mo's eyes looked up in confusion, though he did not dare question Talon's judgment.

Talon walked to the door with hollow, light steps. Koz-Mo was sharp to follow.

11:46am

Rusty's wispy strawberry blond bangs flickered over her fuzzy scalp as she gripped tightly to Jobie's waist. She had never noticed their size difference, but it was suddenly apparent at such close quarters—on the back of Ol' Bessie. She could easily defeat him in a confrontation simply by sitting on him. She determined that a man of his stature would have to depend on a much different approach in a skirmish. Then again, she decided that his deplorable odor could be enough of an assault on his enemies to ward off any tangible danger.

Ol' Bessie slowly edged down United Street toward Smathers Beach—just blocks from their destination. Barring any problems, such as crushing the dainty bike under their combined weight, they would arrive with minutes to spare.

Jobie steered right onto George Street with his haphazardly designed cloak flapping in the wind around them like a cape.

"I want you to stay at a distance," he told her loudly over his shoulder as the bike buzzed down the street. "If we stay too close together, we could be easily surrounded. We don't want that. Keep spread out at all times, but close enough for safety. Did you bring a weapon?"

"No," she told him loudly. "I don't need one myself." She tightened her fists and playfully punched his kidneys. "See?"

He smiled to himself. He did not doubt that she could handle her own. That was his very first impression of her, after all.

11:53am

Koz-Mo steered the rental car through the back streets of Key West, quietly watching the road as Talon sat in the passenger seat. They passed through the lazy old neighborhoods with the casually elegant houses crammed tightly together. Second story balconies once offered seafaring shipwreckers a perfect view of the clear blue ocean—an empire based on other men's tragedies. The fascinating histories of the grandiose houses were reduced to a mere mention on a tram tour or a pricey overnight stay in a bed and breakfast.

Koz-Mo found himself drifting into the riches of the life he had made for himself. He shook out of it with a deep breath that trailed into maniacal laughter. If his agent only knew what he was about to embark upon, the destination of their short road trip...

"What do you want to do?" Koz-Mo asked Talon. "Once you meet this person from your past?"

"Make up for old times."

"What about the girl?"

"What about her?" he muttered as if the point was irrelevant.

"We can't keep her, and obviously we aren't letting her go with them today."

"Just drive."

Koz-Mo asked no more questions, trusting Talon unequivocally.

12:05pm

Jobie leaned his back against the concrete wall that separated the beach from Roosevelt Boulevard. Sweat poured down his body as the thick, ratty cloth clung to his skin. He ran his wiry fingers along the warm metal surface of the disabled butterfly knife—unable to feel anything with his sense of touch, yet knowing it was there within reach, ready to serve him.

It had killed for him before. It could do it again.

Rusty stood at a distance of no less than fifteen feet, waiting for the NRF to show up. She rocked back and forth nervously on her toes to her heels. She had no idea what to expect, and she knew asking Jobie would not help. He, too, was in the dark.

Tourists with pale skin and sunburned children passed along the sidewalk, crowding the small walkway to the beach. Children screamed in the distance, splashing in the clear ocean water. Cars passed both ways down the busy road, each slowing to make sense of Jobie's unusual combat wear. The children, with their floaties and fluorescent-rimmed sunglasses, gave Rusty equal attention, staring up at her as though she were a giant.

Rusty could not imagine a more inappropriate time and location for such a confrontation to occur. She had to assume it was part of a plan, and that whomever they were to meet had no interest in a physical challenge. The busy atmosphere enforced neutrality. She gazed around at all the people when suddenly she exploded with excitement. "Koz-Mo!" she belted out. "Jobie, look! It's Koz-Mo from *Far Out!*"

Jobie shrugged his shoulders, unfamiliar with the name or the television show. He peeked through the hood of his cloak and cocked his head to catch a glimpse, but there were too many pedestrians passing between them. He shrugged his shoulders once again.

Rusty stammered while doing a frenzied little dance like a child with bladder problems. She jabbed at the air, pointing across the street hysterically to grab their attention. Jobie scrunched his brow in annoyance and growled at her to stop making such a scene. Yet it was her hero—alive and in the flesh—sharing her space along with the other mortals. She could barely contain herself.

When Jobie finally laid eyes upon them, he gasped. Instinctively, he drew the butterfly knife, opening it under his terrycloth battle wear, poised for attack.

It was a blast from his past, and the worst of its kind. The kind that could capsize his life. The kind that knew his secrets, yet knew nothing about him personally. He stared with fear and dread as they crossed the street where motorists paused without hesitation. Talon embodied strength in all it denominations. His only apparent weakness was having none.

Jobie's mouth had suddenly dried. Panic shot through his sweaty little body, tensing his feeble muscles and pressing him to fight or flee. He was certain that the Freemasons were behind it all. He had no doubt that Talon was affiliated somehow, and if he was the best they could send for the job, they chose well.

Jobie's reality was crumbling before his eyes. His hands shook so violently that the butterfly knife nearly shook loose. He did not stand a chance, and it was potently clear that they could pulverize him in a matter of seconds, should they have chosen to do so.

Talon approached with a firm and venomous expression that seemed to hiss with blasphemous fire. "I have waited a long time…"

Jobie crinkled his lips furiously at him.

"Where's the car?" Talon spoke softly as his eyes ripped him apart with rage.

Jobie snarled back. "Where's Josephine?" He pulled the hood from his head. His disheveled hair stuck to his sweaty scalp like an orange ball of wax.

Rusty sheepishly scampered in the distance, noticing only Koz-Mo, waiting for her chance to speak with him once again. She scanned her surroundings for the NRF, invigorated and star-struck. She was perfectly unaware of the circumstances at hand.

"I've waited for this moment," Talon breathed lightly, "to find you, and kill you." His tone was almost pleasurable, as if his words could be anything but warm and sincere.

Children passed by, stopping to examine each of them as their parents scooted them along cautiously. They did not want them to be corrupted with the sight of their own worst nightmares—that their children could turn out in such a way.

"Very few people know what happened that night," Talon seethed, "but I know. I was on your heels, she was supposed to have met me...I was on your trail before you left Austin, before you had taken her life and taken my car to escape."

Jobie pulled the butterfly knife into the bright sun, fully extended. Its shiny blade shimmered in the harsh light of day. "This knife," he began as he waved it back and forth with slow and even strokes. "It's what was used to kill your girlfriend. Not by me, though. I didn't touch her. Treva killed her."

Talon's face remained perfectly stoic. "Your death will be slow. I will make you suffer, you will beg me to let you die." He reached inside the pocket of his thick black coat. "A gift for you," he told him as he held out a fist closed around an object.

Jobie apprehensively backed away, holding the knife out in front of him.

"Please, take it. I picked it just for you."

Jobie opened his hand below Talon's fist as another severed finger dropped into his palm. It was Josephine's other pinky finger. He let it slide between his red fingertips onto the ground where it rolled into the concrete crevices.

Jobie cringed, slashing violently at the air between them. "What do you want of me?" he growled. "What?"

"It's simple, really," Talon responded slowly, unimpressed with Jobie's threatening posture. "I want you dead. Very soon. And I wouldn't mind having the car back, either."

"No, you are wrong," Jobie hissed, trembling in their overbearing shadow. "You will be joining her soon...I don't even recall her name, just another dead whore."

"You're not in a bartering position," Koz-Mo inserted awkwardly. "We have your little lady friend locked up, and we're dismembering her piece by piece!"

"Who the hell are you?" Jobie snarled fervently.

Koz-Mo liked that—it had been years since he had been asked such a thing.

Jobie clutched the butterfly knife with an anxious and quivering hand. Children passed, watching intently.

"Should we call the police?" one mother whispered to her husband.

"No, let's just go...and get the kids," the husband responded.

"Big prize waiting for you at your *mailbox*," Talon informed Jobie. "You'll love it."

"I had my way with her dead body," Jobie fibbed. His words cut deeper than his knife possibly could, as intended. "Yeah, Phaedra—that was her name. I sodomized her corpse."

Talon glanced down the street, noticing a police car slowly approaching. He turned his fierce gaze back to Jobie, drilling him with murderous hatred. "Bring the car tonight," he instructed. "No games."

263

"Set Josephine free," Jobie demanded. He tucked the knife under the sleeve of his cloak, away from the view of the police. They slowed as they passed, watching the small gathering suspiciously.

Talon backed away, scowling with malicious intent. "Midnight. Right here. Bring the car."

The police continued down the street.

"I will be here," Jobie assured him.

12:21pm

Rusty watched Koz-Mo chauffeur Talon away from the beach. She plopped herself on the curb, distraught. She cupped her head in her tattooed hands and squeezed tightly. Her sighs of resignation were drowned out by the tourists on Smathers Beach.

"Koz-Mo is the one," she exhaled in defeat. "How could that be?"

Jobie sat down on the curb next to her. "We can't stay here, we need to go."

"I can't believe it," Rusty repeated helplessly.

"Well, believe it. The world is full of burst bubbles. Welcome to reality."

"I don't understand, I just don't get it." She gasped with remorse. She turned to him with a bent expression. "How do you know that strange guy anyway?"

He took a deep breath and slowly let it out as he collected his thoughts. "I don't."

"Then who is he?"

"How much do you really want to know?" he asked cautiously.

"Is it that bad?"

He let go of a beleaguered breath. "Treva did it. The person he wants is already dead. Yes, I left Texas with his car, but also with Treva's dead body. He seeks revenge…well, I'm not the one."

"How did Treva die? I mean, really?"

"I've already told you."

She shook her head. "Never mind, I don't want to know."

"Good choice."

"You have a lot of skeletons in your closet," she determined.

He raised his brow with a forceful nod. "To say the least."

"Why Josephine? Why have they taken her and done these things?" She raised her head with closed eyes, and then let go of a deep breath. "I thought this was about Strickland's boys."

"I didn't know. I still don't know."

264

"What are we going to do?" she asked.

"Are you still in this with me?"

"More now than ever."

"But it's not with Strickland or the NRF," he reminded her.

"Obviously. And it doesn't matter. I want Josephine returned safely before they kill her."

"How do you know that hasn't already happened?" Jobie mused gravely.

Rusty gasped. "She's dead, isn't she?"

"I have no idea. It's hard to say what we'll find at the mailbox. That may be our answer."

Rusty took in a shaky breath. "So what are we going to do?"

"Exactly what he wants. We're bringing the car to him."

"We're not going to fight back?"

He scoffed. "I didn't say that. We have one ace in the hole—they never saw you with me. They think I'm alone." He quickly stood, brushing the sand off his tattered cloak. He raised the hood over his head to pointlessly conceal his identity. "Let's go. We need to check the mailbox."

12:51pm

Rusty and Jobie crept nervously down Whitehead Street, sharing a deep sense of dread. They busied themselves through the congregations of camera-flashing tourists that lined the sidewalk in front of Truman's Little White House.

Jobie visualized the carnage that awaited them in his makeshift mailbox. He stopped before crossing the street, standing with his heels on the curb. The duct-taped toes of his shoes were bent over the edge, pointing downward toward the gutter.

His heart suddenly began racing, his breathing erratic with panic. His eyes were widened like saucers, as though the claws of death were ripping at his body.

"What is it?" Rusty asked.

"I did this," he responded with a shaky voice. His rigid fingers clutched the fabric of his ragtag cloak. "Everything that has happened to her."

Rusty reached out to grab his stiff hand, but he resisted. She then placed her large hand on his frail shoulder and squeezed gently. "How?" she asked calmly, pleasantly. "How did you do this? You didn't do this, you know that."

He stared forward to the white fence across the street. "What are we going to find there?" he grumbled to the wind.

She looked forward as a car passed her line of vision momentarily. Her tone had changed, quieter, more defeated. "I don't know."

265

"Yeah," he continued with his self-loathing, "this is my fault. I was there when his girlfriend was killed, I helped plan it all."

Rusty quickly turned to him, staring deep into his frightened eyes. "Did you kill her?"

"No...but I didn't stop it from happening, either." He bent down to the ground and sat on the curb, never allowing his eyes to leave the white picket fence that hid his mailbox and all its unknown contents. "I really loved her."

"Who?"

"Treva, the girl who killed her."

Rusty took a seat next to him, dwarfing him like a child. "She sounds crazy to me."

"No more crazy than me, I guess. Have you ever been in love?"

She wiped some dust off the leather of her boots. "No. I love my family. Even more than I love myself, to be honest. I've never given myself a reason to love myself. I'm still waiting for that."

"Well...I loved her. I've never really loved anything. And I can't let go of that, still, to this day...it's still with me. Love never dies. I still sleep with the memory of her."

"You probably have better sleep than I have, then," she admitted. "I envy you."

The sight of the white fence pained him. "Thanks for being here, Rusty. I've never had someone stand by me like this. I can't tell you what it means to me."

"Ah, you're going to get me all teary eyed, and you can't do that now," she said as she pointed across the street. "I'm afraid to get up and take this step."

"Me too."

"Jobie, someday you will have an army of friends to back you in all your dreams, whatever they may be. The words you write, they will move people someday. You're passionate, you believe in your vision, what more is there?" She could sense his entire chemistry relaxing with every word. His cardboard posture loosened next to her, yet his eyes never looked away from their destination. "We could be heroes, Jobie."

"As though our names were written in sand on the beach," he joked.

She choked out a stifled laugh. "Come on, let's go. We've got to be brave."

He stepped up from the curb like an explosion, forthright with determination and confidence. He helped her to her feet and together they trekked across the street toward the mailbox. Visions of severed limbs and teeth and eyes danced wickedly in their minds. Each step brought them closer to reality.

"He is evil," Rusty murmured as they reached the other side.

"I know," he agreed passionately. "There was a reason Treva did what she did."

They stepped up to the tree, looking down upon the rock that covered the secret mailbox.

"I could kill him," she growled. "Easily. Is that bad?"

"I think it's good. A public improvement to be rid of him." He cleared his throat uncomfortably. "And speaking of *him*, your idol is no better. He is *not* our friend."

She struggled with the changing face behind her eyes. Her sanitized world of mundane life in rural Illinois was long gone. She had escaped to make a difference, to make a change. But the only change that occurred was internal.

"I know," she replied as they both hesitated to look inside the mailbox. "And that tears me apart."

"Why?"

"Because when I said I could kill him, I wasn't talking about your old friend. I was talking about Koz-Mo."

He slowly reached down and lifted the rock, revealing the tin can. He looked up at Rusty with wide eyes. She nodded apprehensively.

He picked up the tin can and tipped it upside down. A cockroach fell out onto the ground and crawled frantically away.

It was otherwise empty.

Monday, September 20, 1999
12:01am

The beachfront was dark and empty when Talon and Koz-Mo returned to Smathers Beach at midnight. Only one car awaited their arrival, a black convertible 1956 Plymouth Fury. Talon's face brightened, but he could not smile. Not until Jobie was dead.

Koz-Mo pulled alongside the Fury and parked. Together they waited for an ambush. There was nothing. No sound, no noise. Nothing.

Talon slowly stepped out of the car, cautiously looking over his shoulder. He opened the door of the Fury and stuck his head inside. It was empty, yet the keys were stuck in the ignition. A wretched foul stench filled the cab. He held his breath as he grabbed the keys and dropped them inside his coat pocket.

He stepped out into the dim light and looked to Koz-Mo. "The keys are in it."

"Where is he?" Koz-Mo asked.

"Oh, he's here," Talon spoke softly with confidence. "Watching us right now." He removed the sharp chisel from his pocket and slowly headed to the beach. "Stay here and watch the car."

Talon rolled weightlessly up the steps like fog. The beach was dark, and as he passed through the dense foliage and palm trees that withheld the sandy beach from the road, he kept his senses alive, waiting for that strike.

It never came.

Instead, he walked safely onto the beach where the moonlight ricocheted off the calm ocean waters, lighting the world with a peaceful glow. The beach was vacant except for one person sitting on the shoreline facing the ocean. A person covered with a shanty, hand-made cloak.

Talon quietly approached with his bloodstained chisel leading the way. The only sound was the wind and the squawking seagulls that drifted through it. There were no waves, yet there was the faint sound of water chopping against the shore. Nothing out of the ordinary.

He edged closer and closer, creeping through the sand, holding the chisel out in front of him. His steps were calm and calculated—he had no interest in a brawl, he just wanted to kill him. The scenario would be perfect.

Closer he stepped until he could see the individual stitches of floss that held the cloak together. He could see the thin shoulders beneath the thick fabric. He

268

could see the bottoms of his duck-taped boots as he sat with crossed legs, completely unaware of the danger that lurked within arm's reach.

Talon lunged at him, driving the chisel deep into his back. Sand flowed in place of blood as the entire upper portion of it crumbled from the impact. Its coconut head rolled down into the warm ocean water.

Talon rushed to his feet and turned around with the chisel pressed in front of him. Standing between him and the road, partially hidden in the thick foliage behind the palm trees was Jobie dressed in stealthy black, carrying a rusted chain and a vicious smile.

Talon found himself trapped between the ocean and his lascivious opponent. The only way out was through him. Jobie slowly stepped out into the moonlight, rattling the chain as he prowled with overbearing confidence. His cheeks were puffy as though he were holding his breath.

No words were exchanged.

Talon edged closer, limiting the distance between them. Their eyes were locked in one single line of vision. Talon stared deeply into Jobie's hostile eyes. His hatred struggled with respect for his adversary's bravery, yet it all came together with a unified vengeance. Talon was stone cold and perfectly under control. Jobie envied this. In another life, he would be honored to share the same cause with this devilish man. There was an unusual level of respect that rivaled their hatred.

Jobie lashed out at his foe, slashing his ankle with the tip of the chain, and then pulling it back quickly. Talon hobbled forward, grimacing. It was the first sign of weakness or expression Jobie had ever seen of him. Jobie pulled a lighter from his pocket and flicked it twice before a tall flame danced over his clenched fist.

Talon rushed at him with his chisel outstretched and slashing the air with firm, swift strokes.

Jobie puffed his cheeks and spit a steady flow of lighter fluid from his lips and through the lighter's flame. The fluid exploded into an enormous fire that engulfed Talon's attack like a glove. Talon emerged from the flames with his thick coat smoldering, only to find Jobie's rusted chain rapping his arm, knocking the chisel loose. Talon dove into the sand to retrieve it as Jobie lashed at him once more with the chain. It smashed against his back with a bone-crushing thud, but Talon was able to grab hold of the end and pull Jobie to the sand with him. Talon slid the chisel across Jobie's stomach, slicing his shirt and nicking his skin. Blood dripped down his belly and onto the sand.

Jobie grabbed a handful of sand and threw it into Talon's face—undeterred by his new injury, unable to feel it or anything else with his dead senses. He squirmed away, pulling the chain free as he rushed to his feet once again. The blood dampened his clothes and covered his skin with a shade of red much darker and thicker than his own unnatural complexion.

Talon scrambled to his feet, rubbing his eyes and preparing for hand-to-hand combat. To his surprise, Jobie had retreated into the dark foliage. Talon chased after him, but the distance was already too great. He shook his head in disappointment as he made his way back to the street where Koz-Mo waited calmly in the rental car.

"Did you see him?" Talon asked as he limped into the street.

"Who?"

Talon looked around, scanning Roosevelt Boulevard. Shadows crawled across the pavement from trees twisting in the streetlights.

Jobie was nowhere to be seen.

Talon gripped the chisel tightly. He could not leave without finding him, yet he knew that it was very unlikely that he would be able to track him down. He had the car, and he still had his hostage. They would meet again.

"Come on," Talon told Koz-Mo as he stepped up to the Fury and fished the key from his pocket. He slid into the driver's seat and turned the ignition, bringing the old engine to life. "We'll find him again."

Koz-Mo followed the Fury back to the inn, disappointed with the turn of events, hoping for a more dramatic conclusion.

Talon pulled up alongside the curb and quickly shut down the engine. The car felt tainted, like it was no longer his. The putrid stench of it sickened him. He lumbered out of it angrily, enraged at what had just transpired.

"I'm taking that bitch's hand off," Talon grumbled to himself as he stomped up to the door of the inn.

Koz-Mo pulled up behind the Fury just as Talon slammed the door behind him. He shut off the lights and turned off the engine. The street was unusually quiet. He opened the door and stepped onto the moist ground just as the trunk of the Fury flew open. Rusty sprang forth onto the sidewalk, standing face to face with Koz-Mo.

She grabbed him by the neck with one firm hand and rammed her meaty fist directly into his nose. A crunching sound let loose the flow of blood as Koz-Mo batted wildly at the air, disabled by his own confusion.

Rusty took him by the mesh shirt and dragged him into the yard, beating him with bloodied knuckles and steel-toed boots. She stopped, adjusting her collar and straightening her thin red braces as she assessed the damage. It was severe. She brushed her strawberry blond wispy hair to one side as she wiped the sweat and blood from her brow. Koz-Mo lay in a heap of broken down flesh at her feet—at her mercy. She reached into his pockets and fished out his cell phone, the keys to the rental car, and most importantly, to the inn.

She brushed her hands off and swaggered up the steps.

She could not wait to meet Talon.

12:31am

Jobie stepped forward from the foliage after the cars had driven away with Rusty safely inside the trunk of the Fury, soon to discover Josephine's mysterious whereabouts. Jobie ran across Roosevelt Boulevard where Ol' Bessie was parked deep inside the hotel parking lot. He climbed aboard and started the engine. A trail of fresh droplets of white paint ran the length of the street. It was the same color as the paint on his hidden shed. In fact, it was the same paint. The can was strapped to the bottom of the Fury and punctured with a small hole. It was just large enough to leave a substantial trail to follow all the way back to Josephine.

Everything was going exactly as planned.

12:41am

Talon hastily unlocked the door and bounded through the darkness toward the bathroom. He turned on the lights, pausing a moment until his eyes could adjust. Josephine was curled up inside the bathtub, hog-tied—her face alive with terror. Her frazzled braids covered her shoulders, disheveled and coming apart.

Talon wasted no time disassembling the ties that bound her arms and legs, pulling her up on the toilet seat as he restrained her with his powerful hands. He yanked her bandaged right hand up to the counter and steadied it as he reached for the chisel. She shrieked in horror—her voice raspy and worn thin. She struggled to free herself from his clutches, but to no avail. He was too strong.

He placed the chisel's sharp edge against her wrist.

"Your friends didn't follow through," he whispered as he prepared to drive the chisel into her flesh. "They abandoned you."

Her cries were shrill and savage. She watched through tears, aghast at the horror of losing her right hand when suddenly the bathroom door burst wide open like an explosion.

It was Rusty.

She grabbed Talon by the throat and shoved him firmly into the bathtub with her merciless strength. She punched him in the mouth, jarring his head to one side. His eyes were wide with shock.

Hers were calm and steady, though filled with rage. "Go!" she screamed at Josephine.

Josephine stood abruptly, hesitating a moment to help, but overwhelmed with the desire to be free. She stumbled to the door, steadying herself with both bandaged hands as she fled through the bathroom door.

She made it all the way to the front door, and then stopped. She had to help Rusty. Together they could destroy him. She fumbled her way back to the bathroom to see Rusty and Talon struggling together, banging from one wall to the other. She watched Rusty send a swift uppercut to Talon's jaw, releasing an explosion of blood, yet freeing his armed hand. The chisel rushed through the air, stabbing her in the neck. Rusty put her hand to her injury as the blood sprayed like a fountain. She loosely grabbed his neck with her other hand, but it was not enough. He shoved the chisel into her chest, crunching through the bones.

Rusty fell to her knees, waving her free hand wildly before collapsing to the ground.

Josephine screamed in terror as she covered her mouth and shielded her eyes. Talon stepped toward her, his lips dripping of blood like a vampire. She scrambled back out the door, racing down the stairs, sobbing with each step as Talon trailed right behind her, reaching desperately for her. She burst through the front door of the inn and stumbled clumsily onto the lawn just as a blinding light blazed in her wide eyes.

"Josephine!" Jobie screamed from the light—the headlight of Ol' Bessie.

He jumped off the scooter with his chain rattling wildly in his hands. She lunged at him, wrapping her arms around his neck. Her bandaged paws clung to his bony shoulders.

"Let's go!" she cried wildly.

Talon stepped out of the door, his chisel in hand with blood dripping from his chin, staining his stark white shirt.

Jobie stepped forward, poised for attack.

"No," Josephine exclaimed, "let's go!"

Talon glided down the steps, skulking in a semi-circle around them. Koz-Mo lay in a mangled mess of bloodied limbs on the lawn beside them.

Josephine clawed at Jobie's back, urging him to leave with desperate whimpers.

"Fight to the death," Jobie suggested. "Seems you've already lost."

Talon shook his head calmly as he circled around them, edging closer to the street. Blood seeped from his smile. "You're mistaken."

"He killed Rusty!" Josephine shrieked.

Jobie's tense posture fell limp for a moment.

"Let's go!" Josephine insisted.

"We're even," Talon offered. "You go…and I will go."

"No," Jobie growled furiously.

"The police are coming. Is that really what you want?"

Jobie nodded. "I'm innocent."

"Are you?" Talon asked. "I bet not."

Jobie recalled his grave secrets stowed away inside his shack. He lowered his chain and motioned to the Fury, allowing him to leave.

Talon wasted no time climbing inside his old car and fleeing the scene, leaving Koz-Mo alone on the lawn to deal with the mess that was made—the crimes that were committed.

Jobie and Josephine rushed up the stairs and into Talon's room where Rusty's body was struggling on the floor. She had crawled a few feet into the dark living room, leaving a bloody trail behind her. She raised her head to greet them, smiling as they entered. She felt them gather her in their arms. Their touch was so warm, so soft. She shivered on the floor, huddled against an impending darkness that caved in around her.

She looked into Jobie's bloodshot eyes with a peace she had never known. "We did it."

"No," he corrected her with a quivering voice, "you did it."

"Back page of the *Olney Register*," she muttered with a blood-spewing cough. "Ma will be so proud."

"Come on," Josephine insisted. "We need to get her out of here."

As her words fell into a cavern of silence, Rusty's body violently convulsed until death suddenly and unmistakably claimed her.

An unusual smile graced her lifeless face. One of peace and contentment. Of pride and conviction.

2:11am

Josephine sat trembling in the corner of her well-lit room at the Merlinn Inn, staring at the floor with eyes like ice cubes. Her face was vacant, her mind numb. Her bandaged hands were wrapped around her lean body, shaking, suffering the loss of Rusty.

"I'm sorry," Jobie offered sternly, breaking the silence with his offensively frothy tone. He was overwhelmed with guilt. He carefully stitched the blood-encrusted gash on his stomach together with black thread that crisscrossed his red skin. "If I could have done anything more to help you, I would have. If there was any way I could have prevented this, I would have."

She swallowed hoarsely with a loud and painful gulp.

"I understand if you don't want me around," Jobie told her as he closed the minor surgery and threw his torn black shirt over his scrawny neck, pushing his arms through the proper holes as the worn fabric tumbled over his scant torso. "I don't blame you for being angry."

"Are we safe?" she mumbled under her breath to the floor.

273

Jobie perked up with optimism. "Very safe. I promise you."

"I don't blame you at all," she said lightly with a distilled breath. "You didn't do it."

"He's an animal," Jobie growled. "A monster."

Josephine sat quietly a moment. She pulled her hands up to her face where she looked at the bandages with no obvious change of expression. "What do you plan to do?"

"How are your hands?" Jobie asked, avoiding her question. "Do you need to see a doctor?"

"I think he was a doctor," she grumbled coldly. "He had done this before to someone else, and maybe many others. He knew what he was doing." She closed her eyes, revealing the torment in lines across her forehead. "There's no infection, I just look like a cartoon character now."

"How's that?" he asked.

She raised her wrapped hands in the air. "Four fingers, each hand. Like Bart Simpson."

He laughed.

"What are you going to do?" she repeated more vigorously.

He did not reply, but continued laughing, reveling in the lightened atmosphere.

"I'm not one for vengeance," she said. "But I'm not taking this lightly, either. What are you going to do?"

He took a moment to stand, pacing across the hardwood floors to the dresser where Rusty's rolls of film remained untouched. He clicked on the television with the remote control. A weatherman stood in front of a map of southern Florida splattered with treacherous tropical storms painted with vibrantly digital colors. He immediately turned it off again. "First, I want you to know that I can permanently take you somewhere safe, if you want. You'd be welcome, and you'd be anonymous."

"Where?"

"With my brother Rik," he told her. "In Austin, Texas."

"Texas, huh…"

"Secondly," he began as he fumbled through his pockets and pulled out a cell phone, "this." He walked over to her and sat on the cold floor in front of her, creating a third wall for her. He turned it on and flipped through the saved phone numbers. "This one comes up often…we need to know where he's heading. Maybe someone at this number will know."

"Is that from the house?"

He nodded affirmatively before closing the phone and looking deeply into her eyes. "It's Koz-Mo's. Rusty had taken it from him, and I took it from her before she died." He glanced down at her hands and stumbled back into sorrow and hopelessness. "We need to get some new bandage and disinfectant for you. If your hands get infected, it'll turn way worse."

274

She reached forward with clubbed hands and stiff muscles and wrapped her arms firmly around his head.

He patted her knee gently in return. "I'm glad you're okay."

"Let me know what I need to do to help you," she urged.

He rushed to his feet, handing her the cell phone. "You can make the call. Your voice will be much less suspicious than mine. Are you going to be okay here if I go to the store to get you supplies?"

"No!" she screamed frantically. "Don't leave!"

He hesitated momentarily, and then knelt before her once again.

"Please, don't leave me. Don't leave tonight at all. Stay with me, I can't be alone. We can get all that stuff tomorrow...okay?"

"Sure," he said as he plopped down on the floor once again.

She closed her eyes and released a long-winded sigh. "Tell me about Austin."

Tuesday, September 21, 1999
7:12am

Los Angeles, California

Felina rolled over in bed, staring into the darkness with narrowly slit eyes. She reached over to the nightstand, fumbling with the digital alarm clock, reaching for the ringing telephone. The red lights of the clock revealed it to be seven o'clock in the morning.

"Who could be calling this early?" X grumbled from the opposite side of the bed.

She let out a begrudged sigh, thick with exhaustion. "I was having a really bad dream about…" her words trailed with another grating ring from the phone.

"About who?"

She picked up the phone and raised it to her fatigued face. "Do you know what time it is?" she demanded of the caller.

"I'm sorry, ma'am," the friendly female voice gently offered on the other end. "It's ten in the morning here, I must've called out of the time zone—my bad. I'm in Key West, Florida, I am the manager of the Flagler Inn where your acquaintances were staying the past couple days. They left several important items behind, including their credit cards and cell phone. Do you know how I can get in touch with them? They won't be getting very far without—"

"Just a minute," Felina roared. She cupped her hand to the phone and turned to X. "What was the name of the place Koz-Mo and Talon going to be staying at in Key Largo?"

X groaned as he rubbed his eyes with clenched, tattooed knuckles. "Something Neptune…"

"Neptune something," Felina grumbled into the phone. "In Key Largo. Look, it's seven in the morning here, I'm pregnant—" she stopped talking immediately and lowered the phone dormant against the pillow as she turned to X, exasperated. "That bitch hung up on me!"

5:10pm

Vaca Key, Florida

"Get off the road!" an irritated motorist shouted in Jobie's rearview mirror.

He stared forward to Highway 1, steering Ol' Bessie into her own single headlight beam, chasing his preternatural instinct. The cars lined up behind him as though he were leading an impressive motorcade or kicking off a poorly planned parade. At full speed, the moped's rapped-out engine failed to exceed the minimum speed limit.

He scowled with great determination, painfully aware that Ol' Bessie was being pushed beyond her limits. He could smell the heat rising from the engine, filling his nostrils with sufferable warmth. His limited resources were tapped at the slightest opposition, which infuriated him. Two hours on the road, two roadside stops to relax the engine, and such little headway in distance traveled. He anticipated Ol' Bessie to protest living once and for all, leaving him stranded in an unfamiliar and potentially hostile environment of common folk.

More importantly, he feared his plight was in vain. It was a gamble to leave Josephine unprotected, yet he followed his one and only lead. He depended on its reliability, knowing nothing of its source.

He veered off the highway into a well-lit service station to once again relax the engine. The stretch of cars that followed him so closely accelerated at once—many honking as they passed. The single headlight condensed from the size of an enormous veil of light that covered the highway to a compressed ball flattened against the wall of the small concrete service station. He shut down the labored engine and placed a duct-taped boot onto the oil-stained pavement, hoisting himself vertically. The black padded vinyl seat was imprinted with the shape of his bony buttocks. He stretched, raising his clenched crimson fists skyward while deeply inhaling the salty oceanic air. He tugged at his loosely fitting black jeans, and then nervously rummaged through the contents of Ol' Bessie's baskets, making sure his items were still secured.

He glanced up at the northern sky, facing his desired destination. Dark storm clouds draped the horizon, seemingly crushing the silver sunset, bringing forth a premature nightfall. The wind was cool and thick with the smell of rain. Early evening had transformed into the dead of night.

He backed himself against the wall and slid down onto the stained concrete. Circular flats of crushed and discarded bubblegum spotted the cement in an impressive array of colors like random polka dots. Customers walked over them with stiff and abrupt steps as they skirted around him, ill at ease in his presence.

277

They diverted the focus of their attention and conversations to the approaching tropical storm.

He scowled at them from time to time to fend off stares. He realized that in Key West he was no longer considered a spectacle to the locals. But the everyday people of the mainland were far less open to his eccentricities. To his surprise, the negative attention bothered him in ways that never had before. It disappointed him that he had been drawn to complacency so easily. Being away from his home—only a brief jaunt up the Keys—he had stumbled upon an old familiar world. The world he had successfully avoided since he stepped into the topsy-turvy looking glass of Key West.

Succumbing to discomfort, he impatiently rose to his feet, choosing to trust the stamina of Ol' Bessie once again.

He had no other choice.

He wiggled his ass into the imprint on the old vinyl seat once again and kick-started the moped back to life. It responded with a disengaging quiver and a hacking belch of smoke. The entire frame buzzed uneasily between his legs like a maimed mosquito. He revved the engine and steered it through the oil-stained lot, zigzagging between smashed wads of gum like slaloms. Without signaling, he merged into traffic as a new trail of cars reduced their speed behind him in a cloud of smoky exhaust.

7:50pm

Key Largo, Florida

Silver rays of sunlight burst skyward from the horizon, piercing the ominous storm clouds that swept the sky like a circumfusion of boiling black ink. Lightning shimmied across the rippling ocean waves, zigzagging back and forth over the surface of the choppy water. The entire world seemed compressed to shades of gray and black, tunneling toward absolute darkness. The turbulent whitecaps crashed against the rocky shoreline, folding over the land in explosions of salt tinged vapor. The rising ocean mists tumbled into the proportionate rows of palm trees that lined the coastal front. The cold, brackish wind violently shook them like organic pompons.

Talon stood on the edge of the dock at Neptune's Hideaway with his toes curled over the edge of the wooden structure. He draped a relaxed arm over the center support beam, comforting himself in his tumultuous surroundings, watching the storm devour the natural light of the world. The blustery winds screeched through the moist air with a grinding rhythmic pulse akin to a locomotive. In the distance, a wall of rain rolled over the vacillating brine, aggravating the ebb and flow of tide with its unrelenting descent. The horizon had vanished to black.

Talon stood unflinching, eager for the elements to be thrust upon him in a cleansing gust of wind.

"Satisfied?" a familiar voice broke through the howling wind.

Talon turned away from the undulating seascape to face the bleakness of dry land. Standing on the edge of the shoreline was Jobie, holding his rusted chain in one hand and a gas can in the other. His spidery body was comically padded with poorly fitting clothes, seemingly dressed for a child's backyard war games. The menacing anger that contorted his boyish face was deliciously primitive. Talon forfeited a condescending chuckle at Jobie's expense.

"Not yet," Talon replied shortly, still choked with laughter. "You're still alive."

Jobie stepped forward onto the damp wooden planks of the dock, trapping Talon against the oncoming storm that viciously smashed against the wooden framework. Jobie frantically poured the combustible contents of the gas can over the surface of the dock as he advanced toward his adversary. As the last drops fell from the can, he tossed it into the water where it was sucked into the undulating pelagic churn.

"You killed my friend," Jobie snarled as he dangled the chain with outstretched hands. He approached with steady, calm steps. "Killing you will be easy."

Talon chuckled, crossing his arms and raising his nose to the air. He stared down the bridge of his narrow nose at Jobie, fawning at the intimidation. He shook his head as if to dismiss the threat outright.

"I'm glad you arrived," Talon told him. "Saves me trouble." He belted out a belittling guffaw as Jobie stepped within hand's reach.

Jobie whipped him across the abdomen with the chain. A jagged welt quickly arose. Talon smiled, clearly unmoved.

"You'll need to do better than that," Talon proposed lightly.

Jobie's eyes tightened and his face contorted wildly. His spindly body was hunched as though his spine was furrowed with plate armor. He stared viciously into Talon's eyes while wrapping the chain around his hand to secure it for another attack. He lashed at him once again with the chain, wrapping it around Talon's leg and pulling with all his strength.

Talon did not budge.

Instead, he yanked the end of the chain and reeled Jobie like a helpless fish on a line. Jobie's flailing arms scratched and clawed the air between them in vain. For Talon, there was no challenge.

Talon gripped his neck and forced him to the dock, all the while wrestling his floundering little body into submission. Taking hold of the chain, he wrapped it several times around Jobie's neck and shoved him to the edge where the black water churned and erupted, waiting to devour him.

Jobie's breathing restricted. It would be nearly impossible for him to find the surface once in the violent turbulence of the water, especially while hanging from a chain. His own chain. He could not fathom a more wretched death. As his face was pushed over the edge of the dock and his body was being slowly scooted closer to the edge, he looked back at the storm, at the wall of rain that crept so closely. Too close. There was only so much time to turn the tides.

His shoulder blades rolled off the wood as the vicious ocean waves lapped at him like hungry dogs. His spine scraped along the edge of the dock. His hands reached toward the dock, and then into the pocket of his poorly fitted pants. His spidery claws quickly emerged from his pockets, frantically clicking his lighter as his hips arrived at the edge. He lowered the flame to the wooden planks, into the fumes of gasoline.

The dock erupted in a blanketing inferno. The fire danced up Talon's black cotton shorts, rushing him to his feet in a frenetic furor. Jobie held tightly to the wood that blazed with fire, securing himself on the dock as he yanked Talon back onto him, back into the flames. Jobie smiled at Talon's shock and terror. His skin was numb and free of the pain of his own burning clothing. He could see the fire covering his legs and stomach, but his focus was on the chain wrapped around Talon's arm—the chain that held them both inside the inferno. Only Jobie was immune.

The rain suddenly rushed over them, drowning the fire into submission. Jobie scooted himself back onto the dock and scrambled to his feet. His black clothing was singed and hanging from his frail body in smoldering strips. His legs and torso were wrapped in the discarded towels that had once comprised his cloak, now a rudimentary form of insulation that protected him from his own crude arsenal.

He stepped over Talon's blistering and burnt body and looked down upon him with a sheepish smile of victory. Talon's screams of pain were awash in the deafening drum of rain that ravaged the coastline. With a duct-taped boot, Jobie kicked Talon off the dock and into the dark waters that slammed against the rocky shore. His trembling body splashed into the ocean, submerged within the treacherous current beneath the white-capped waves.

Jobie stood momentarily in place as the wind hammered prickly droplets of rain against his red flesh. Lightning danced along the ocean in the distance, scarcely visible through the violent storm that cradled the scene of Jobie's latest crime.

Key West, Florida

Taking aim, Reaction
I have once again taken the life of another human being. In many ways, it's like sex. The first time is always the most awkward. But that second time, the euphoria was overwhelming. Maybe it was simply the knowledge that the world would be a better place with that one life removed. Or maybe I have become a living nightmare.

The world's soul corrodes before my eyes. It corrodes the soul behind my eyes as well, fevered by the poisonous venom of the Malcontents who plot my demise. They envy my purity, adding it to the list of their evasive desires. As they have sought commodity, I have coveted only the simple pleasures of life. Love, happiness, understanding, acceptance. I live as nothing, I avoid the trappings of the modern world, yet their venom corrupts me. I see my face in their eyes, and I see myself in them. In my tropical retreat I myself have become lagged into complacency. The curse ends now. Today I sever myself entirely from society's corruption. Commerce exists on the science of subservience, preying on the desire for material wealth and the pretense of contentedness. It's easy to be sucked away by the corporate undertow. Buy your happiness, sell your soul. You'll love yourself for it.

It is time the demons were unmasked. The real enemy must be destroyed. They have made a monster of me, though I was born of pure innocence. I never chose to kill. Yet murder has become my trade. I am a killer, vicious and cunning. It is time for me to focus this energy. It is time to give back the soul that was stripped away from my fellow man. The Enemies of Progress will be destroyed. I may die trying, but I will have given my best shot. And what more could I ever hope for? Today I pack my arsenal. In time I will wash my hands with the blood of the Enemies of Progress. And in doing so, break free the shackles of the Malcontents. My destiny is that of World Savior.

281

Jobie stared down at his poor penmanship while crunching the lid of the ballpoint pen between his yellow stained teeth. Beads of sweat slithered down his fiery skin into bloodshot eyes. A single worn boot tapped the dirty floor in a nervously syncopated rhythm. His hunched body cradled his words with pointed elbows stabbing knobby knees. His daring blue eyes dragged across the handwritten lines. With a devious smirk, he closed the notebook and dusted the front cover with a gentle caress. In large black letters, *The Apolitical Manifesto*.

He rose to his flat feet and packed his writings inside his shanty old knapsack along with a few superstitious keepsakes and weathered clothing. He turned to a stack of milk crates against the wall where the last of his personal possessions remained unpacked. Streaks of sunlight burst through the cracks before him, striping his vermilion skin with a linear and luminous grid.

He reached inside his bowl of red *female* M&M's—which he was convinced were laced with a poisonous red dye—and let them slip between his wiry fingers. An oily residue from the partially melted coating remained on his fingertips—greasy to the touch. He could not feel a thing. He visualized the fictitious Freemason Army breaking into the old shed and finding nothing but the bowl of candies laced with the governmentally mandated recipe-of-death. Poison for children. Just one of many unspeakable crimes initiated upon the world by a non-existent fabrication of his delusional imagination. He could only hope that their notorious craving for sweets would bring about their own demise by negligence. Yet he knew they would never fall for such an obvious ploy, but wishful thinking nonetheless.

He tied the knapsack closed and strung it over his shoulder, giving his old fortress one last sentimental look. He found great relief in knowing that he would be long gone by the time the Freemasons arrived. Foiled again…

Yet at the same time he was riddled with deep remorse and dread. He felt ripped at the seams. This was his home. He loved his home. He loved the island and the town on top of it.

"You got me into this," he growled at the dark figure lying motionless on the bed. His eyes narrowed into hostile slits, creased by a furrowed brow. "It's all your fault."

Silence followed, as he knew it would. His treasure of unequaled value stared southward into the shambled wooden rafters known as the *Dry Fixins*.

His lifeblood, his love—the corpse of Treva Rifkin. His bed partner.

Her dilapidated body had been painstakingly reconstructed and held intact with shellacked gauze like a paper-machete puppet of human proportions. Her body was painted the color of soft supple skin, her lips an unnaturally bright red. Her eyes were nothing more than dark empty cavities that gazed horridly into the *Dry Fixins*. A ratty, tangled Cleopatra wig covered her skull, painted a glowing magenta as best as he could recollect. Although the stench of rotting flesh was abundantly present, it was not overbearing. Soon after her demise, he performed a relatively simple taxidermy procedure, replacing her internal organs with old discarded rags. The gauze cast was nothing more than a clever afterthought. All in all, he was quite pleased with his work. He could not let her go then. Leaving her would have been self-punishment. He felt he had no choice.

He stepped forward and kissed her gristly cheek, all the while staring into the depths of her empty eye sockets where once he found a semblance of hope, love, and normalcy.

"I must leave," he whispered in her ear cavity, "and you must stay." His chin crinkled as tears swelled in his eyes. He wrestled to conceal them deep inside his tormented soul. He could not imagine life without her. He lowered his head to her chest, unable to feel the rough gauze against his insensitive skin. His mind envisioned soft delicate flesh, as it once was. Her skin was the last human touch his senses ever felt—the memory of her was eternal.

Her dead body had become his shrine, a lifeless replication of his own fleeting dreams. It was all he could believe in. He knew she was dead, there was no confusion regarding the state of her health. After all, he was the one who killed her. But on those frequently lonely nights, having her by his side was a taste of heaven. Someday he would join her there.

"Goodbye," he whispered to the dust as he stood to journey into the outside world once again.

1:54pm

Josephine walked along Simonton Street in the heat of the day, swaying her bandaged hands with a calm fluidity. A plastic shopping bag containing all her belongings hung over her shoulder, teetering against the direction of each smooth footfall. The stubby filter of a cigarette dangled between her thick dark lips. She exhaled a breath of smoke that rose through her gold-rimmed sunglasses and climbed the stone steps of the post office.

She crept through its silent halls, pleased to be alone in life for the first time. She removed her shopping bag from her shoulder and fumbled through her few, yet brand new belongings, searching for the letter. She clutched it with bandaged paws and held it up in the light that streamed through the tall windows. The package was thick and inflexible, and as she dropped it in the outgoing mailbox, she paused a moment to rekindle the awkward smile of Rusty in her mind. She relaxed her hand, allowing the envelope to begin its journey to Illinois.

Each step away from the mailbox echoed throughout the cold atmosphere of her surroundings. Like every other location in Key West, the post office felt haunted, too.

She checked her watch just minutes before the hour of two o'clock in the afternoon.

She returned to the sun once again and sat down on the building's front steps. As she sat in silence waiting for Jobie, she lit another cigarette and imagined life in Austin, Texas. She was eager for change, to fall into a routine that would bring stability to her life for the very first time.

Her mind drifted to the mysterious mid-west plains that Rusty had spoken of with such high regard. She tried to visualize an Ayrshire cow, a grain silo, or a stretch of land so vast and remote that one could believe humans were nothing more than a dream. At the same time, she felt she had not truly given in to the possibilities of the land on which she had fled to, the land below her feet. She could easily find work as a tour guide or a fast food worker.

It suddenly hit her that she had truly found freedom. The road was wide open.

She smiled to herself, and then for some strange and unknown reason, the cherry of her cigarette sizzled in a plume of smoke and yellow flame. A repulsive taste of sulfur filled her mouth, and she tossed the sabotaged cigarette onto the ground, vowing at that moment to never smoke again.

Jobie came buzzing up on Ol' Bessie, stirring birds into flight as he approached with a trail of exhaust. He stepped off the bike, leaving it to idle by the road where it sputtered and quaked in the hot sun.

"What have you decided?" Jobie asked as he joined her on the steps. His hands and ankles were swollen and blistered from the fire. "Are you going to join me?"

She stared pensively into the blue sky while spitting the wretched taste of sulfur from her mouth. "You want me to go to Texas, huh…sure. Let's do it."

He turned to her. "Are you sure?"

She nodded her head slowly, yet assuredly. "Positive. What about you?"

"Gotta go," he told her flatly. "I have a mission."

"I don't think I want to know…" she grumbled.

"Yeah," he agreed. "You don't want to know."

They sat quietly, staring at the vibrating moped that ruined all peace in the area. It was immersed in its own cloud of smoke.

"Guess I'll leave Ol' Bessie at the bus station." He quickly stood and brushed himself off. "Well, Josephine…shall we?"

She stepped up and hugged him tightly, squeezing his lean body like an old ragged and smelly doll. "Ready." She glanced into the street at Ol' Bessie, at its convulsive quakes and sporadic bursts of smoky plumes that polluted the otherwise clean ocean air.

"Did you send the letter?" he asked as he descended a few steps.

"Yes."

He looked to the ground and nodded with tense lips. "Good."

"I sure hope you don't have anything stupid planned for yourself."

He stumbled clumsily down the rest of the steps and turned to her as he reached Ol' Bessie. "I'm going to change the world," he revealed to her with a sinister grin as he climbed aboard. "Is that stupid or what?" He waved his hand over his head, luring her back to the mainland once again.

She slid onto the back of the moped and they raced into the countless possible futures that beckoned their arrival.

Monday, September 27, 1999
2:10pm

Olney, Illinois

Swirling winds of dust raced down the gravel road, splitting through acres of livestock farms. As Thelma Kern walked across the cracked brown earth to the edge of the narrow, rutted driveway, she could still see the distant rise of dust from the postal truck's tires. She shielded her eyes from the bright sun as flies circled her head. Her face was puffy and distraught under the burden of the ghastly news. She felt guilty—ultimately responsible for not saying no when given the chance to prevent the trip that would bring her daughter's untimely death.

She unlatched the mailbox that had once been part of a giant snow penis, and pulled out a single envelope postmarked from Key West. Her eyes widened in the harsh sunlight as she held it close to her face to observe the unfamiliar handwriting. The package was thick and bulky.

She ripped it open with anticipation and dread, unsure of what to expect. Inside it was a stack of photographs and a short note. Her daughter's face smiled from the topmost photograph of her standing before the Southernmost Point of the continental United States. A tear rolled down Ma's cheek as she flipped through the pictures at the unfamiliar faces that seemed to bring her daughter such happiness. It made her smile from deep within.

Then she brought the note close to her face as she squinted to read the illegible handwriting.

Dear Mrs. Kern,

I know that we have never met, and odds are we never will. As I am sure that by now you have learned of the passing of your only daughter, Sharon "Rusty" Kern. I am writing to not only send my deepest regards, but to give you these photographs that she intended to share with you upon her return. She spoke often of you—you meant the world to her. I just wanted you to know the true circumstances of her passing—she died a hero, saving my life while risking her own. If there was anything I feel she would like for you to have known, it is that you were right. She

286

did make a tremendous difference in the world—my world. I am the living proof. And for as long as I live, and for as long as my future children shall walk the earth, so shall her memory.

With Sympathy,
Josephine Ott

THE
STICKLER

Monday, September 4, 2000
9:40pm

Austin, Texas

Mark Maxwell found himself staring directly into the eyes of the Devil. They glowed with extreme voracity like burning embers, floating in a faceless void of shadow from within a black satin hood. They pierced with an unbridled rage that Maxwell had never before witnessed in his middleclass sterility. They would haunt him for years to come.

"No words," the Devil hissed. "I talk, you listen."

Two unseen men forced Maxwell into genuflection before the hooded beast. His knees burned from the futile struggle he initially gave. A knife scraped at his clean neck, keeping his posture staunch, yet perfectly submissive at the same time.

Maxwell brought his attention helplessly into the dark alley that entombed him. He wished to be awakened from this all too vivid nightmare. Perspiration collected on his brow, zigzagging down his face as his body trembled.

He had heard the tales of the Shadowmen, but like most, he did not believe them. He dismissed them as rumors spun by the Drag's homeless population in an attempt to rid their turf of riffraff and highfalutin college students. Now, the moment it was too late, he realized the truth. The Shadowmen were real—as real as the cold metal blade pressed against his neck.

Memories of recent petty crimes on the Drag surfaced in his mind, coming together as a warning sign received too late. Claims of robberies and bizarre interrogations. Rumors of bloody and violent conflicts between the factions of vagrants and runaways on the Drag. It all seemed to be preceded by a strange mid-summer incident that occurred at the Scottish Rite Freemason Temple just one block off the Drag. An arsonist had set fire to the building after burglarizing it. The damage was significant, yet lacking a clear motive. Objects with considerable value were left intact, while an old fire extinguisher was taken with the words *Jobie Lives* spray-painted in its place.

Maxwell gazed into the distant traffic lights that bathed the street like a bloodstain. Splashes of vibrant greens, whites, and blues pulsed from neon signs, reflecting off the cracked and weathered asphalt. He imagined the passengers inside the climate-controlled vehicles at the stoplight, oblivious to the crime within their range of senses. A stifling heat still remained in the night air, long after the day's record temperature of one hundred ten degrees. It was the most important news story that day in Austin, Texas. One would be led to believe there was nothing of greater significance worthy of being reported.

Meanwhile, the Devil loomed over Maxwell. Black satin cascaded over the beast's shoulders, creating a curtain that concealed his human identity. To Maxwell he appeared enormous.

"What do you want?" Maxwell asked with trepidation, straining to convey a false sense of self-control.

"Cut him," the beast snipped. He extended a misshapen finger that appeared to be stained by tomato soup. His skin looked to have truly come from the bowels of hell, marred by the eternal flames of damnation.

Maxwell could feel the blade slide, cutting through his flesh. The blood flowed down his neck, staining his wrinkled T-shirt.

One of the unseen henchmen, known to his peers as IX, placed his lips over the cut, suckling the wound like a ravenous piglet. Maxwell trembled uncontrollably as he listened to each throaty swallow that relinquished more and more of his blood. He could smell IX's long, straight black hair. It was clean with the faint scent of hair dye. Completely human.

"The cut is closing," IX gurgled.

"Cut him again," his accomplice suggested calmly from behind Maxwell's shoulder. "Deeper."

Before Maxwell could fathom the words, he felt the blade slice into his skin. The Devil's henchmen pushed at one another, squabbling over the blood that seeped from his split-out flesh. He could feel their lips on his neck, sucking at the blood, licking the wound with sticky wet tongues. Razor stubble scratched his skin. He could smell their breaths.

The beast grabbed Maxwell's face with his discolored and gnarled hand, forcing mutual eye contact. "I'm looking for something."

"It's closing again," IX grumbled callously. "Where's the knife?"

Tears rolled down Maxwell's pasty cheeks as the two men had their way with his flesh and blood. They swiped at his skin repeatedly, releasing more blood for their eager mouths. Maxwell looked into the menacing and scrofulous eyes of their leader, certain to have finally come face to face with the Grim Reaper himself.

"Who do you know?" the beast hissed.

"He's an Oogle," IX reluctantly concluded. His speech pattern was very slow and succinct. Almost mechanized in its drone. "He doesn't know anything. He was at the Spider House drinking coffee. He's not from the streets. He's phony. A wannabe. Lives in the suburbs, probably."

"I do," Maxwell confirmed with a desperate cry. "I live with my parents, I'm still in high school."

"Who are you going to tell about this, kid?" the other henchman asked. His voice was jittery, quick with speech and followed by a demeaning cackle. "Because you know we can find you."

"Kiss the ground," the Devil demanded. "Look up, and we'll kill you."

They pushed Maxwell face down into the pavement. He hugged the cracked concrete as he listened to their fading footsteps and his own defeated sobbing. He vowed, as he remained perfectly still for an unaccountable time, that he would never step foot on the Drag. True to his word, he remained in seclusion until moving to attend an out-of-state college a year later.

10:21pm

Frank Smith stumbled out the back door of The Bagel Shop, struggling with two heaping bags of day-old bagels. He paused a moment to adjust to the heat and darkness that stood between himself and the dumpster. Shapes began to take form around him. Rusted stairwells. Graffiti on brick or cracked stone walls. He descended down the stained concrete steps toward his destination, guided by its foul stench. The air smelled of moldy bread and motor oil, accentuated by the unseasonable heat that remained so long after nightfall.

Then he heard a voice thrumming quietly in the darkness. He remained perfectly still with his senses completely alive. He held his breath and listened. The sound was coming from the huge metal trash bin directly in front of him. A pair of scrawny legs were sticking straight out of the dumpster, kicking at the air. Frank let loose a sigh of relief. It was just a vagrant rummaging through the trash. Very typical for the Drag at such an hour.

He placed the bags on the ground and calmly approached the ruckus. He could hear communication, but from only one voice. A voice of madness. Words and phrases shot out from a disconnected flow of energy. It seemed as if the dumpster-diver was responding to a shower of compliments and flattery, all the while maintaining focus on whatever frantic business they had inside the garbage heap.

Frank tiptoed stealthily up to the dumpster and kicked the side of it. "Hey!" he screamed with a hearty growl. "What's going on in there?"

The pair of legs quickly slid inside the dumpster, making an awful mess of sound in the process. A thin hand thrust upward and yanked on the dumpster's cover. It smashed against the bin with a thunderous racket. The person retreated inside the mound of garbage like vermin.

"Come on, now," Frank coaxed, "I know you're in there. There's no trouble. You can come out, you just scared the crap out of me."

Silence.

"It has to smell like an ass in there," Frank surmised, softening his tone even further. "Come on out. Seriously, I didn't mean to scare you. I'm throwing out the day-old bagels. If you want any, they're here."

The dumpster cover slowly raised just enough for the person to gaze out.

"I'm armed," a gravelly voice threatened from within the rubbish. "And dangerous."

"Well, I'm not armed, and I'm not dangerous," Frank calmly informed them. "No need for problems, you can have the bagels, just come out of there before you get sick."

The dumpster cover flew open, and an emaciated head ascended from the trash.

"Oh," Frank sighed, "it's you. I was worried for a second. Do you need help out?"

Jobie Wallace stepped over the trash inside the dumpster, climbing toward the highest level to leap out onto the asphalt. He landed on his weathered old combat boots that were bandaged entirely with duct tape. The skin of his legs sagged from what appeared to be a grotesque flesh-eating virus that had feasted plenty on his haggard little body. They were like two red-stained broomsticks emerging from his blue/green kilt. His black T-shirt had been ripped into a sleeveless half-shirt—seemingly unintentional. The tattoos of cobwebs that had once covered his cheeks were almost completely invisible beneath the red plague that ate at his skin.

They had grown familiar with each other's presence over the previous year. Jobie spent quite a bit of time in The Bagel Shop when he first returned from Florida, simply because Tamika worked there and he knew she was good for handouts. From time to time he would take bagels from the bins when no one was looking while he read the *Austin Chronicle* on quiet afternoons. Each time before leaving, he would circle several perverse classified ads and leave the page open on the table for the next unsuspecting patron to discover. He loved to watch their reactions at a distance. Other times he would simply sit on the outside deck in the summer's intense mid-day heat and talk to himself, laughing frequently and often rambling hours on end about vacationing in Key West with his one true love. The Bagel Shop was the only place where Jobie was welcome as a loiterer, and to show his appreciation he would occasionally, though infrequently, offer a hand with closing tasks.

He brushed pieces of browned lettuce off his torn shirt. His kilt was wet from whatever he had stooped into inside the dumpster. "I was looking for something."

Frank watched his reddish-orange hands graze the dirty fabric of his clothing, as if the new stains would stand out anymore than the old ones. His skin was practically transparent, and looked too wretched for Frank to remain tactfully silent on the matter.

"You know, a doctor can probably help you."

"A doctor?" Jobie groaned as he flicked tomato seeds off his shoulder. "To clean my shirt?"

"You seem to have a bit of a sunburn...or something."

"A doctor *caused* this," he bitterly revealed. "No thanks."

Frank had no idea that the doctor he was referring to was none other than the late Doctor Schtepp—a frequent customer before he had died. "Well, no offense, but you don't look too good. I mean, it couldn't hurt to go talk to a doctor. I'd even drive you, if you need it."

The words seemed to drift right over his head. He gazed down at the ground and smiled as he ran his fingers through his messy yellow hair. It looked like a blooming marigold. Or a dandelion. He mumbled to himself, "Soon enough, okay...right." He then looked up at Frank with a deadpan expression. "I liked your record."

Frank cocked his prominent brow, unsure which conversation he was in, if any.

"You were in the Jerk Offs, Tamika told me about you," Jobie explained. "I had your record, I thought it was cool. Really great and powerful stuff. So...why?"

"Why what?"

"Why are you here serving bagels to rich, anorexic white girls? You should be doing music."

"I appreciate the compliment, but no. Whatever I had, I lost."

"That's ridiculous."

Frank shook his head and smiled. He did not have the time or desire to elaborate. "It's a long story. Where did you get the record? I didn't know they even existed still."

"Got it in Tucson two years ago. I don't know what happened to it, but I liked it. I wish I still had it."

"Well, thanks," Frank offered sincerely before addressing him with a wry smile. "Did you want the day-old bagels, or should I find some bimbos from a sorority to take them?"

"Don't do that, give them to me." The humor went right past him. "I'll feed them to my dog, she loves bagels. Especially when they get hard like biscuits." His tone softened as he thought of her. "She had puppies, if you want one. They're really cool dogs."

"You really shouldn't feed bagels to puppies."

"You really shouldn't give so much advice," Jobie snapped. He was clearly getting frustrated. He was ready to bash him over the head with a trashcan lid, but none were around. "It's probably not a good idea to hang out here like this." He threw a quick and deliberate glance down the dark alley. "Wouldn't want to meet up with those Shadowmen, now would we?"

"I don't know where everyone is getting these wild ideas. There are no elusive 'shadow' people out here."

294

Jobie walked his direction, passing him with a scent of sweat and garbage. It was clear that he had not bathed in weeks. "These are the bagels, in these bags?"

"Yeah," Frank responded.

"Can I have both bags? I have lots of friends."

"I suppose," Frank shrugged grudgingly.

Jobie struggled to lift them, but was not about to ask for help. He turned to Frank and nodded with an unusually restrained contention. "Thanks."

"Don't mention it."

Frank watched him disappear around the corner toward West Campus. He shook his head with a smirk before lumbering up the concrete steps and back inside The Bagel Shop. He locked the door behind him.

10:21pm

Tamika Tovar rushed through the University of Texas campus, lugging her camera equipment over her shoulder in a black vinyl bag. Canisters of film rattled against one another, keeping rhythm with each forceful and confident step. The wind blew through her short and stylish black curls, bouncing with each footfall. A thin cotton dress the shade of lilacs covered her lean body, flattering her well-proportioned figure.

She was happy to find herself alone. Especially from the wandering eyes of men. She still had not grown accustom to their stares and catcalls. They made her feel cheap and insignificant. When she first started losing weight, the attention was a pleasant change for her. She even took up a few offers, acquiring the sexual experience she had always felt would give her the confidence and validation she so desperately sought at the time. It only proved to worsen her self-esteem. After several brief and uninspiring liaisons with men, she had the good fortune of being introduced to a soft-spoken teacher's assistant named Vanessa. They had met in an informal photography class and became inseparable—except on rare occasions like this particular night.

She looked over her shoulder at the giant clock Tower on campus, certain that she would be late to the photo shoot. She hustled past the fountain and waited at the crosswalk that separated the university grounds from the Drag. The reflection of neon lights was far more plentiful on the streets than people at such an hour. Tiny bubbles drifted through the hot air—a sight she hoped to have avoided. She turned to backtrack through campus just as the crosswalk light offered access.

"Hey, Tamika!"

Her shoulders tensed when she heard his gnawing voice. She reluctantly proceeded across the street, walking under stoplights that covered the asphalt like a red satin sheet.

Ahead of her was a Crusty known as Pip Squeak. He leaned slovenly against a wall, holding a bright pink plastic bottle in one hand and a plastic stick in the other from which he earned the title of the Bubble Man. The bubbles, as he claimed, was a gift to the people of the Drag. He spent many hours a day offering his trade to the passersby for spare change. His face was thin and fiercely energetic. He was thrilled to have stumbled upon a chance encounter with her. His dirty brown hair was covered with a blue and white pinstriped engineer's cap, puffy and poorly fitted like a lopsided mushroom. His torn red vest had been salvaged from the video arcade's dumpster. Its bright coloration separated him from the drab styles of his peers. It still had a large green button on it with the bright yellow words: *Ask Me For Change!* His corduroy pants were long and baggy, held up by rainbow-colored suspenders. The waistline sagged like a hobo's. He was equal to Tamika in both age and stature.

"Good seeing ya!" he told her as he smacked his gum with loose friendly lips.

She kept walking, which provoked him to step away from the wall to pursue her. "Hi, Pip."

He took a second to blow a succession of bubbles in her face. They popped against her dark skin. "Bubbles for you! Happy day, isn't it?"

She kept her brisk pace, shaking her head. "It's been okay, I suppose."

"Hey," he returned politely, "you know what Jobie told me?"

She cringed at the sound of his name. Jobie. It was synonymous with the word headache.

"He told me that you used to be one of us. Is that true? Were you a Crusty?"

She sighed as she continued down the Drag toward West Campus. For some reason, which she could not understand, it bothered her to be referred to as *one of us* in regard to anything. Especially homelessness. "I was out here for a while. Very *short* while."

"Whew, no way!" he said with a leap and stomp. "I can't believe it! I bet all the guys wanted to hang out with you."

"You know, Pip Squeak, I'm in a hurry."

She turned the corner down 22nd Street. He kept following.

"I need to be at a photo shoot, and I'm late."

"So I guess you don't want to go on a date, then?" he boldly offered. "I'd pay."

She laughed and blushed, flattered, but uninterested. "I'm taken."

"Okay, then what about your roommate? Is she single? She sure is pretty."

"Josephine has a boyfriend, too."

"Oh," he replied, dejected. He quickly snapped his fingers as he struggled to keep up with her steady gait. "Has anyone ever told you that you look exactly like Marilyn Monroe?"

She belted out a boisterous laugh.

"Seriously, you do."

She turned to him, yet never slowing her pace. "Pip, I'm not white, for starters. And I have thick and curly black hair...I look nothing like her."

"You're just being hard on yourself."

"You are insane."

He chuckled proudly. "Oh, guess what else?"

She could only imagine. One of his lesser qualities was his ability to fabricate the most incredible tales. He lied simply for the sake of lying. He would lie even when the truth would have sounded better.

"The Shadowmen attacked!" he declared with his silly giggle to follow. He took a second to cheerfully blow more bubbles into the night air. "Yeah, no more than an hour ago. I saw the kid myself, walking away, all bloody at the neck."

"Pip," she irritably protested, "you can't possibly believe all that stuff."

"Believe it? I've seen them myself! And trust me, I don't want to see them again!"

"Really?" she asked suspiciously, still chugging forward. "What did they look like?"

"Long black hair, black clothes—typical Heshers. Metalheads, you know. There were only two of them, but I have heard that there is one more, the leader of them. The worst of all. He's supposedly out here looking for something. Maybe something he lost..."

"Maybe a life?" she interjected.

He giggled with a snort. "Yeah, maybe. I just wanted you to know it's probably not too safe to be out here like this."

"And that's why you're walking with me?" she asked snidely, though with a polite smile. "You're going to protect me?"

"Of course."

"What are you going to do, blow bubbles in their faces?"

"If they mess with me," he said sharply, "they are messing with Jobie, too. And that means trouble."

She was slow to reply. It still baffled her how legendary Jobie had become during his year's absence. Stories of his violence and callousness had been blown way out of proportion. He practically returned to Austin on a throne. She was no fan of him when she had first met him. Since he had come back to town, she was far less happy to have him back. It bothered her that he claimed to know nothing of Treva Rifkin's whereabouts. She saw him as nothing more than a charismatic hooligan, and the Crusties on the Drag had become his cult, willing to do whatever he felt was right.

"Pip, crime sure has gone up since Jobie came back to town," she told him casually, hoping that it would provoke some introspective thoughts. She did not find it a coincidence that the day after the Scottish Rite Freemason Temple was burned, Jobie spent the next day tinkering with a fire extinguisher in their backyard.

"Crime, or self-defense?" he speculated as they walked through the tree-lined streets of West Campus.

"Like a little organized crime unit. I would say crime, not self-defense. How long has this Shadowmen thing been going on?"

"I heard from a cop that they've been on the Drag for as long as the Drag has been here. Hundreds of years. Maybe thousands. Ghosts, or vampires, or something unexplained."

Tamika knew the answer herself. It had been no more than a few months. "Crime begets crime. Maybe if you guys had a 'leader' who acted less like a thug, people wouldn't be coming down to the Drag to rough people up."

"I don't see any connection in what you're saying," he dismissed with a quick sweep of his bony hand. "Anyway, will you take my picture?"

"No. Film is expensive."

"Oh, come on!" he protested lightly, smiling with all his crooked teeth visible. "I walked you all this way, and you won't take my picture?"

She sighed and stopped just as they had reached the sidewalk to her rented house.

"Come on." He looked at the dimly lit house where they stood. "Is this where you and Josephine live?"

Tamika cringed. "Okay, I'll take your picture if you promise to stay away from here. No window peeking. I'm serious."

"Hey now, I would *never* do that."

"Sure you wouldn't. Don't forget, Jobie stays here sometimes, and his brother is my other roommate. You don't want to make Jobie mad, do you?"

"Come on, you know me better than that."

She rolled her eyes.

"Take my picture and I won't come back here. I promise."

She quickly took her shabby, though functional, 35mm camera out of her bag as he posed next to an elm tree, blowing as many bubbles as he could possibly muster.

"Hurry," he urged her, "before they drift away."

She knelt onto one knee and snapped the picture with a bright flash.

"I'll let you know when I have it developed." She picked up her bag and watched him leave. "Pip, thanks for walking me home."

He waved. "Any time, doll."

She savored a breath of silence before walking up the sidewalk to the front door. As she gripped the doorknob—still warm from the day's heat—she could hear the droning beat of Opaque's first recording with a DeeJay known as

Krunk—a song entitled *A Mid-Autumn's Nightmare*. It had become a house favorite at Ohms where Krunk was the Friday night DeeJay. Following its unexpected success among the club patrons, the two decided to take the effort a little more seriously. They dedicated the entire summer to creating the perfect dance song. After the music was finally in place, Opaque devised the gimmick for it. It would be called *One With The Stars* and would "finish the trilogy" that was started with David Bowie's space epic, *Space Oddity*, and updated in the 1980s with Peter Schilling's *Major Tom*. Tamika had little doubt that Opaque was onto bigger and better things. She was thrilled when he asked her to be the photographer for the pictures that would be used for his portfolio.

She twisted the doorknob and unleashed a blast of cold air that teased her hot and sweaty skin. The living room was dark and sparsely furnished. The walls were covered with posters of glam rock and hip-hop stars appeasing the interests of both her roommates.

The kitchen was lit like a basket of oranges and cherries. Thin white sheets were stretched from floor to ceiling as a backdrop for the photo shoot, absorbing the splashes of color from strategically placed lights.

"Hey everybody," she said as she entered. "Sorry I'm late."

Opaque slouched in his La-Z-Boy chair as Josephine Ott sat on the edge of the wooden coffee table, manicuring and painting his fingernails. His black hair looked like a massive explosion caught on film. His face was flushed white, giving his skin the texture of porcelain. Thick black eyeliner encircled his eyes, hollowing out his already gaunt features. His lips were painted vibrantly red, matching his colored contacts that made his eyes look like a coil of flame. A skin-tight black bodysuit with long sleeves and an extremely low-cut neckline that arced down to his navel seemed almost painted on. His bony and hairless chest glistened with baby oil. He looked like a demonic ballerina. Effeminate and evil. Ready for the camera.

One With The Stars played loudly over the stereo system. Opaque's vocal tracks were thin and heavily effected to sound more synthetic than human. Combined with the grating, clever beats provided by Krunk, the song was indeed destined to find a home in many dance clubs. Just as its creators had.

"It's about time, sistah," Opaque lisped.

"My class ran late."

"You're always *on the go*," he returned lightly. "You need some time off."

Tamika nodded to herself as she quickly assembled her gear, setting up the tripod for the camera.

"Tamika, I'm just messing with you...you know how much I appreciate you doing this for me."

"Oh, I know. I think it will be fun."

"Whassup, Tamika," Josephine rolled off casually as she filed away at his fingernails. Her long black braids rested on her arched back, spilling over her smooth coppery shoulders. At her side were two files, half a dozen cotton

299

swabs, and a container of purple fingernail polish. Her own fingernails, all eight of them, were impeccably groomed. "Howzit?"

"Ah…busy, busy."

"I hear ya," she said dismissively.

Although Opaque never openly spoke of it, he loved being the minority Caucasian in their humble household. It was unusual to have Tamika present, and it made Opaque very pleased to see her again. He did not necessarily feel that they had drifted, but rather they developed lives independent of one another. It was a good thing. But he still felt a deep-rooted connection with her. Seeing her on those rare occasions was always a treat for him.

"I saw Pip Squeak, he walked me home," she told them.

"Lucky you," Josephine replied snidely.

"Yeah, I felt really safe with him there," Tamika joked. "You know how he tells the tall tales…well, he told me that the Shadowmen attacked some kid earlier tonight."

Opaque's eyes perked up, alert and pensive. "I thought that was all over…" His face fell dour with devastation. "Did they get caught?"

"Don't know," Tamika replied. "Didn't ask. Hard to tell if it even happened when coming from Pip Squeak."

Opaque nodded, fretting over a hunch. He thought a moment to himself, and then let out a deep and rugged sigh. "Has anyone seen my brother lately, by chance?"

"It's been a few days," Tamika said optimistically, unable to contain the relief in her voice. No sign of Jobie was a good sign to her.

"Been a while," Josephine added, a bit more respectful than Tamika.

Opaque's face scrunched with concern as he contemplated Jobie's whereabouts and declining health. He pushed it all to the back of his mind. He had no doubt that the subject of how to deal with his brother would surface again, sooner than later.

"Do my eyebrows need to be plucked?"

Josephine closely examined him, and then shook her head. "Nuh-uh."

"I'm ready when you are," Tamika announced as she carried the tripod and camera into the kitchen.

"These pictures better make me famous."

"I thought you said that it's all about the hype?" Tamika chided. "That it's hype, not music, that makes the star."

"That's true. You just wait and see," he assured her.

He stepped in front of the stretched sheets that seemed to vibrate with dizzying waves of reds and oranges. His red lips and artificially fiery eyes matched perfectly, just as he had planned. The camera followed his fluid motions from one pose to the next, a perfect natural. A whore for the spotlight.

Twenty minutes later, as everyone was crowding in the kitchen, Jobie entered through the front door unnoticed. He stood watching the three of them busily organizing the photo session. He remained in the darkness, holding his garbage bags of bagels as he listened to their happy banter. If they knew he was there, they made no mention and gave no greeting. He quietly walked to the backdoor, careful not to disturb them.

He knew they did not prefer to have him around. He could see it in their eyes. It was a combination of fear and concern, and it did nothing good for his ego. Even Josephine, whom he felt he had forged such a deep connection with when they moved in a year ago, seemed uncomfortable in his presence anymore.

He shuffled quietly through the backdoor and into the darkness. He began walking before his eyes adjusted, finding his way to the dogs by their happy little yelps. His feet scraped across the lawn, which was nothing more than weeds, rocks, and clay-colored dirt. Piles of dog dung and fire ant mounds were a natural repellent to visitors, which made it an ideal location for his place of solitude. During the day the small fenced yard saw very little sunlight due to the intertwining branches of elm and pecan trees overhead.

"Mama," he called out.

There was a quick response in the form of a bark.

"Good girl."

He reached out after twelve steps, which he knew was the distance from the backdoor to the mingle-mangled mess of construction he called *The Kennel.* He could hear the three yelping puppies, and the familiar loud and happy panting of their mother waiting patiently inside.

The Kennel was his home, no larger than the average doghouse. Everything he owned fit comfortably inside.

He originally intended *The Kennel* to be entirely underground, but after three days of shoveling in the Texas heat, battling against rocks and bricks buried beneath the hard dry earth, he altered his plans. The hole he had dug was roughly six feet by four feet, and two and a half feet deep. It was little more than an arm's reach from the house itself. He scavenged enough cinderblocks from a nearby construction-site to build the walls. It looked something like an igloo with an ill-fitting plywood sheet placed over the top as a roof. The dirt and debris, which he had shoveled out of the hole, had been thrown back against the exterior cinderblock walls to keep it cooler inside. The doorway faced the house, making it a challenge to reach the entrance, which then required crawling low enough to enter the partially underground fortress. Colorful plastic beads leftover from Austin's last Mardi Gras were strung over the gap that comprised the entryway. Inside, old discarded blankets covered the cool earth, making a reasonably comfortable floor. From the outside, it appeared to be a shabby doghouse, no more than three feet tall. Inside, it was roomy enough for him to stand in a crouching position.

He removed a few bagels from the trash bags and slinked along the wall of the house, lowering himself slowly inside the shanty little dwelling. It smelled dusky, like mold and dirty wet dogs. The blankets on which they slept harbored the odors, trapping them inside the tiny hovel. A nightlight, which was duct taped to the plywood ceiling and powered by a long extension cord, gave off a very faint orange glow.

Mama was lying against the cinderblock wall, her tail wagging, pounding against it with a dull thud. Three little puppies crawled over her, wrestling and biting each other's floppy ears. Mama licked at Jobie's knees as he knelt before her. He could not feel her sloppy kisses on his nearly translucent red skin, but he could feel the sentiment. It made him smile.

Mama was a short little terrier mix that he had acquired from a fellow Crusty en route to Las Vegas from Minneapolis. Mama came into Jobie's possession when she bit two students that tried to pet her puppies from a previous litter. The Drag was full of her offspring, each owned by different Crusties who used the dogs to increase the probability of getting money from the more liberal and compassionate passersby. Mama proved too unruly for the streets, and had since retired to Jobie's secret fortress. As far as he knew, its precise location was a complete mystery to his peers.

Mama crawled up onto Jobie's lap, allowing him to scratch her dry skin. Her fur was thick and coarse, and looked like rust due to her brindle coloration. Her dark and expressive eyes were barely visible through the dirty hair that covered her face. Her ears were perky and alert, and her legs were shorter than Jobie's hand. Her teeth, in true terrier form, were large and strong with powerful jaws that were bred to hunt and kill small animals.

"Hey, Mama!" he declared cheerfully. "Look what I got for you!"

He held out one of the cinnamon raisin bagels, allowing her to sniff it. She quickly pulled it from his hands and ripped it apart with her strong mandibles, swallowing the torn pieces whole in a matter of seconds.

"Good girl," he praised.

He reached out to a plywood shelf that was covered with candles in glass jars, matches, stacks of papers, and *The Apolitical Manifesto*. He picked up a book of matches and struck one. Mama's pupils shrank as she stared directly into the flame, tilting her head curiously as he lit two candles. Sitting with crossed legs, he picked up a piece of paper, which contained the latest entry in *The Apolitical Manifesto*. It was entitled *Goddamn Christians*.

He turned quickly, realizing that he was being watched.

"That is so great!" Treva Rifkin told him as she appeared out of nowhere, a ghost existing only in his deteriorating mind. "You are so smart, Jobie!"

Her smile entranced him. Just like the day he met her. Her skin was soft and supple, almost luminous. She looked longingly into his eyes as if nothing else mattered to her. Her plum-colored hair seemed to glow like soft candlelight.

"Do you like it?" he asked desperately, nodding to his writing.

"Like it? I love it!" She leaned forward and kissed him on the cheek.

His sense of touch had died long ago, but when she touched him, he could feel it throughout his entire body.

302

"You're going to save the world, Jobie," she assured him with absolute conviction. "Just like how you saved me. Do you remember that?"

He smiled coyly. She knew exactly what to say to make him happy.

"Remember our place in Key West?" she asked him. "Remember how nice it was? How you took care of me there?"

He nodded proudly.

"Are we going back sometime? I never got to swim in the ocean."

His lips crinkled, as did his forehead. "No, we aren't going back."

"Darn…oh well, that's okay. I like it here, too. I just like being wherever you are."

"I like being with you, too," he admitted. He rarely allowed himself to be so disarmed, but only in her presence. He knew he could trust her.

"Sweetie, are you feeling okay? You look sad. Are you sad?"

He shrugged his shoulders and stiffened his face in an attempt to ward off the tears. His chin crinkled and his lips tensed together.

"Can I be honest with you?" she asked without pausing for an answer. "I think you're dying, Jobie."

He shook his head defiantly. "What do you know?"

Her skin changed, practically disintegrating before his eyes. She suddenly looked as if she had bathed in battery acid. It was exactly how she appeared to him in her last living breath. "You know what I know." With those words, she transformed back to perfect health.

"You left me all alone!" he protested aloud. Mama and her puppies all looked up at him, intrigued with his wild outburst. "And now who is going to help me like I helped you?"

"I know what you have in mind," she whispered softly to him, offering a mischievous smile. "I know your plan. I think it's a good one. You're at least going out in style."

He nodded to himself with a surge of confidence. "It's a good plan. A *great* plan. Too late to turn back, even if I wanted to."

"I know. I can't wait to watch it all unfold."

"Yeah," he said with tearful eyes.

"Everything will work out okay," she promised him. "And soon we'll be together. Look at it that way."

"There's no other way to look at it, Treva," he grumbled remorsefully.

"Are you afraid to die, sweetie?" she asked with utmost sincerity, giving him all her attention as he slouched in his wretched little cave. "I was afraid, too. You were there for me, and I will be there for you."

He smiled at her, staring directly into thin air. He heard a rustling noise outside that dragged his attention away from his delusion. When he turned back, she was gone. He looked over to the stolen fire extinguisher hidden in the corner beneath a stack of stained and musty blankets. The *Dragon*, as he called it.

"Jobie," Opaque called out from the backyard. "Are you out there?"

He sat quiet a moment as Mama stared up at him, wagging her tail. Mama loved Opaque because he often allowed her to come indoors while Jobie was not there.

"Jobie, I can see the light through the cracks, I know you're out there. Not to mention the fact that you're back here screaming to yourself. Talking to yourself, I can deal with that...but the screaming...we have neighbors, you know."

Jobie could hear him walking across the lawn. He double-checked the *Dragon*, making sure that it was properly concealed. It was the last thing he wanted Opaque to know about. Not that his brother would enter *The Kennel*, especially with its capacity of one person filled.

"Jobie...would you come out here, please?" Opaque demanded shortly. "I'm not coming inside there, it stinks worse than you do."

Jobie crawled through the entrance and slithered outside. His black T-shirt was snagged by the corner of the cinderblocks, adding another small tear in his ragtag attire.

"Where have you been?" Opaque asked him shortly, staring directly into his striking pale blue eyes. A black leather biker jacket covered Opaque's thin torso, concealing his skin-tight one-piece form-fitting bodysuit.

"When?"

Opaque sighed and tapped his foot on the dusty ground. Small clouds rose around his glossy black leather boots from the impact.

"Hanging out on the Drag," Jobie responded with a growl that had no effect on his sibling. In a strange sort of way, he respected the fact that Opaque did not find him at all threatening. "Why?"

"Then you probably heard about the attack earlier?"

Jobie gazed off into the darkness. "The Drag just isn't very safe anymore, is it?"

"Never was," Opaque added with a sneer, "but now it's gotten worse."

"Are you asking me to do something about it?"

Opaque protested with an aggravated stomp. His wrists were firm against his narrow hips. "No! I want you to stay the hell away from there. For your own good. Your luck is running thin, and all this wild hellion *save the world* stuff is going to catch up to you. I have no idea what you are up to now, but I know you have something going on. And I can tell you right now, I don't like it."

Jobie looked to the ground, slouching a bit. "Thanks for the support."

"Jobie, I will support you in whatever you do, but—"

"But you don't even know what I *am* doing!"

Opaque gave a long, exasperated sigh of defeat. "Who were you talking to out here?"

"When?"

"Before I came out here. I heard you say her name," Opaque revealed, speaking of Treva, whom he had not seen in nearly two full years, and at the time she was not in the best of health. "Did you want to talk about it?"

"About what?"

"About what happened to her. Josephine says that when she first met you a year ago in Key West, you were saying that you had killed your girlfriend. The girlfriend who gave you this disease you have all over your body."

"So?"

"So!" Opaque squealed. "So, you killed someone. So? Does that not strike you as a little weird, Jobie?"

"That's kind of weird, I guess. But remember when we were kids, we put the dog to sleep when we knew he had cancer."

"Ah, I see. So I should kill you, then, now that you have the same problem Treva had. Right?"

Jobie shrugged his shoulders, unsure of his immediate response. It was not entirely that bad of an idea to him.

"Wrong!" Opaque declared loudly. His painted red lips tensed together. "What happened to her?"

Silence.

"What you did...it was a *serious* crime. The position you have put me in with this knowledge it makes me an accomplice to your crime. How do you feel about that?"

"I feel that you're wrong," Jobie told him. "You don't know anything, Rik. You think you do, but you don't."

"You underestimate my intelligence," Opaque countered swiftly. "I know you well, Jobie, and I have my suspicions..." His voice faded as he suddenly realized he was going nowhere with this. He felt burdened with the knowledge that his brother had taken someone's life, and he was torn with how to handle the situation. He had ideas, but could not decide what exactly was the right thing to do—to keep his silence, or notify the authorities in Key West of a missing person. He changed his train of thought as the two of them stood facing one another—a connection of blue and red eyes. "Tell me what you loved about her."

Jobie's eyes wandered, focusing on the darkness, and then smiling. "Everything."

"Everything?" Opaque asked. "What did you *really* know about her?"

Jobie shook his head and smiled. "You have no idea."

"Actually," Opaque returned with a condescending tone, "I think I do. I think that you fell head over heels for an ideal. I think that you had just enough time to become *really* interested in her, but not enough time to really *know* her. It's like when a musician or artist dies in their prime, people always assume that greater things were on the way. She was psycho! A nutcase. But you saw what you wanted to see, and when she died before you got to the deeper levels, your imagination filled in the rest. You supplied the details that were missing, which was probably a lot of details to fill in. You created her in your own image, designed to be exactly what you wanted her to be. And with her being dead, as we all know she is, she never was able to let you know how wrong you were, and still are. So you hold onto this image of who she is when really that image is more *you* than *her*. You're in love with yourself, with your own ideal. You just put it all inside the false memory of a real person whom you just happened to have *murdered!* Doesn't really make a lot of sense, does it? You take someone's life, then you go on about how you were so much in love."

Jobie took a deep breath, keeping his eyes on his brother's washed-out, made-up face. "Like I said, you really don't know."

"Okay, did you ever talk to her about her family?"

"Yes, actually, we did." Jobie sent him a victorious smile. "And you think you know what's going on? If you knew the whole story, saw the whole picture, you'd understand."

"What was the name of her best friend when she was growing up?"

Jobie's eyes widened and his confident smile faded.

"You don't know. See what I'm saying? How could you not know such a thing about the person you have been in love with nearly *two years* after her death? Did she have any boyfriends before she left home?"

Jobie's face was awash. His eyes squinted in the darkness, and his expression slowly turned fierce. "What is your point with all this?"

"I've made my point," Opaque said slowly, assuredly. "I just want you to take your own advice, the advice you want to give to the world through your *Manifesto*...look at yourself, Jobie, look at your life. Take a long hard look at where you are, and where you are going. It's not too late to change things. Take a different path. Publish your *Manifesto*, I think it's a wonderful thing. I would help you in any way that I could. You know this is true. I so completely support you, and I think you have great things to say, to share with the world. But these destructive schemes you have, I don't see how they can help."

"If you knew what the *scheme* was, you wouldn't disagree. Trust me, Rik, I know you just as you claim to know me. You would help me. You wouldn't try to stand in the way. Not if you knew the whole story. Just give me time, and don't do anything crazy. I can tell you're struggling with all this, and I think that you are even considering betraying me, but don't. I'm your brother, Rik. If you can't support me, then avoid me."

Opaque was silent for a moment as he looked out into the street. It was a very quiet night for West Campus. "What is happening on the Drag, Jobie? This Shadowmen thing, what is this all about?"

Jobie shook his head. "Beats me."

Opaque sneered at him. "If you don't get it together on your own, I will have to take it on my own to help you." He turned to walk away. "Goodnight."

Wednesday, September 6, 2000
9:41am

Barron's Bluff, Colorado

Kinsman Torben Kale leaned passively against the front steps of the NRF Headquarters, looking out at the mountain terrain that stretched beyond Barron's Bluff. Reverend Strickland always boasted that on a clear day, you could see as far as Boulder, Colorado. After several years on the Reverend's private land, Kinsman Kale had never been able to back that claim, despite the weather. In fact, judging by the map of the area, the front porch faced a little too much to the east for such an event to even take place. Nonetheless, the view from Headquarters was astounding.

Up the rocky northern side of Barron's Bluff was the Reverend's own humble ranch house, built in the 1980s when he was still happily married. The southern side had a gradual slope that collected snow in the winter and pinecones in the warmer months. A gravel road meandered at a great distance like a winding stream, stopping one hundred yards away at the chain-linked fence that surrounded the premise.

Very few people were granted access to Headquarters. Even fewer had keys. All visitors and volunteers were under immediate supervision of Kinsman Kale, who reported directly and only to the Reverend himself.

Kale sipped his black coffee while gazing out into the vast stretches of wilderness. A calm breeze blew in from the north, cooling his weathered face and freshly shaved head. His firm biceps flexed involuntarily each time he raised the mug to his thin lips, stretching the fabric of his black Ben Sherman tightly against his barrel chest.

He took a deep breath of clean mountain air, reeling in tranquility, when suddenly the front door burst open with a thunderous racket. His muscular body tensed, spilling hot coffee on his jeans.

He turned with an angry scowl smeared across his heavily lined face. Brother Perry loomed over his bulky shoulder, smiling mischievously at the minor pain he had unwittingly inflicted upon his superior.

"Awww...that really sucks, man," Brother Perry sarcastically lamented. "I guess you need to get up off your ass and go get a refill, then, huh?"

"You're a bastard...and you best watch it."

307

Brother Perry plopped his wiry body on the bottom step. He placed his freckled hands on his bent knees, partially covering the intentional holes in his acid-washed jeans. He smiled at Kinsman Kale, nudging him, but was unable to alter his mood.

"Oh, come on, man," Perry offered playfully as the cool wind shifted his scraggly blond hair. "It's not as if you were stopping with that one cup. If I know you..."

Kale finally smiled. Not at Perry's humor, but at the fact that the same was true for Perry when it came to alcohol consumption. To make matters worse, Perry tended to be an angry drunk, letting his hostility flow when not wearing his happy face during rare bouts of sobriety.

"Ready for a busy day?" Perry groaned.

"Always," Kale asserted with a certain level of confidence and authority. His tone of voice was steely and cold. He was anything but friendly. "Mail-outs a week from Monday."

Perry exhaled a dramatically belabored sigh. He leaned forward and whispered, "Between the two of us..." he paused to make sure Strickland was nowhere around, "I don't know how you handle this mindless, boring crap after all the years you've been out here."

Kinsman Kale cracked a rigid smile before taking a sip of coffee. Perry was not entirely sure if his expression was in compliance or at his expense. Perry found him impossible to read, which he assumed was entirely the point.

"Just between us, of course," Perry repeated cautiously.

"Planning on leaving?"

"Nah," Perry said with a flick of the wrist that fanned away such a suggestion. "I'm in it, brother."

"Good."

They sat quietly, watching an elk pass through the huge evergreens in the distance. It was not an uncommon sight in their neck of the woods, but no less intriguing each time.

"Would you go back to Washington?" Kinsman finally asked.

"What?"

"If you left here. Would you go back to Tacoma?"

"Probably," Perry responded with reluctance, unsure if he was stepping into a loaded question. He gave a subtle smile that Kale half expected. "It's Puyallup, by the way. Not Tacoma."

"Oh, right," Kinsman replied, not really concerned with the specifics of his life.

"Haven't seen my friends in a while," Perry said lightly. "They think I joined a cult."

Kale laughed out loud. "That's ridiculous."

"That's what I tell them!"

"Stay out of trouble—if you end up going back."

"Well," Perry replied shortly with a snort, "I don't plan on leaving. Didn't I just tell you that? Like twice?"

Kale laughed, this time clearly to ridicule him. He could not tell which part of his statement seemed to rub the raw nerve. That he assumed Perry would soon be departing, or that he would no doubt return to his criminal ways back in Washington. Truth be known, Kinsman Kale would be eager to see him go. There was something shifty about him. Something that Kale just could not put his finger on. He was not what Kale would refer to as a straight shooter. The organization was plagued with the type, though. People slim on principle, heavy on talk and blind rage. It was enough to disillusion someone with lesser convictions.

The door opened once again, and out stepped Jimmy Paglea. Or, as he preferred to be called, Pokerface. He was the best-dressed man Kinsman Kale had ever known. He strutted down the steps of the porch and turned to face his comrades, flaunting his debonair style. The sun was edging over the mountain, and his wide-brimmed black fedora cast a hard shadow over his face. His olive skin blended well with the old-style zoot suit—black with white pinstripes. His shoes were glossy as though perfectly new. He did not have a large selection of clothing, but what much he had, he wore with excesses of finesse.

Pokerface put on his black sunglasses and set his sights to the gravel road. Although he recognized the beauty of his surroundings, the great outdoors represented nothing but isolation and vulnerability to him. The mountains, in all its lushness, teeming with life, seemed like a desert with its lack of human intervention. He was always eager to make his way into Boulder for supplies, which he did as often as possible.

"Seeya, fellas!" he sang gruffly with a thick Chicago accent. He added his own personalized inflections—a hybrid of Chicago and east coast ghetto slang. "Takin' da cah down ta Bouldah. Groceries."

Perry winced with envy. "Have fun, man."

"Heya, Torben," Pokerface barked with his cold northern accent, "Chief wansa seeya."

"About what?" Kale asked him.

Pokerface shook his head, which shifted the shadow that crossed his hairless chin. "Dunno." He waved, and then strolled down the stone path toward the road.

"Wonder what's up?" Perry pondered aloud, never taking his eyes off Pokerface until he left the fenced compound.

"Probably giving us a new assignment for the day." Kale stood up and brushed his coffee-stained jeans. "I bet he's going to have us clean the toilets."

Perry chuckled with an unusual amount of concern. "No thanks. I'll stick with the fliers and mailings for the queer's funeral."

He was referring to the NRF's latest crusade of organizing a protest for a man who had died of AIDS. The funeral was to be the following weekend in

Denver. Such things were highly effective publicity stunts that drummed up more new memberships than one would initially suspect.

Kale walked inside Headquarters, which was originally designed to be a small Baptist church. The function of the building changed when the Reverend's wife left him for another man. Her departure prompted him to abandon all plans and devote his energy to his growing organization—the National Reclamation Front. The would-be church became its headquarters for operation.

The building was long and slender with lots of tall and narrow windows, wooden floors, and no furnishings. Boxes of paper filled the empty space like a maze. Folding tables lined both the front and back walls. The front tables acted as the mailing station for the newsletter, while the rear tables were used for assembly, stapling, and packaging. Alongside the back wall was a brand new computer with a color printer feeding from it. Kinsman Kale spent most of his time staring into its large color monitor, printing off the newsletter, responding to online inquiries, or keeping track of the organization's general accounting.

The Reverend's personal office was in the rear of the building. Although he kept his door closed most of the time, Kale had come to assume that he tended to the layouts, press releases, and business matters while locked away in solitude, day after day.

Kale made his way through the building and stepped up to the Reverend's closed office door. He took a deep breath before knocking.

"Come in, Torben," the Reverend instructed from the other side. "It's unlocked."

"Good morning," Kinsman Kale offered politely as he entered.

"Morning," Strickland replied shortly. He stroked his graying facial hair and gestured to the chair in front of his desk. "Have a seat."

Kale did as he was told. He could not help but notice the pistol lying on the Reverend's desk.

"Is there a problem?"

The Reverend nodded his narrow head. "Yes. Yes, there is."

Kale raised his eyebrows. His heart began banging inside his chest. He glanced around the office at the filing cabinets, the desk, the Rolodex, and the pictures on the wall of Strickland's once-happy family. Most of them were taken less than a year before the separation. Before the heavily publicized abduction of his only child on Independence Day, 1998. It was a subject he never brought up.

"What kind of trouble?" Kinsman asked him uneasily.

"Someone has been in here tampering with things, moving things around."

Kale's face went flush. "Really?"

"I think we have a traitor here. Someone not looking out for our best interest."

Kale suddenly felt unusually vulnerable. It crossed his mind how far away they really were from the rest of the world. "Any ideas who?"

"What do you know about these two guys? Jimmy and Perry."

"Well, they seem like good enough guys to me," Kinsman offered up quickly as he took a moment to think further. "Perry has a criminal record, as you know. Took out some liquor stores, served some time…"

"Shot a mud," Strickland added with a smirk. "Shows how flawed the system is that he had to serve time for that."

"He seems really fickle to me," Kinsman admitted with a straight face. "I'm not convinced his heart is in this at all. But a traitor? Hard to say what his real beliefs are or who his friends were back in Puyallup."

"No," the Reverend said firmly. "The other guy. Jimmy." He hissed his name with disdain. "What's he all about?"

"You know that he's a pivotal member in the Great Lakes Division. They do a lot of good work up there. Seems like a good guy to me."

The Reverend pointed a narrow finger at Kale. "Watch him."

"Yes, sir." He sat quietly, waiting for further instructions. "What about just cleaning house and putting a request out for new volunteers from other divisions?"

Strickland leaned forward and gave a wry smile. "No, that won't be necessary. I have my suspicions—I plan to take him down personally. Just let it be common knowledge to everyone out here that I am armed."

Kale glanced uncomfortably at the pistol. The thought crossed his mind that maybe the Reverend had finally lost it and was about to pull a Jonestown on them. "Yes, sir. I will."

There was a moment of silence to clear the air and shift the conversation.

"Do you suppose you'll have the signs done this afternoon for the funeral?" Strickland asked.

Kale nodded, happy that the conversation had lightened its tone. "Definitely."

"How many members do you anticipate being there?"

"Well," Kinsman said with a pause to gather his thoughts, "I've heard from twenty, but I would guess no more than twelve actually showing up."

"That's plenty," Strickland said with a mischievous grin. "Contacted the press?"

"Working on it."

"Well, get to it," Strickland said coldly, dismissing him with a flicking wrist. "And don't forget our little talk here. We need to be extra cautious. There's a wolf in sheep's clothing mulling around. We'll know soon enough who it is, once he makes a wrong move. And trust me, he will."

Kale nodded with a furrowed brow. "I'll keep an eye out."

3:15pm

Austin, Texas

Jobie sat shivering inside *The Kennel,* holding himself with quivering, nervous arms as the sweltering mid-day heat basted him with his own perspiration. Sunlight shined through the cracks between the cinderblocks, making it unbearably hot inside his little fortress of solitude. He was unaware of the temperature, due to his deadened nerves. The only thing that mattered to him was his safe concealment away from society.

The three little puppies played outside beneath the shade of the old pecan tree. Mama was with them, lying motionless beside the trunk, panting furiously from the heat.

Jobie stared into the cinderblocks, smiling, shaking, laughing, and crying. He kept his hand close to the *Dragon,* just in case trouble should arise.

His mind drifted to an endless stretch of white sandy beaches where he walked hand in hand with his one true love. Events of the day changed with his passing whims—sometimes it was at sunset, other times in the late afternoon under puffy white clouds and blue skies. Always with her. Speechless, locked in harmony with an expansive stretch of years left for both of them to live.

He looked over to the collection of papers placed loosely inside the new folder Opaque had purchased for him. Scribbled on the front in black ink were the words, *The Apolitical Manifesto.*

Reaching out with a slack and shaking hand, he opened the folder. An unfinished work rested on top of the heap of entries. He picked up his ballpoint pen and pulled the folder across his lap. He quickly reread his passage, and then went to finish it, making corrections by blotting out words and writing on the edge of the margins with arrows showing the path of the revisions. It made it very difficult to follow for anyone other than him.

Goddamn Christians
The most destructive of human impulses is the urge to belief. Belief poisons minds and turns good people into bloodthirsty murderers, justifying their acts in the name of deities fabricated by men for such justifications. A human with a true religious faith, empowered with spiritual strength and self-awareness, would not care to covert and change the world to meet their personal agendas.

The United States is owned by a group of spiritually blind Christians known as the religious right. Their faith is based on nothing more than proper attire and Sunday morning attendance. Pomp and arrogance and archaic traditions. It has

312

nothing to do with spiritualism. It has nothing to do with soul-searching. We are a species comprised of childish minds with more power than we can philosophically and spiritually handle. Humans are not rational. Humans rationalize. Self-awareness has been neglected in favor of a book of fantastical tales, similar to the ones children read. Our culture does not understand the power of self-judgment because it is not something you can study in a book or a church. It is learned through solitude and introspection, in deep contemplation of one's own true identity and place in the world. We fear criticism and judgment, and would not dare to judge or criticize our own actions. Reason being, we are liars, to ourselves and to the world. It is the way the Church has taught us to be. The path of denial is their righteous path. This gross and absurd character flaw that is so commonly practiced will be society's undoing. Until we can accept ourselves for who and what we are, in all our flaws and all our glory, we are doomed to a catastrophic downfall. And who will be to blame? The spiritually blind Christians who own our lives.

Jobie's eyes were watering from the heat. He felt ill and tired. His vision wavered through light and dark. He put his writing aside and let his head fall against the cinderblocks.

Then he heard a shuffling in the backyard. He perked at once, startled back into reality. He instinctively reached down for the *Dragon*.

"Hey!" Josephine screamed from the backdoor. "You out there?"

The puppies scrambled over to greet her. Mama was right behind them.

"Jobie?" she hollered at *The Kennel*. "You got a letter."

"Who is it from?" he slurred from exhaustion. His mouth was nearly too dry to speak. "Terminal?"

She knew exactly who he was talking about—the informant of his who had gained access to the NRF Headquarters in Colorado. "No, it's from..." She paused to look at the return address. "Pistol Whip Press. In Portland, Oregon."

His eyes widened with excitement. "Hold on a minute! I'll be right out."

He crawled out of his little cave where he had been the entire day. As he rushed to his feet, he nearly fell over, but kept advancing with his hand against the wall.

"Boy," she said while shaking her head, "you look awful. Just plain awful."

He pulled the letter from her hands, and prepared to turn around.

"Nope," she declared as she grabbed his ratty old shirt and pulled him back, nearly tripping him. "Get your ass inside. You eaten?"

"Not hungry." He kept his eyes on the letter. His body swayed as he did.

"I don't think so, now come on. I'll make you up some noodles or somethin'." She led him inside by his shirt and steered him to the kitchen table. "Sit down."

He did as he was told.

"What you want to eat? Macaroni? I have a chicken potpie in here...does that sound good?"

He ignored her. The only thing in the world to him was the letter from the small independent publisher that could decide the future of his writing. He tore the handwritten letter out of the envelope and looked it over with so much optimism that his red face seemed as luminous as a Christmas light.

"Chicken potpie it is," she mumbled to herself as she turned on the stove and retrieved the meal from the freezer. "Thick-headed honky..."

She pulled it from the box and glanced back at him. His expression was long and dour, lifeless as it had been for so long.

"Bad news?"

He did not respond. He folded up the letter neatly and put it back inside the envelope.

"Third one," he eventually mumbled with defeat.

She took a moment to pour a glass of lemonade for him. She even delivered it to his trembling hands. As she did, she noticed that his skin seemed unattached, hanging thinly from his scrawny muscles and bones. It seemed torn in places and covered with so many orange and red lesions that they truly covered his entire body. From the looks of him, he had very little life left.

Her eyes began to moisten at the thought of his passing. After so much he had done for her in the past. Even saving her life.

"Can I tell you what's wrong?" she asked.

"Can I tell you to shut up?" he growled at her.

"Sure, we have a deal, then," she said briskly, unmoved by his spouts of anger. She had grown accustomed to them. "Drink your lemonade, I went out of my way to pour it for you, you thankless little shit."

He looked up at her, surprised to hear her scolding him.

"Go on, now," she screeched. "Drink the damn lemonade, and listen to what I have to say. After I finish, then you can tell me to shut up, if you feel you need to."

"I'd rather have a beer...or six."

"Too bad."

Keeping his eyes on her, he lifted the glass to his chapped and damaged lips. He took a big gulp, and then followed it with another, and another, until the entire glass was empty. She removed the pitcher from the refrigerator and refilled his glass.

"Your letter...sucks," she confided as she replaced the pitcher inside the fridge. She then opened the oven and put the potpie on the center rack amidst a pale orange glow. "Your presentation...sucks. You need to make yourself look like a professional. A bona fide writer."

He swallowed every drop of lemonade, listening while staring into his empty glass.

314

"I tell you what," she said after a long pause for contemplation, "I'll type your letter, we can do an experiment. Let me put together your portfolio, and we'll send it to a couple of these publishers, see what they think."

He thought to himself.

"You don't have to do anything," she explained. "I'd write your letter. All you'd need to do is let me type up some of your writing, and present the whole thing to them in a really nice package."

As he listened to her talk, he realized that he was hungry after all. He glanced over at the oven, eager to eat the potpie.

"So?"

"Huh?" he asked as he stared at the oven.

"Are you interested?"

He imagined poking the top of the potpie with a fork, allowing the steam to carry the scent of chicken and peas and carrots up to his nostrils. He wanted nothing more. "Sounds yummy."

She smiled. "Good. We'll give it a try this afternoon."

8:41pm

Pip Squeak looked over at Karen Wovey and said, "Has anyone ever told you that you look exactly like Madonna?"

She kept her eyes on the millions of Mexican short-tailed bats that fluttered over their heads. Her fingers were interlocked behind her neck as she lay flat on the grass, surrounded by the hundreds of people appreciating one of Austin's biggest tourist attractions. The sun was setting, leaving the sky a shade of purple that grew increasingly darker toward the eastern horizon where the bats clustered like an enormous pulsating cloud. Their numbers were so great that they even showed up on the Doppler radar on the nightly news weathercast.

"Madonna?" she replied. "Are you blind?"

Karen Wovey, known as "Wolfie" since the age of seven, was born and raised in an upper-middleclass Austin home in the Lakeway suburbs. She was tall and painfully thin, somewhat awkward in her presentation, but always impeccably dressed. What she lacked in physical beauty, she more than overcompensated with a strong sexual prowess. Her natural red hair was thin and long and wispy. She had a small mouth and recessed lips with an excessively large nose and narrow chin. Her makeup accentuated the odd proportions of her face rather than subdued them, giving her an unusually exotic appearance.

Pip Squeak gazed longingly at her slender legs. Her pale skin was almost too enticing for him to resist touching. His eyes followed the curves of her thighs up to her leopard skin skirt. He would be satisfied to simply smell her, if not actually taste her, but his goal was far more explicit than that. She meant nothing else to him. He stared at her pierced naval and pierced nipples, slightly bulging from beneath her tight black Satan's Cheerleaders T-shirt. Her breasts were small, just how he liked them. Actually, he had very little preference, but at the moment, he was strongly opinionated about the subject, just watching her.

Wolfie was a student at the more prestigious St. Edwards University in South Austin. In her spare time, she hung out with the punks at a bar called Emo's and the Crusties on the Drag. She cared little for their music, but absolutely loved their sense of fashion and attitude. She was frequently courted by the more debonair males from the punk scene, simply because she was known to be dependable for one-night stands. After continuous badgering, Pip Squeak had surprisingly convinced her to spend an afternoon with him. She chose a neutral setting with large amounts of people and an event that would be brief but interesting. Watching the bats in their nightly departure from beneath the Congress Bridge seemed perfect.

"What are we doing later?" Pip Squeak asked her.

"I need to study," she replied quickly without recourse. "In fact, we need to leave soon."

He kept quiet a moment as if concentrating on the flight of the bats. He hardly noticed them, although he could definitely smell them. He was merely taking a break from eyeing her body so lustfully. And so obviously. Knowing that his time was limited, he felt pressured to hasten his advances.

"Who is Jobie?" she asked.

"Why?"

"I've heard people talking about him, and I've seen his name around."

"Where have you seen his name?"

Her forthcoming answer both amused and intrigued her. "Spray-painted on walls. Like the one off 26th on the Drag that reads, *Jobie Lives*. And the one behind El Mercado on Lavaca—*Jobie Saves*. I like a guy who doesn't take himself too seriously."

He chuckled. "He's a very close friend of mine, actually."

"How come he's never anywhere I go?"

He thought to himself before answering. "He's really busy. He's working on something, I can't say what it is, but it requires a lot of time...I guess."

"My dad's a Freemason," she revealed. "I heard that that name was spray-painted at the Scottish Rite Temple when it caught fire a few months ago."

"Hmm, imagine that."

"I won't tell," she promised him. "So who is he? And why don't I know him?"

"He used to live in Austin for a while, and then he left," Pip began. "I think he and his girlfriend broke up wherever they went because he told everyone that he left her in Florida. He's a really cool guy. He's been sort of the glue for the Crusties since he came back last year. But he hasn't been around much lately."

"Since about the time where he burned the Temple?"

"I suppose so."

"Well, I'd like to meet him."

Pip thought about her reputation for conquering the more outspoken and eccentric iconoclastic types. Jobie definitely fit the bill. "I bet you would."

"What does that mean?"

"Nothing."

The sky was getting more and more dark. Many of the tourists that were lined up on the bridge were walking away, as well as those sitting in lawn chairs on the grass.

"Should we be going?" she asked.

"Already?"

"I have things to do." She stood and brushed herself off. "Ready?"

He remained on the grass for a moment simply because he could partially see up her skirt. She was wearing red panties. He wondered how many different men had stripped those off her. He hoped to be one of them.

"Can I show you where I stay at on the Drag?"

"I'm really busy," she told him. "Maybe some other time."

He stood, wishing he had the courage to make a pass at her. "Have I told you that I used to be a pickpocket in San Francisco?"

She had already learned of his knack for stretching the truth, but she humored him anyway. His lies intrigued her. They were always so colorful and strange and creative. "No, you never have."

He followed her to the parking lot, amidst all the other sightseers. "Yeah, you wouldn't believe the amount of money we would bring in at Fisherman's Wharf."

"Really?"

"Oh yeah. Hundreds of dollars a day. Sometimes even thousands."

She unlocked the door of her new white Toyota and let him inside.

"What did you do with all that money?" she asked him as she started the car.

"Spent it on stupid things usually."

It was not the type of response he typically gave. It actually made some sort of sense.

"No trips to Paris?" she asked, egging him on a little.

"Maybe once. To Amsterdam. Oh, and we also went to Boston, I forgot about that."

She smiled. That was more like it.

He kept his eye on her legs as she drove the car back through the city. The way her calves flexed each time she shifted gears. He could watch her do that all night long and never get bored with it.

"Where do you want to be dropped off?" she asked him as she turned onto the Drag.

His eyes roamed her body. "Are you sure you don't want to see where I sleep? It's pretty cool. It's in the alley behind the Drag."

"No, not this time."

"I'd pay you."

She tapped the brake instinctively. "What?"

He looked at her right pierced nipple protruding from within her tight black T-shirt. "Have you had sex in a while?"

She laughed out loud—a knee-jerk reaction from being taken aback by his sudden boldness. "Why would you ask something like that?"

"Just wondering. Is that weird?"

"Sort of."

"Well?"

She shook her head, truly shocked by his tactlessness, yet nowhere in the vicinity of being aroused. "A few weeks."

"That long?"

"Maybe longer. Why?" She pulled up to the Drag at 22nd Street. "Okay, here we are."

"Do you mind taking me down the street a little ways?" he asked politely.

She rolled her eyes.

"I need to see my girlfriend," he explained.

"I bet you do."

"Do you have a boyfriend?" he asked.

"No. I don't believe in boyfriends."

"Do you swallow?"

She stepped firmly on the brake. "Okay, that's enough. I need you to get out of the car."

"Why?"

"Because you're acting extremely weird and freaking me out."

"Asking you about sex?" he clarified. "That's weird? I thought you weren't so easily offended."

"I hardly even know you." She looked to the passenger door as if beckoning him to open it. "So…"

"So?"

"Can you go ahead and get out?"

"You're prude," he told her lightly. "I can't believe you're afraid of the question. You let me down, Wolfie."

"No, I don't *swallow*." She nearly spat the word at him. "Not that you'll ever need to know that."

He was disappointed. His illusion of her was blown, and there was no regaining the image of her that he had built inside his imagination. He wished he had never asked. "You don't?"

She sighed and shook her head. "What is this all about?"

"Just asking a question."

"And I answered it," she hissed with a much more catty tone of voice. "This is as far as I'm taking you, so please... *leave*."

He opened the door, but resisted stepping out. "Do you drink milk or eat cheese?"

Her eyes tensed into narrow slits that accentuated the amount of eyeliner she was wearing.

"Are you afraid to answer that, too?"

She laughed. If he were the least bit threatening, she would have punched him. Instead, it was simply humorous to watch him try so hard and fail so miserably.

"Yes, I drink milk, I'm not a vegan. Good seeing you, Pip Squeak, and goodnight."

He put one foot on the pavement, and then said, "So you'll drink the body fluids of an animal that eats where it shits, but you won't swallow a few drops of fluids from a man you've chosen to go down on? That doesn't make any sense, Wolfie."

Her smile slowly went away as she pondered it for a moment. "Goodnight, Pip Squeak, and good try. Be more tactful next time, and maybe you'll get somewhere."

He stepped out of the car. "Bye. Come by tomorrow if you aren't busy. This was fun."

She quickly sped away, leaving him alone on 22nd Street. He walked a few blocks to the west, wishing things had turned out differently. Then he came to Tamika's house.

He walked around the side where one of the lights was on. He ducked into the shrubs that grew along the side of the house and peeked through the window. Josephine stood in the closet of her bedroom, folding clothes and stacking them neatly on the shelves. He backed away from the light, making sure that she could not see him.

After the clothes were all properly folded, she left the room and turned off the light. He sighed, and then prepared to leave, just as another light came on in a small window at the front corner of the house. He crept along the bushes very quietly, although the puppies in the backyard were well aware of his presence and were beginning to bark and yelp at him.

He placed one foot on the house's foundation and the other in the thick shrubbery until he had decent enough to traction to lift himself desperately up to the high window. He could see pastel linens hanging over the edge of the bathtub. The water was already beginning to fill the bathtub. Steam billowed over its edge. Josephine was sitting on the toilet, reading a magazine with her shorts down around her ankles. She was practically out of his view. He gritted his teeth and waited impatiently for her to stand. Time seemed to stretch into eternity as the hormones exploded through his gangly body, tormenting him and holding reason captive. The small window slowly began to collect steam, distorting everything beyond it like an Impressionist painting.

She finally flushed the toilet and wiped herself, though he could only see so well by then. His heart raced with excitement and dread. He hoped that he would catch a view before the steam prevented it, but his optimism waned with each passing second. It was a race against time, and his hormones could barely handle the stress of it all.

She stood and faced the mirror. He could tell she was wearing no pants, only a shirt, but he could only see the shape of her buttocks. It was enough for him. Her skin was a creamy caramel color with the vague streaks of stretch marks across her hips. The bulbous shape of her ass was perfect—something he would remember for a very long time.

She washed her face while staring into the mirror. She began singing a popular hip-hop song, humming the words she did not know. The window fogged more and more with each passing second, driving Pip Squeak insane with frustration. By the time she had pulled off her shirt and bra, he could barely see anything. What he could see was the firm muscles of her stomach and the perfect shape of her breasts. Her copper-colored skin glistened from the steam billowing up from the bathtub. Her nipples were much darker in contrast, giving him the view he so desperately hoped to get.

Within two seconds, she had stepped down into the tub and out of sight. Two seconds he would cherish for years.

His breathing was shaky. His entire body seemed to be made of putty. He drifted quietly away from the bushes, drunk on the hormones flooding his skinny body.

"Who's out there?" a voice growled from the backyard.

Pip Squeak sped off in a mad dash, racing through the front yard and down the street.

Jobie glared into the darkness, holding the *Dragon* with both hands as he watched and waited. He stood there for several minutes, brooding with paranoia, eager to kill a trespasser.

He never saw who it was.

9:49pm

Jonathan Wranger knelt before an upturned black pentagram painted on his bedroom wall. Rose-colored candles surrounded him, encompassing him in a shell of soft warm light. On a small wooden alter were nine Wanga Dolls with frayed black hair and wrapped in tiny white robes. Nine Power Wanga Dolls to summon the dark spirits. His lucky number. He had acquired them from a woman he had met in a local bar who claimed the title of Voodoo Priestess. Mistress Lakasha. A knife with a wooden handle was in front of him on the floor, pointed directly toward the center of the pentagram.

"Bring me the power," he hissed quietly to himself as he knelt with his nose close to the floor. He could smell his roommate's dog's urine in the carpet. "Bring the power."

A black silk robe draped over his bony shoulders, descending to the floor around him. His dyed black hair blended with the material, giving his form the appearance of a blob of tar. Illuminated by candlelight.

On the dresser by his twin bed was a stack of *Venom* and *Spawn* comic books and graphic novels. Ratty old copies of Poppy Z. Brite and Anne Rice novels rested on the nightstand, alongside paycheck stubs from his dishwashing job. A letter from his mother was opened and in the trashcan, with her check already cashed and spent. The walls were covered with posters from slasher horror films, along with gory pictures from back issues of *Fangoria*. Next to his small stereo system, CDs were strewn about the floor—Black Sabbath, Mayhem, Slayer. Photographs with graphic images of rape and bondage were stashed underneath his bed, saved for more intimate viewings.

His vanity swelled. He felt famous. Infamous. Feared by the common man. Like Jack the Ripper, or Zodiac. He was IX, the number nine. But to the residents of central Austin, he was one of the fearsome Shadowmen.

With his hands clasped together, fingers tight on his fair skin, knuckles white, he begged for power from the dark underworld. He chanted in Latin to summon the beyond to ordain the Shadowmen into the realm of darkness. He praised the One, the leader of the Shadowmen. The modern legend—the man to whom their strength and power was owed. Ruler of the underworld, ruler of the streets. The One, as they called him.

He ran his tongue over his teeth, wishing his canines were more pronounced, more fierce. More vampiric. He leaned forward to the knife that had been used in all four of the Shadowmen attacks. He wished to own the hands of death. He fantasized about murder. He fantasized of his own criminal independence from the group, a sole demon set free in the world of the living and pure. The one and only Shadowman. IX.

The knife reflected the candlelight as he brought it closer to his face. Bloodstains were still visible on the serrated blade, yet it was the blood of minor injuries, not death. He wished upon it a great sacrifice to come. An instrument of death. He gripped its handle and fell deep into a homicidal fantasy.

He visualized a woman on a dark and empty street. He saw himself emerge from the night, taking her by the collar and slicing her throat wide open. He could almost feel the blood pouring down his thin white hands. Her screams were drowned in a pathetic gurgle as her lungs filled with her own blood. Soon her body fell limp, and he dragged her off into the night, to keep him company, to succumb to his sadistic whims.

His breath quivered, and his pants bulged uncomfortably. He raised himself up from the floor and took a deep breath. He wanted desperately to live out his dreams. He wanted the fame that would go with it. To become legend. Like Dahmer and Gacy.

He crawled across the floor to the telephone. His silk robe fell around him with his head bobbing over a pit of blackness. He dialed Thomas Patterson, one of the other Shadowmen.

"Hello?" Thomas answered.

"Hey," IX breathed into the phone. "Come over here."

"Why?" he asked insipidly.

IX held out the knife, caressing the blade tenderly. "I want to try something."

"What?"

"I want to kill someone."

There was a pause as Thomas tried to interpret the statement as a joke or a reality. "Who?"

"Anyone." He took a deep and seemingly sensual breath. "Doesn't matter. Come on over here."

"Are you serious?"

He did not answer.

Thomas thought to himself for a moment, not sure what to make of the statement. He knew that he could not murder someone in cold blood, but at the same time he was not against watching it. Maybe even filming it.

"I need to wait until my parents go to bed," Thomas told him.

IX sighed. He was overcome with impatience. "Hurry up."

"I'll see you tonight, later on." He hung up the phone, leaving IX tense and frustrated.

IX stood up and hastily stomped to his closet. He pulled down a bundle of folded bedspreads, comforters, and towels. He laid them out on the floor in the center of the circle of candles, stacking them on top of one another so that the blood from his victim would not saturate into the carpet, leaving a stain that would trace him to the murder.

11:45pm

Barron's Bluff, Colorado

Kinsman Kale sat bleary-eyed in front of the computer, transferring funds from the smaller regional accounts into the main corporate account. The monthly dues had yet been distributed properly, and Kale was the only one Reverend Strickland could trust with such information.

He pondered the conversation he had with the Reverend earlier in the day, contemplating the ramifications of such a revelation. Was Strickland simply being overly paranoid, or did he truly have grounds for his suspicions? Before he could consider it any further, there came a loud thumping on the porch. Awkward clumsy steps that approached the unlocked door.

He quickly logged off the computer and reached for the industrial strength stapler. There was nothing else worthy of defense.

The door swung open with a loud bang. It was Brother Perry. Drunk.

"Hey...Torben...what's gone on?"

Kale stood upright with his thick chest bulging forward to give the impression of confidence. His hands trembled. The stapler rattled.

"Just closing shop," Kale told him casually. "Where you been? Out late, huh?"

"Shhhh," Perry said as he stumbled inside Headquarters, slamming the door behind him.

Aside from a lamp by the computer, the large room was very dim, lit only by moonlight.

"Come on, Perry," Kale coaxed him as he stepped away from the computer. "Time for bed."

"Messing with the money, huh?" Perry asked with a belligerent slur. His head seemed to swivel on his lazy shoulders. "We should run this place, you and me."

"We pretty much do, Perry," he told him calmly as he stepped toward him. "Sending out all the newsletters, that's the real backbone of the operation, isn't it?"

"*You* run this place, man, and you know it."

Kale stared at him with a deadpan expression.

"I'm not gone stay here, man, I decided tonight," Perry drawled. He swaggered forward. "What if I told you that I plan to split from you guys? Do my own thing?"

Kale shrugged his shoulders. He knew he was bluffing. Kale had noticed him slip on more than one occasion, revealing his true lack of interest in the NRF's agenda. "You're free to do what you want. Are you that unsatisfied?"

"All I need is the database you keep," Perry told him in a near threatening tone. "Where is it? I've looked on the system, man, but it's not there."

Kale stepped up to him, blocking his path. He was close enough to smell the whiskey on his breath. "Why would you do that, Perry?"

"Why not? It's here."

"No," Kale told him flatly. "It doesn't work that way."

"Come on, man," Perry slurred with a crooked smile. He scratched his scraggly hair with a flat palm that made a swirling mess of his dirty blond hair. "You and I could make good money that way. Think of it."

Kale quickly grabbed Perry's collar and lifted him up off the ground. "Say it again, Perry. Say it again and I'll smear you across the mountain." He lowered him to the wooden floor, staring into his incoherent line of vision. "You're a miserable drunk, Perry. Sober up. Get yourself together. You're an idiot. Stop acting like one. Makes you look bad."

"You called me an idiot?" He tried to break free of his grip, but Kale did not budge. When Kale finally let go, he lost his balance and stumbled backward toward the door. "We should be out beatin' people down, man. You know? All we do is send out letters."

Kale glared at him. "Get to bed, Perry, you're drunk, and talking in circles. You know what? You're completely full of shit, and I know it."

"It's a desk job, man," Perry groaned as he stumbled to the front door. "Do you like being here?"

"Get to bed, Perry."

"You're a pawn, man."

Kale laughed.

"You and I could run this place, man," Perry tried one last time. "It wouldn't be hard to get rid of the old man."

Kale pushed him through the door where he stumbled down the front steps. "You best be packing your bags."

Perry grabbed onto the stairs and pulled himself awkwardly to his feet. He stood at the bottom of the steps in front of Kale, and then backed away into the darkness that surrounded them.

"Nice knowing you, Perry."

11:58pm

At the rear of Headquarters was a trailer with three bedrooms—one for each in-house volunteer. Pokerface reclined on his twin-sized bed, reading a magazine article about a man named X, the new host of the television show *Far Out*. A cassette tape of a band called Skrewdriver played loudly over the portable stereo system on the nightstand. The singer's growl and the band's high volume music relaxed him more than anything else.

The walls of his tiny room were covered with caricatures of Friedrich Nietzsche, Ayn Rand, and Karl Marx. His small closet was packed with clothes, all neatly organized and hanging from plastic hangers. The ironing board was still out with one of his cotton shirts splayed over it like a bedspread. Five different pairs of leather shoes lined the narrow wall by the door. The whole room appeared like the interior of a packed suitcase with very little floor not covered with some piece of furniture or clothing. The room was the smallest living space he had ever claimed, even smaller than the dorm room he occupied for the two years he spent in college.

Unlike his compatriots at Headquarters, Pokerface had come from a respectable and educated family. He grew up in the Lake Forest suburbs of Chicago, an only-child raised by loving parents who owned a small regional clothing chain. They did their best to shelter him from the evils of the world, shielding him with money and affection. Unbeknownst to them, their actions were so successful that they created in him an unjustifiable fear and hatred for anything that differed from his wholesome and sterile sensibilities. They were shocked when he became interested in the NRF. His life and ambitions slowly transformed into something they deeply abhorred.

To further their dismay, he chose to spend the first two years out of high school working for the Great Lakes branch of the NRF rather than attending college. After persistent talks and badgering, they were finally able to convince him to pursue higher education.

He was accepted by several schools, but chose to go with the one that had the largest enrollment in the nation, the University of Texas. It seemed to his parents that his life was on the right track for the first time in years. In support of his decision, their suburban house became a shrine for Texas Longhorns knickknacks and paraphernalia. All seemed well with the Paglea household until the summer following his sophomore year. It was then that he announced he would be quitting school to volunteer his time at the Headquarters of the NRF. The day he left was the last time he had spoken to either of them.

He was determined to prove his worth on his own terms. He had a plan, one that would take some time to set in motion, but a reasonable plan nonetheless. He would become an independent book publisher. Only catch was the large amount of revenue required to start the business. He was penniless, but luckily for him, he was certain he had discovered a way to acquire an exorbitant amount of money.

The front door opened and Perry came stumbling inside the trailer's narrow living room. Pokerface closed his magazine and quickly turned off the music and the lamp. He crossed his arms behind the pillow and waited for the knocking at the door. He had grown to know his colleagues well, and he was happy to note that he was on good standings with both Kinsman Kale and Brother Perry. Nonetheless, he knew that Perry would be drunk, as he was most every night. He also knew that Perry would want to sit on the edge of his bed and ramble for hours in a drunken stupor. It was the last thing he wanted.

There came the anticipated tapping at the door.

"You awake?" Perry asked from behind the closed door.

Pokerface waited a few seconds to respond. "Nah," he grumbled in a phony raspy bedtime voice. "Do ya need sompun?"

"I guess not," Perry concluded rather glumly. "I'll talk to you tomorrow, man. Goodnight."

Pokerface sighed with relief. He rolled over and looked at the clock. He was happy to see that it was finally late enough to go to sleep. He closed his eyes and concentrated on the noise Perry was making in his own tiny living space. It was just the type of commotion he needed to help him fall asleep.

11:59pm

Austin, Texas

Thomas Patterson gently tapped on the front door. He waited patiently, unwrapping his new CD with eager fingers. The door opened and he walked inside, never looking away from the CD that he had finally managed to break free from the shrink-wrap packaging.

"Check it out," Thomas bellowed with excitement, "it's the new Deicide." He looked up at IX, finally getting a glimpse of his clothing. He was dressed in old ill-fitting gray sweats with at least two pairs of knee-high tube socks. He laughed. "What's with this costume?"

"I don't want to get bloodstains on my good clothes."

The smile on Thomas's face melted into icy confusion. "Are you really serious about this?"

IX presented the knife.

Thomas was shocked. He had known Jonathan Wranger his whole life. In fact, Thomas was the person who introduced him not only to Dungeons & Dragons in their early teens, but also opened him to the world of black metal. It struck him momentarily that Jonathan was taking this too far, and too seriously.

"Who do you plan to kill?" Thomas asked.

"Come here and see what I've done with my room," IX instructed his old friend as he led him into his dark lair. "You'll be impressed." The circle of red candles were still blazing, though mostly burned down to small stumps immersed in puddles of wax. He pointed to the layers of blankets, towels, and old pillows. "This is where the body will go."

"You're going to take the person up here?"

He leaned against the doorframe and said, "I've thought about this a lot, actually. How to kill someone and get away with it. I think I have some good ideas on it."

"Oh yeah?" Thomas said casually, though not sure how seriously he should take him. He was certain that he had no intentions of being any part of it. "You never told me any of this."

"First, you need to not have a motive, if you're doing it for sport. Should be totally random."

"Yeah, what else?"

"Second thing, leave no trace," IX told him partner. "You know how on those crime shows on TV they always are able to trace the killer because of the evidence they have left behind? A good premeditated crime can remedy that."

Thomas nodded his head. He had drawn these conclusions on his own. He was only moderately impressed. "Can I put on the CD?"

IX pointed to the stereo system across the room.

Thomas eagerly walked around the stacks of blankets and placed the CD inside the player. He then pressed *Play*. As he stood up, IX grabbed his hair and yanked him backward onto him, plunging the knife into his throat, slicing deeply, and then pulling the blade from one ear to the other.

Blood spilled all over both of them. Thomas writhed wildly on top of his old friend, struggling to stop the knife that was slamming over and over into his chest. Somehow, he broke free.

Thomas crawled forward, feeling an unbearable loss of breath. He stood nervously and caught a quick glimpse of the blood that was draining from the wounds on his chest.

"You...you're insane!" he said to IX as he backed over to the door.

IX climbed to his feet, sliding uneasily on all the blood that had spilled, and threw the knife with brute force at him. It bounced off the wall.

Thomas opened the door, holding himself up with what little strength he had left as he stared, horrified by the monster whom he had spent so much of his life confiding in and defending.

IX leapt forward, ramming him in the belly with his shoulder. The impact caused the wounds to rupture. IX wrestled him to the ground and listened to his cries and he gripped his sliced throat and squeezed with all his strength. He could feel his fingers penetrating the gash, digging deeply beneath the skin into slick tissue.

Eventually Thomas's movements stopped, aside from a few spasms and twitches. The blood spilled over his shoulders like a trickling fountain that drained upon the piles of sheets that covered the floor. He rolled over, pushing his lifelong friend's body onto the spot he had designated.

He rushed to his feet and stood akimbo as the evil music throbbed in the darkness that surrounded him. His sweatpants were covered with blood. He could feel it on his skin. It was still warm.

He slowly pulled his tube socks off and threw them on the corpse's mutilated chest. The blood soaked into them immediately, coloring them a soft shade of pink.

A wicked smile stretched across his face. The situation was one that had increasingly grown in appeal over the years of his young life, turning from passing thought to absolute obsession. It was nearly too powerful for him to contain himself. He felt strangely compelled to masturbate, but instead he stood immobile, living purely in the moment. It was a high he never knew possible.

He studied the body, reenacting the incident over and over in his mind. There were two wounds to the neck that IX could not remember. His inability to recollect that particular stabbing frustrated him. His smile washed away briefly until he looked at Thomas's face. He had the most horrific expression imaginable on his colorless face. It was as if he had been frozen at the gates of hell after having gotten a glimpse inside. His hands were still clutched and bent in oddly twisting angles like oak branches.

IX quickly pulled off his garments and tossed them onto the body. He began beating on his chest with his bloodstained fists, lumbering like a gorilla, or Tarzan. He stood naked over the lifeless and bloody body, feeling invincible. It was every bit as gratifying as he hoped it would be. He ran his fingertips across his shoulders, sliding easily through the streaks of blood.

"You know, Thomas," he said matter-of-factly, "there was no reason for this. No motive, totally random." He picked up one of the towels and wiped his pale skin, doing little more than smearing its gruesome aftermath. "It's always the guy you'd never suspect."

He knelt before the corpse and wrapped it with the layers of blankets, leaving it in the center of the room—a tight bundle of carnage. He calmly blew out each candle, bringing darkness to the room as the music played on.

"Hey, Tommy-boy," he chided playfully, "you stupid-ass, you're my first victim! Dumbass…"

He stepped over the body, bobbing his head to the music with a menacing scowl. He walked to the bathroom and stood before the mirror, flexing his feeble muscles and feeling ultimately powerful. The realization was almost too much—his body was covered with the blood of his childhood friend. It empowered him with a false sense of control and strength. To him, it carried a profoundly deep meaning. He saw it as a rite of passage, a test of his own dark conviction. His first sacrifice. His first killing. He knew there would be more. He had no doubts in his deranged mind that he could outsmart the police and become famous. World famous. If he played his cards right, he could kill and never be caught. He humored the idea of sending letters to the police and to the newspapers, letting them know whom to fear. IX. The cunning serial killer that even the cops could never catch.

He smiled proudly to himself, overwhelmed with confidence and adrenaline. He stepped into the shower and washed the blood off his thin and pasty skin. His dyed black hair hung over his shoulders, slipping onto his chest in a stream of blood. He stood under the warm water for several minutes, recapturing the murder over and over in his mind. When the water finally turned cold, he shut it off and dried himself, taking a moment to flex his unimpressive muscles in front of the mirror once again. He preferred the blood splatter look from before.

He strutted into his bedroom with his fists clenched tightly together. He turned on the light, ready for anything unexpected. He knew that sometimes death did not come as quickly as the murderer would hope. But in this case, he had done the job right the first time. The body had not moved.

He went into his closet and found some old black garments, proper for the hours of digging that he had ahead of him that night. He took his time dressing, taking several breaks to admire his gruesome work. Eventually he carried the wrapped body outdoors to his car. He rolled it off his shoulder and into the trunk where the shovel had already been placed. It would take forty minutes to drive out to the Hill Country land owned by his uncle, but as far as he could imagine, it was the perfect place for a shallow grave. He even had the spot located from a previous visit. It was all part of a well-crafted plan. Flawless.

Or so it seemed.

He had not noticed the tiny droplets of blood on the bathroom's baseboard, as well as three tiny specks of blood waiting to dry inside the shower over the faucet handles. It would only be a matter of time before a missing persons report was filed, tracing Thomas Patterson's last moments in the company of Jonathan Wranger. The Luminol would light up the tub like a dance club, professing his guilt with hardly an investigation.

Friday, September 8, 2000
11:17am

Key West, Florida

Detective Marlen Esparanza stared intently at her computer screen as she filed a report on a domestic disturbance from the previous night. She was familiar with the address and the subjects of the case due to the small number of people who actually claimed Key West as their home. The warm tropical sun shined through an open window that allowed a gentle salty breeze into the stuffy office. Her desk was scattered with reports from other complaints on the household, pulled from her filing cabinet earlier that morning.

It was grunt work, and not the type that had lured her to law enforcement in the first place. During the long and hot summers, very little happened in the community. She found herself secretly awaiting the tourists that would soon be coming in droves, bringing along their crimes of passions and lewd behavior.

There came a knocking at the door.

"Come in, Theresa," she said blandly with a slight Cuban accent. She recognized the knock to be the receptionist. She did not even have to look up to greet her when the door opened.

"You got a strange letter here," Theresa announced as she stepped up to her desk. "No return address, either. Postmarked from Austin, Texas."

Detective Esparanza shifted her deep dark eyes to the envelope. Her thick eyebrows rose slightly. "Thank you, Theresa."

"You're welcome." The receptionist left the room in the same quiet state it was in before she entered.

Detective Esparanza slowly opened the envelope and pulled out the contents—two pages. One was a typed letter, the other a crude map, which she recognized to be part of a Key West neighborhood. As she read through the letter, her heart rate quickened. She could feel herself beginning to perspire under her blue denim shirt. It was not the type of letter she was accustomed to receiving, and if its grisly claim was true...

She stepped up out of her chair and grabbed her purse. She fumbled for her keys and sunglasses as she made her way to the door.

"Take messages from anyone who calls," she told Theresa as she passed the receptionist's desk. "Anything important, page me."

She strolled eagerly through the front doors, shielding her eyes briefly from the sun before putting on her large black sunglasses. Her salt and pepper hair blew gently in the warm ocean breeze as she bounded to her car, shaking her wide shifty hips with each determined step. She quickly unlocked the door and slid inside, first checking her sparse makeup in the rearview before starting the engine.

The map proved to be useful, and took her to an old house with peeling white paint and an overgrown yard. She parked out front and sat quietly for a moment, pausing to survey her surroundings. Although the letter deeply implied that there was no danger to be found there, she relayed her whereabouts back to the station as proper protocol. She denied a request for backup, and approached the decrepit old house on her own.

The lawn was in an extreme shape of mismanagement, making it a task to reach the front steps. She stepped up onto the porch that creaked noisily. The house appeared vacant. There were absolutely no sounds coming from within. She knocked loudly on the front door and waited.

No answer.

She knocked again, doubling the rhythm and volume. A cold chill ran the length of her spine. Just as she decided to request assistance after all, the front door slowly opened. An old woman stood hunched over, staring up at Detective Esparanza through thick glasses.

"Mrs. Reinbrandt?" Detective Esparanza asked. It was the name given in the letter.

"Yes?" the old woman replied.

"Hi," she said with deep sigh of relief, "I'm Detective Marlen Esparanza from the Key West police department." She paused to show her badge. "Can I ask you a few questions?"

"I done talked with an officer about the yard. I have a boy coming to cut the grass day after tomorr-ah."

"No, actually it's not about the grass. It's about a shed that you have in the backyard."

"Oh…" She looked up at Detective Esparanza, and said, "Oh dear. Is that gentleman in trouble with the law?"

Detective Esparanza raised her thick and dark eyebrows. "What gentleman?"

"The feller who rents it. I ain't had no problems. He paid a year's rent last year this time. Haven't seen him since, and if you want the truth, he is the one who agreed to keep the yard up."

"Seems like he hasn't been around in a while. Do you know his name?"

She looked over Detective Esparanza's shoulder with a bent brow. "Reckon I don't."

"You have some records, right?"

Mrs. Reinbrandt shook her head. "Can't rightfully say I do."

331

"So you don't know who is using your shed?"

"Nah, ma'am."

"Okay…" Detective Esparanza said with an exasperated sigh. The letter she had received gave the name and current address of the man who had rented it. She was hoping that the old woman could corroborate the information provided in the letter. "Would you mind me taking a look around?"

"Go right ahead," Mrs. Reinbrandt offered politely. "Would you care for a glass of tea? Or lemonade?"

"No, thanks."

"Let me show you the way through the house," Mrs. Reinbrandt offered as she scooted very slowly out of the way. "The gentleman kept it locked real good. Padlocked it, had some wire over the top of the fence, too. You need to go through the house to get there."

Detective Esparanza stepped inside the stuffy little house that smelled of mold and wet newspaper. Mrs. Reinbrandt hobbled along, speaking too low to be understood, though apparently apologizing for the mess.

They passed through the main room, which was dark and filled with old furniture, ancient ceramic knickknacks, and a large bookshelf filled with old hardbacks. Everything was covered with dust.

Mrs. Reinbrandt led her slowly through the dining room that had only a stainless steel table with a Formica top. Four stainless steel seats with vinyl cushions surrounded the table, and only one of them appeared to have had any use in years.

As they reached the kitchen, the backdoor was finally visible. The kitchen smelled of oil and spices, which was a nice contrast to the rest of the house.

"Out here," Mrs. Reinbrandt said politely as she came upon the backdoor. She unlocked it and gave the door a brief and ineffective struggle. "It's too hard to open myself, if you don't mind…"

Detective Esparanza reached out and clutched the old metal doorknob. She twisted it and gave it a brisk tug. By the sound of it, no one had opened it in a very long time.

The backyard was fenced in, just as she had been told by the old woman. In the center of the overgrown and neglected yard was an old wooden shed practically in shambles. Its paint was peeling, revealing the gray wood beneath it. She stepped out onto the back porch and walked down the steps into the thick green grass and weeds.

"Just let me know what you may need," the old woman said before closing the door.

"Thanks," Detective Esparanza muttered to the air as she opened her purse and took out the envelope once again. She kept her hand close to her concealed weapon at all times.

As she reached the shed, she found that the small door was bolted and padlocked and covered with chains. But the old rusted hinges were in such poor condition that she decided it would be easier to simply unhinge the door than to try to get through the barricade.

She took a moment to contact the police station. She requested backup, feeling certain that the letter's claim was likely going to turn out to be true. She gave them the address, and told them that the resident of the old house seemed harmless.

She then took a metal fingernail file out of her purse and began unscrewing the hinges. They came easier than she would have suspected. She assumed that the wood had undergone quite a bit of natural deterioration from the oceanic elements. As she unscrewed the last one, the door fell over to the side with dust and a ghastly stench pouring out from inside. It was an odor she knew from past experience in the force. The smell of death.

She pulled her denim shirt up over her mouth and slowly peeked inside. She found exactly what she was looking for—a partially decomposed body laying on makeshift bed.

Her eyes widened as she was struck with a jolt of morbid excitement. She stepped one foot inside the shed while drawing her gun with her free right hand. Red milk crates were stacked up against the walls where sunlight crept through, illuminating the swirling dust with streaks of light.

The body was that of young woman. According to the letter, her name was Treva Rifkin.

She took a closer look and realized that the body had been altered. It looked as if someone had tried to preserve it somehow by filling its decayed remains with gauze. It glistened from some sort of enamel that was painted the color of pasty Caucasian skin. Even her makeup had been carefully and painstakingly applied with paint. A bright pinkish wig covered the skull, and the eye sockets were deep and empty. Although she could not be absolutely sure, it appeared that the body had been adjusted so that it could be used for sexual gratification. The legs were spread wide, and there appeared to be some sort of apparatus wedged where her genitalia had once been.

Detective Esparanza could feel her body shaking. She looked around the room to see what evidence could lead her to the culprit of this abomination. The letter gave a name, but she wanted something that would alleviate any doubt. The room was empty except for a bowl of melted red M&M's, the body on the bed, a large wasp nest, and a flier penned to the wall. It was for a protest of a Drag Queen beauty pageant. The protestors called themselves the National Reclamation Front, or the NRF.

She backed out of the shed and stepped out into the warm, yet clean air. Wasps buzzed overhead, surrounding the shed they had claimed as their home.

The backdoor burst open and two officers rushed down the steps, kicking through the grass and weeds in an attempt to forge a path.

"We can take a missing person's name off a milk carton now," she gravely informed them with a foreboding sense of dread. "Wait until you see this."

"How'd you find out?" one of them asked her as he passed.

"Got a tip in the mail today," she told them. "They even gave the name and address of the person responsible."

4:46pm

Austin, Texas

"Jobie!" Josephine yelled from the backdoor.

He opened his eyes and lifted his head cautiously. He slowly reached for the *Dragon*, making sure it was at his side. He held his breath and listened for the voice once again. Flies swarmed around his head, buzzing in his ears. He had gotten used to the sounds of all the insects that shared his shanty little dirt home. He considered them allies. To him they were a good group to befriend. As he saw it, they were the next in line to take power after the humans had wiped themselves out of existence. He could only wish to be so lucky to begin again, to be given a fresh start as a bug.

"Hello, Mama," Josephine called out to the yard. "Din, din!"

His head was spinning, and he wondered, was it Treva? Or someone else. Someone from the Freemasons searching for their fire extinguisher. The *Dragon*. He had it in his hands, ready to strike. Ready to kill again.

He could hear the puppies yelping happily. Mama had even gotten up from her lazy slumber beneath the old pecan tree to greet the intruder. He knew those dogs were traitors...

"Come on out of there, Jobie," Josephine screamed in a shrill voice. "You got a letter from your man. *Terminal.*"

Jobie dropped the *Dragon* and scrambled to the entrance of The Kennel, crawling out of it like some wild rodent. He reared his head to look at the backdoor. Josephine stared back at him, holding a glass of lemonade in one hand and a UPS package in the other. Her long braids hung down over her smooth copper-toned shoulders. Her lips were painted a dark brown that seemed almost purple in the sunlight. She had on a pair of knee-length overalls that were folded to her upper thigh. Her shirt was tightly fitting with white and burgundy horizontal stripes. She looked clean and healthy.

He shuffled slovenly against the wall, holding himself up with a feeble bony hand. His skin seemed to be made of a watery tomato paste with touches of Parmesan and flakes of melted cheddar. His clothes were in such disrepair that they were practically hanging from his skeletal body, just like his skin. Josephine

334

could not remember the last time he had changed his clothes. His body odor had moved into a new realm of revulsion. She kept her distance.

He reached out for the package, but she yanked it away at the last second. "Drink the lemonade," she insisted.

He quickly ripped the glass from her hand and scowled at her. He wondered if she was trying to somehow poison him with all the lemonade. If so, he would almost be grateful. He took a big gulp, keeping his eye on her to see any change of expression that might validate his suspicions.

"Don't you get fussy with me, boy," she scolded him before handing the UPS package. "I'm your mailroom clerk, and don't you forget it." She watched him walk back to *The Kennel*, spilling some of his lemonade as he staggered along the wall. "I think I do enough for you to get some respect. Do you hear me?"

He raised his hand in the air to acknowledge that he did.

"I'm making myself a hotdog," she yelled into the yard before she retreated back inside the house. "I'll bring you out one, so you best have your appetite on when I come back out here."

He crawled back inside *The Kennel* and took his seat in the corner, near his weapon—the converted old fire extinguisher.

He looked at the return address. He smiled, just as he did each time. It was from the NRF Headquarters in Colorado. Somewhere called Barron's Bluff. It was his informant. Codename: *Terminal.*

He ripped open the package and let the contents spill out on the tattered old blankets that comprised the floor.

Dear Friend,

Mission accomplished! It wasn't easy finding these. View with discretion. I didn't expect to find more than I was looking for, but I did. I found a list of names and numbers. They were stashed in a manila folder taped to the backside of the filing cabinets in his office. It took some time, but the payoff speaks for itself. We have the names and contact information of the entire ring.

But the bad news—I think they're getting suspicious. It's only a matter of time before my cover is blown. Please do not waste any time. My life could truly be at risk. I had some doubts about all this—as I have told you—and finding these, I see that I was right after all. And so were you. I know that I have done the right thing now.

Page me when you receive this. Enter the code 9357. I will know it is you and that this package reached its destination. I will not rest well until I know it arrived safely. Like I said before, they are onto me. It's only a matter of time. It's not safe for me to remain here much longer. I have no idea what they would do if they were to find out.

Sincerely,
"Terminal"

Jobie picked up the photographs that were enclosed. There were only two. The first was of a small boy, probably part of the parish. The boy's face was sullen, petrified with fear and confusion. Jobie could imagine the boy's thoughts, wondering how someone that he trusted so much could put him in such an appalling position. Jobie sneered at the photograph, having never seen such a horrendous sight in all his life.

The second photograph made Jobie's heart pound like the drums of war. It was a lewd photograph of Reverend Strickland's own child, appearing to be no more than eleven years old. Naked and vulnerable.

Jobie's fists clenched into curled red balls. He forced a deep breath, closing his eyes to ward off the hatred that exploded inside his head. He struggled to calm himself. He now had exactly what he hoped to obtain—a reason to kill *The Stickler*, the false prophet known as Reverend Strickland. Child molester. Kiddie porn peddler.

He picked up the list of offenders. It was extensive. Nationwide, and some Canadian addresses as well. He knew his hands clutched a very coveted piece of information. Something that the authorities would love to possess. But he had his own agenda, his own plan to initiate. This was merely the proof needed to fulfill his plan.

"Poochie, poochie!" screamed a male voice from the backdoor.

Jobie swiveled his head erratically as if suffering from shellshock.

"You mangy little mutts ready for some chow?" Opaque sang to the dogs.

Jobie stuffed the contents back inside the package and hid it underneath *The Apolitical Manifesto*.

"Jobie," Opaque wailed cheerfully. "Get in here, we're eating weiners."

"Just a minute," he called back to his brother.

He listened as Opaque filled the dog bowls with food and water. He could nearly hear their happy little tails wagging with delight, just as they did every morning and evening when breakfast and dinner were served to them.

He gave one last glance at the UPS package. He would take care of it first thing in the morning.

4:46pm

Barron's Bluff, Colorado

Brother Perry slouched against the rocks on the edge of Barron's Bluff, overlooking a valley of blue spruce. Lying close to his side was a six-pack with only two beers remaining. He tipped his head back and drained the last of the fourth beer down his throat. He let out a belch as he tossed the empty can into the valley. The spruce trees below the cliff sparkled as though they were dressed for Christmas. It was merely the sunlight reflecting off the empty beer cans he had discarded over the months since he arrived at the NRF Headquarters.

He loved sitting alone on the edge of the expansive property, drinking beer and savoring the freedom. It was a far cry from the confines of prison he had grown too accustomed to. It seemed to him that every phase in his life was a vain attempt to battle the demons he unwittingly befriended in the previous phase.

Freebasing cocaine became his entire world in his late teens, ending in an arrest after a botched liquor store robbery. The prison sentence that followed forced him to quit cocaine in all its forms cold turkey. By the time he was ready for release, he was convinced that he had finally kicked the habit. He stayed clean for no more than two weeks.

His family decided that it was time they intervened, but were staggered by the high cost of sending him away to a drug rehabilitation center. His ever-so-thrifty uncle came up with a reasonable and cost effective solution. As a member of the NRF, he was able to pull some strings to arrange that Perry become an in-house volunteer. It all seemed like a good way to remove him from the proverbial wrong crowd and to allow him to focus on working toward a goal. His parents were comforted in knowing that he would be reporting directly to a man of God, Reverend Strickland. Although Perry had no affiliation with the organization, he obliged. At the time, it was definitely the lesser of two evils.

In the solitude of the Rockies, he kicked the drug habit once again. Unfortunately, not a day passed without thoughts and cravings of his old lifestyle. Often times in his dreams he was drifting weightlessly over an endless stretch of smoldering tar on shiny tinfoil. He always awoke fresh and inspired.

He cracked open another beer and stared blankly into the valley. He took a quick swig and dove into the memory of the woman whom he knew could change his life. To him, she was a good luck charm, like a beacon of hope over the vast desolation he knew awaited him on the outside world. He had met her through an old acquaintance from Puyallup. Visiting with her on those rare

337

three-day excursions over the past year had filled him with a sense of purpose and direction. He was eager to leave Headquarters, to join her in a new life.

The time was coming soon.

8:35pm

Jimmy Paglea crept silently through Headquarters. Moonlight trickled in through the tall and narrow windows, giving just enough pale blue light to make out shapes. Boxes of varying sizes were scattered throughout the large room, creating somewhat of a maze. He ran his fingertips from one to the next, sliding closer to Reverend Strickland's office. His destination.

The wooden floor creaked below his smooth leather brogue wingtip shoes. His black jacket fit like a curtain across his broad padded shoulders. His black pleated pants draped over his black and white shoes with nearly an inch to spare.

He reached the door and took one last turn over his shoulder to make sure that no one else was inside the large building. He turned the knob. Slowly, he pushed the door open, waiting until the last squeak before he took a cautious step inside the dark little office.

A harsh light blasted his face. He brought his hand up to cover his eyes.

"Don't move," Strickland said from behind his desk, holding a flashlight on Paglea's eyes. "Brother Jimmy. Or Mr. Pokerface, as you prefer to be known…take another step, and I will shoot you dead."

Pokerface kept his hand over his face. His heavy breathing could be heard in the silence. It gave away his fear and vulnerability.

"I knew it," Strickland announced proudly. "I just knew it."

Pokerface's mouth was suddenly dry. His tongue felt heavy and useless. "Wha?"

"Turn on the light."

He stood perfectly still.

"Do it!" Strickland insisted.

He turned to the light switch and flipped it on. He allowed his vision to adjust, and then lowered his hand. The rim of his black fedora placed a harsh shadow over his face.

Strickland clicked off his flashlight and placed it on the desk. He kept the gun aimed directly at him.

"How many times you been in here?"

Pokerface did not answer. His eyes avoided any personal contact. He noticed that the base of the tall pane window had been dislodged from the wall, leaving an empty little cavity. He assumed this to be the gun's hiding place. It would be easy to stash, and nearly impossible to find.

"Why are you in here?" Strickland asked. "Lie to me, and you just may die."

"Came for-da pen."

Strickland's brow crinkled, trying to understand him.

"Pen," Pokerface said, pointing at an ink pen on his desk. "Gonna write a letta."

"To who?" Strickland hissed. His teeth grated with anger. "Someone I know? Someone I *should* know about?"

"My goil."

"Your girl, huh?" Strickland said with a mocking smile of disbelief.

"Yup."

"Come get it, then," Strickland challenged him. "Get it, big man. I dare you."

Pokerface looked at the gun, and then up at the Reverend's angry glare. He took one step forward. It surprised Strickland. He stepped once again, closer to the gun. He leaned forward to the desk with his olive colored hand outstretched.

Strickland smiled, clearly impressed with his courage. "Go ahead, get it."

He slowly reached out to the pen, watching Strickland's paranoid expression change. "You's a good man, Chief. You don't do dat. You ain't dat way." He picked up the pen and slowly backed away from the desk.

Strickland closed one eye and aimed it at his head. "No, I *am* that way. I'll kill you if ever I find you in here again. You or anyone else messing with my flock."

Sweat beads covered his olive skin. His faux accent slipped slightly as he said, "Next time, I'll knock."

"Next time?" Strickland threatened angrily. "There won't be a next time, Brother Jimmy. First and last warning, right here. Is that clear?"

He nodded. "Oh yeah. Not again."

"Leave," Strickland demanded. "Leave!"

Pokerface rushed out the door, taking the pen with him.

Strickland's face was tense with anger. He kept the loaded gun in his grip, holding it tightly, aiming it at the door. He kept it there until the sun began to rise the following morning.

Monday, September 11, 2000
11:07am

Key West, Florida

Detective Marlen Esparanza hung up the phone and rubbed her eyes with her fingertips, careful not to smear her eyeliner and mascara. She had been on the phone with the medical examiner in the Treva Rifkin case all morning. She was happy to hear that the dental records had been received and that they would have a positive ID on the body very soon. But for her, it was not soon enough.

She was wide-awake with enthusiasm, and the adrenaline that had kept her sleepless throughout the weekend was starting to take its toll on her. Between phone conversations with the police department, the family of the deceased, the coroners, the crime unit investigating the scene for evidence, and the medical examiner, she barely had enough time to keep her coffee mug refilled.

The crime unit had come across some unexpected pitfalls in the investigation. Very little evidence remained, but it did not appear that a mass cleanup was involved. The fingerprints that were found were all unusable, giving them no conclusive leads. It was almost as if the person was either using layers of partially shredded rubber gloves, or that the person had somehow "lost" their fingerprints. It was unclear how such a thing could occur, as there was no known skin condition that would cause what they seemed to be finding in their investigation. And what they seemed to be finding was just enough evidence of an individual being present, but one that had somehow cleverly covered their skin, or had no more than a partial epidermis remaining on their hands and feet. The only conclusion they could draw was that the person responsible for this had so far evaded detection, with or without their knowledge of doing so.

Detective Esparanza considered the letter she had received from Austin, Texas just a few days earlier. Its claim to the guilty party was the only lead they seemed to have. But to chase that lead would require out-of-state intervention.

A dull tapping on the door brought her back to her present surroundings.

"Come in, Theresa," she called out in her slight Cuban accent.

The receptionist walked into the small office, bug-eyed and eager, holding a package. "You're going to want this."

Detective Esparanza did not even ask. Somehow she knew. The informant was back again.

She reached out across the desk and swapped it out of Theresa's hands. She haphazardly covered her hands with rubber gloves and tore open the package. Its contents spilled onto her workspace. It took only a second to confirm the legitimacy of the previous letter's claim.

She took her rubber gloves off by yanking forcefully on each finger. She threw them onto her desk and took a deep breath. "Thank you, Theresa."

Theresa shut the door, leaving Detective Esparanza in silence.

The phone rang once again. She turned to her desk and picked it up on the second ring. She listened intently to the words that she now knew she would hear. It was the medical examiner. The body had been positively identified as Treva Rifkin.

What she did not expect to hear was that the body seemed to have in fact been used for sexual purposes, offering their first tangible lead. He was not entirely positive, but if his hunch would prove correct, DNA evidence would be present in whatever fluids were left inside the body.

After thanking the examiner for his speedy work, she called her supervisor, letting him know that they now had enough circumstantial evidence to obtain the search warrant for the suspect given by the anonymous informant. The anonymous tip from Austin, Texas.

11:58am

Austin, Texas

Jobie clutched his ink pen tightly as he huddled over *The Apolitical Manifesto*, adding a new entry. The *Dragon* was at his side, just an arm stretch away.

He pitied anyone that would face the *Dragon*, no matter how evil their intentions. After the fire extinguisher had been stolen from the Scottish Rite temple off the Drag, he had emptied its contents inside a drainage pipe and began its transformation from life-saving device to life-threatening. He filled the chamber of the extinguisher with Styrofoam peanuts and saturated them with gasoline, creating a highly flammable gel-like substance. Once reassembled, he fixed a Zippo lighter to automatically ignite when the handle was pressed to activate the extinguisher. When the flammable gel passed through the flame, it became napalm—capable of scorching anything within a radius of twenty feet. Any stranger stumbling into his backyard would be burned beyond human recognition with homemade chemical weapon. To make matters worse for them, any attempts to wipe the gel off their burning bodies would only smear and spread the fire, hastening their own death.

341

He had been anticipating a visit from the Freemasons, and he was happy to turn their own materials against them. He knew that it was only a matter of time before they had tracked him down. And when they did, they would face the *Dragon*.

He dragged the pen across the notebook paper, scratching his thoughts in swift, illegible strokes.

> *The Stickler*
>
> *I carry with me a list of organizations that I must destroy in order for my species to survive. The first on my list, The Stickler—the false prophet known as Reverend Strickland, a man who uses the Bible to justify his hatred. The flames of hell seek to reclaim him, and I must only assume that I am that soldier of the underworld sent to carry him to his fiery destination. Does this make me a terrorist? Or is The Stickler a terrorist? Are modern corporations not a form of slow and silent terrorism, concealing their evildoings through their control of the media? These organizations are not out for the best interest of mankind, but rather the interest of men. A few men. Pushing their agenda or beliefs upon the world. Maybe I am the one worthy of being called The Stickler—a stickler to a principle and a high expectation of what I feel my species is capable of being. Yet so rarely lives up to. The National Reclamation Front will soon crumble, and I will be there to witness its unraveling. The wheels of destruction are already in motion. Reverend Strickland is a marked man.*

"Hi there," a voice squeaked from over his shoulder.

He swiveled his head nervously, unaware that his cramped little quarters had been shared by another. He reached for the *Dragon*, preparing for the worst. As if mist had pulled together to form a living being, Treva appeared behind him in an impossibly compact posture, shimmering like sunlight on water, smiling joyously at him.

He gave her a bashful grin and said, "Oh, hi. It's you. I've been wanting to talk to you, to ask you questions."

"Okay!" she sang sweetly with her youthful voice. She smiled pleasantly, and looked down at his quivering hands holding the *Dragon*. "You plan to use that?"

"You know I do."

She giggled passively. "What questions?"

He thought to himself, digging through his memory, trying to figure out which to ask first. "What was the name of your best friend when you were growing up?"

"Hmmm…" she hummed aloud, tapping her temple with a thin index finger. "Who cares?"

He let out a sigh of relief. "My brother said I should know…"

"What does he know?" she giggled like a child. "What other questions?"

342

"Did you have any boyfriends?"

"No," she declared with assurance. "You were the only one. The *only* one."

Her words made him smile, as they always did.

She turned the question back onto him. "Did *you* have any girlfriends before we met?"

"Yeah, there were a couple girls. I dated a girl from Seattle for a while. It didn't work out too well. She expected all these things of me…"

"That's no good," she told him. "What was her name?"

"Rhonda."

"Did you have a close friend growing up?" she asked.

"Not really. I spent a lot of time with my brother, I suppose. He had more friends than me. Sometimes that bothered me. There were some guys I used to hang out with, they skated a lot."

"Did you skate?"

He shook his head. "Nah. I did have this friend in Puyallup whose dad was a cop."

"A cop? Sorry to hear that," Treva teased.

Jobie smiled. "Me too. When we were really young, I used to go with him and his dad on camping trips to Mount Rainier. I used to hate taking the showers with his dad and all of his cop buddies because I knew they'd be able to tell that I was jacking off all the time. They all had these little mushroom caps for dicks, and even my friend was that way. Hung like a fly. Mine was much longer, and I just assumed it looked different than theirs because I had pulled it too much, stretched it out from all the jacking off. I figured that I'd end up pulling it so much that in time I'd have this enormously long schlong that hung down to my knees. At that age, I thought that would be a bad thing." He laughed to himself, and then sat awkwardly, thinking of what to say next. He was afraid to say something that might upset her, despite the fact that she was a fabrication of his own imagination. "Are you mad about what I did to your body in Key West?"

"I thought you were so romantic. The way you treated me, the way you touched me. When can we go back?"

He sneered. "Probably never."

"That's okay," she casually replied, alleviating his anger. "Are you excited about the trip you have planned?"

"Very excited."

His ears perked to the sound of police sirens. The puppies howled as they grew louder, closer. Treva altogether disappeared, leaving not a trace.

Jobie grabbed the *Dragon* and peeked through the cracks in his tiny fortress. It suddenly occurred to him that all his dreams could come crumbling down if the authorities were more astute than he had assumed. He was certain that his past crimes left no trail, but then he was not entirely certain.

The sirens rushed through West Campus, edging closer and closer. The puppies cried out, soon joined by Mama.

Jobie's heart raced. He considered running away, but he knew that if they were after him, they would eventually find him. All he could do was fight back. He held the *Dragon* tightly, waiting for the police to enter the backyard. He did not want to be caught by them. He would rather be gunned down in defense than to be taken into custody, questioned, and eventually sentenced to life in prison for the murder of Treva Rifkin. And Talon, of course.

He could hear the sirens turn the corner, blocks away. Then the noise stopped. The dogs quit howling.

"That was close," he heard Treva say as though her voice had drifted through the air.

"Sure was," Jobie replied.

He fell back onto the soiled blankets, breathing heavily. His head was light from the combination of stress and heat. The air around him began to cloud. Then everything went black.

12:17pm

Barron's Bluff, Colorado

"What are they here for?" Brother Perry asked Kinsman Kale as the two of them stood with Pokerface on the porch of Headquarters, watching the police search the premise.

"They have a search warrant," Kale replied. "They said it was about his missing child. They found her body in Key West. She was murdered. They seem to think Strickland did it somehow."

Pokerface jeered. "Dat's crazy."

"When the newspapers carry the story, he's ruined," Kale told them frankly. "Doesn't matter what they find out after that."

"Ain't good," Brother Perry agreed.

Kale looked out at the police car where the Reverend sat hunched over in the backseat. Several officers were carrying boxes and filing cabinets out of the office and loading them into unmarked vehicles.

"They're going to want to talk to us, too, aren't they?" Brother Perry resolved with discomfort.

Kale shook his head while gazing out upon the sprawling mountains he had grown to love. He knew in that instant that his days on Barron's Bluff were numbered. "Hard to say."

Kale knelt down on the porch and watched the officers gathering outside the patrol cars, snickering and talking in tight little huddles. One of them held the missing persons poster for Strickland's stepdaughter, Treva Rifkin.

He drifted into memories of her, of sensual late nights in Headquarters, the two of them intertwined, their pale bodies locked together as one. He remembered every detail of her body with perfect clarity. As far as he knew, the Reverend never suspected anything. He had no idea what would have happened to him had the truth come out. Luckily for him, it was now buried with the only other person who knew.

Kale wondered how the news of Treva's death would be handled by her mother, Sandra. It had been years since she had been at Barron's Bluff. In fact, he had no idea where she even lived anymore. As far as he knew, no one did.

Like most, Kale had very little respect for Sandra Rifkin. She was a notoriously short-tempered woman who had a tendency to hold grudges indefinitely. She tended to be the type of woman that sized a person up in a matter of seconds and never forgave that impression, whether good or bad. As he sat there recalling her in memory, he felt old aggravations resurface.

Sandra was a very young mother, and very pretty. Some claimed that before she met the Reverend she had been a stripper, while others claimed that she had been a prostitute. From all that Kale could gather from Treva, Sandra was nothing more than a wild spitfire who got pregnant at sixteen, dropped out of high school, and lived with her mother for the first five years of Treva's life. During that time, Treva was mostly raised by her grandmother since Sandra spent most of her time in bars and nightclubs, seeking a man to father and financially support her child. Treva remembered a list of men who had been in and out of Sandra's life, none of them staying more than a few weeks at a time.

Sandra's negligence wore thin on the family after five years of dependency and unemployment, and she was eventually asked to leave. As Treva had recounted to Kale, it was a firestorm of a moment, and the last time Treva ever saw her beloved grandmother.

Lost and desperate, Sandra left the city, heading aimlessly into the mountains. When she passed a small church nestled on a picturesque bluff, something compelled her to stop, hoping to find salvation for her and her five-year-old daughter. It was there that she met Reverend Strickland.

Overnight her identity changed from hypersexual bar wench to upscale born-again Christian. Her relationship with the Reverend happened almost overnight, and within six months, they were married.

As the wife of the Reverend, Sandra's condescending attitude toward the parish resulted in periodic fallouts with church members, slimming the attendance numbers as the years progressed. Rumors of extramarital affairs with men from the congregation spread from time to time, but none were substantiated. The marriage lasted for nine years until one day she ran off with a married man, never to be heard from again.

Treva, abandoned by her mother, remained with the Reverend for the next two years until that fateful Independence Day celebration in Boulder where she suddenly vanished. Like her mother, no one had heard from her.

Until this day.

Kale's mind wandered back to the lustful nights shared with Treva. Her lack of inhibition, and her desire to please. He was always amazed at how sexually advanced she was at such a young age—half his own age, and illegally so. She had skills that would inspire the most perverse whore, and although Kale had his suspicions on the role Strickland played in her life and her experience, he never voiced them.

Kale watched the police car drive down the rutted road, en route to Boulder with the Reverend in the backseat, cowering shamefully away from the window. He was certain that the press would be there to greet him upon arrival, eager to bring down his white power legacy.

"I think we've just witnessed the fall of Reverend Strickland," Kale muttered gravely to his comrades. "And probably the NRF, too."

10:02pm

Austin, Texas

Pip Squeak nudged the girl, tempting her away from the lights of the Drag. He tried listening to her rambling one-sided conversation, but failed to focus on anything other than the thought of her naked body sprawled lustfully beneath him. He had even forgotten her name for a moment. Then it came back to him, with little significance to anything other than his perverse intentions. He would have to remember it to get anywhere with her, so he repeated it in his mind over and over. Petra Steuben. Some random Crusty on the Drag.

"I don't think I want to stay in Austin," she said to him amidst her longwinded dissertation. "I want to go to New York."

He turned to her, tipping his pinstriped engineer's cap so that the sparse light could catch his bright-eyed expression. It was to let her know that he was deeply interested in her senseless babble. His eyes roamed her thick body, concentrating on her wide hips and full breasts. He could almost taste her. Without any doubt, he could certainly smell her. She had not bathed in weeks, and it was quite evident.

She habitually stroked her greasy bangs, pulling them opposite directions against the part that zigzagged across the center of her head. Her haircut had large chunks hacked near the scalp while other random pieces dangled at great length over her face. Her eyebrows were thick and joined in the center as one. She had beautiful green eyes and long thick lashes.

"I used to live in uptown Manhattan," he lied to her. "My dad has an apartment there."

"Wow…" she mumbled excitedly. "That'd be so cool if I could stay there."

"Has anyone ever told you that you look exactly like Julia Roberts?"

She cocked her head at him and laughed. "Are you crazy or blind?"

"I'm serious. You look exactly like her. Exactly."

He grabbed her by the hand and pulled her down the sidewalk. The wind rustled through 24th Street where giant colorful murals rose over both sides of the street. He brought her to the alley, out of reach of the city lights.

"Come on," he beckoned, nodding to the darkness behind him.

She stood steadfast in the streetlights. "No. This isn't good."

"Why not?"

"The Shadowmen." She shook her head defiantly. "It's not safe."

He reached inside his hobo-styled corduroy pants pocket to retrieve a slender plastic pocketknife. He flashed the three-inch blade for her approval.

"I know how to use it," he assured her. "I spent eight years in self-defense classes."

"Really?"

"Oh yeah," he boasted, almost believing his own wild claim. "I could use practically any household device to kill a man. We're safe. Trust me. Besides, I know people. *Important* people."

She grudgingly followed him into the alley. Before her eyes adjusted to the darkness, she felt his lips pressing against hers. She resisted somewhat, caught off guard by his forwardness. He was clearly more enthusiastic than she was.

He pulled her further into the alley.

"This is where I sleep sometimes," he told her as they arrived at a stairwell blocked by an iron grate. There was a mattress propped against the brick wall, sandwiched between it and the grate. He pulled on the end of it until it slid out onto the cement. It was covered with stains. "Have a seat."

She looked down upon it without moving a muscle. "I really don't know about all this…"

Pip Squeak flopped his gangly body onto the mattress, crossing his legs at the ankle while placing his hands behind his head. He smiled up at her, calm and sedate.

"It's perfectly safe," he reassured her. His smile washed away as he stared longingly at her chest. "Take off your shirt."

She laughed.

He extended his hand in the hopes that she would take it.

She refused.

He sat up abruptly, frustrated. "What's your problem?"

347

Before she could answer, she was startled by the sound of footsteps. She turned to a thin man in a long black trench coat creeping through the shadows toward her. Silver buckles on black boots shimmered with each methodical step. As he came closer, she caught a glimpse of his wicked eyes peering through strands of black hair. In his hand was a long serrated knife.

It was IX, the Shadowman.

Petra turned to run, only to find a mysterious robed entity leaning on a knobby walking stick, blocking the other entrance. She stammered, twisting her head from one side to the other, weighing out her limited options.

Pip Squeak, on the other hand, had not noticed anything other than her heaving chest. He watched her composure breakdown, and her sudden intensified breathing. It appeared to him that for the first time in his life, his mojo was actually working. *Really* working. His hormones went wild.

"You aren't going anywhere," IX snarled at her.

The sound of his voice shocked Pip Squeak back into reality. He scampered backward, lodging himself as tightly against the iron grate as humanly possible. He curled his knees up to his chest and wrapped his arms around his legs.

IX rushed at her with an unrelenting velocity, trapping her against the brick wall. He raised the knife to her face. The blade smelled of rust and rotten flesh. He pressed its sharp metal edge against her smooth neck and smiled at the sound of her staggered breathing.

Without turning his head, he addressed Pip Squeak with a hostile bark. "Stand up."

Pip Squeak burst into tears, whimpering and babbling incoherently.

She could feel IX's breath on her face. He smelled like pepperoni pizza and aftershave lotion. She could see his straight white teeth through his tense and fearsome lips, and the homicidal intentions raging in his unsettling eyes.

Pip Squeak cowered into a trembling ball, sobbing and shrieking. "I don't wanna die, I don't wanna die…"

"Shut him up," IX growled at Petra.

"I can't."

"If you don't, I will."

With tears swelling in her eyes, she said, "Pip, shut up!"

"I don't wanna die," he wailed shamelessly. "You can have her, just let me go. I won't tell anyone."

Petra cringed. Her sense of self-worth was crushed. She felt subhuman, as she had her whole life. It made it worse that it was on her turf, among her own chosen kind. Tears streaked her puffy cheeks. "What are you waiting for, then?" she cried out as anger swelled beyond her control. "Go ahead and do it."

IX laughed in her face. "Gladly."

A blind rage overcame her. Without thinking, she furiously rammed her knee into his crotch. His eyes sparked in shock and pain, and then he slid the knife across her throat, releasing a thin streak of blood. It barely broke the surface of her skin.

She threw a swift and wild uppercut to his jaw, knocking him two steps back and onto the pavement. He gasped and winced, holding his groin with one hand and the knife loosely with the other. Blood dripped from his broken lip as he coughed and choked.

She stood watching him, boiling with rage as she held her bleeding throat. She wanted to kill him. And she knew in that instant she could.

"Kill her!" IX screamed.

She looked up to see the black robe fluttering like the wings of a grackle in flight, ready to attack her. His devilishly red hands clutched the walking stick that he held outward like a lance.

She scrambled away, racing toward the city lights. She could feel him fast on her heels, swiping the knobby misshapen stick at her. It smashed against her hip, but she stared forward with wide and hopeful eyes, charging clumsily to the light. His heavy breathing loomed over her shoulder. She could almost feel his body heat reaching out to her. The walking stick smashed against her ankle, but failed to trip her as she reached the lights. She kept running, cackling as she stumbled onto the well-lit paved surface of 24th Street. She ran westward beneath the streetlights, and when she was certain she had lost the Shadowmen for good, she kept running, never once looking back.

Pip Squeak's eyes were too full of tears to see his surroundings. He clung to himself, shivering in the dark. The large green button on his tattered red vest rattled with his quaking body. Voices gathered around him, whispering obscenities at him and one another.

He felt a breath on his ear. He cowered away from it, but could only recoil so much. He kept his eyes tightly closed.

"You are going to help me," the raspy voice informed him.

Pip Squeak sniffled and wiped away the tears. "Okay…"

11:11pm

An unhealthy red hand reached out from beneath the black robe, unlatching the gate. The three puppies perked at the sight of him, and came bouncing up to greet him. They playfully jumped at his robe, biting and nipping at his heels as he crept toward *The Kennel*. His black garments seemed to disappear into the night air.

Faint light could be seen breaking through the space between the cinderblocks. To the untrained eye, it looked like a ramshackle doghouse, lopsided and off-center—positioned far too close to the house, and facing the wrong direction. The house itself seemed vacant aside from one bedroom light. The air was unusually still.

He slowly reached out to the plywood that comprised the roofing of *The Kennel* and lifted it so that it slid off the cinderblock dwelling. Candlelight burst forth, as did Jobie with the *Dragon*. A stream of gelatinous fire exploded from his hands, partially burning the Shadowman's black robe, albeit so briefly. Before the flames could spread a respectable fire on the intruder, Jobie let loose of the weapon's trigger. He looked upon the hooded specter with wide and curious eyes. He was stunned—had Death finally come to claim him, only to have him attack Death? He struggled to see into the shadows of the smoldering satin hood to find a face, but to no avail.

Taking no time to give a formal greeting, the Shadowman swung his knobby walking stick, knocking the *Dragon* out of Jobie's hands and onto the blanketed dirt floor. Jobie fell backward into the cinderblock wall from the impact. He struggled to orient himself as he reached for the *Dragon* among the soiled blankets. Then he heard a loud thump, followed by a vision of stars.

He shook his dizzied head as he drifted in and out of consciousness. He could tell he was being dragged out of *The Kennel* and thrown down onto the clay-like ground. The Shadowman towered over him with the walking stick poised to strike.

As he reared the walking stick back, Mama gave a futile attack, jumping at the smoking satin robe, ripping it with her powerful jaws. The seam split up the side of the robe as she struggled hopelessly to protect her master.

Jobie crawled on all fours to the pecan tree throughout the brief diversion. His head throbbed and his vision clouded. He nearly lost consciousness, and then he heard the walking stick crack against Mama's skull. As he watched her body topple over into a lifeless mass of fur and blood, his senses sharpened with fury.

The Shadowman turned to Jobie.

"You're next," the Shadowman promised him.

His gnarled fingers slowly removed the hood, revealing a horrific face burned practically beyond recognition. His scarred red skin seemed melted to the bone. His nose and ears were nothing more than narrow slits, and his mouth was so misshapen and scarred that he appeared to have no lips—only a set of white snarling teeth. But it was his devious eyes that Jobie recognized. Talon. Back from the grave.

Jobie jumped upward at the pecan tree, flabbergasted. It was just not possible. He had killed him, he was certain of this. Yet here he stood in front of him, just as alive as he had ever been. Not quite so attractive, or as healthy, but nevertheless alive.

Jobie sprang upward and grabbed onto a branch, hoping to rip it off for defense. Instead, his body just bobbed with the warm breeze as his feet dangled over the ground like a marionette.

Talon bounded toward him with sheer force, wielding the thick stick like a club.

"I've killed you once," Jobie reminded him awkwardly as he jumped down from the tree. He lost his balance briefly, and then scurried behind the tree for safety. "I'll kill you again."

Talon stomped over the mounds of dog turds scattered throughout the yard, waiting for the right moment to strike.

It suddenly occurred to Jobie that he never had a substantial reason to believe that Talon did perish in Key Largo. He never saw his body surface, and in retrospect realized he had assumed way too much. The cold and salty water did not take his life, but rather saved it. Underneath the docks on which Jobie had stood on that fateful night, he would not have seen Talon come up for air. Obviously he did. Obviously he survived.

It made no sense to Jobie how he possibly could have tracked him down, though. Unless someone ratted him out. But who knew where he lived?

Talon slashed the air with the stick, taunting his squirrelly little nemesis.

"This isn't good," Jobie resolved under his breath as he stood empty-handed, waiting to be bludgeoned to death by a former dead guy.

Talon kept himself between Jobie and *The Kennel*, slowly cornering him into the fence.

Jobie knew that he had no possibility of surviving. He would either have to resign himself to death, or take his chances and do something stupid. He chose to do something stupid. He ran straight at Talon with his head down like a battling ram. Talon swatted him like a fly into the fence. He crashed to the ground, disoriented and overwhelmed with a pain in his shoulder that exploded well beneath the surface of his ruined skin. He rose haphazardly to his feet, teetered back, and prepared to run again—but not before Talon grabbed his forearm and yanked violently. To Talon's bewilderment, Jobie's skin—from elbow to wrist—ripped off in his hands like wax paper. Talon fell backward from the momentum, crashing against the ground with nothing more than a handful of Jobie's diseased skin.

Jobie looked down at his forearm, shocked to see his glistening tender muscles completely exposed. He staggered to his feet, and leapt forward with Talon right on his heels, reaching out to stop him. He grabbed hold of Jobie's shirt and pulled, ripping the thin material right off his back. Shirtless but still mobile, Jobie kept running.

He dove over the cinderblock structure and smashed into the wall with his lame shoulder. With his one good hand, he picked up the *Dragon* and aimed it at the tops of the cinderblocks. He squeezed the trigger, flooding the air with a sludgy stream of fire. Talon unwittingly emerged under a shower of flames that stuck to his flesh like paste. He fell backward onto the dusty ground, slithering and writhing in vain to relinquish the fire. But unlike the cold waters of the Atlantic that had once spared his life, these flames refused to subside, feeding on

351

the oxygen in the air that surrounded him—suffocating and burning him at the same time. The flames relentlessly fed on his flesh, cauterizing the damage so completely that virtually no blood had been shed.

Jobie watched safely from behind his disassembled fortress. He leaned his head against the cinderblocks, beaten and frazzled, but thoroughly captivated by the intensity of the flames. They had a calming effect on him. So much so that he drifted completely out of consciousness for an unaccountable duration of time.

When he awoke some time later, the fire was gone and the backyard was quiet and dark. All that remained of Talon was a skeleton covered in stinking black goo that looked more like excrement than flesh.

No doubt about it this time, Talon was dead.

Jobie hobbled to his feet and stumbled across the yard, holding his lame shoulder with his other arm—his skinless "good" arm. Although his sense of touch was no longer of any use, he had no problem feeling the damage beneath the ruined skin, in his muscle tissue and bones. A different set of nerves, just as strong as they ever were. The pain was relentless. He was not accustomed to it anymore. It made him feel weak and vulnerable. It was a good reality check.

He opened the backdoor and clumsily walked inside the house to Josephine's room. He could hear her talking on the phone. He tapped his bony red knuckle against the door.

"Josephine," he mumbled sheepishly. "I hurt myself…and there's a dead guy in the backyard. I think I need some aspirin."

She covered the mouthpiece, looked over to him, and then gasped.

"Oh Lord!" she cried out. "What happened?"

He stepped inside her room, holding his shoulder while the muscle on his forearm glistened like freshly butchered meat. "It's my shoulder."

"It's your arm!"

"Do you have some aspirin?"

She held up one of her four fingers to quiet him. Her eyes were wide with terror. "Okay…okay…calm down," she said more to herself than to him, "you said someone is dead in the backyard?"

He nodded. "My shoulder really hurts." Then his face brightened with a sudden recollection. "Wait, you remember. It's Talon. He's out back…but it ain't pretty."

Her face cringed when she heard his name. She looked down at her hands, at her missing pinky fingers. "I thought you already killed him?"

"Well," he replied slowly as his attention wandered to the intricate layers of exposed muscle on his forearm. The damage caused to his useless skin seemed far less important to him than the sharp pain deep inside his shoulder. "I killed him again, I guess. This time for real. It's gross, you probably don't want to see what I did to him."

She thought back on her horrific memories of Talon. Her eyes tensed with rage. "I think I do want to see what you did to that son of a bitch." She suddenly remembered the phone. She paused to address the person on the other end. "Hey, it's me, I'm back. Yeah, it was Jobie. Something bad has happened." She looked up at Jobie and said, "It's your man *Terminal.* He's on the cell phone out in Colorado."

"Can I talk to him?" Jobie asked.

"Hey, he wants to talk to you." She waited for a response, and then held it out to him. "Here you go. I'll go get something for your arm."

She handed him the phone and sprang to her feet. She threw him a sleeveless black sweatshirt from her closet before she stepped out of the room.

He took a moment to sniff the sweatshirt before putting it on. He was not used to something that smelled so clean and fresh. It even had a feminine scent to it, which he could not place, but enjoyed very much.

"Hey," he said into the telephone. "It's me. How's it going out there?"

"You okay?" the tinny and static voice asked.

"Yeah," Jobie replied with a deep exhalation. His posture calmed when he heard his voice. Although he had not seen him in several months, he felt as if he was right there, listening to him as he did so well. And so often. "I got in a fight. Got roughed up pretty good, but you should see the other guy." He refrained from a deeper explanation. "Ready for my visit?"

"Can't wait."

Jobie studied his own exposed flesh, enamored with what had always existed just beneath his skin. "Any problems out there?"

"None. Just hurry. And be safe. I think they're starting to see through my façade."

Josephine came into the room with a roll of gauze and a pack of bandages in her hands.

"Okay, I gotta go, the nurse arrived," Jobie said into the phone. "I'll see you soon. The train leaves tomorrow. I'll be on it."

"Tell my girl I'll talk to her later."

"I will," Jobie said as he hung up. He turned to Josephine who was already unrolling the gauze. "He told me to tell *his girl* he'd talk to her later."

She smiled, somewhat blushing, and then returned her attention to his arm. She could not help but fall back on memories of the previous spring when *Terminal* had come to visit Jobie, and an unexpected romance flourished between them. Her thoughts of him were evident in her blissful smile. "Sit down."

He sat on the edge of her bed, allowing her to wrap his arm several times with gauze so that it appeared like a flexible cast.

"It's my shoulder that really hurts," he told her.

"We'll get some ice on it."

He looked down at his wrapped arm, twisting it around to get a better look at it. "It won't be long before my whole body will need this. My mind is made up once and for all—I'm going to be a mummy for Halloween. I guess that solves that nagging problem, now, doesn't it?"

She smiled, but her sorrowful eyes revealed the inner turmoil she felt in witnessing his rapidly declining health. He clearly had one foot in the grave. It made her deeply upset.

"How about that letter to the publishers?" He stood up from the bed with great discomfort. "Gotten very far with that?"

Her chin crinkled and her eyes filled with tears. They ran down her copper-toned cheeks. "I'll have it done tomorrow."

"Don't sweat it." He hobbled to the door, holding his lame shoulder tenderly. "I'm not sure it's worth it at this point."

"Don't you dare start with that. I can't handle it. Not now. It *is* worth it—if not to you, then it is to me. Your stuff will be published, I promise." She sniffled, took a deep breath, and struggled to regain her composure. "Okay, now…the backyard…do I dare take a look? Is it *really* bad?"

"Well, it's not really good. But we do need to get out there before my brother starts snooping around. He'll have a shit-fit if he finds out."

He led her to the backdoor.

She paused before he opened it, and said, "I hope you're right about him being dead."

He watched her hand tremble. "Trust me, when you see him, you won't have any doubt if he's dead. And relax, will you?"

"Relax? Are you kidding?" She sent him an evil eye. "I trusted you last time when you told me he died. I can't believe he's been out here wandering around…"

"I made a mistake that time, give me a break…" He opened the door and stepped out into the warm night air. Talon's body was right where he had left it. Like a skeleton covered in glistening hot tar. In a very low voice, he whispered, "Here he is."

Josephine crept over to him, cringing at the sight. The face she made was as foul as the odor that came off the simmering corpse. "Yeah, you're right," she replied under her breath, "he's not going anywhere." The stench stopped her from taking another step. "He's dead all right. I think I'm going to get sick…"

"Should we bury him?"

"Where?" she asked softly. Before she got an answer, she spotted Mama's badly beaten body. Her fragmented skull was strewn about the dusty ground. "Oh my God, what happened to her?" she exclaimed loudly.

"Shhh!" he hushed her. When he spoke again, he could barely be heard. "The bastard killed her." He looked at Mama's lifeless body and took a deep and uneasy breath.

She clenched her teeth, scowling at the corpse with intense hatred. "That son of a bitch," she grumbled to herself. "What about the puppies?"

"I think they hid somewhere."

She walked out into the darkness, calling nervously, "Here, babies. Here, babies."

One by one they came to greet her with an uncharacteristic apprehension. She gathered all three of them up in her arms and let them nuzzle into her neck. She stepped up to him and whispered in his ear. "We aren't going to bury him out here, so don't even *think* about it."

"Where, then? In the country?"

"That never works," she murmured as she coddled the yelping puppies. "I can't believe this is happening."

The kitchen light came on, bringing a warm glow over the backyard. Slow shuffling footsteps came to the backdoor.

"Jobie!" Opaque called out loudly, breaking the silence they had tried so hard to maintain. He peeked his head out the door. "Are you out here?"

Jobie rolled his eyes and gnashed his teeth. He placed his one good hand over his forehead and grumbled aloud to acknowledge his presence.

"Guess what I heard on the news," Opaque hollered, having not yet adjusted to the dark. "That guy you always complain about, the Reverend who says that God hates minorities...he got busted for child pornography! It was just on the radio!"

Josephine and Jobie looked at one another, communicating their deeper knowledge of the arrest with a slight, though uneasy nod.

"Smells like something is burnt, what are you guys cooking out here?" He stepped out into the backyard. His white terrycloth bathrobe seemed almost luminous in the dark. He shuffled his pink slippers along the dusty ground until he caught sight of the charred body. "Oh my...tell me that's not real."

"It's real," Jobie confessed softly.

Opaque swallowed hard. He pulled his bathrobe tightly around his waist. He put his hand over his mouth, muffling his volume dramatically. "Tell me that's not someone I know."

Josephine and Jobie looked at one another, and then Jobie said, "I don't think so."

Josephine said, "Let's go inside the kitchen and talk about this where no one can hear."

She led them through the backdoor. They stood by the door, huddled in the dark, looking out upon the smoldering body.

"What happened?" Opaque asked, distraught and nervous. "How did they die?"

"Napalm," Jobie replied frankly.

Opaque was too shocked to respond.

"It was in self-defense, right?" Josephine added swiftly. "Right?"

Jobie agreed.

Opaque shook his head contemptuously. He ran a limp wrist across his sweaty forehead as he scrunched his face sourly. "Well," he finally said with a breathy sigh. He tapped his slipper anxiously on the linoleum floor while shaking his head. "Now what? What are we supposed to do? Call the cops?"

"Are you nuts?" Jobie hissed at him. "Do you realize what will happen to me if you do that?"

"You said it was in self-defense, right?"

"He's dead, Rik," Jobie pointed out. "I would walk out of that courtroom in shackles, never to see the light of day again."

Opaque grumbled. "I can't believe this. You want to dispose of it, don't you?"

"Yes."

"Me, too," Josephine quickly added, to his surprise. "Not only for Jobie, but because I don't want this man having the honor of a proper burial."

"We need to do it now," Jobie insisted. "Before the birds start eating him and get sick...and you know the dogs would be trying to play with him all day...they'd probably try to eat him, too."

"Okay, enough!" Opaque screeched. "I don't need the extra visuals, okay? Okay?"

"Whatever," Jobie grumbled.

Opaque rubbed his temples and shut his eyes in deep contemplation.

"We done thought all this through already," Josephine told him as the puppies chewed on her braids. "We aren't burying him out here or anywhere else."

Opaque opened his eyes and groaned. His face was awash with panic. "Let me guess which of you thought it'd be a good idea to bury a dead body in our backyard."

Jobie shrugged defensively. He looked to Opaque and said, "I think he broke my collarbone."

Josephine added, "Broke a little skin, too."

Jobie was happy that he could not see the damage beneath the gauze cast.

"I thought you couldn't feel anything?" Opaque asked.

"Oh, I can feel this," Jobie insisted. "We're not talking flesh wounds here—this is deep tissue destruction. Beneath the skin, I can feel it all."

"Do you need a doctor?" Opaque asked him, knowing the answer, and expecting none.

"How's about we take the body out to Lake Austin," Josephine suggested as she shifted the puppies from one arm to the other. "We could bring that big pink raft we used at Barton Springs last summer to take him to the center of the lake. If he's wrapped in trash bags and weighted with rocks, he'll sink to the bottom. Gone for good."

"And we use my car to get out there, I suppose?" Opaque asked, dreading the answer.

"How else?" Jobie responded.

"May I ask who this person is first?" Opaque demanded. "And why they're in my backyard burnt to a crisp?"

Josephine held up one of her maimed hands and said, "The guy that did this."

"I thought that guy died?"

"I thought that, too," Jobie replied. "I guess I didn't wait long enough to find out."

"Anyway, here he is—or what's left of him—and we need to get him out of here," Josephine told them.

They all stared out the window at the body, dedicating a considerable amount of time for silence and contemplation.

"I'll get the trash bags," Jobie said.

"I'll get my keys," Opaque reluctantly added.

"And I'll start blowing up that pink floatie," Josephine finished. She opened the door and placed the puppies onto the ground, allowing them to investigate and cope with their mother's dead body. "Meet back here, outside."

Jobie watched the two of them walk away, leaving him alone in the kitchen. His shoulder had swelled like a zit, splitting his fetid and useless skin like wet construction paper. His muscles were faintly visible between the cracks of his deteriorating skin.

He slowly descended to his knees from stress and fatigue. He had the sudden realization that death would be soon and inevitable, and it petrified him with fear. He held his face with his hands, feeling nothing in his dead nerves. He noticed a trail of blood gathering on the linoleum floor. It was coming from his knees. The impact onto the floor had ripped his thin and corroded skin wide open.

He crawled forward to the cabinet doors beneath the sink, leaving a trail of blood. He tore through the cleaning supplies until he found a box of trash bags and a roll of electrical tape that Opaque had once used to cover his nipples during a provocative—though artistic—photo session for one of Tamika's class assignments. He slowly and carefully pulled himself to his feet when he suddenly realized Treva standing at the door, looking at him.

"Hiya, Sport!" she said gleefully.

He smiled at her, holding himself up against the sink with a shaking hand.

"Looking a little rough, huh?" she observed. "Don't worry, I'll be there to meet you."

His sharp blue eyes began to water. "I don't want to die."

"I didn't either. But you'll be okay. Look at me." Her smile loosened a bit. Her face seemed to resonate with compassion and understanding in a way he had never before seen. "When you are gone, your words will live on."

He shook his head in aggravation.

"Don't doubt me," she playfully impressed upon him. "I've seen the other side. *I know.*"

His breathing relaxed a bit as he watched her. She glowed with a magnificent radiance that touched the deepest part of his soul. He could almost feel the demons burning away inside his tormented heart.

Then she faded.

"Jobie," Josephine cautiously whispered as she entered the kitchen with the deflated pink raft in her hands. She suspiciously investigated the room. "Was someone else in here?"

He looked to the empty doorway where Treva had stood. It was as dark and barren as ever before. He stumbled outside, dour once again. She followed him with a confused expression, lugging the limp plastic raft through the backdoor. She plopped herself down on the clay-like earth and crossed her legs with the raft lying across her lap.

By the time he had sealed the body, she had also finished blowing up the raft. She stood, brushed her clean garments, and brought the raft to him so they could transport the corpse with minimal physical contact.

The getaway car waited in the street with the trunk open and the lights off. Opaque sat quietly behind the wheel, griping and cursing and hating to be involved, but loving the excitement. He kept a watchful eye on the street as they crammed the body into the trunk. When they were all safely inside the cab, he turned on the headlights and sped westward down the more poorly lit back streets. They remained silent all the way to Pennybacker/360 Bridge on the Capital of Texas highway.

Opaque steered off the highway to the boat ramp beneath the bridge. It was quiet and still and perfectly desolate. He turned off the headlights, leaving only the pink sky and the trail of taillights that bled over the top of the bridge.

"Ready?" Josephine mumbled sprightly.

Opaque shut off the engine. After a long and exasperated sigh, he pulled the keys from the ignition and dangled them in his firm right hand.

"Here you go, dear," he said to her. "Have at it. I'm not messing with any of this."

"I understand," she replied as she snatched the keys. "And I hope you understand why I am."

She stepped outside the car and went to unlock the trunk. She grabbed the corpse by what remained of its shoulders and dragged it out onto the pavement. Jobie hobbled up beside her to offer a hand, but he was too late. He picked up the raft and followed her to the waterfront.

Opaque stood close to the car with his hands tucked inside the pockets of his terrycloth bathrobe. He tapped his pink slipper nervously on the pavement.

"I'll take it out there," Jobie told her. His voice could barely be heard over the cars passing at high-speed on the bridge. "I'm the one that killed him."

She shook her head. "You can barely stand up, you sure ain't swimming out there in the dark. You should be in the hospital right now. Move aside. I'm doing this."

She pulled her shirt off and tossed it at Opaque's feet. She stripped down to a sports bra and satin jogging shorts, leaving her shoes and socks by the water's edge. She then walked down the boat ramp and plunged herself into the dark waters.

"Push it out to me," she hollered with chattering teeth.

Jobie steadied the corpse on the raft and launched it in the direction of her voice. She grabbed its plastic edge and swam the floating body away from shore. She could see the black outlines of cliffs in front of her—a huge limestone wall on the edge of Hill Country. It was on these very cliffs where Treva had burned Phaedra Lin's corpse nearly two years earlier. Jobie had been too drunk to remember. Now he struggled to remain conscious.

The night sky was pink and starless, just like almost any other night in Austin. She believed a city was as much a living entity as its own population. To her, Austin was without a doubt feminine—smart, vivacious, and wickedly beautiful. It thrived on aesthetics, from its tasteful floral landscaping to the Texas State Capitol—a feminine replica of the nation's Capitol, except slightly larger and made entirely of pink granite. The Pennybacker/360 Bridge that blocked most of the sky over her head even had a slight rusted pink coloration to it. No matter where you looked in the city, you could find something painted pink.

She looked up at the grand steel arches of the bridge, using its crested peak as a guide to finding the centermost point of the narrow lake. Once there, she pressed her weight onto the raft, capsizing it. The corpse toppled silently under the calamity of the highway traffic overhead—witnessed by no one other than herself.

She gazed upward toward the dark underbelly of the bridge and visualized the body sinking into an eternal darkness. This time she knew it would remain there.

She casually paddled the raft back to shore, and the three of them returned home in silence, never to mention this night again.

11:40pm

Pip Squeak stood in the center of the food court in the Dobie Mall, waiting. He jerked his head from side to side, fearfully chasing his blind spot. He was shaking with fear, but grateful to be alive.

He knew that he would never be able to erase the memory of Talon walking away with his black robe flapping in the gentle breeze, on his way to destroy his friend Jobie. It was very clear to Pip that he would share Jobie's fate as soon as IX gathered his composure.

At that moment, IX was still on his knees holding his crotch and wincing as the knife lie at his side. He looked up at Pip Squeak with menacing eyes that forecasted his insidious intentions. Only three feet separated them. IX lowered his head and took a deep breath. His long black hair cascaded over his face. When he reached out for the knife, it was gone. His head shot up at Pip Squeak, who appeared to have not moved a muscle, yet the bloodstained knife was now in his hands.

Pip Squeak slowly rose to his feet, and said, "Don't move."

He kept the knife pointed at IX, who raised his hands passively in submission.

Pip Squeak backed out of the alley, never allowing IX to leave his sights. As soon as he reached the streetlight, he took off running down the Drag, passing pedestrians who kept their distance from what appeared to be a knife-wielding maniac. Once he reached 21st Street, he turned to look over his shoulder. IX was nowhere to be found.

It was no lie that Pip Squeak had once been a prolific pickpocket on the streets of San Francisco. It was a skill that, once perfected, was no less than streetwise magic. He never could have imagined that the sleight of hand he had learned during those times would someday save his life.

There was an etiquette to pickpockets that he and his comrades abided by—drop the ransacked items in a random mailbox so that the identification would allow the individual to get back everything that lacked monetary value, such as driver's license, proof of insurance, and social security cards.

Pip Squeak dropped the knife into the mailbox on the corner of 21st Street as proper protocol, just before taking the crosswalk to Dobie Mall. Little did he know that the authorities would soon be seeking that particular weapon for the Thomas Patterson murder case.

A few Asian students were studying at tables near the Dobie Mall's movie theater, minding him no business. The arcade had a constant flow of foot traffic, but none seemed too interested in him. It was as crowded and well lit as he hoped it would be.

He felt nervous and ill as he watched the clock and waited. He had vomited already, and if he had anything left in his stomach, he would have made another trip to the restroom. Instead, he watched his shoulder, keeping an eye on the exit at all times.

Never in his life had he wished to be invisible, or even non-existent, until that moment. He recalled Penelope, an old friend of his from San Francisco. She was fascinated with a sort of escapism that she could only achieve with depressants. It was fanciful, though dangerous thinking for someone whose only intention with it was to evade the demons of the past. He suddenly and completely understood her motivations. He, too, wished to be ripped out of his physical existence and given a fresh start elsewhere.

"Pip Squeak!" a female voice called out to him.

He was aghast with terror. He nearly wet himself just hearing his name spoken in public. He frightfully craned his neck, and then smiled at the sight of her.

"Wolfie!" he joyously cried out.

She, on the other hand, was not so thrilled to see him. When he had called her from a payphone, she was nearly asleep. He was the last person she would have expected it to be, begging for help.

"What is this all about?" she demanded.

She had on a large floppy hat to cover her disheveled bedtime hair. A long black fur-lined coat was buttoned from knee to neck, revealing only a pair of knee-high leather boots. Her face had no makeup. He never noticed just how freckled she was because his eyes were always roaming her body. Had he not been so overwhelmed with terror at the moment, he would have given her one of his typically hollow compliments. Sexual persuasion, for the first time in a long time, was not his motive.

"I *need* a ride."

She rolled her eyes at him. "You dragged me out of bed, begging me for help, and all you want is a ride somewhere? Are you kidding?"

His eyes shot back and forth, checking and rechecking any movement in his peripheral vision. "Not just somewhere. I need to get out of town *fast*."

She grimaced. "What did you do?"

"I didn't do anything!"

"What happened?"

His chin began to crinkle and his eyes filled with tears once again. "I just got jumped by the Shadowmen."

She failed to hide her disbelief. "Really?"

"I'm *very* serious, Wolfie. I wouldn't lie."

She had to laugh. "Where are you wanting to go?"

"To the train tracks. I need to get on a freight train and get the hell out of here."

She loved the way he made it all sound so dramatic.

"Can you take me?"

She paused to think. "There used to be a club called the Electric Lounge. It was right next to the tracks, and very near the train station. It's not far from here. Would that work?"

"That's perfect...*excellent*...let's go."

She followed his lead toward the rear entrance, but quickly moved ahead of him. "I hope you know that you woke me up the night before a major exam."

"Sorry. But you're saving my life. Doesn't that count for anything?"

He followed her out the rear doors to the parking garage. He never kept his eyes off his back. He was not sure if he was more afraid of the Shadowmen returning, or Jobie's vengeance for ratting him out. At the same time, he was also very concerned about Jobie's welfare. When it was all too late, he understood who and what the Shadowmen were, and what they were seeking. It was Jobie that they were searching for all along. Now that he had pointed the way for them, he could only hope that Jobie and his housemates had somehow evaded harm. Or even death.

He climbed the steps behind Wolfie, keeping close to her heels while constantly checking corners. His imagination was getting the best of him.

They pushed through the metal doors on the second floor of the parking garage. There were only a handful of cars, one of them being Wolfie's new white Toyota. She unlocked the door for him as he stood next to her, trembling. His face was colorless. She suddenly realized that something tragic had actually happened to him, despite whether or not she believed his specific claim.

"Am I safe to be helping you like this?" she asked him.

He knew that her willingness to help him was only so strong. Anything negative that she could acquire from such a favor would definitely send her away. He could not risk that.

"Yes," he assured her. "You're fine." He climbed inside the car and quickly fabricated a story. He waited until she had slipped into the driver's seat to tell it to her. "I got a girl pregnant."

She turned on the engine and locked the doors. "Right."

He allowed her to exit the parking garage before continuing. "Yes. Well, not really. What happened was that I got this girl pregnant, and then her boyfriend found out that it's mine, not his."

She laughed. "That must suck for him, huh?"

"Yeah, probably."

"I can tell you're flustered, but you're going to be fine. You don't have a scratch on you."

Her revelation made him cringe. It was true, the Shadowmen did him no harm whatsoever, yet he gave them all they needed to know to destroy Jobie. He wanted to shrivel away.

"I'm just not a good friend, or really even a good person."

To her, he was speaking as if he was drunk, making absolutely no sense. But to him, it was one of the most reflective and honest statements he had made in his life. From that moment on he knew things were going to change for the better. He just had to get away and start over.

He was relieved to see how well the lights were timed down Guadalupe Street. Making one green light meant making them all from the Drag down to 6th Street. She turned off 6th Street onto a poorly lit road named Bowie Street. She followed it to the end where the headlights shined over a ditch and onto the railroad tracks.

"Here we are." She gazed fondly at the building that had once been the Electric Lounge. "Lot's of good memories out here." Her eyes wandered out to the ditch alongside the railroad tracks. It was in that ravine that she had lost her virginity. She kept that information to herself. "It's safe down there, no one will see you. Trust me."

He quickly opened the door, but turned to her first. He looked her in the eye and said, "Wolfie, you just may have saved my life."

"Sure." She reached into her purse and pulled out a twenty-dollar bill. "Here, take this. It isn't much, but it will get you some food until you get where you're going."

He snatched it quickly from her hands. "You are the best. I mean it."

She shook her head and snorted. "Whatever."

He sprinted to the tracks and ducked beneath the ravine. He could see her headlights vanish, leaving him all by himself. Town Lake stretched beyond the tracks, reflecting the city lights on its timid waters. He would miss Austin. As he sat alone in the darkness, he began weeping once again.

11:42pm

Barron's Bluff, Colorado

Pokerface stood in the shadows on the porch of Headquarters, gazing out upon the rugged mountain terrain. It was quiet and still, aside from a cool gentle breeze. As far as he could tell, he was alone.

He opened the front door and slipped quietly inside. Moonlight shined from the tall and narrow windows, striping the floor with faint blue lines. It was just enough light to find a path between the stacks of paper and boxes scattered haphazardly throughout the workspace. If his calculations were correct, there was a wealth of undocumented contributions hidden somewhere inside Strickland's office, just waiting for him to take custody. He could walk away a very wealthy man, never to be seen or heard from again.

The wooden floors creaked as he made his way through the building. His eyes flipped in all directions, searching for movement in the shadows. It was not the lack of light that unnerved him. It was the silence. The complete absence of noise, testing his nerves as it had since he arrived on Barron's Bluff. He focused on the steady breeze that rustled outside as he mustered the courage to move forward.

When he finally reached the office door, he took a deep breath to calm himself. He clutched the door handle with a shaky hand that rattled the doorknob. He slowly opened it. Its creaking broke the paralyzing silence, sending a chill up his spine. He tried to make out shapes in the dark, but the police had seized almost everything. Everything except a dark shape in front of him which he knew to be the desk.

"Turn on the light, Paglea," a thunderous voice barked from the darkness.

He gasped. His terrified eyes shot back and forth through the room, searching for a stranger in the shadows. A slender strip of moonlight revealed a shaved head covered with nicks and scars, sitting behind the desk, watching him. The posture was enough for him to realize that it was Kinsman Kale.

"Did you not hear me?" Kale growled at him.

Pokerface grudgingly flipped on the light switch and shielded his eyes, almost shamefully. He shifted his weight nervously from one foot to the other, back and forth. He remained quiet, knowing that there was nothing he could say in his favor. So he waited to be spoken to.

"Strickland asked me to keep an eye on you," Kale informed him. "I guess he was right with his suspicions."

"You know me better'n dat."

Kale glared at him. The lines of his face were tense and unforgiving. The look in his eye was at best skeptical, at worst paranoid. Any respect he once had was gone.

"I don't think I do," Kale admitted regretfully. "Who are you *really*, Mr. James Paglea?"

"You're overreacting," Pokerface insisted, briefly faltering with the accent.

Kale shot him a wicked and interrogating face. "Am I?"

The front door of Headquarters burst open, and then quickly slammed shut, followed by staggered footsteps. It was Brother Perry, drunk as usual. He stumbled up to the doorway, bringing the faint scent of alcohol on his breath and the fragrance of wilderness on his clothes. His shoes were caked with fresh mud.

"Whassup?" Perry slurred as he squinted into the well-lit room. "You guys busy?"

"Nah," Pokerface assured him. "C'mon in."

Kale sneered. He was ready to beat them both senseless. "Where have you been at this hour?"

"Wandering around," Perry replied defensively. "What's it to you?"

"Just aimlessly wandering around in the dark? Like Pokerface here?"

"I was talking to my girl on the phone," Perry responded shortly. His anger escalated with each word spoken. "If you *need* to know, your Excellency. Are we forbidden to take a walk now? Or use our cell phones?!"

Kale raised his hands to ease Perry's temper. "Take it easy, Perry, I'm just asking."

"Why are you both in here?" he snapped back. "Shouldn't we *not* be hanging out in here right now with the police still investigating this place?"

Kale looked to Pokerface. "No, we shouldn't be."

Pokerface seized the opportunity at once. "Let's leave." Without waiting for a response, he stormed out of the room as if leading an inmate revolt.

Perry trailed him like a lost puppy all the way to the porch.

"I'm tired," Pokerface declared as he rushed down the steps. "Goodnight, brotha's."

Perry waved. "See you tomorrow, man." He grabbed hold of the banister to steady himself. He turned to find Kinsman Kale leaning inside the doorway, glowering at him. "Did I miss something?" Perry asked him.

"Always." Kale locked the front door of Headquarters and descended down the steps, leaving him alone on the porch. "I'm staying in Strickland's house tonight."

"You can't do that," Perry objected loudly.

Kale turned to him with a vile expression. "I can do anything I want out here. I'm in charge. Watch yourself, Perry. And tell your pal to do the same."

"*You* watch yourself," Perry grumbled under his breath.

He wanted to scream out at him, to tell him of his plans to leave the National Reclamation Front, but he remained silent. There would be no use in arguing since his decision had been made a long time ago. He would soon be gone, free to pursue his true aspirations.

He watched Kale march defiantly to the quiet little property, locking himself safely inside. The cautious gesture made him laugh out loud. It seemed perfectly futile to him.

"Nice knowing you, Kale."

Tuesday, September 12, 2000
6:55pm

West Texas

Jobie stared out the window of the Amtrak train, watching tumbleweeds roll across the dry land. Funnels of dust twirled in solitary positions over the inhospitable land, mesmerizing him into tranquil memories of better days. It had been two years since he had arrived on the same system of rails, along with Opaque and Treva, traveling from Arizona. He could still remember their hopeful optimism—three runaways embarking on a wild adventure that would be all too short. The image of Treva on the freight train with the raspberry-colored clouds resting on the horizon behind her was permanently etched in his memory. Looking out on the barren landscape once again gave him an extreme mix of emotions.

Hours earlier, he swore that he had seen Pip Squeak sitting in the shade of a Mesquite, sipping from bottled water, watching the train go by. Jobie took it as just another sign that his mind was not what it once had been.

He looked down at an empty sheet of notebook paper on his lap. His red scaly hands rested on the clean page as a constant reminder of his deteriorating health. His body appeared to have been boiled in saltwater and left out to dry in the hot Texas sun—cracked like a brittle piece of red clay.

He reached into the small carry-on bag Josephine had packed for him. It was filled with spare clean clothes, several liters of bottled water, and peanut butter sandwiches. He pulled out a pair of thin leather gloves and gently covered his hands, careful not to rip what little skin remained. A black sweatshirt hung loosely on his shoulders with the hood drawn to cover the patches of abscess skin and missing clumps of hair on his head. It was the first time in years that he had worn a pair of blue jeans, and it was simply to hide his legs from the wandering glares of strangers. Despite all his effort, the seat next to him remained vacant. Before the train had even left the station, he overheard passengers complaining about an unusual foul odor. Not just body odor, but something more repulsive. Something that resembled death.

He concentrated on the blank page, eager to write what would likely be the very last entry in *The Apolitical Manifesto*. He wanted to write about the need to return the Federal Reserve to a gold standard, but became frustrated by his lack of secondhand knowledge on the subject. All of his books and resources were back in Austin where he would probably never return.

He took the cap off his pen and began writing the first thing that came to mind.

Thinking Outside The Box
Isn't that a lovely term? Makes us all feel so full of positive and creative energy. What a joke. Our society does everything in its power to destroy anyone who dares to live by those words. Such as myself. But what am I to you? Am I not spawned out of your own sewage of thought? Here's to me—the best man you'll never meet. May the status quo be better in the next world.

He then scribbled at the bottom of the page: *Last entry, 9-12-2000.*

He dropped the pen on the page and closed his eyes. He felt old and decrepit. Ready to face the final curtain. But one more task remained on Barron's Bluff.

**Friday, September 15, 2000
10:21pm**

Barron's Bluff, Colorado

Brother Perry stumbled through the front gate, calling out to his two comrades with a wild shriek. He fumbled with the padlock before giving up in fear and frustration. He limped up the sloping mountainside, screaming wildly into the night with flailing arms.

"Kinsman! Pokerface!"

He stumbled desperately toward Headquarters, slipping on the pinecones strewn across the rocky ground. His face was scratched, his knees scraped, and his arms covered with small bloody abrasions. When he saw Kinsman Kale on the porch of Headquarters, he gave a hearty sigh of relief.

"Kinsman," he cried out to him, "I've been attacked!"

Kale gave a quick glance and scoffed. "*Attacked?* By what? A raccoon?"

"A person," Brother Perry shouted. "A madman without skin."

Kale laughed. "That's crazy."

Perry reached the steps and held himself up against the banister. He took a moment to calm his heavy breathing.

"I'm serious," Perry assured him. "Just look at me, if you don't believe it."

Kale eyed him up and down, raising a suspicious brow. "You don't look that...*attacked*...to me," he acknowledged lightly.

Pokerface came wandering around the corner, rubbing his eyes, but fully clothed and completely alert. "What's happ'n out heya? I 'as asleep."

"A madman is out there, he attacked me while I was on the phone with my lady..." he paused to wipe his mouth, checking his hand for the remains of blood. There was none. "Kale here doesn't seem to care. We're being stalked by a lunatic right now, and *he* doesn't care."

Kale laughed. "It's not that I don't care. It's that I think you're full of shit."

Pokerface smiled, pleased to find a situation where he could speak out against Kinsman Kale, their self-proclaimed new leader. "We needta look, jus' in case. You wit' us, Kale?"

Kale shot them both a condescending smile. "If it will make you happy...sure, I'll play along."

367

Brother Perry climbed the steps and pushed his way into Headquarters. "We need some weapons."

Pokerface was right behind him.

Kale cringed at the thought of the three of them alone in the wilderness—armed, angry, and paranoid. He was certain that this was a trap. He followed them inside and switched on all the lights.

"Was this person armed?" Kale asked Brother Perry.

"I don't think so. I could barely see, it was dark."

"Then I don't think we should get carried away with this," Kale suggested. "How about we get some rocks, or maybe some big sticks? We'd be less likely to have some fatal accident out there, seeking this crazed wildebeest, mountain goat, or whatever it is…"

Pokerface mulled it over, and then nodded. "Dat's a good point. Let's keep our cool."

Kale was relieved to finally get consent. He retreated outside once again, followed by Perry.

"I'm grabbin' my hat," Pokerface called out from inside Headquarters.

Kale and Perry walked down the steps in a race to find the more potent weapon. In their frantic search, they failed to notice that Pokerface had quietly entered Strickland's office. He went straight for the tall window and pulled on the bottom frame of the windowsill until it came loose. The pistol rested in the empty cavity, still loaded. As he suspected, the police knew nothing about it. He stuffed it inside his loose-fitting pants and rushed out of the room. He grabbed his hat on the way out the front door.

"Hurry up," Perry yelled at him. "Get down here and find something."

Pokerface calmly strolled down the steps and picked up the first flimsy stick he could find. He pointed to the open gate where the padlock dangled from the chain links.

"Did ya leave dat op'n?" Pokerface asked Perry.

"I told you I was attacked! What do you expect?"

"I expect you to be less stupid," Kale snarled. "If there really is someone out there, they're probably inside here now."

"I doubt that," Perry snapped back.

"Nah, dat'd be too risky," Pokerface replied mildly, unmoved by the circumstances. "Let's go out'n find 'em."

The three of them walked to the swinging front gate and locked it before heading into the densely forested mountainside.

"We should spread out," Kale suggested. He pointed opposite directions. "I'll take the more rocky path, and you guys go along the sides. If you come across something, scream out to the rest of us."

They both looked to each other.

"That doesn't sound very safe," Perry objected.

Pokerface kept his mind on the pistol concealed in his pants. "It's safe. We won' be too fah."

"You sure?" Perry asked.

"Positive."

"Okay, let's meet back at Headquarters in a half-hour," Kale said.

They agreed.

As they went their separate ways, Kale kept a close eye on them while he drifted into the shadows. He was not about to be played by either of them. The time had come for him to take matters in his own hand. He climbed down the rocky embankment and trailed Pokerface at a safe distance, waiting for the first opportunity to take him out. Perry would be next.

10:46pm

Jobie sat on the porch of Headquarters, watching the three of them disappear into the trees. He trusted that *Terminal* would be able to handle himself should any problems arise. He ambled down the steps and crawled beneath the porch into a void of darkness. He reached out with his gloved hand to find exactly what he had come for—six cans of gasoline and a brand new converted extinguisher for protection. All courtesy of his man *Terminal*. The new flame-thrower was considerably smaller than the one he had left behind in Austin, but would be no less effective at close range. The *Dragon Jr.*

One by one, he carried the cans of gasoline inside Headquarters, emptying them on every box, every stack of paper, and every inch of wooden floor space. He saturated the computers, knowing for a fact that no backups had been saved. Once burned, the entire framework of the organization would be reduced to ash.

He walked inside the Reverend's office, finding only a desk and a chair. The floor was discolored where filing cabinets once stood. He wondered if his descriptions of them in his letters to the Key West police department were a close match. He would probably never know.

Then he noticed something out of place. Something that just did not fit. The bottommost windowsill had been hastily removed and tossed onto the floor, leaving an opening just beneath the tall glass pane. He walked forward and reached inside. Nothing. He backed off and looked up at the window. It stretched nearly to the ceiling. Acting on a notion, he climbed onto the desk and pulled at the topmost panel of the windowsill. With little effort, it fell off in his hands. Inside the space was a bank deposit bag stuffed to capacity. He pulled it out and plopped it onto the desk. To his surprise, it was brimming with tens and twenties, all neatly sorted and stacked. Thousands and thousands of dollars. Unbeknownst to him, it was exactly what Pokerface had been searching for.

He stuffed the bank bag under his arm—ecstatic with his discovery—but far more thrilled with the business at hand. He emptied the last can of gasoline onto the desk and chair and walked back through the building. He inhaled deeply, savoring the fumes of the coming destruction. It made him smile. It was the pinnacle of all his hopes and dreams. His life, in its twilight, was suddenly complete.

He stepped onto the front porch and stashed the money inside his carry-on bag. His head was light and his body ached, but he never felt so alive.

He gazed into the wilderness that surrounded the compound. The forest seemed restrained by the surrounding fence, leaving the grounds stark and empty in contrast. In its own way, it was a miserable place to be. So close to beauty, yet so truly removed from it. A prison for insecure people too frightened to live in the modern age of reason and understanding.

Then it occurred to him that this was Treva's childhood home. Where she skinned her knees and ran wildly on warm summer days. Where she entertained slumber parties and learned to skip rope and read.

"Nice view, huh?" he heard her whisper from behind his back.

He turned to see her standing casually in the doorway, happy and healthy. He grinned sheepishly.

"Yeah, it's nice."

"I want you to see my bedroom."

He looked over to the darkened house. It looked strangely cold. Eerie and unwelcoming.

"Come on, you can see all my yearbooks. I'll even show you pictures from when I was young and had really stupid hairstyles."

He smiled.

"I still have pictures of my old friends, my family, my grandparents, my old dog…it's all in there. You can see the teddy bears I snuggled with at night, and the clothes I can no longer wear—or would care to, even if I could. You can see the brush I used to comb my hair in the mornings and the jackets I wore to school on cold days. I bet they still smell like me. And in my sock drawer, in the back, I still have notes that my friends and I passed in school. Everything you'd want to know about me, it's all there."

He looked to the house once again. It looked creepy and uninviting. It looked dead. Just like her.

"And if I don't like what I find in there?"

He noticed that his statement caused her image to flicker and fade. When she reformed, she looked different to him. Unfamiliar. Young and innocent and naïvely pure. Not at all the vivacious, happy-go-lucky sexpot he had grown to love.

Her voice stunned him when she responded. It was Opaque's voice. "But you don't really *know* me."

He reached into his pocket for a match. "I need to burn this place down. Leave me alone."

Her image immediately dispersed like vapor.

He struck the match and tossed it inside the building. The fire erupted in an instant, racing across the wooden floors and over the boxes of papers. In a matter of seconds, the Headquarters of the National Reclamation Front was a raging inferno.

With his bag strung over his one good shoulder, he climbed down the sloping mountainside toward the padlocked gate from whence he had come. He stopped briefly, and turned to face the fire, to bask in his glory. He let out a devious laugh, but his moment was all too brief. *Terminal* remained out there, and he had to help him.

10:48pm

Pokerface took a seat on the rocky embankment that overlooked the steep tree-lined cliffs. He took off his black fedora and placed it at his side while he rubbed his eyes with his palms. He took a deep breath, wishing that time would pass more quickly. In the morning, he would be gone. It was simply to endure the night, for whatever could be expected of it.

There was a hint of smoke in the air. He took a deeper breath and noticed the sky glowing orange in the distance. He put his hat back on his head and prepared to stand up when he felt a gentle tug on his shirttail. He turned, just before he was dragged over the edge of the rocky embankment—five feet onto rich fertile ground. He landed on his back and gasped for air, certain that a bear was attacking him. He reached for the pistol, but it was no longer there.

He looked up to see Kinsman Kale's fist smashing into his nose. Stunned and short of breath, he stared up at Kale with wild eyes.

"What are you doing?" Pokerface wheezed. "Have you lost your goddamned mind?!"

Kale kicked him in the ribcage with his steel-toed boot.

"Where did your ridiculous accent go?" Kinsman Kale growled. "You're a phony. Everything about you is a lie. I should have known better than to have trusted you for so long."

Kale bashed him on the head with the thick tree limb he had found in the yard at Headquarters. He beat him mercilessly, cracking the limb against his back and legs and shoulders until he had no more energy or anger to spend. He stood over Pokerface's beaten body and held tightly onto the tree limb with his thick and powerful hands. The limb's splintered ends dripped of fresh blood.

The scent of smoke dragged his attention away from Pokerface. He looked up to the bright orange glow radiating from the direction of Headquarters. With the bloody tree limb in hand, he walked toward the fire, leaving Pokerface alone on the rocks.

Pokerface held himself with trembling arms. His legs throbbed with excruciating pain and the whole world seemed to be tipping and turning on end. His left arm fell passively to his side, thumping against a hard and cold object. He grabbed it with his bloodied hand and slowly raised it to his line of vision. It was the pistol.

The sight of it sent a surge of hope throughout his beaten body. He struggled to move his legs underneath him. His skin and muscles screamed in resistance as he steadied his bloody body against the rocks. He pulled himself upright and took a shaky step forward, nearly losing his balance. He stumbled onward through the woods, following Kale.

"You're a dead man, Kale. You're a dead man…"

11:02pm

Brother Perry found what he was looking for, but a little too late and under the wrong circumstances.

In the distance, he could see the blazing fire. He knew exactly what it was and what it meant. It was the end of the National Reclamation Front, plain and simple. He took a deep breath of the smoky air, and laughed.

"There goes your dream, Kinsman," he mumbled to himself with a steady chuckle.

Then he heard footsteps approaching through the brush.

He ducked behind a large pine tree and waited. It was exactly who he thought it would be. Kinsman Kale. At almost exactly the same time, another set of footsteps came crashing through the trees from Headquarters.

It was Jobie. His hood was drawn tightly to conceal his face and the fire was directly behind him, covering him completely in shadow. In his gloved hands was the *Dragon Jr.* He limped feebly toward Kinsman Kale, kicking rocks with each clumsy step.

Brother Perry shifted his gaze between the two of them, and then shot out from behind the tree to reveal himself to his comrade. As he made his presence known, they all stopped and faced one another in perfect silence. The fire on Barron's Bluff cast hard shadows on Kale and Perry's uneasy expressions.

Kale clutched an enormous tree limb that was broken at the end and splintering—moist with the blood of Jimmy Paglea. His firm muscles flexed with his grip. The lines on his face were tense with confidence.

Brother Perry slapped a thin and compact branch in his open hand, allowing its thud to be a warning. He was ready for attack. He just needed his ally to join him.

Each of them took one step forward when suddenly a gunshot exploded from the trees. Jobie fell to the ground, holding his stomach with both hands as the *Dragon Jr.* rolled at his side. He clutched his belly and floundered on the dark and rugged rocks. His hood concealed his expression as well as his identity. Only one of them knew.

Pokerface hobbled from the trees, beaten and bloody and wielding a pistol. He aimed it at Kale and snarled as best he could with his bruised fat lip. "This asshole jumped me!" he called out to Brother Perry without the slightest hint of an accent. He wiped some blood from his face as he gave a bold and belligerent smile. "He thought he did me in. He was wrong."

Perry stared uneasily at the pistol. "Where did you get that?"

"Strickland's. Or it was. Now it's mine."

Perry looked down at Jobie. "I think you shot him." Even the shadows could not withhold the deep concern written across Perry's face. He swallowed hard. "He may die."

Pokerface kept the gun on Kale. "He won't be the only one."

Hasty words poured from Kale's twitching lips. "He's been lying to us, Perry. Think about it," he pleaded. "Think about everything."

Perry stepped back from Pokerface, eyeing him with caution. "Wait a minute...Pokerface, if you broke into the office and got that gun, then...*you* are the one that caused *all* of this, aren't you? It was you all along."

"That's right," Kale added desperately. "When could he have gotten the gun? Don't you get it—it's a trap and we're right in the middle of it. Do you honestly think he really shot this guy? It's a setup, Perry."

"Good try, Kale," Pokerface interjected with a sinister laugh. "Where were *you* just now, Perry? Burning down Headquarters? You lured us out here with this phony story. Now your man's been shot. Got a new plan?"

Perry was deeply frazzled. He kept his frightened eyes on Jobie. "I don't even *know* this person. But we can't leave him out here to die."

"We should all take a deep breath and think about this," Kale desperately shouted. "Before this gets any worse."

Pokerface laughed, keeping the gun on Kinsman Kale. "You aren't walking out of here alive." He pulled the gun to a neutral position between them. "Neither are you, Perry, if you side with him."

"He can't take us both at once," Kale begged Brother Perry. "Are you with me or not?"

A shower of flames suddenly erupted from the ground like a volcano, exploding from Jobie's gloved hands, spreading gelatinous flames over Pokerface's body. The pistol fired wildly in the air before he dropped it to the ground.

Right at Perry's feet.

He reached down and picked it up with a gleeful smile on his face. He had underestimated Kale's quick reaction. He trampled across the rocks with enough speed to smash his fist into Perry's face, busting his lip. The blood came quickly. Perry pointed the pistol at Kale and fired. Somehow he missed. Did it have blanks?

Kale tackled him onto the rocks and quickly overpowered him. There was a struggle for the pistol just before it went off. Brother Perry's skull burst open and splattered the rocky ground. The eerie expression on his lifeless face was one of absolute terror. The pistol was still in hands.

Kale rushed to his feet, aghast at the steady flow of blood that poured from Brother Perry's disembodied skull. Kale stripped the gun from his hands and turned to Jobie.

Pokerface's fiery body toppled over, tainting the mountain air with the odor of burnt flesh. Small strips of orange flames danced over his back, feeding on his expensive attire.

Jobie held his stomach. His fingers were covered with blood. He was barely alive.

Kale clasped the pistol and looked down upon Jobie's face—the face of the Devil. He had seen these particular striking eyes in Key West when he had nearly been beaten to death. Days later, Jobie reappeared in his hospital room. The same red skin, the same cold monotone he had always assumed the Devil would speak.

"Your boss is a child molester," Jobie had told Kale as he watched him drift in and out of consciousness that fateful day in the Key West hospital room. "Treva Rifkin is dead."

These words had sent a jolt throughout Kale's beaten body. "How do you know this?"

"The question is, how much of it did you know?"

"Very little," Kale replied honestly as he struggled to remain awake. His pain was unbearable. He gazed uneasily out the window, into the bright Key West sunlight. "But I always had a feeling."

"You can help me avenge her," Jobie had suggested. "In return I will help pay for this damage we caused so you can get back to health. Is it worth it to you?"

Kale had decided that it was.

Jobie kept to his promise, covering his hospital expenses with the money he had saved as a street performer on Sunset Pier. He visited Kale as frequently as possible. Strickland, on the other hand, never once checked on him. It had become painfully clear to Torben Kale that he was never anything more than an expendable foot soldier under the leadership of a very selfish and devious man.

With a new perspective on life, Kale came to believe that justice had to be served to the victims of Reverend Strickland. The only conceivable way was to return to Headquarters to search for the proof that would convict him. And that is exactly what he did.

Torben Kale lowered his hand to help Jobie up.

"I ain't going anywhere," Jobie informed him. His teeth were stained with blood. "This is it, lights out. Right here in Treva's playground."

"No." Torben's voice was shaky. He emphatically shook his head. "No."

"Better to burn out," Jobie whispered with a wry smile on his face, "than fade away."

Torben's face brightened for just a moment.

"Take care of Josephine," Jobie wheezed, "like she did for you."

"I will."

"I found some money in the office. *Lots* of money."

Kale knew exactly what he meant. The elusive unaccounted contributions.

"I can use it to publish your writing," Torben suggested.

"No. Don't do that. I'll be dead, I won't care." He coughed, splattering some blood on his cracked and scaly cheeks. "Spend that money on my brother's music. Make him a star. I want him happy."

Torben nodded. "I will."

Jobie closed his eyes and drifted momentarily. "Give me the gun."

"Why?"

His face came alert, ever so briefly. "Are you kidding? I want credit for all this. This is my moment of glory."

Torben cracked a brief smile that crumbled beneath overwhelming despair. He placed the pistol in Jobie's hand.

"You're officially off the hook," Jobie told him. He closed his eyes for a very long time, smiling throughout. "May the status quo be better in the next world."

These were his final words.

His eyes, sharp and piercing even in death, stared heavenward. He was smiling like a child that had robbed the candy store—and gotten away with it.

Saturday, February 10, 2001
3:45pm

Josephine stood over the grave of Treva Rifkin, holding in her gloved and shivering hands an urn containing Jobie's ashes. She knelt down and brushed away the snow that covered the gravesite. Using the granite headstone to shield the frigid wind, she slowly spread his ashes over the frozen soil.

Although Jobie had found his fifteen minutes of postmortem fame when the national news carried the arson and double murder story, her recollection differed dramatically from how the press had presented him. She had wisely used the public interest to grant his final wish—the publication of *The Apolitical Manifesto*. She sold the rights for a substantial amount of money to a major publishing house's true crime subsidiary. It went to print immediately, pandering to the public's thirst for sensationalism. Its sales upon release were well beyond anything he could have dreamt in life.

She retrieved a lighter and a mass-market paperback from her deep coat pockets. The cover of the book was completely white with the words *The Apolitical Manifesto* scrawled like graffiti in black. At the bottom was the name Jobie Wallace as though it was printed on a cheap old typewriter and copied several times over, losing most of its definition with each copy. The subheading read, *Inside the Mind of an Environmentalist Assassin*. For a final touch, on the upper right corner was a red fingerprint, faintly visible, as though the author himself had handled it.

She placed the book in the lighter's flame, slowly burning it so that the dark black ashes spread over Jobie's ashes, covering the grave like a mix of salt and pepper.

Joined for all eternity.

"The Apolitical Manifesto"
By Jobie Wallace

Available Summer 2004

To view weekly updated excerpts, go to:
www.laymanbooks.com

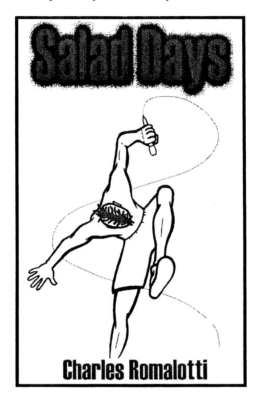

Salad Days keeps your heart pumping high-octane gasoline and your emotions running high. Romalotti's debut novel is quite an accomplishment...a great book.
- Maximum RockNRoll

A fast-paced, engrossing, and thoroughly enjoyable read.
- Ramsey Kanaan, President of AK Press distribution

One of the finest books I've ever read.
- punkrockreviews.com

I cannot explain how much I thoroughly enjoyed this book. No kidding, this is *good* reading.
- Boots fanzine

Charles Romalotti's debut novel is an excellent first stab at punk authorship.
- Willamette Week (Portland, Oregon)

Salad Days...how things were when it all really mattered.
- LA Weekly

Charles Romalotti is the author of *Salad Days*. He lives in Austin, Texas and is currently working on his next novel entitled *Blood of Stone*.
Two spin-offs from *Pariah* are also in the works: *IX*, and *The War Pigs*.